THE MIRROR VISITOR
BOOK 4

THE STORM
OF ECHOES

Christelle Dabos

THE MIRROR VISITOR
BOOK 4

THE STORM
OF ECHOES

*Translated from the French
by Hildegarde Serle*

Europa
editions

Europa Editions
1 Penn Plaza, Suite 6282
New York, N.Y. 10019
www.europaeditions.com
info@europaeditions.com

Copyright © 2019 by Gallimard Jeunesse
First Publication 2021 by Europa Editions

Translation by Hildegarde Serle
Original title: *La Passe-miroir. Livre 4. La Tempête des échos*
Translation copyright © 2021 by Europa Editions

Library of Congress Cataloging in Publication Data is available
ISBN 978-1-60945-697-9

Dabos, Christelle
The Storm of Echoes

Book design by Emanuele Ragnisco
www.mekkanografici.com

Cover illustration by Laurent Gapaillard © Gallimard Jeunesse

Prepress by Grafica Punto Print – Rome

Printed in Italy, at Puntoweb

Contents

Volume 3 Recalled: *The Memory of Babel*   11

Characters   13

Recto   31

  In the Wings   33

  The Void   38

  The Signature   48

  The Home   58

  The Messenger   67

  Solitude   83

  The Whiteness   94

  The Chosen Ones   109

  The Fabrication   122

  In the Wings   134

  The Trap   135

  The Glasses   148

  The Attraction   157

  Communion   172

The Deviation 182

The Meeting 196

The Shadow 210

The Collaborators 226

The Mistake 241

(Parenthesis) 254

The Conjuring Trick 261

In the Wings 275

Verso 277

The Unspeakable 279

The Loop 290

The Role 303

The Platform 313

The Renunciation 331

In the Wings 340

The Airship 345

Whirlwind 353

Adrift 362

The Ark 375

The Strangers 387

The Count 400

The Reunion 414

Plenty 425

The Fall 436

The Wrong Side 453

(Sisehtnerap) 465

The Counterpart 473

CONTENTS

In the Wings   484

The Imposture   485

Identity   500

The Space   510

The Mirror Visitors   527

Acknowledgments   539

VOLUME 3 RECALLED
THE MEMORY OF BABEL

After languishing for almost three years, Ophelia picks up Thorn's trail once again on Babel, an ark that is both cosmopolitan and a jewel of modernity. She gets to Babel with the help of Gail Fox, and Archibald, who, for months, have been searching for LandmArk using the Compass Roses.

As soon as she arrives on the ark of the twins, Pollux and Helen, Ophelia enrolls, under a false name, at the Good Family conservatoire in order to pursue her investigation into the true identity of God. She is then confronted by the omnipotence of the Lords of LUX, and the law of silence that, paradoxically, seems to prevail in this hub of information. In the wake of her investigation, strange deaths occur, people are struck down with sheer terror etched on their faces . . .

Ophelia's strenuous research finally enables her to find Thorn at the very heart of the Babel Memorial, a huge library claiming to be "the memory of the world," in which he had taken refuge to try to track down God. But against all expectations, God's identity lies hidden in some books for children, or rather, in their author, Eulalia Gonde. The distortion of her surname, Gonde, had gradually elevated her to the rank of God.

But if God is Eulalia, then who is the Other, that alter ego that Ophelia glimpses in the mirror, and who will cause the definitive disintegration of the arks? And what are those echoes that Lazarus, one of God's allies, deems to be "the key to it all"?

CHARACTERS

OPHELIA

Born on the ark of Anima, Ophelia turned down two marriage proposals before finding herself obliged to marry Thorn, from the Pole. Her particular family power enables her to read the past of objects and to travel through mirrors. Due to an accident with a mirror when young, she has remained unusually clumsy, her voice is reedy, and she has a disarming propensity to get into scrapes. Small in stature, she hides her shyness behind her rectangular glasses, whose lenses change color according to her mood, and behind her old three-colored scarf, which her animism has contaminated, and from which she is never apart. Her family moans about her severe, outmoded dresses; and as for her reader's gloves, precious as they are, they fall apart at the seams thanks to the nervous nibbling of their owner. However, in order to pass unnoticed on the ark of Babel, she will sacrifice her thick brown curls for a short, yet still unruly, cut, and will hide her coat and scarf to don the midnight-blue uniform of the company of Forerunners.

Behind her discreet manner, Ophelia conceals determination and staunch resilience. Although initially staggered by the cruelty at the Pole, she remains as motivated as ever by a deep sense of fairness and truth and refuses to bow to the will of others when that will counters her own. Stubborn and headstrong, she spent more than two years searching for the slightest trace of Thorn, her missing husband, and crossed the arks to finally be able to admit her feelings to him and make him her closest ally. She proves ever more intrepid and ingenious in her quest to discover both the identity of "God" and the cause of the cataclysm that divided the old world into many arks.

THORN

As Treasurer of the Pole, Thorn is ostensibly nothing more than a brusque, sullen accountant, as tall and surly as Ophelia is short and friendly. The bastard descendant of the Dragons clan, he was placed under the protection of his aunt, Berenilde, and also inherited, from his mother, the power of the Chroniclers, a fallen clan endowed with exceptional memories. Thorn's appearance reflects his character: reserved, and as cold as the ice covering his ark. Deeply misanthropic, he respects only numbers and cannot tolerate disorder. His every action is timed by the hands of the fob watch he always wears, and the weight of a difficult childhood seems to drag his smile downwards. However, he gradually reveals a true revulsion for violence, a fierce desire to protect his loved ones, and an unshakeable sense of duty. Obsessed with the desire to rehabilitate his family, he was counting on Ophelia's object-reading powers to unlock the secrets of the Book belonging to Farouk, the Pole's family spirit. Alas, events escaped his control: the dreadful plot in which he embroils his fiancée, his aunt, and others close to him almost leads all of them, more than once, to their death.

Determined not to involve Ophelia anymore against her will, Thorn chooses to disappear in order to investigate the identity of "God," and the implacable force that, secretly, seems to be governing life on the arks. And yet, it is when he teams up with Ophelia that they both reveal the best of themselves, as though cured of their flaws and insecurities by how they see each other. Thorn's scar-riddled, and now maimed, body proves to be the exact opposite of his brilliant mind, and testifies to his ultimate desire to do good, to do the best for his family and the world he inhabits.

15

ARCHIBALD

A member of the Web clan, endowed with a version of the telepathy that is characteristic of members of the Pole family, Archibald is the Pole's ambassador, but the exact nature of his duties is unclear since an ambassador would be expected to have a certain sense of . . . diplomacy. He, however, devotes himself, body and soul, to doing the exact opposite. Scruffy, cavalier, and a skirt-chaser, he also makes a habit of never lying, and doesn't always care about the feelings of whomever he's speaking to. Paradoxically, he is both greatly respected and greatly disdained for his escapades. Maybe his angelic beauty makes people quicker to forgive his erring ways, or maybe his position at court, and the deferential fear his family inspires, give him a prestige that he does his utmost not to deserve. All the same, Archibald's irreverence actually conceals a keen intelligence and a profound melancholy. Behind his nonchalant exterior, the ambassador is a formidable political strategist, and is adept at giving the impression of serving only his own interests, when, in fact, most of his actions enable Ophelia, Berenilde, and even Thorn to survive in the face of their enemies. Since he was abducted from the heart of his estate of Clairdelune, supposedly the most secure place in Citaceleste, the Web has cut its ties with him. Archibald, severed from all his points of reference, is now a free agent, and is able to find routes between the Compass Roses, those conduits that enable travel from one side of the world to the other . . .

ROSALINE

Aunt Rosaline asked nothing of anyone when she was dispatched to the Pole as Ophelia's chaperone. Grouchy, and stiff as an unoiled door hinge, she is known for her unwavering practicality.

Behind her severe hair bun there does, indeed, hide a fiercely protective instinct and incorruptible morals, even in a hostile setting. Aunt Rosaline's particular power gives her a singular affinity with paper, so it's not unusual to see her keeping boredom, or nervousness, at bay by repairing any books or wallpaper she can lay her hands on. She loathes the bitter cold of the Pole, but she really loves her goddaughter Ophelia, and she adores Berenilde, with whom she has forged a strong and sincere friendship. When, having fulfilled her chaperoning duties, she is obliged to return to Anima, she misses Berenilde and the Pole terribly, even if she would sooner swallow her precious papers than admit it. So, as soon as the opportunity arises, Aunt Rosaline dives, without hesitation, into the first available Compass Rose to rejoin her adoptive family and support it in adversity.

BERENILDE AND VICTORIA

Beautiful and ruthless—those are the first words that spring to mind to describe the dazzling Berenilde, sole survivor of the Dragons clan, and Thorn's aunt. As Farouk's favorite, she is admired for her beauty, and feared for her scheming at the heart of Citaceleste. Warring clans and court conspiracies snatched away the lives of her husband, Nicholas, and her three children, Thomas, Marian, and Peter. Stoked by anger, grief, and the need to be a mother again, Berenilde shrinks from nothing to consolidate her position in court. Her capricious moods often land Ophelia in tricky situations, but, behind her sometimes abrasive manner, Berenilde is deeply attached to her.

Her pregnancy puts her in a very particular position, since she gives birth to the first direct descendant of a family spirit for centuries. Although she appears to disdain Archibald, she has blind faith in his loyalty and goodness, and makes him godfather to her daughter, Victoria. It is said that Berenilde and Victoria are the only two people Farouk truly cares about. Which is fortunate, since Victoria's newfound power enables her to duplicate herself, and send, hither and thither, her astral double, whom only "God" and Farouk seem able to see. But to save the last child remaining to her, Berenilde won't hesitate to use her claws.

GAIL AND FOX

Fox—real name Foster—is a servant at Clairdelune, in the service of Lady Clothilde, Archibald's grandmother. He's a red-haired giant, with a character as fiery as his mane. When Ophelia arrives at Clairdelune with a false identity—that of Mime, Berenilde's valet—Fox takes her under his wing and agrees to initiate her into the mysteries of the court, in exchange for her first ten green sandglasses. When he becomes the victim of a technicality following the death of his mistress, Ophelia takes him into her service as an adviser. Fox is a faithful friend, a loyal guide, and a solid shoulder on which to lean. For years, he has harbored an affection, mixed with admiration, for Gail, Clairdelune's mechanic.

Mother Hildegarde's protégée, Gail is the last surviving member of the Nihilists, a clan whose power was that of annihilating the powers of other clans. To conceal her origins, she dyes her short hair jet black, and wears a black monocle over what she calls her "bad eye." More reserved than Fox, she nevertheless reciprocates his feelings for her, while never having really admitted so to him. Fundamentally honest, Gail detests court intrigues, and gives Ophelia her unfailing support.

ELIZABETH AND OCTAVIO

An aspiring virtuoso, Elizabeth is in charge of the division of apprentice Forerunners that Ophelia joins in Babel. Tall, slender, and with a face sprinkled with freckles, her grasp of humor is as poor as her grasp of information is great. Indeed, she specializes in databases. Elizabeth is Helen's goddaughter, and was born among the powerless, but she proves to be one of Ophelia's rare allies among the Forerunners.

As for Octavio, he descends from Pollux. He belongs to the family branch of the Visionaries: like his mother, Lady Septima, a professor at the Good Family, he benefits from phenomenally sharp eyesight. He is studying to become an apprentice virtuoso within the company of Forerunners. While his mother has every intention of making him top of his division, Octavio is determined to gain his position on his own merits. Uninvolved in Lady Septima's scheming, he befriends Ophelia, and then desperately tries to prove to her that he is "a good person," even to the extent of getting embroiled in some perilous situations that are beyond him.

AMBROSE AND LAZARUS

Lazarus travels from ark to ark, like the renowned explorer that he is. He recounts how, one day, wearing a diving suit, he had attempted to jump from the edge of the world, but had to be brought back up before he could see anything other than clouds. When he isn't roaming the world, he devotes himself to his inventions: it's thanks to him that Babel boasts many automatons, to combat "the servitude of man by man." Unfortunately, his cheerful and friendly demeanor conceals his loyalty to "God." His intentions may not be as pure as he makes them out to be.

By contrast, his son Ambrose is innocence and goodness personified. Disabled at birth, he has his left arm where his right should be, and his legs are similarly reversed. So, he gets around in a wheelchair and harbors the ambition of being a "whaxi" driver, to ferry people across Babel. He is the first to welcome and help Ophelia when she arrives on this unfamiliar ark. Nevertheless, he is aware of the existence of "God," and of his father's involvement in this vast conspiracy that governs the order of the world. When Ophelia enters the Good Family, and sends him desperate messages, the young man's laconic telegrams are few and far between. So she thinks he has abandoned her, whereas Ambrose, indoctrinated by his father, thinks that she is the "Other," that mysterious being that caused the disintegration of the arks.

FAMILY SPIRITS

No one really knows how the family spirits were born, or exactly which catastrophe cost them their memories. They have been around for centuries, immortal and omnipotent, with, as sole points of reference, their Books: ancient tomes made of a material similar to human skin; disturbing, mysterious, written in a language no one understands anymore, holding secrets that even Anima's most able readers haven't managed to unlock. The family spirits passed their powers on to their human descendants, and they rule, each in their own way, over their respective arks, which they never leave.

Artemis, the red-haired giantess who watches over Anima, has immersed herself in the stars, which she studies with fascination. She has very little contact with her descendants but endeavors to be a benevolent spirit on their behalf. She seems to have no interest whatsoever in anything concerning the past.

Farouk, the Pole's spirit, is capricious and irascible, like a child. His memory is so weak that he consigns all his thoughts and decisions to a notebook, kept for him by an Aide-memoire, but his psychic powers are inordinately strong. He has never really bothered to control them, and, often, the mental shock waves he sends out trigger searing migraines in those around him. Farouk, like most of the family spirits, is incredibly beautiful, but it's a beauty so cold that he seems to be hewn from marble. He tends to lounge around, in an attitude of total indifference to everything. He has just one obsession: unlocking the secrets of his Book, and his past.

On Babel, the twins Pollux and Helen form a complementary duo. Pollux is beauty, Helen intelligence. Unlike the other family spirits, Helen's physique is unsightly, out of proportion, and she moves with the help of a crinoline on castors, or mechanical limbs. Since she cannot have any descendants, she dedicates herself to the protection of the powerless, known as the Goddaughters of Helen. As for Pollux, he shows an almost paternal interest in his descendants, and they are known as the Sons of Pollux. With both Helen and Pollux being passionate about knowledge, they direct the establishment of the Good Family, which trains the elite of the nation, and supervises the running of the Memorial, the vast library incorporating all the books and knowledge accumulated since the Rupture of the world. They rule over the most cosmopolitan ark, but also the most militaristic, that Ophelia has explored.

If life on Anima is lighthearted, and that on the Pole is all intrigues and debauchery, life on Babel is bound by respect for rigid laws and the pursuit of knowledge. However, the Lords of LUX seem to be pulling the strings from the shadows and beware those who pry a little too closely!

GOD

He can take on the appearance and the power of all humans to whom he gets close enough.

He wants to obtain the final power that he's missing: the Arkadians' mastery of space.

He was, originally, a little female author from Babel.

Her true name is Eulalia Gonde.

He has no reflection.

He's looking for the Other.

THE OTHER

No one, apart from God, knows who he really is, or what he looks like.

Ophelia released him during her first passage through a mirror.

He destroyed, almost entirely, the old world.

And today, he's at it again.

THE MIRROR VISITOR
BOOK 4

THE STORM
OF ECHOES

To you, Maman.
Your courage inspires mine.
C.D.

"You're impossible."

"*Impossible?*"

"Improbable, if you prefer."

"*. . .*"

"Are you still there?"

"*Still there.*"

"Good. I'm feeling a bit lonely."

"*A bit?*"

"A lot, in fact. My suppers . . . superiors . . . they don't come down to see me often. I've not yet spoken to them about you."

"*About you?*"

"No, not about me. About you."

"*About me.*"

"Exactly. I don't know if they will strand udder . . . if they will understand you. Even me, I'm not really sure I understand you. I struggle enough to understand myself."

"*. . .*"

"You've not yet told me your name."

"*Not yet.*"

"And yet I think we're smarting . . . starting to know each other well. Me, I'm Eulalia."

"*I'm me.*"

"That's an interesting reply. Where have you sprung from?"

"*. . .*"

"Okay, my question was a little complicated. Where are you, right now?"

"*Here.*"

"Where's here?"

"*Behind.*"

"Behind? But behind what?"

"*Behind behind.*"

RECTO

IN THE WINGS

He looks at the mirror; he has no reflection. Not important, all that matters is the mirror. It's very modest, not very big, and not very straight, either, on its wall. Rather like Ophelia.

His finger slides across the reflective surface without leaving a trace. It's here that everything started, or, depending on one's point of view, that everything ended. In any case, it's here that things really became interesting. He remembers, as if it were yesterday, Ophelia's first passage through a mirror, on that memorable night.

He walks a few steps in the bedroom, casts a familiar eye over the old toys as they stir on the shelves, and stops in front of the bunk bed. Ophelia had shared it first with her big sister, then with her little brother, before leaving Anima in a hurry. He should know; he's been watching her closely from the wings for years now. She always preferred the bottom bunk. Her family has left the rumpled sheets and flattened pillow just as they found them, as though they all expected her to return home from one moment to the next.

He bends over and studies, with amusement, the maps of the twenty-one major arks that are pinned under the top bunk. Trapped here due to the Doyennes, Ophelia had long scoured the maps for her lost husband.

He goes downstairs and crosses the dining room, where plates of food are getting cold. There's no one about. They all left in the middle of supper—because of the hole, obviously. In these empty rooms he almost feels as if he's present, as if he's really there. The house itself seems to sense his intrusion: the chandeliers jingle as he passes, the furniture creaks, the clock lets out a loud, questioning chime. That's what amuses him about the Animists. One ends up no longer knowing who, between object and owner, really belongs to whom.

Once outside, he calmly strolls up the road. He's in no hurry. Curious, yes, but never in a hurry. And yet, there's not much time left now. For everyone, including him.

He joins the gathering of neighbors around what they have dubbed "the hole," as they exchange anxious looks. It's like some manhole in the middle of the pavement, except that, when they move their lanterns closer, no light penetrates it. To gauge how deep it is, someone unwinds a bobbin, which is soon out of thread. The hole wasn't there during the day; it was a Doyenne who gave the alert after almost falling into it.

He can't stop himself from smiling. This, madam, is just the beginning.

He notices Ophelia's mother and father in the crowd; they, as ever, don't notice him. Shining from their staring eyes is the same unspoken question. They don't know where their daughter is hiding—any more than they know that it's her fault, partly, that there's this chasm in the pavement—but it's obvious that, this evening, they are thinking of her more than ever. Just as they hug their other children closer than ever, even as they are unable to answer their questions. Bonny, strapping children, bursting with health. The streetlamps make their golden locks gleam as one.

He never tires of observing how different Ophelia is to them, and for good reason.

He continues with his walk. A couple of steps, and here he is at the other end of the world, at the Pole, somewhere between the upper levels and lowest depths of Citaceleste, just outside the entrance to Berenilde's manor house. This estate, plunged in a perpetual autumn, is as familiar to him as the house in Anima. Everywhere Ophelia has been, he has been, too. When she served as a valet to Berenilde, he was there. When she became Farouk's Vice-storyteller, he was there. When she investigated the missing of Clairdelune, he was there. He witnessed the spectacle of her misadventures with increasing curiosity, without ever leaving the wings.

He often likes to reconsider decisive moments in history, the important history, their collective history. What would have become of Ophelia if, among all the female object-readers in Anima, Berenilde hadn't chosen her to be her nephew's fiancée? Would she never have crossed paths with what they call "God?" Of course she would. History would simply have taken a different route. Everyone must play their role, as he will play his.

As he walks through the hall, a voice reaches him from the red sitting room. He looks through the half-open doors. Within this narrow field of vision, he sees Ophelia's aunt pacing up and down on the exotic carpet, as much of an illusion as the hunting paintings and the porcelain vases. She crosses and uncrosses her arms, waves a telegram that has stiffened thanks to her animism, talks of a lake drained like a sink, calls Farouk a "laundry basket," Archibald a "bar of soap," Ophelia a "cuckoo clock," and the entire medical profession "public latrines." Seated in a wingback chair, Berenilde isn't listening to her. She's humming while brushing the long, white hair of her daughter, whose little body is gently slumped against hers. Nothing seems to reach her ears apart from this light swishing between her hands.

He immediately looks away. He looks away whenever things get too personal. He has always been curious, never a voyeur.

Only then does he notice the man beside him, sitting on the floor in the half-light of the corridor, his back to the wall, furiously polishing the barrel of a hunting gun. It seemed these ladies had found themselves a bodyguard.

He continues with his walk. In a single stride he leaves the hall, the manor, Citaceleste, the Pole, for another part of the world. And here he is now in Babel. Ah, Babel! His favorite field of study. The ark where history and time will reach their conclusion, the point at which everything converges.

It was evening on Anima, it's morning here. Heavy rain falls on the roofs.

He paces up and down the covered walkways at the Good Family, just as Ophelia paced up and down them during her Forerunner apprenticeship. She came within a whisker of gaining her wings, and becoming a citizen of Babel, a situation that would have opened a good many doors for her next investigation. She failed, most fortunately in his opinion. It made his observation from the wings even more stimulating.

He climbs the spiral staircase of a watchtower. From up there, despite the rain, he can make out, in the distance, the neighboring minor arks. The Memorial in front, the Deviations Observatory behind. The two buildings will have an essential role to play in history.

At this time, the Good Family's apprentice virtuosos should already be in uniform, radio-lesson headphones on their heads, Sons of Pollux on one side, Goddaughters of Helen on the other. Instead, they are all mixed together, up on the walls of the minor ark. Their pajamas are sodden from the rain. They are letting out horrified cries, pointing the city out to each other, beyond the sea of clouds. Even the principal, Helen herself, the only family spirit never to have had descendants, has joined them under an enormous umbrella, and is focusing on the anomalous scene with piercing intensity.

From his privileged observation post, he looks at all of them. Or rather, he tries to look through their terrified eyes, to see as they do this void that, today, has gained ground.

Once again, he can't help smiling. He's benefited enough from being in the wings, the time has come to take to the stage.

THE VOID

Ophelia's memory of Pollux's botanical gardens remained vivid. It was the first place she had visited on Babel. She could still see the imposing tiers of terraces and countless steps she had to climb to get herself out of the jungle.

She remembered the smells. The colors. The sounds.

There was nothing left of it.

A landslide had swept everything into the void, down to the last blade of grass. It had also swallowed up a whole bridge, half of the neighboring market, and several minor arks. Along with the lives of all those who happened to be there.

Ophelia should have been horrified. She was merely dumbfounded. She gazed at the abyss through the makeshift railings along the new frontier between land and sky. At least, she tried to. The rain had stopped, but the sea of clouds had started to spill over the entire city. This seething tide, as well as reducing visibility, had misted up her glasses.

"The Other really does exist," she stated. "Until now, it was an abstract concept. Much as it was repeated to me that I'd messed up by releasing him, that he would cause the destruction of the arks because of me, that I was linked to him whether I liked it or not, I never really felt involved. How could I have let out an apocalyptic creature from the mirror in my own bedroom, and not be able to remember it properly?

I don't even know what he looks like, what he's doing, and why he does so."

The fog around Ophelia was so dense, she felt like a disembodied voice in the midst of the void. She gripped the railings when a gap in the clouds revealed a fragment of sky, exactly where the northwestern district of the city had previously stood.

"There's nothing left. And what if Anima . . . perhaps even the Pole . . ."

She left her sentence hanging in the air. Men, women, and children had plunged into the void that was before her, but her first thoughts were for her own family.

A great swirl of disorientated birds searched for the trees that had disappeared. Where did everything jettisoned end up? All the arks, both major and minor, gravitated around a vast ocean of clouds to which the living never ventured. The core of the world was said to be nothing but a concentration of perpetual storms. Even Lazarus, the famous explorer, had never been that far.

Ophelia hoped that no one had suffered.

Only the previous day, she had felt so calm. So complete. She had discovered the true identity of the multifaceted God who controlled all of their lives. *Eulalia Gonde.* Finally knowing her name, realizing that she was originally an idealistic little author, understanding that this woman had never had any right to decide what was good and what bad: all that had lifted such a weight from Ophelia! Except that the most formidable enemy was, perhaps, not whom she thought it was.

You will lead me to him.

"The Other used me to escape from the control of Eulalia Gonde, and today, Eulalia Gonde is using me to find the Other. Since those two are involving me in their crimes, I take it personally."

"We."

Ophelia turned her head toward Thorn without seeing him. In this fog, he was himself but a distant, rather eerie murmur, and yet to her, his voice seemed more tangible than the ground beneath her sandals. With just one word, he had made her feel better.

"If it turns out that this Other is linked at once to the Rupture of the old world, to the destruction of the arks, and to the transformation of a simple human being into an omnipotent one," Thorn continued, in the tone of a ledger, "then he becomes an essential part of the equation with which I've been grappling for years."

There was a metallic click. It was the familiar sound of his fob watch opening and closing its cover as a reminder of the time. Since becoming animated, it had adopted the tics of its owner.

"The countdown continues," said Thorn. "For ordinary mortals, destruction such as this is a natural disaster. But us, we now know that not only is it no such thing, but, in addition, it's going to continue. We cannot speak of it to anyone so long as we don't know whom to trust, and how to prove it. So we must establish the precise nature of the relationship linking Eulalia Gonde to the Other, understand what they want, what they are about, where they are, why and how they do what they do, in order to use all this knowledge against them. And, preferably, we must do it fast."

Ophelia screwed up her eyes. The sea of clouds had just dispersed around them due to the wind, and, without warning, the light fell on them in a blazing cascade.

She saw Thorn very clearly now. He was standing, like her, in front of the railings, watch in hand, gaze lost in the endless sky, extremely upright, excessively tall. The gold decorations on his uniform became blinding in the sun, but that wasn't enough to make Ophelia look away. On the contrary, she opened her eyes even wider to let all that brilliance inside her. The determination Thorn exuded was as palpable as an electric current.

With her whole body, Ophelia sensed what he had become to her, what she had become to him, and nothing in the world seemed as solid.

She made very sure not to move closer to him, however. There was no one in the vicinity—the area had been evacuated by the authorities—but they maintained the same formal distance between them as they always had in public. They were each at opposite extremes of the social scale. Since her failure at the Good Family conservatoire, Ophelia no longer had much status in Babel. Thorn, on the other hand, was "Sir Henry," a respectable Lord of LUX.

"Eulalia Gonde has thousands of different identities, the Other doesn't have a single one," he added. "We don't know what those two will look like when our paths cross, but we must be ready to face them before finding them. Or being found by them."

Thorn suddenly noticed how insistently Ophelia was staring at him. He cleared his throat.

"It's impossible for me to keep you away from them, but I can keep them away from you."

It was almost word for word what he had already told her in the Memorial's Secretarium—minus the formal "you" this time. What worried Ophelia was that she took his word for it. Thorn had sacrificed his name and his free will to liberate her, once and for all, from the surveillance she had so struggled to extricate herself from, and that she could be back under if she just put a foot wrong. Yes, she knew that Thorn was capable of giving up everything if it allowed him to fulfill this one objective. He had even accepted the idea that Ophelia might put herself in danger by his side, as long as it was *her* choice.

"We're not alone, Thorn. Against them, I mean. As we speak, Archibald, Gail, and Fox are busy looking for LandmArk. Maybe they've already found it. If they manage to persuade the Arkadians to be on our side, it could make all the difference."

Thorn frowned, unconvinced. He and Ophelia had already broached the subject the previous day, before the sirens had forced them out of bed, but the mere mention of Archibald's name invariably prompted this reaction.

"He's the last person in the world in whom I put my trust."

The sunny interlude was over; the sea of clouds engulfed them up once more.

"I'm going on ahead," Thorn announced, as his watch clicked impatiently. "I have another meeting with the Genealogists. Knowing them, the next mission they assign me will have a direct bearing on the business that concerns us. See you this evening."

A mechanical grating sound told Ophelia that he had set off. The caliper stopped him from limping, but that was the sole benefit the Genealogists had brought to his life. Thorn hoped to get closer to Eulalia Gonde's secrets through them, since they also wanted to bring an end to her reign. But working for the Genealogists was like juggling with sticks of dynamite. Having given Thorn a fake identity, they could take it from him at any moment, and, without the facade of being Sir Henry, he was back to being a fugitive.

"Take care."

Thorn's step halted and Ophelia could make out the angular outline of his silhouette.

"You too. A little more than that, even."

He moved off and was then totally swallowed up by the fog. Ophelia had got the hint. She searched the pockets of her gown. In them were the keys to Lazarus's home, entrusted to her by Ambrose, and the little note that Helen, her former apprenticeship director, had sent her: *Come and see me some time, your hands and you.*

Ophelia finally found what she was looking for: an aluminum plate. Upon it were engraved the same arabesques as in the family spirits' Books, a code invented by Eulalia Gonde that remained indecipherable. This plate, punctured in the middle by a shotgun bullet, was all that remained of the old sweeper from the Memorial. Ophelia felt nauseous just thinking about him. He had turned out to be a family spirit of a totally different kind, the guardian of Eulalia Gonde's past, and he had almost terrified her, literally, to death. The son of Fearless-and-Almost-Blameless had saved her through wanting to avenge his father. Luckily for her, he had fired at the head on which the plate was bolted. Barely had the code been shattered than the old sweeper had faded away, like a nightmare. A life that depended on just a few engraved lines . . . Thorn really hadn't appreciated this story when Ophelia had told it to him.

She flung the plate through a gap in the railings. The aluminum glinted one last time before disappearing beneath the clouds and joining the poor souls who had plunged into the void.

She thought, painfully, of her false papers. *Eulalia.* She had chosen, unintentionally, the same name for herself as that of her enemy. It went even further: she was sometimes assailed by unknown memories. Where did Eulalia's memory begin and where did hers end? How could she progress in the present when her past was a puzzle? How could she think of the future when the world was collapsing? And how could she feel free when her path was destined to cross, once again, that of the Other? She had released him; she felt obliged to take responsibility for that; but she held it against both of them—Eulalia and this Other—that they had deprived her of what she could have been without them.

Ophelia blew on the fog to chase it away from her. She would take advantage of every lead this second memory offered her in order to discover their weak points. It was in Babel that the story of Eulalia, of the Other, of the family spirits, and of the new world had begun. Regardless of the collapse, Ophelia wouldn't leave this ark before she had dragged everything out of it, down to its last secret.

She turned on her heels to leave the void behind her.

Someone was standing right beside her. An undefined shadow due to the fog.

The area was out of bounds to the public. Since when had this person been there? Had they eavesdropped on Thorn's and Ophelia's earlier conversation? Or were they innocently collecting their thoughts on the site of the catastrophe?

"Hello?"

The shadow didn't reply, but it slowly moved away through the fog. Ophelia allowed it to get ahead, then decided to follow it between what could be glimpsed of the deserted stalls. Maybe she was imagining things, but if this nosy man—or woman—had deliberately listened to them, she at least wanted to see his—or her—face.

The mist-shrouded market, cut in half by the collapse, had an end-of-time feel. An automaton that was supposed to distribute the newspapers but had not been wound up stood as still as a statue in the middle of the square, holding aloft a paper from the previous day. Disturbing, in this silence, were the tiny noises that Ophelia wouldn't have noticed in normal times. The gurgling of the water along the gutter. The buzzing of the flies around the produce just left where it was. The sound of her own breathing. On the other hand, she heard nothing from the shadow that she was now losing sight of.

She sped up.

When a gust of wind cleared the fog, Ophelia jumped at her own reflection. A few steps further, and she would have banged into the window of a store.

GLAZING—MIRRORS

Much as Ophelia swiveled her glasses in all directions, there was no longer anyone around. The shadow had shaken her off. Never mind.

She went up to the entrance of the glazing-and-mirror store. The owner, terrified by the collapse, had left without even closing the door. From inside there came the murmur of a radio that was still on:

". . . is with us on the *Official Bulletin*. Citizen, you are among the rare witnesses of the tragedy . . . a tragedy that plunged Babel into grief yesterday morning. Tell us about it."

"I still can't believe it, and yet, *vraiment*, I saw it. Or rather, no, I didn't see it. It's complicated."

"Just tell us what happened, citizen."

"I was at my spot. I'd put up my stall. It was pouring as never before. A torrent from the sky . . . from the sky. We were wondering whether to pack up our stock again. And then, I felt a kind of hiccup."

"A hiccup?"

"A very slight jolt. I didn't see, didn't hear, but that, yes, I felt it."

"And after that, citizen?"

"After that, I realized the others had also felt it, that hiccup. We all came out of our stalls . . . stalls. What a shock! The neighboring stand, it had disappeared. Nothing left of it, just clouds. That could've been me."

"Thank you, citizen. Dear listeners . . . listeners, you are

tuned in to the *Official Bulletin*. The Lords of LUX have designated the northwestern district out of bounds, for your safety.
They recommend, above all, that you refrain from reading
the banned leaflets that disrupt public order. We also remind
you that a census . . . census is taking place at the Memorial
right now."

Ophelia decided not to listen to any more; the echoes disturbed her. This phenomenon, once rare, occasional just two
days ago, now affected all transmissions. Before flying off on
a new voyage, Lazarus had stated that the echoes were "the
key to it all." But then, he had also told Ophelia that she
was *inverted*, as he was himself, that he explored the arks on
God's behalf, and had created the automatons to contribute
to making his world even more perfect. In short, Lazarus came
out with all sorts of nonsense, but he did have a lovely home
in the center of town that she and Thorn had made their base.

Ophelia held her own gaze in the mirror in the store
window. The last time she had passed through a mirror, she
had done an enormous leap in space, as though her family
power had matured at the same time as she had. Travelling
through mirrors had got her out of a good many impasses, but
the world would have been in a better state had she refrained
from doing so that very first time. If only she could recall
what precisely had happened in the mirror of her childhood
bedroom! Of her encounter with the Other, she retained mere
crumbs. A presence behind her reflection. A call that had
woken her in the middle of the night.

"Release me."

She had released him, apparently, but from where had he
emerged, and in what form? No one, as far as she knew, neither on Anima nor elsewhere, had reported the arrival of an
apocalyptic creature.

Ophelia stared wide-eyed. Something didn't make sense in

the mirror in the store window. She saw herself wearing her scarf, when she knew for certain that she had left it at Lazarus's house. Babel's dress code forbade her from wearing any color in public and she hadn't wanted to draw attention to herself. She then noticed that this wasn't the only anomaly in this mirror. Her gown was covered in blood, her glasses were in pieces. She was dying. Eulalia Gonde and the Other were there, too, with no precise form, and everywhere, everywhere around them, there was just the void.

"Your identity papers, *s'il vous plaît.*"

Ophelia turned from the vision, her heart on fire. A guard was holding out an authoritarian hand in her direction.

"The district is out of bounds to civilians."

While he was examining the false papers, Ophelia glanced again at the mirror in the store window. Her image had returned to normal. No more scarf, no more blood, no more void. She had already experienced, when living in the Pole, being tricked by illusions. First a shadow, then her reflection: had she been prey to hallucination? Or worse, manipulation?

"Animist of the eighth degree," the guard commented, handing her back her papers. "You're not a native of the city, Mademoiselle Eulalia."

Patrolling this close to the collapse made him uneasy. His long ears twitched, and twitched again, like those of an agitated cat. Each descendant of Pollux, Babel's family spirit, possessed an overdeveloped sense. This guard was an Acoustic.

"But I do have accommodation," Ophelia replied. "May I return to it?"

The guard looked hard at her forehead, as though searching for something that should have been there.

"No. You're not authorized. Didn't you hear the announcements? You have to go to the Memorial for the census. *Maintenant.*"

THE SIGNATURE

The birdtrain was packed. But Ophelia was still shoved in by the guard before the doors closed. She couldn't change position without squashing a babouche. It was boiling hot, and the smell of sweat was stronger than the smell of the giant fowl on the roof, which was itself pungent. Somewhere, a baby was screaming. Everyone around Ophelia seemed to be suffering from the same confusion. Why were they being taken to the Memorial? What was this sudden census all about? Was it to do with the landslide? Despite all the anxiety, no one dared raise a voice. If Ophelia went by the dress code, crammed in here were Totemists, Florins, Seers, Heliopolitains, Metamorphosers, Necromancers, and Phantoms, men and women from all four corners of the arks, as was so common in Babel. Every invention in the city was the fruit of their combined family expertise, starting with this birdtrain they were all suffocating in, which was taking forever to get going.

If they were nervous, Ophelia was even more so. She had no desire to take part in a census, not with false papers in her pocket and an apocalypse to prevent. The reflection in that store's mirror, whether she had imagined it or not, had shaken her.

Flattened against the glass of the door, she gazed at the crowd outside. A tradesman was tying up his carpets on a trolley, an old lady was maneuvering a small van loaded with children, and a zebu in the middle of the road was stopping the traffic. It wasn't just from the district affected by the landslide that everyone was running away; it was from the precipice, the void. People were scared. Ophelia didn't blame them for that. The Other could have been any one of them . . . She was supposedly linked to him, but she wouldn't have recognized him along a pavement.

An automaton riding a bicycle suddenly appeared. It was a singular spectacle, this mannequin without eyes, nose, or mouth pedaling straight ahead while a rasping, gramophone-like voice boomed from its midriff:

"I PULL YOUR WEEDS, I POLISH YOUR BRASSES, I MEND YOUR BABOUCHES . . . BABOUCHES . . . AND I NEVER GET TIRED. HIRE ME TO PUT AN END TO THE SERVITUDE OF MAN BY MAN."

Through the glass, Ophelia's eyes met those of a gentleman, sitting on a trunk that was too heavy for him. He had the distraught expression of someone who doesn't know where he will be spending the night. He shouted at Ophelia, and at the other passengers on the birdtrain:

"Find yourselves another ark! Leave Babel to its true citizens!"

Finally, the birdtrain left the platform. Ophelia was all shaken up, and not merely by the bumpy flight. Throughout the journey, she tried hard not to look at the void beneath the sea of clouds. She breathed more easily once the doors opened onto the forecourt of the Memorial.

She raised her glasses as high as she could to take in this architectural folly, part lighthouse, part library, and so colossal it took up the entire ark—give or take a few mimosa trees. Ophelia had spent days within its walls, sometimes nights, cataloguing, evaluating, classifying, and card-punching.

Here she felt almost at home.

Pollux's family guard broadcast its orders. "Alight, *s'il vous plaît*! Move along, *s'il vous plaît*! Wait, *s'il vous plaît*!" No sooner had all the passengers got off than a flood of citizens, having completed their registration, were replacing them on the birdtrain to return to town. They all bore a strange mark on their foreheads.

Ophelia became trapped in an endless queue under the blazing sun. She envied the old Water-diviner behind her, going around with that little rain cloud above his head.

She was stuck for a long time in front of the statue of the headless soldier, which was as ancient as the rest of the place. The Memorial already existed at the time of the old world. It was in this very place that Eulalia Gonde had brought up the family spirits. Was it also here that she had met the Other? Here that, together, they had triggered the Rupture? The Memorial bore the scar. Half of it had collapsed into the void and had since been ambitiously rebuilt above the sea of clouds. Every time Ophelia looked at the building, she wondered how it managed not to tip over.

Suddenly, she couldn't see a thing anymore. A gust of wind had slapped an orange leaflet against her glasses.

WE'RE GOING TO DRINK. WE'RE GOING TO SMOKE.
WE'RE GOING TO BREAK ALL THE TABOOS.
AND YOU, HOW ARE YOU GOING TO CELEBRATE
THE END OF THE WORLD?

Ophelia turned the leaflet over. A single line was printed on the other side:

JOIN THE BRATS OF BABEL!

Fearless-and-Almost-Blameless was dead, but his followers were pulling out all the stops.

A guard snatched the leaflet from Ophelia's hands.

"Enter, *s'il vous plaît!*"

At last, she was moving between the doors of the Memorial. As always, she at first felt dwarfed by the gigantic scale of the place, by the vast atrium, the towering circular stories, the vertical corridors of the transcendiums, the reading rooms set up on the ceilings, the terrestrial globe of the Secretarium floating beneath the cupola, and, maybe more even than all the rest, by the multitude of bookcases brimming with knowledge. Then, once this initial crushing impression had passed, Ophelia felt aggrandized by the united message of all these pages, all these quiet voices that seemed to whisper to her that she, too, had the right to make her own voice heard.

The queue was divided into several branches, stretching to the back of the atrium. The few Memorialists that Ophelia spotted on the floors above moved furtively, glancing down surreptitiously, as though embarrassed by this census being carried out at their place. Ophelia looked for Blaise's familiar face among them, but soon knew that he wasn't there: the poor assistant was cursed with such bad luck that he never went unnoticed. There were, on the other hand, many automatons coming and going with portable typewriters.

She let out an "Oh, no" when, after an eternity, she finally saw the counter her queue was leading to. In charge of it was a tall, slim Forerunner, with tawny hair tied in a messy ponytail.

Elizabeth.

This young woman had been in charge of Ophelia's division. Ophelia liked her singularity and admired her intelligence but found her blind loyalty to the city's ruling class exasperating. If her false papers did indeed prove problematic, Elizabeth wouldn't be sentimental about it.

51

"You again?" she said, by way of greeting, when Ophelia's turn arrived. "Welcome to the counter for non-natives of Babel."

She barely smiled, which was typical of her. Her eyelids, thick and gray, half-covered her eyes, like lampshades. Her freckles didn't succeed in brightening up her pallor. Ophelia was caught in the sun's rays and looked more Babelian than she did.

"You're not looking your best," Elizabeth said, pointing her fountain pen at Ophelia's nose as it dripped with perspiration.

"You don't look that great, either," retorted Ophelia.

It was a bit too easy; Elizabeth never looked that great. She raised her eyebrows a little, doubtless surprised at Ophelia's informality, but must have remembered that she was no longer her superior, because she cheered up.

"We're not allowed to wear makeup. We have to show complete transparency while performing our duties. Hand me your identity papers, then, so I can check your own transparency, Eulalia."

"What's going on? Why have we all been summoned here?"

"Hmm?" said Elizabeth, without looking up from the papers she was going through. "The Lords of LUX decided to conduct a mandatory census of those who arrived in Babel less than ten years ago. And believe me, that's a whole lot of people," she added, gesturing casually at the queues disappearing into the distance. "I volunteered to help out. It's obviously only temporary; I should find out soon where I'm being transferred to next. I've already received several proposals."

Right now, Ophelia was less concerned about Elizabeth's future than her own. Her false papers had been cobbled together by Archibald. A mere stamp in the wrong place could reveal her deception.

"But why?" she insisted. "Why are the Lords doing a census?"

"Why wouldn't they?"

Ophelia suspected as much. Even having gained her final grade, Elizabeth was no initiate. Like all the Babelians, she was unaware that the Lords of LUX were secretly serving Eulalia Gonde. Ophelia couldn't believe that their organizing such an extensive survey the day after a landslide was a coincidence. Something was definitely brewing.

"Elizabeth," murmured Ophelia, leaning on the counter, "do you know if there were any landslides anywhere other than Babel?"

"Hmm? Why would I know such a thing?"

"Because you're a Forerunner."

Faced with her impassive expression, Ophelia felt exasperated. She needed a better source of information. She looked around at the neighboring counters.

"Is Octavio here, too?"

It wasn't just the son of Lady Septima, herself a member of the LUX caste, that Ophelia wished to see. It was mainly someone she could trust—which was pretty ironic considering her and Octavio's mutual mistrust during their shared apprenticeship at the Good Family.

"He's just started on a part-time contract at the *Official Journal*," Elizabeth replied. "And it's not for us to give information to you. I'm going to ask you a series of questions to complete your file; you answer with as few words as possible."

Ophelia had to endure an interrogation such as she had never experienced before. When had she arrived in Babel? For what reason had she settled there? From which ark had she come? What was her family power? Was she currently under contract? Did she have a criminal record? Was any member of her family physically or mentally disabled? On a scale of one to ten, how attached was she to the city? Which was her favorite brand of candy?

Much as Ophelia had prepared herself for one day being questioned on her false origins, answering took all her sang-froid. She did, however, struggle to maintain it when she saw a couple approaching who, by their mere arrival, prompted a respectful silence along every queue; suddenly, people had stopped whispering, complaining, yawning, coughing. Ophelia had only ever seen the Genealogists from a distance, at the grade-awarding ceremony that had taken place right here, at the Memorial, but she recognized them without the slightest difficulty: they were clad entirely in gold. Even their faces and hair were that color. They were smiling as they strolled, close together, hand in hand, as though it were quite usual for them to take a walk in an administrative setting rather than in a park.

Thorn was supposed to have a meeting with them, but he wasn't around, which naturally concerned Ophelia. Was he waiting for her, as planned, at Lazarus's house? She hoped he'd had fewer problems than she had. The Genealogists were accompanied by a young Pharoan girl, who jumped with fright whenever one of them brushed her arm or whispered something in her ear.

Ophelia tensed up as they moved in her direction. Why, of all the counters in the Memorial, were they interested in precisely the one she was at?

The Genealogists leaned forward on either side of Elizabeth.

"What is the winner of the top prize doing in a role so unworthy of her?" lamented the man.

"You single-handedly revolutionized the Memorial's data-base," continued the woman. "Your talents are totally wasted here, citizen!"

Unexpressive as Elizabeth was, she was visibly disconcerted to be the focus of their attention like this. She got up to stand to attention and give them the obligatory greeting: "Knowledge serves peace!" But they indicated for her to sit back down by laying their hands on her shoulders.

"Don't put yourself out for us, young *dame*. Just tell us whether you have considered our proposal."

"It's just that I haven't had time to—"

"A mere 'yes' will suffice," said the woman.

"It's right up your street," said the man.

"And you will be doing a great service to the city!" they concluded, in unison.

Ophelia had no idea what they were talking about, but was grateful not to be Elizabeth, whose cheeks had suddenly gained some color. Now that she could see the Genealogists close up, she noticed the strange texture of their skin, under the golden powder they covered it in, as if they suffered from permanent goose pimples. They were Tactiles. She knew nothing about this variant of Pollux's family power.

"*En fait*, my first choice was the post of personal assistant to Lady Helen," Elizabeth explained to them, respectfully. "Without her I would be on the street, I owe her every one of my stripes."

The Genealogists exchanged a knowing look.

"A *très* moving story, citizen, but your work at the observatory will also concern Lady Helen. You couldn't be more useful to her than by accepting this offer!"

Elizabeth's composed mask cracked. Ophelia's glasses turned briefly to the young Pharoan girl, who, staring intently at her babouches, was pretending to stay out of the conversation. Ophelia could easily guess her role in this surprise encounter. The Pharoans' charm enabled them gently to modify the emotions of others, so as to win their trust. They generally worked in a medical setting, to calm patients down, but that was clearly not this one's function.

"You shouldn't decide right now."

Ophelia hadn't managed to hold back this warning, seeing Elizabeth overcome with indecision, but she instantly regretted it. The Genealogists, who hadn't so much as glanced at her until now, had both just turned towards her in one fluid movement. Their eyelashes were also tinted gold.

"Did you have something to say, *mademoiselle?*" the man asked, while perusing her false papers.

"Some change you would like to make to your file, perhaps?" the woman suggested, stroking the form.

They aroused such a visceral dislike in Ophelia that she drew back. Since her marriage to Thorn, during which they had shared their family powers, she had inherited some Dragons' claws. And although hers weren't malign, they played tricks on her when she got angry. The Genealogists didn't know her, but she knew them. They didn't seek the good of the city, they sought to become what Eulalia Gonde had herself become. Ophelia needed to remain just an insignificant little foreigner in their eyes, otherwise she would cause problems, as much for Thorn as for herself.

She swallowed both saliva and pride and calmed her claws.

"No."

"So?" the Genealogists persisted, returning to Elizabeth. "Do you accept our offer, citizen?"

"My lady, my lord, I . . . I would be honored to."

The woman plucked a contract from her cleavage and unrolled it on the counter. The man offered Elizabeth a fountain pen.

She signed.

"Good girl."

With these words, which they each whispered in one of Elizabeth's ears, the Genealogists moved off, hand in hand, their golden cloaks fluttering behind them, followed, at a good distance, by the young Pharoan girl. Ophelia realized that her mouth had gone dry in their presence.

Elizabeth wiped her forehead, to which her hair was sticking.

"I . . . maybe I was a bit too quick to sign."

"What was it about, that offer?" Ophelia asked her.

There was a sudden chorus of complaints. Now that the Genealogists were far away, all those waiting in her queue were losing patience. The old Diviner threatened to trigger a storm. As for Elizabeth, she was still totally shaken.

"It's confidential, I can't talk about it. I really did sign too quickly."

She kept blinking with such bewilderment that Ophelia felt sorry for her.

"That Pharoan made sure of that."

"I hope, for you sake, that you aren't insinuating that there was some kind of manipulation going on," Elizabeth warned her, sternly returning her papers to her. "We're talking about the Lords of LUX. That's an extremely serious accusation, particularly coming from a person whose file isn't in order. You're going to have to face a tribunal."

Without giving Ophelia time to react, the Forerunner leaned over the counter and applied a stamp to the middle of her forehead.

"I'm kidding. Everything is in order for now. You've just a medical examination to get through and you can go home."

THE HOME

"At least you're not ordinary."

Perched on a stool, Ophelia considered the blurred face of the doctor in front of her. She had had to take her glasses off for the checkup, so all she could see clearly of him were two eyes shining in the half-light. Several makeshift consulting rooms had been set up in the reprographics department, on the first floor of the Memorial. Ophelia was there in her underwear, surrounded by mimeographs, cyclostyles, and roneos. Without her reader's gloves, placed on an automaton's tray with the rest of her things, she felt vulnerable.

Elizabeth had told her that her papers were in order for now. It was that "for now" that worried her. What would happen if she was deemed not to conform to the requirements of the Babelian administration? Daylight was fading behind the windows, and Ophelia was seriously starting to wonder whether she'd ever see the end of this census. She wanted to get back to Thorn so they could start doing their research together.

"May I go? I'm expected elsewhere."

The doctor drew closer. As a Visionary, his eyes, luminous as lightbulbs, were worth all the medical-imaging equipment combined. He hadn't touched Ophelia once since she had entered, not even to take her pulse, but there was something disturbing about his way of looking.

"Have you been the victim of an accident, Mademoiselle Eulalia?" he asked, studying her file.

He had pronounced the word "accident" with a particular intonation that wasn't just a matter of the Babelian accent.

Ophelia frowned. Was he referring to the traces of cuts scattered over her body since the Seers had poured broken glass over her while she was taking a shower? Or to the scar on her cheek, dating further back, which she owed to Thorn's half-sister? Or to her bones, which had suffered multiple fractures in recent years?

She realized that it was in her interest not to come across as someone of fragile health. Her forehead bore Elizabeth's stamp, but she would only truly feel out of trouble once she was out of here.

"A few," she replied, evasively. "That never stopped me doing what I had to do."

The doctor nodded. Ophelia then noticed that it was her lower abdomen that he was examining with the least discretion.

"I was thinking of an accident of . . . a particular kind," he said, choosing his words carefully. "Mademoiselle Eulalia, according to your file, you're not matrimonially committed. Can you confirm that to me?"

"That's my private life."

She didn't appreciate one bit the way this conversation was going. In fact, she didn't appreciate any of what she had been put through since she had been forcibly taken to the Memorial. The Babel administration was invading her privacy more and more, and the intrusive approach of this doctor was too much for her.

"I'm going to put my clothes back on."

"You're suffering from a malformation, mademoiselle."

Ophelia, who had got off the stool to grab her things from

the automaton, slowly sat down again. She put her gloves and then glasses back on, as if that would enable her to hear better.

The doctor's eyes shone more brightly as he studied her, not without a certain fascination.

"I've observed some curious things in my time, but never anything comparable. It's rather as if all the parts of your body had . . . *je ne sais pas* . . . turned back on themselves. I have no idea what kind of accident could cause that to happen."

A mirror accident, Ophelia replied in her head. The very first one. The one that had released the Other.

"I also don't know how you manage to coordinate your movements," continued the doctor, his eyes going out like lamps. "You must have been young when that happened to you, your organism has managed to repair itself almost *entière-ment*. Almost," he stressed with a very paternal kindliness. "Do you see what I'm getting at, dear girl?"

"I'm inverted. I know, I've already been—"

"You will never be able to have children," he interrupted her. "It's physically impossible for you."

Ophelia watched the doctor filling in her file. She understood the words he had just used, but they made absolutely no sense to her. She could think of no other reply than:

"May I go?"

"You should make an appointment at the Deviations Observatory. They won't be able to do anything for you, but they will undoubtedly be interested in studying you close up. They specialize in cases such as yours. Get dressed," he added, with an offhand gesture. "We're done here."

Ophelia had to make several attempts at fastening her sandals, as if her hands could no longer agree on anything. She went out, to let the next person take her place. The first floor of the Memorial was heaving with men and women waiting their turn. Seeing all those foreheads branded with a stamp made Ophelia feel as if she were in an abattoir. The family guard was herding all those who had passed their medical examination toward the exit. Ophelia had no intention of allowing herself to be locked inside another birdtrain.

She must isolate herself. Now.

There was neither staircase nor lift at the Memorial, but she was used to the artificial gravity of its transcendiums. Discreetly, she slipped into a vertical corridor, which took her away from the crowd, and then hid in the toilets. Apart from a monkey lapping water from a sink, she was, at last, alone.

Ophelia looked hard at herself in one of the mirrors. She no longer feared seeing something there that didn't exist, as had happened to her that morning at the glazing-and-mirror store. She feared what she couldn't see and that really did exist.

She placed a hand on her stomach with care, as if she risked further damaging herself by pressing too hard. Not content with tearing apart the world, the Other had also torn apart her body. So why did she no longer feel anything, all of a sudden? There was no howl of outrage within her, only silence.

"I never imagined myself as a mother and Thorn detests children," she muttered, looking her reflection straight in the face. "So there's no problem."

She clambered awkwardly up on to the sink, thought "home," and dived into her reflection.

Ophelia was diverted. Literally. On entering the Memorial mirror, she had expected to reemerge through the mirror in Lazarus's house. Instead of which, she had the sensation of falling, dizzyingly, incomprehensibly, as though she were falling from down below to up above.

Everything had become blurred.

Images.

Sounds.

Her thoughts.

Ophelia suddenly realized that someone was holding her hand, firmly. She felt herself being pulled, step by step, through some indefinable setting. She tried to concentrate on each fragment of reality her senses grasped. There was a statue. The statue of the headless soldier. The statue of the headless soldier when he still had his head. So she was back on the forecourt of the Memorial, at the time when it wasn't yet the Memorial.

The military academy.

By associating words with objects, their contours became more precise. The building she was moving toward didn't yet have the majestic appearance that the architects of Babel had given it later, much later, but it was already imposing. All that blue and gold surrounding it, that was sea and mimosa. An island. Ophelia could almost smell that heady scent, half-salty, half-sweet. Almost. Her nose was blocked, she was struggling to breathe.

Steps. The woman holding her hand now made her move up toward the entrance. A woman? Yes, that voice whispering to her to hurry up definitely belonged to a woman. She was speaking to her in a language that wasn't her own, but that Ophelia could have understood had everything not been so distorted by the general haziness.

The woman made her sit down in what she supposed was a hall; the surroundings were too blurry for Ophelia to be sure. She felt as if she were in a watercolor painting on which a glass of water had been spilt. She was pretty shocked to notice that her own feet no longer touched the ground. Had she shrunk? And where had the woman gone? Ophelia could no longer feel her hand gripping her own, but her voice was still reaching her from afar. It was no longer to her that she was speaking now. By really applying herself, Ophelia finally managed to translate the conversation she was hearing into comprehensible words:

"And then, I've already got all my children to look after, how am I, like, supposed to feed another one? And then me husband has gone off to war, what am I, like, supposed to do, me, with no money? And then, don't get me wrong, she's hard-working, polite, and clever with it! Very clever. Yes, yes, she speaks the language perfectly. Several of them, in fact. Her favorite pastime is inventing new ones, believe it or not! And then she goes and types it all up for you, like a grown-up. She does have mood swings, that I can't deny, but the poor girl . . . She lost her parents, her brothers, her sisters, her uncles, her aunts, her cousins—all deported! Family of printers, I believe. Must have printed something they shouldn't have, and what's more, that's no joke over there. Miracle she managed to survive it. What? Gonde. No, no, not God! *Gonde*, with an 'n' in the middle. Yes, it's a name from where she's from, everyone round here made the same mistake. So, I know you're looking for children with . . . how do you, like, say it, again? Children with *great potential*, that's it. I'm no expert, like you all are, but that girl, there, she's got lots to offer, and she only wants to help out with the war effort."

Ophelia looked up when someone approached her. It wasn't the woman anymore, but a man. Even though Ophelia couldn't see him clearly, there was something familiar about him. Instinctively, she understood that she had to go with him, so duly followed him through a maze of stairs that were as hazy as everything else. The man marched in a military way, wore a turban, muttered strangely to himself. Ophelia knew him, she was sure of it. By focusing her attention on him and not on herself, just as she would when reading an object, he became clearer. The fabric of his turban was being used, not very successfully, to conceal his lower face, where a ghastly wound, evidently recent and not fully healed, had obliterated part of his jaw. The old caretaker. The old caretaker who wasn't yet old.

Ophelia was then led into a place, on the very top floor, that gave her a bittersweet feeling. She was going to spend many, very many, nights here.

Home.

Boys and girls of all ages gathered around her, curious and wary at the same time. Orphans, like Ophelia. She couldn't see any of their faces but could hear their questions.

"What's your name?"

"Where do you come from?"

"Are you a spy?"

"Did you see the war?"

Ophelia heard herself replying to them very seriously, in a voice that was hers without being hers:

"My name is Eulalia and I'm going to save the world."

The orphans all disappeared in a cloud of dust. Ophelia coughed again and again, swallowing cobwebs as soon as she tried to breathe in. She had collapsed onto a wooden floor and its splinters were piercing her skin.

Dazed, she glanced at the mirror from which she had fallen. The vision she'd just had was already fading. The mother, the caretaker, the orphans, they had all been contained in the tiniest fraction of a second, the duration of a simple mirror passage.

It had been nothing like a hallucination this time. She had witnessed a scene that had actually taken place, several centuries ago.

Ophelia got back up on her feet. The mirror, hanging in the air, was the sole item of furniture in the room. No door, no window. A small opening in the ceiling was all that allowed a thin shaft of light to enter. She knew this place. It was a secret room, entirely contained within a floating globe in the center of the Secretarium, which itself floated in the center of Babel's Memorial.

She moved closer to the hanging mirror, which reflected back a dusty image of her. Just as on her first visit there, she could make out the ghostly contours of the wall on which it had once been hung. Ophelia knew, having already read this mirror, that Eulalia Gonde had lived here at a time when she hadn't yet become God. She saw once again that little woman, who so resembled her while still being so different, busy typing up her stories for children. Ophelia understood now that this room represented much more than a writing place for Eulalia Gonde. Prior to being the peace school where she had brought up the family spirits, the Memorial had been the military orphanage where she had spent her childhood.

Home.

That was what Ophelia had wished for before passing through the mirror in the toilets. And it had brought her here, awakening in her that other memory that wasn't her own.

"This isn't my home," Ophelia reproached her reflection, as if they no longer understood one another. "I am not her."

The obvious truth hit her just as she spoke these words. When she had first visited this place, she had seen Eulalia facing her own reflection in the mirror, a reflection that Eulalia had herself directly addressed, a reflection that, today, Eulalia no longer possessed.

What had she said to it, again?

"'Soon, but not today,'" Ophelia recited.

It was then that she understood something very simple and completely insane. Something she had to speak to Thorn about.

She dived back into the mirror, with as much attention

and as little intention as possible. She tried her utmost to be open to all destinations without choosing one in particular. She felt herself tipping into a space that was hard to put into words; within it, shapes and colors fluctuated, like those one sees when pressing hard on one's eyelids.

The in-between. The narrow space within mirrors. The Other's prison, she now understood, from which she had released him.

She had accidentally visited this "bidimension" when she had found herself consigned to the Good Family's isolation chamber. Right now, she was starting to understand, instinctively, how to slip into it. It seemed almost possible for her to detect from here the resonance of all the mirrors in the world, however far away they were.

Ophelia chose one without a second's hesitation: the mirror hanging in Lazurus's atrium. And yet, when she reemerged above a sideboard, awkwardly placing her sandals between the censers, she wondered whether she hadn't somehow got it wrong again.

She found Thorn having a tête-à-tête with a doll.

THE MESSENGER

"You're here at last, *mademoiselle*!"

A joyful Ambrose had suddenly appeared, in his wheel-chair, upon hearing Ophelia tumbling off the dresser. His eyes, shaded by long antelope lashes, shone out against the darkness of his skin. The scarf lay, rolled in a ball, on his knees.

"We heard about the census. They didn't give you too hard a time?"

Helpfully, Ambrose held out both hands to Ophelia—a left hand that was on the right and a right hand on the left. The adolescent suffered from a serious inversion himself, but his couldn't go unnoticed.

Ophelia's was invisible, concealed. Malignant.

"My false papers did the trick," she replied. "I couldn't see the usefulness of the whole procedure."

"It was anything but useless."

Thorn had spoken these words in a deep voice. He was seated on the edge of the impluvium, which was brimming thanks to recent downpours, and he was staring hypnotically at the doll seated on the bench in front of him.

"In any case," he said, slowly, "it certainly won't go unused. The Lords have a plan."

"Which is?"

"I don't know. All that is LUX about me is the garb I wear."

67

Ophelia made a move to retrieve the scarf, but it instantly wound itself around Ambrose, ending up coiled on his head like a tricolored turban. Seeing someone else wearing it disturbed her. Since they had been separated, because of her, their relationship had changed.

Looking guilty, Ambrose offered Ophelia a bowl of rice.

"You must be famished; I asked our kitchen automaton to prepare something for you to eat. *Désolé*," he sighed, seeing her eyes water after the first mouthful, "he's a bit heavy on the spices. What happened to your forehead?"

"The Memorial was short of paper," Ophelia replied, ironically.

She rubbed at the stamp mark, peering into the mirror she had just emerged from. Not only could she not remove it, but now she had added a yellow curry streak to it, too.

"It's Alchemist's ink, *mademoiselle*," Ambrose explained to her. "It only fades away on the date and at the time designated by the Babel administration. Be patient."

This boy was sweetness personified. He in no way resembled Lazarus, his eccentric and dynamic father, who had chosen to be the pawn of a god rather than look after his only child. Ophelia couldn't bring herself to reproach Ambrose either for his relation or for the scarf's favors. She returned his smile.

He indicated Thorn, who hadn't taken his steely eyes off the doll's glass ones.

"Your husband arrived with this new guest. I'm *très* curious to know more, but he didn't wish to confide in me. I've passed the time coming up with thirty-four theories that might explain what such a serious man could be thinking of doing with this toy."

Thorn let out a snort of irritation.

"He came up with all of them out loud."

Ophelia gobbled up her rice with gusto, suddenly aware of how hungry she was. The pressure weighing down her stomach had just diminished. *Home*, that was here.

"May I?"

Thorn went from staring at the doll to staring at Ophelia. He agreed, while knowing that she wasn't really asking his permission to sit beside him.

It was an agreement between them. Ophelia must never do anything that might take him by surprise.

She sat on the edge of the impluvium and, in turn, looked at the doll on the stone bench. With her lovely black fringe, porcelain face, and oriental features, she reminded her a little of Zen, her old friend in the Forerunner division.

"Is it a present from the Genealogists?"

"Their messenger," said Thorn, "They never address me directly with their instructions. They have a questionable sense of humor."

"I wasn't that far from the truth with my nineteenth theory," commented Ambrose, approaching them with a tea tray balanced on his lap.

In Babel, the hotter the weather, the hotter the beverages. Ophelia blew on the cup she had just seized. The smell of her mint tea was soon overpowered by the strong, camphoric smell of disinfectant coming from Thorn, beside her. Even the rainwater filling the water-lily pool behind them reeked less. Ophelia was used to his odd habits, but this one had assumed worrying proportions since he had become Sir Henry.

"What did the message say?"

Thorn unfolded his arm to take the doll from the bench. He uncovered a mechanism concealed under the little kimono, on the doll's porcelain back.

"I don't know. It's a voice recording that can only be played once. I was awaiting your return to find out."

Being invited to listen to a doll wasn't among the conjugal scenes Ophelia would have imagined experiencing one day. More than at the doll itself, she gazed at the long, bony hands holding it. The rolled-up sleeves revealed a few of the fifty-five scars that riddled Thorn's body.

Ophelia had seen every one of them. She still felt awed. And privileged.

As soon as he noticed her looking, Thorn cleared his throat. He pushed back the only lock threatening to escape from his strictly regimented hair, and added, in a voice even more stilted than usual:

"Together."

Ophelia nodded.

"Together."

Ambrose's eyes darted from the one to the other, and then he put his chair into reverse.

"I . . . *eh bien* . . . I'll leave you two alone. Call me if you need anything at all."

"Best to be careful," warned Thorn, when the sound of the wheels had faded between the colonnades. "Simply because this kid has to know most of our secrets, or because he opens the doors of his home to us, doesn't mean he is our ally. I wouldn't be surprised if his father asked him to keep an eye on us in his absence."

His hard Northern accent had returned. Ambrose knew Thorn's true origins, but all the same, Thorn only took off his Sir Henry mask in private. Ophelia glanced at the uniform jacket that he had meticulously folded in a corner; he had shed it like someone else's skin. Pinned on the white-and-gold fabric, the LUX insignia of a sun gleamed in the light from the electric lamps.

Night had fallen as fast as a theater curtain. Looking up at the open roof, Ophelia couldn't see a single star. A fresh tide of clouds had risen over the city and its fog reached right into the atrium.

"Let's listen to the message," she suggested, putting her cup down.

Thorn turned the wind-up key on the doll's back for a long time. As soon as he released it, a shrill sound rang out from the porcelain:

"Greetings, *cher ami*."

Ophelia pushed her glasses up on her nose. If it was the voice of one of the Genealogists, it had been so distorted in the recording that it was unrecognizable.

"You have now been promoted to chief family inspector," the doll continued. "Tomorrow, at dawn, you will be welcomed into the Deviations Observatory, which will accommodate you within its walls . . . its walls for the weeks to come. Officially, you are appointed there to check that the generous subsidies granted by the LUX patrons are being put to good use. Your expertise in accountancy makes you the perfect official for this inspection. It is a *très* lengthy procedure, which will allow you the time to carry out another inquiry . . . inquiry alongside it.

"The Deviations Observatory was founded to study and correct certain pathologies, but we know that that is but a façade, cleverly constructed, almost impossible to penetrate. Despite all of our influence . . . influence, we found ourselves being refused on-site access, under the pretext of *medical confidentiality*. For a long time now, we have suspected the observatory of carrying out behind-the-scenes activities. One of our informers succeeded in infiltrating the premises. In his last report, he brought to our attention a project being secretly run by the observatory.

"It has been named PROJECT CORNUCOPIANISM.

"The informer didn't get a chance to reveal any more about it to us; he has since disappeared without a trace. We have every reason to believe . . . believe that the answers to our questions, and also to yours, are linked to this project.

"You fulfilled your first mission by providing a name to us, *cher ami*. We have carried out some minor research in some very old archives to which the public are not permitted access. The Deviations Observatory was formerly a military base, much before those words were condemned by our Index. That military base was also working on a research project that was highly . . . highly confidential.

"Guess which name features on this old register.

"Yes. That very one.

"You understand, *cher ami*? The secret that made this woman what we know her to be—the power of having all the powers, including that of thwarting death . . . death and of saving our world from the great collapse—this secret is to be found at the Deviations Observatory.

"Those who really are in charge of the observatory are well ahead of us. It's for you, *cher ami*, to reverse the trend. All your belongings are already packed, and they await you there. We won't insult you by explaining to you what will become . . . become of good old Sir Henry in the event of failure."

With a final resounding gurgle, indicating that the vocal mechanism had just disintegrated, the doll went quiet.

Ophelia did her best not to show the intense emotion that had overcome her as she listened to the message, even if the darkening of her glasses gave it away. She realized how much she hated the Genealogists. Much as they opened doors to Thorn that would otherwise have been closed to him, they showed such pleasure in using him, in playing with him, as if he were the real doll, that she was disgusted.

Thorn appeared not to attach any importance to it. On the contrary, his eyes narrowed in concentration, glinting with a certain satisfaction. He put the doll back in its place on the bench, and immediately took out, from a pocket, his bottle of surgical spirit to disinfect his hands.

"The Deviations Observatory," he repeated. "If the Genealogists are right, if it's over there that Eulalia Gonde became God, then we have a highly significant lead."

Ophelia focused on the disturbingly realistic almond-shaped eyes on the doll's porcelain face. So, that observatory once again! She thought back to what the doctor had told her, at the Memorial, on the subject of her malformation: "They won't be able to do anything for you, but they will undoubtedly be interested in studying you close up." Just remembering this triggered a spasm in her stomach. It was a subject she had to broach with Thorn.

"I've already been to the Deviations Observatory," she said, instead.

She hadn't been any further than the visitors' conservatory. Mediana, her most formidable rival during her apprenticeship as a Forerunner, had been interned there after being petrified by the old sweeper at the Memorial. Ophelia had wanted to question her but had managed to get almost nothing out of her, so traumatized was she.

"It's an impressive establishment, taking up a minor ark all to itself. I must admit, they are pretty enigmatic over there. They told me they had a file in my name but answered not one of my questions. Oh," she let out, suddenly struck by a thought. "So that's where they want to send Elizabeth? The Genealogists mentioned an observatory, but I didn't make the connection."

"The Genealogists?"

Thorn was forever frowning, but he had a certain ability to modulate that frown according to his degree of irritation.

"I came across them at the Memorial."

"As long as there was no interaction whatsoever between you."

Ophelia went cautiously silent, which deepened Thorn's frown, drawing together the two parts of his scar until they formed just the one.

"I didn't cause any disaster," she assured him. "In fact, they were only interested in Elizabeth. It's not as if they had appointed me Vice-storyteller."

"Why were they interested in her?"

"They wanted her to accept the offer of a job at the observatory. They told her that by doing so, she would be helping not only the city, but also Lady Helen. I didn't understand a thing."

Thorn leaned his elbows back on his knees and rested his chin on his linked fingers. His eyes traced the geometric patterns of the floor tiles before him.

"They are positioning their pawns."

"It ended badly for one of them," Ophelia recalled. "The Genealogists' informer did, after all, disappear while investigating that Project Carno . . . Copra—"

"Cornucopianism," Thorn corrected. "It's a reference to the 'Horn of Plenty.'"

Ophelia was baffled. The Horn of Plenty? She specialized more in history than in mythology, but she had, of course, heard of this legendary object that furnished endless food. Different arks had different versions of it. On Anima, where practicality ruled, it was represented in the form of an inexhaustible shopping bag. What did it have to do with Eulalia Gonde and the Other? Neither had spread plenty around them. They had sacrificed lands, seas, and lives.

She wished she could listen to the Genealogists' message again. The untimely echoes had distracted her, and she didn't have Thorn's memory.

"'The power of having all the powers,'" she recited, carefully handling the doll as she searched for another vocal mechanism. "Can something so important be studied in a renowned observatory without anyone knowing about it?"

Ophelia shuddered on spotting a mosquito on Thorn's wrist: the insect had barely landed before an invisible little blade cut it in two with surgical precision. As he studied the pattern of the flooring, deep in thought, Thorn hadn't even noticed. His claws lashed out indiscriminately at anything in the dead angle of his conscience, whether the threat was real or not. A primitive, uncontrollable hunting instinct of which he was ashamed. Ophelia couldn't really fathom what could have caused such a defect in him.

"Eulalia Gonde created twenty-one immortal family spirits," Thorn declared. "She described how each one of them functioned in a Book unchanged by time. Directly or indirectly, she caused the Rupture of the world. She disseminated the family powers across all the arks. And finally," he concluded, with a disdain that suddenly altered his steady tone of voice, "she elevated herself to the rank of a divinity who, today, has a stranglehold on all the families. And yet, who knows her name? For posterity, she remained but an anonymous author of tales for children—mediocre ones at that. If such an insignificant human was able to accomplish so many feats, it is not unreasonable to think that others can do so today."

He clenched his linked fingers so hard that his nails dug into his flesh. Ophelia understood his reaction when she noticed a flaw in the atrium's flooring, which broke up the harmony of the whole design. Thorn had a pathological need for symmetry. His stare intensified, as if he were seeking to correct the problem tile through sheer willpower.

"The Genealogists made out that the observatory contained

the answers to my questions," he said, separating each syllable. "I have a considerable number of them. How did Eulalia
Gonde become God? What is her true share of responsibility for the Rupture? Why endow the family spirits with free
will and a memory at first, if only to withdraw it from them
afterwards? Why does she possess all the family powers today,
except that of the inhabitants of LandmArk? If she really did
create the family spirits with her own hands, why wouldn't
she possess all of their capabilities? And by what right does she
pass herself off as God? How does she dare to claim concern
for the good of humanity when she has lost the essence of all
that constituted her own humanity?"

His voice had gradually intensified, shaking with sup-
pressed rage, and Ophelia could feel her own skin quivering
under the galvanic effect of the claws. She was hoping not to
end up like the mosquito. Every time Thorn said the word
"God," he did so reluctantly and barely audibly, but she still
cast her eyes around the atrium to reassure herself that they
really were alone. Lazarus's automatons had been designed
to transform themselves into a prison of blades when that
word was spoken in his home. There were so many machines
among the antique furnishings that it was difficult to determine which might be traps. That graphoscope, on the marble
desk, was it as innocent as it seemed? And that chronometric
teapot? And the statue-fountain, in the center of the impluvium, with its cymbals clashing on the hour?

Thorn closed his eyes to stop seeing the flaw in the flooring.

"I detest contradictions. And yet I have to put up with
them since my mother infected me with Farouk's memories.
There is no 'Other' in these snatches of memory, but I am
convinced . . . Farouk was convinced," he corrected himself,
"that Eulalia Gonde was punished on the day of the Rupture.
It sometimes seems to me that I can almost remember what

really happened at that moment. Farouk was the sole witness. Of that I am certain. It's for that reason that Eulalia didn't want anyone to 'read' his Book's past."

Ophelia listened to him, refraining from interrupting for now. Thorn was a man who spoke sparingly, to a degree that sometimes made him difficult to fathom, but this evening he was anxious to give substance to his thoughts. With his eyes closed, he seemed to be watching a scene unfolding behind his eyelids.

"When the Rupture took place, Eulalia was shut away in a room. She had forbidden Farouk from entering, but he ended up opening the door."

Thorn's broad, migraine-afflicted forehead furrowed with the effort, glistening with perspiration, as if he were trying to bring back up to the surface fragments of a submerged memory.

"On one side, the parquet floor, on the other the sky. The room has been sliced right down the middle. Nothing is left inside it. Nothing, except for Eulalia and . . . and what?" he asked himself, sounding annoyed as the memory slipped away once more.

"A hanging mirror."

Thorn reopened his eyes and straightened his shoulders.

"Indeed," he finally conceded. "There was a hanging mirror."

"There's always one there," said Ophelia. "I visited the room by accident. It's at the Memorial, in the Secretarium, inside the floating globe."

"At the exact center of the building's circumference," continued Thorn, with a flash of understanding in his eyes. "Just where half of the building was swept away by the Rupture. It wouldn't surprise me if Eulalia Gonde had instructed the Babel architects to wall in that room during the reconstruction.

When we discover what really happened, first at the Deviations Observatory, then in the secret room at the Memorial, we will have solved the whole equation."

Ophelia suddenly thought of her vision at the glazing-and-mirror store: the blood, the void, the terrible reunion with Eulalia and the Other against an apocalyptic backdrop. Wasn't it, in the end, her own fears she had projected onto that mirror? She noticed her own shadow and Thorn's, exaggerated by the lamps, stretching out at their feet and superimposed, one upon the other.

"I, too, am asking myself many questions. I have often wondered why I resembled her to that extent. Eulalia," she clarified, as Thorn looked questioningly at her. "I have much more in common with her than with my own sisters. I even share some of her memories, memories that haven't been inflicted on me, like yours have."

She went quiet for a moment. All around them, Lazarus's home was profoundly calm, barely disturbed by the rustle of the mosquito screens, stirred by the breeze, and the distant activity of the automatons. Not a sound reached them from the surrounding streets. Babel nights were never blighted by party music, or noisy neighbors, or the sounding of horns.

"I think I've finally understood why," Ophelia continued. "That Other I released from my bedroom mirror, with whom I *blended* myself," she said, stressing that word. "It's Eulalia Gonde's reflection."

This statement would have been enough to make Thorn snigger, if he were capable of doing such a thing, but, on the contrary, he started to think very hard about it.

Ophelia then slowly raised her left hand and watched her shadow copy her with its right hand.

"A reflection that Eulalia would have lost at the same time as her humanity," she murmured, in a shaky voice. "One part of me subscribes to this theory, certainly for longer than I care to admit, and another part rejects it. I know we live in a world where miracles have become the norm, but . . . a reflection capable of escaping from a mirror? Capable of acting and thinking for itself? Capable of wiping out entire arks? Would there be no limit, then, to the acceptable reality that could be transgressed? And then where would the observatory project come into it? Did Eulalia Gonde help herself to that Horn of Plenty, so as to have a multitude of faces and powers? Is that why she came into conflict with her reflection in the mirror? Is it due to that conflict that the Other appeared, and the Rupture took place?"

Thorn consulted his fob watch, hanging from the chain on his shirt; it opened and closed its lid itself to give him the time.

"We will have to find all the answers for ourselves," he declared, pragmatically. "If Eulalia Gonde worked on a project that made her and the Other what they are today, then that project must be understood from the inside. What has been done can be undone, one just needs to know how. I will be off at first light, to investigate at the observatory."

Ophelia scrunched her gown in her fists. She really had to tell him, now. Thorn had the right to know all the implications of that mirror accident. I can't have children. It was only a few words, after all, they weren't even that important, in fact, so why did they refuse to come out?

Ophelia decided that it was, doubtless, not the best moment.

"I'm going there with you."

Thorn tensed up, but there was no disapproval at all in his voice:

"I can't take you."

"I know. Sir Henry mustn't flaunt himself in the company of a foreigner with this in the middle of her forehead." With a half-smile, Ophelia tapped her stamp. "We would arouse everyone's suspicions. I'll go there under my own steam. After all, Lazarus stated that I would be of interest to this observatory, as someone who is inverted. I could offer myself as a volunteer."

She refrained from adding that the doctor at her physical had also suggested that she do that.

"No one takes themselves voluntarily to that kind of institution without having a very good reason," Thorn warned her. "The Genealogists' spy might have disappeared due to a lack of caution. If he was unmasked, they are going to be doubly vigilant at the observatory, and wary of any newcomers."

"I'll start looking into the best strategy to adopt tomorrow. I, too, have informers."

True to character, Thorn didn't return Ophelia's smile. He focused hard on the stamp behind her messy curls.

"I may wear the insignia of the Lords of LUX, but I have no idea what the point of this census is. The collapse of the city's northeast district will have consequences. Maybe you should avoid being seen in public, at least for a time."

"It would take more than all of Babel's bureaucracy to stop me from joining you."

Thorn's eyebrows relaxed suddenly. He gazed at Ophelia, nonplussed, as if it were incredible that she was still there, sitting close to him on the edge of this impluvium, and totally willingly, at that. A succession of expressions then flashed across his face, so contradictory and so subtle that they were hard to separate, one from the other. Relief. Frustration. Gratitude. Rigor.

He avoided Ophelia's gaze, and had to clear his voice before finally replying to her:

"I will wait for you."

All of a sudden, he looked uncomfortable on that stone ledge, restricted by his own skin, by his too-large arms, too-long legs, and too-heavy caliper.

Ophelia then understood that the intimacy they had shared the previous day hadn't given her all of Thorn; a part of him remained untouchable. The distance between them was small, but it had become too great. She suddenly felt the need to close it, but then remembered her scratched skin and dusty hair. She must be a little disconcerting to someone who made hygiene a top priority.

"Should I disinfect myself?"

Darkness swooped down on Ophelia. Being winded, it took her a moment to understand that Thorn had suddenly clasped her to him. Embraces from him never came with any warning. Distance one moment, closeness the next.

"No," he said.

Ophelia yielded to him without thinking anymore. She listened to the furious beating of his heart. She liked him being so big and her so small. He totally engulfed her, like a wave.

Thorn pulled back as soon as his eyes met hers, wide open behind her skewed glasses. He turned away, pressing hard on the bridge of his nose. His ears were ablaze.

"I am not used to that," he explained. "Being looked at in that way."

"What way?"

Thorn cleared his throat again, embarrassed as Ophelia had never seen him before. He, who was so eloquent in his speech and his reasoning, now seemed lost for words.

"As if, from now on, I was incapable of making mistakes. It so happens that I do make some. A little more than that, even."

Thorn lowered his large nose, still marked by his fingers, toward Ophelia, in order to consider her with utmost seriousness.

"If, at any time, something doesn't suit you . . . a gesture I make, a word I don't say . . . you must tell me so. I don't want to have to wonder why I can't manage to make my wife happy."

Ophelia bit the inside of her cheek. The truth was, they were both in unknown territory.

"I'm already happy. A little more than that, even."

Thorn's stern lips quivered. He leaned over her, resolutely this time, but the joint of his caliper jammed, halting him mid-flourish. This so exasperated him that Ophelia couldn't hold back her laughter any longer.

Yes, despite the world falling apart, she was happy. She wondered whether Eulalia Gonde had ever felt that way, and what she might be up to at this very moment, wherever she might be.

SOLITUDE

The Fake-Ginger-Fellow raised his fists. With no coordination, he stretched out his brawny arms, threw them high above his head, opened his enormous jaws, and yawned.

Victoria drew back in fright. Not too much, though. She didn't want to lose Godfather, who was striding down the street. It was very strange, that street. A terrace full of parasols folded in on itself, finally disappearing altogether. The same thing happened, a bit further along, to stalls of colorful fruits. Then, even further along, to a pretty newspaper kiosk. As soon as they saw Godfather approaching, people took refuge indoors, and their houses followed suit, in a sequence of intricate folds, as though made of paper. In the end, all that remained were white facades, with no doors or windows, as high as the sky.

Soon, the street was totally empty. Apart from Godfather, the Fake-Ginger-Fellow, the Funny-Eyed-Lady, and Victoria, but she didn't really count. The same thing had happened in the previous street, and the one before that, and the one before that.

Godfather paused in a ray of sunshine bursting between the roofs, up on high. A finger poked out through the hole in his pocket, his braces dangled over his thighs. He closed his eyes and breathed in deeply through his nose, as if wanting to sustain himself on light. His skin and beard glistened.

When he turned toward the Fake-Ginger-Fellow and the Funny-Eyed-Lady, he was smiling.

"The saying is true. No one's more elusive than an Arkadian who doesn't want to be found."

Victoria couldn't hear him very well. *Journeying* was like seeing the world through water from the bottom of a bathtub, but it seemed to her that this bathtub was getting deeper and deeper. She had never made such a long *journey*. The voices reaching her were even more distorted, even more distant, often duplicated. Godfather's smile was the only thing here that made her feel a little bit safe.

The Funny-Eyed-Lady rummaged in the toolkit she wore like a belt. With a hammer, she tapped on a facade, putting her ear up close to it.

"Minimal thickness. Hiding, they are, but listening to us."

The Funny-Eyed-Lady spoke with one side of her mouth, the other side clamping a cigarette. She had one, lit or unlit, forever wedged between her teeth, making her even harder to understand.

"Avoiding you, they are, ex-ambassador. Can't deny you collect diplomatic incidents. Maybe we should avoid you, too. Eh, Fox?"

The Funny-Eyed-Lady turned her funny eyes, one very blue, the other very black, on to the Fake-Ginger-Fellow. He made a vague sign with his chin, neither a yes nor a no. His hair looked like fire in the midday light, yet Victoria found nothing warm about him.

Godfather lay down in the middle of the street, in the full sun, one arm folded behind his head, the other flapping his holey hat like a fan. His smile was directed only at the sky.

"I'm afraid I may be entirely unavoidable. Even to myself."

Victoria would have so loved to get closer to him. Even if he could neither see nor hear nor touch her. Even if she herself could only perceive him as a blurred shape and distorted sounds. She didn't dare. The Fake-Ginger-Fellow never left Godfather's side, saying little, listening to everything. He terrified her.

The Funny-Eyed-Lady sent her hammer spinning into the air and caught it by the handle, and then did the same again.

"So that's the plan, is it? Lie on the ground and wait?"

"Precisely."

The Funny-Eyed-Lady let out a swearword that Mommy wouldn't have been happy to hear. She had almost lost her balance due to Twit rubbing against her calves.

"Look after your cat, Fox!"

The Fake-Ginger-Fellow clicked his tongue, but Twit didn't respond to his call; the cat just stared at him without moving. Victoria knew why. She, too, could see the swarm of shadows writhing beneath his shoes. He wasn't the real Big-Ginger-Fellow. He wasn't the one who had walked her around the garden, at home, in her pram, or the one who had caught her when she had almost tumbled off a harpist's stool. No, this Fake-Ginger-Fellow was someone else. Victoria didn't know who, but everything inside her was screaming "danger!" and neither Godfather nor The Funny-Eyed-Lady were aware of it.

Victoria so wished that Father was there. He would have been able to see her. He would have chased away the Fake-Ginger-Fellow, just as he had the Fake-Golden-Lady.

She froze.

The Fake-Ginger-Fellow had just glanced over his shoulder; he seemed to sense her presence out of the corner of his eye. The shadows beneath his shoes instantly began contorting and wildly gesticulating.

Right then, a voice reverberated against the white walls of the street:

"What on earth am I going to do with you?"

It was a voice such as Victoria had never heard before. A man's voice and a woman's voice all at once and seeming to come from the sky. Up there, right up there, someone was sitting on the edge of a roof. Victoria tried harder to make them out, but her *journeying* eyes made anything at a distance even more blurred.

"Don Janus," said Godfather, in greeting, lithely springing to his feet. "I was looking for you."

The person disappeared from the roof. He hadn't fallen; he had simply ceased to be there. He was now standing in the middle of the street, right in front of Godfather. His body, like his voice, was neither really that of a man nor of a woman, or rather, a bit of both at the same time.

"No one looks for me, it's me who finds others. In particular, those who disobey me."

Victoria's curiosity momentarily eclipsed her fear of the Fake-Ginger-Fellow. The man-woman was as huge, as elegant, and as inscrutable as Father was, but apart from that, didn't resemble him at all. His skin was the color of caramel, his moustache like two spiral stairways, and the ruff he wore was so voluminous, his head appeared to be stuck on a meringue.

The man-woman didn't see Victoria, either. In fact, he looked only at Godfather.

"I am well aware of all that goes on in LandmArk, *niño*. I know that you have created a passage between my ark and the Pole, that you have visited the number-one favorite of my brother Farouk, that you intended to bring her here, to introduce her into my home, and that you were counting on your influence to make me change my mind."

The man-woman spoke slowly, without taking a breath.

"My opinion remains unaltered. My orders remain the same. Nothing else must enter LandmArk, and nothing else leave it. Including you, *niño*. Did you really think I wouldn't be aware of anything?"

"I hoped so," replied Godfather. "I was away for less than an hour and returned empty-handed. No point making a great song-and-dance about it."

"Eight of my Compass Roses have disappeared, worldwide."

Victoria was pretty sure that the man-woman was in no mood to joke, but Godfather burst out laughing.

"Aha, that, I didn't touch a thing! I just summoned a short-cut to the Pole. I canceled it as soon as I'd used it."

On one of the facades, a block of white stones detached itself from the wall and opened out, flexible as card, until a window with a balcony appeared. People were leaning over it to watch what was happening down below.

"Eight of my Compass Roses have disappeared," repeated the man-woman. "And the same goes for the ground on which they were situated. I asked the *señores* of the company to double-check, their report is categorical. You set off, and when you return, *niño*, the arks fall to pieces. Personally, I'm tempted to see that as a link of cause to effect."

He leaned his upper body forward in a movement so spectacular, Victoria thought he was going to fall on top of Godfather. She realized that there was a shadow clinging to him like a great cloak of smoke. No one apart from Victoria seemed to notice it, that shadow. Without being the same, it reminded her of the great clawed shadows of Mother and Father.

"I have no other choice but to consider you as a member of my lineage, since a little of my family power flows in your veins. I am, however, going to have to mutilate you for having put it to such bad use."

Victoria became afraid as she saw the man-woman opening a hand with gigantic fingers and moving it toward Godfather, as if wanting to imprison his head inside it.

Then something happened both very slowly and very swiftly. Victoria saw the great shadow detaching itself from the man-woman, twirling in the air in a swirl of smoke, and landing on the pavement, just behind Godfather. An instant later, the man-woman was there in turn. He had taken the shadow's place without needing to move.

He gave Godfather a great slap on the back, sending his hat flying to the ground.

"On second thought, I don't think you're powerful enough to cause such instability in space."

Victoria turned her attention back to the Fake-Ginger-Fellow. While he remained calm and still, his shadows were all going crazy. They were squirming at his feet and stretching their arms—so many arms!—toward the man-woman, as if wanting to snatch away his shadow, but not managing to.

Godfather picked up his hat and, with a twirl of his hand, replaced it on top of his messy hair.

"That instability, Don Janus, is probably the work of God. You should apply yourself to extracting him from his hiding place, instead of lecturing me. You have founded a whole family of Arkadians who mess around with space, and among them, you have an elite group of Needlers capable of finding anyone anywhere. Forcing them to go underground like moles . . . what a waste!"

Victoria didn't know what Godfather had said that was so interesting, but the Fake-Ginger-Fellow's shadows became even more agitated.

The man-woman plunged his fingers between the folds of his giant ruff, as though rummaging inside his actual neck, and pulled out a book that was almost as big as Victoria. Father had a similar one that he carried with him at all times.

"Don't bother coming back at me with that," said the man-woman, shaking his book. "I am not like my brothers and sisters, my memory is in perfect working order. My *Aguyas* will remain impossible to find until I have decided otherwise. As for *that person* whom you call 'God,' I haven't forgotten their real name, either."

"Their real name," Archibald repeated, sounding very intrigued.

"A name I won't give you without getting anything in exchange. You're going to have to win back my trust, *niño*. Know at least this: *that person* and I have never been close. Speaking geographically, of course. Since being old enough to use my family power, I've been incapable of staying put. I wasn't with *that person* on the day the world was torn apart. Neither was I there when *that person* tore away a page from each of my brothers' and sisters' Books, depriving them forever of their memory. I must say, it didn't exactly make me feel like seeing *that person* again. I decided to keep my distance, I hid in LandmArk, in a fold of space, and that was it. I don't get involved in *that person*'s business, they don't get involved in mine, and that's suited everyone fine for centuries."

The Funny-Eyed-Lady, who had remained silent until then, moved forward with a determined look. She let her lit cigarette fall to the ground, crushed it with her heel to put it out, and, with her funny eyes, looked the man-woman straight in the eye.

"Coward."

The people on the balcony started to shout horrid words and hurl oranges. Godfather caught one as it flew past, and calmly began to peel it.

"And I'm the one who collects diplomatic incidents?"

If Godfather's smile hadn't been there, Victoria would have been really worried. As for the Funny-Eyed-Lady, she wasn't laughing at all.

"That has ceased to be true, Janus, and you know it. *That person* is after your family power, and that's why Mother Hildegarde—"

". . . did her duty."

With a slide of his fingers, the man-woman tweaked the spirals of his moustache.

"She may have been my descendant," he added, "but she still betrayed me by changing her name and distancing herself from family politics. Neutrality rules with us. Doña Mercedes Imelda meddled far too much in the business of the other families, yours in particular. She was merely rectifying that mistake. As for *that person*, we're all just going to remain quietly here, between ourselves, until they return to a better frame of mind."

Victoria saw the Funny-Eyed-Lady's fist tighten around the handle of her hammer, but Godfather chose that moment to slip between her and the man-woman.

"I'm offering you a deal, Don Janus. If we succeed in proving to you that LandmArk is already implicated in the machinations of *that person*, we will take them on together, with belt and braces."

Victoria may have understood nothing of all these adult discussions, but she did at least recognize the word "braces," as Godfather was pulling his own up and over his shirt, and gripping them in a determined way. He looked like a hero. He had always been her hero. So why couldn't he see her?

The man-woman thrust his book back into the folds of his ruff.

"It's a deal. In the meantime, *niño*, I forbid anyone on LandmArk to have the slightest dealings with you and your gang. You're far too bad an influence."

The people at their windows immediately withdrew inside;

the balcony folded away again, like pleated paper; and soon all that remained were rows of white stones.

Victoria saw the man-woman's shadow take flight, like a great bird of smoke. The next moment, he, in turn, had disappeared.

The Funny-Eyed-Lady looked hard at Godfather for a long time. She now seemed to want to use her hammer to break his smile.

"We won't be chatting to an Arkadian any time soon, and we'll never prove a thing to them. And you, you don't give a damn!" she muttered angrily, suddenly turning toward the Fake-Ginger-Fellow. "The world's getting blown apart, the Mother died for nothing, and you just stay there, in your corner, not batting an eyelid. Sometimes, you still behave like a valet."

Victoria saw that there was pain in the anger of the Funny-Eyed-Lady. She seemed to expect something of the Fake-Ginger-Fellow that was very important to her.

He didn't even look at her.

"Shame," he said.

He was gazing at the pavement on which the man-woman had just been standing. His shadows still lurked around his feet, reaching out in all directions, as if desperately looking for something they couldn't find.

When Victoria saw one of those shadows creeping toward her, she was torn between the desire to run away and the need to stay.

Suddenly, shadows and sun were all mixed up. Victoria's view of the world, as from the depths of a bathtub, became even more blurred. Forms and colors combined into one giant whirlpool. There was no more Fake-Ginger-Fellow, no more Funny-Eyed-Lady, no more sun, no more street. No more God-father. Victoria had never experienced such a thing on any *journey*. She couldn't understand what was happening. She felt herself being sucked into this whirlpool, as if it sought to dissolve her into the entire universe.

"No!" she thought, and the whirlpool reversed its direction, then slowed its pace. Forms and colors gradually fell back into place. The street regained an almost stable appearance. It was empty. And dark. The sun no longer shone down between the roofs.

Victoria looked all around her. Godfather had gone. Where? She walked straight ahead, turned right, went up some stairs, turned left. The sky, high above the streets, was increasingly less blue. Turning around a park, Victoria spotted a silhouette she thought was Godfather's, but it was in fact a lamplighter, with his pole on his shoulder. Doors sometimes appeared on a façade; they always opened on unknown people going out into the street to exchange murmurs, walk the dog, and return home, wishing each other goodnight.

Victoria stopped in the middle of the highest bridge in the town and looked down onto the dotted lines of lamps below. Masses and masses of streets zigzagged off into the darkness.

She really had lost Godfather.

She looked up at this real sky, something she had always longed to see when at home. It wasn't at all blue anymore. She was alone. Alone, and lost. She thought of the Other-Victoria with all her might—had she real eyelids, she would have closed them with all her might, too—to be as one with her once more. Her *journeying* body curled up tight. She hadn't uttered a word since her birth, but the silence screamed within her.

Mommy. Mommy.

Mommy. Mommy. Mommy. Mommy. Mommy. Mommy. Mommy. Mommy. Mommy. Mommy. Mommy. Mommy. Mommy. Mommy. Mommy.

"I haven't awarded the blurred."

The Fake-Ginger-Fellow was there.

He had leant over Victoria to the point of hiding the stars. His gaze passed through her without seeing her, but he was screwing up his eyes and frowning with his big eyebrows, as if that helped him to make out her presence in the middle of the bridge. Victoria struggled to see him herself, due to the dark and the *journeying*. And yet, strangely, she could make out the shadows beneath his feet very clearly. They were all pointing their fingers in her direction.

"Abandoned the world," continued the Fake-Ginger-Fellow. "I haven't abandoned the world."

His muscular body then began to shrink, while, conversely, his hair grew and grew and grew. The Fake-Ginger-Fellow was now a bespectacled little lady. Victoria had only seen God-mother once, but she reminded her a little of her. But more than anything, she reminded her of Mommy. It was the way her eyes searched for her own in the darkness. Like a void just seeking to be filled.

"My name is Eulalia. And I won't abandon you either, little girl."

The Bespectacled-Little-Lady went back to looking like the Fake-Ginger-Fellow, and turned around with a stumble, as if it were tricky for her—for him—to make their body move in the opposite direction, and then waited.

After much hesitation, Victoria decided to follow them, her—him—and those shadows.

THE WHITENESS

"What do you think they felt?" asked Ambrose. "Those who fell into the void."

Perched on the wheelchair's rear running-board, Ophelia couldn't see his face. She couldn't see a great deal, in fact. The young whaxi driver had opened a mechanical parasol above her, which kept falling in front of her glasses, and when she managed to push it away, a giant turban then obstructed her view. The scarf hadn't wanted Ambrose to go out without it; it had clung on to him with its every stitch, as if wanting to meld with his hair and become part of him. Owing to the dress code, he had swathed it in white fabric, which was now billowing out from his head.

Try as she might to reason with herself, Ophelia still felt deprived of a little part of herself.

"I don't know."

"I already told you my father attempted to explore the void between the arks, didn't I? He wanted to photograph the core of the world but didn't manage to descend that far. No one has ever managed to. Maybe they're not *vraiment* dead, those who fell? Maybe they're all down there, prisoners of those perpetual thunderstorms? Or then," continued Ambrose, having only just avoided a dodo crossing the road, "maybe they reemerged on the other side? Maybe they're now a world away from here,

94

in the vicinity of another ark? That would contradict the principle of planetary memory—you know, the one that says all arks occupy an absolute position among themselves—but I prefer that concept to . . . *eh bien* . . . you know."

Ambrose had at least this in common with Lazarus: he could talk enough for two—and then some.

"My father set off on his travels at the worst time," he sighed, gazing at the sky that stood out between the roofs of Babel. "I hope he's doing well. He's often away, I don't always understand all he's up to, but he loves me," he assured, as if fearing that Ophelia had doubts on the subject. "He always told me I was *très* important, despite my inversion."

"Have you ever been to the Deviations Observatory?"

"Never, *mademoiselle*. When he's back in Babel, my father sometimes goes there to deliver new automatons to them. The directors of the observatory are among his biggest clients! My father says, in jest, that they would find it more interesting actually to dissect him—you know, because of his *situs transversus*—but he'd rather wait until he's dead to donate his organs to science, even if they are on the wrong side."

Ophelia visualized the huge, full-length portrait of Lazarus that had pride of place in his home. Yes, that was just the kind of thing he would say.

"I would like to ask you something else. Something personal."

"*Bien sûr, mademoiselle!*"

"What became of your mother?"

Ambrose looked around at Ophelia with surprise, and almost crashed into the rickshaw that had stopped ahead of him. All the highways were congested. This had been the case since the Babelians had started to flee from the outskirts and the neighboring minor arks. They only felt safe in the town center. Ambrose's wheelchair could thread its way around the omnibuses and carts, but there were also the delivery tricycles, luggage trolleys, animals, machines, and crowds of pedestrians taking up every stretch of public highway to contend with. Some of them made a beeline for the stopped vehicles to beg their occupants to take them in, just until they found somewhere to stay.

Everywhere, the air was ringing with *"S'il vous plaît! S'il vous plaît! S'il vous plaît!"*

Ophelia refused to feel any guilt over the landslide, but that didn't stop her feeling bad for all these people. Several among them had the same stamp as her on their foreheads. She had almost grazed her skin from scrubbing hers with soap, without the ink so much as fading.

Ambrose pulled his wheelchair out of the gridlock by cutting across the jungle of a public garden, where entire families had put up tents.

"I would like to know the answer to that myself," he finally replied. "I didn't know my mother, and my father ceases to be talkative whenever she comes up. I couldn't even tell you which ark she comes from, or whether I look like her."

His voice had lost some of its cheeriness. Ophelia felt silly for having been jealous of him because of the scarf.

He parked his wheelchair in front of a majestic marble building, on the pediment of which was engraved:

OFFICIAL JOURNAL

"You have reached your destination, *mademoiselle*. What took place," he added, gently, "it's not your fault, you do know that?"

Ophelia stepped down from the running board and looked Ambrose straight in the eye.

"Let it be clear, I don't wish to find the Other because I feel at fault, or because I promised your father to do so."

"You're doing so because that's your decision," he finished for her. "I have understood that, *parfaitement*, yes."

Ophelia smiled at them—at him and the enormous turban billowing on his head. She wanted to make her own choices; the scarf had the right to make its choices.

"One day, Ambrose, I really must repay you for your services. You have many qualities, but a business sense isn't one of them."

She went into the journal's offices, alone this time. The hubbub inside was a combination of ringing telephones, clicking rotary presses, competing voices, and, dominating this high-pitched din, the deep counterpoint of the ceiling fans.

"*Désolé, mademoiselle*, we can't tell you anything."

Ophelia hadn't even been given a chance to ask her question. The employee at reception, with one telephone receiver in his hand, and another wedged between chin and shoulder, indicated the exit to her with his elbow.

"I would just like to know—"

"Read our journal," the employee cut in, shoving a dispenser of copies forward with his foot. "It contains all one needs to know."

". . . where I might find aspiring-virtuoso Octavio," continued Ophelia.

"Eulalia?"

A tall stack of files had suddenly turned toward her. Beneath the stack gleamed some boots with silver-wing spurs. When these pivoted around, Ophelia found herself looking straight into Octavio's red eyes. They glowed like embers under two circumflex eyebrows, raised in surprise, before turning to the employee, who instantly put his two receivers down.

"I request your permission to let this person in. I know her."

"Very good, my lord. *Désolé*, my lord."

"That employee addresses you as if you were the editorial director," Ophelia remarked, as she followed Octavio through the various departments of the journal.

He didn't react, as he deposited files on every desk corner, and responded reluctantly to the journalists' excessive expressions of gratitude—"Thank you, my lord! Do present my respects to Lady Septima!"—until his entire pile was distributed. He then took Ophelia into a room that was amazingly quiet compared with the other departments, and on the door of which a plaque was fixed saying "ARTS CRITICISM." A radio was broadcasting a piano piece in there, a performance Ophelia would have found splendid had it not been endlessly marred by echoes. An Acoustic was listening to it with a dubious expression, ears pricked up like a cat's, and letting out the odd "ooh" and "aah."

Octavio indicated to Ophelia to sit at a vacant meeting table, in the light divided by a curtain at the window. The piano, and the "oohs" and "aahs," immediately stopped. Here they were in a soundproof zone. For as long as they remained seated there, they wouldn't hear the rest of the world, and wouldn't be heard by it, either.

"I'm relieved to see you," Octavio declared, straight off. "When that landslide occurred in the northwestern district, I realized I had no idea where you were living, since your departure from the Good Family."

Ophelia studied the patina on the table, in which their two faces were reflected. She had put Ambrose through the same scrutiny on the silver salvers at breakfast. It was a disagreeable precaution, but necessary. She had to put her feelings aside, and never consider the identity of the person before her as authentic. She didn't know how the Other and Eulalia Gonde would appear to her when the time came, but if the former really was the reflection that the latter had lost, only mirrors could reveal their identity and make the masks fall.

It was only once she was sure Octavio really was Octavio that she felt touched by his words. She noticed that he hadn't replaced the gold chain that Fearless-and-Almost-Blameless had torn off him and knew instantly that he never would. That item of jewelry was the visible sign of his filiation to a Lord of LUX. Ophelia considered Octavio her equal—and not only because he was the same age and size as her—but that wasn't the case for all those who put him on a pedestal.

"I'm so sorry," she told him, sincerely. "Even here, people see you first and foremost as Lady Septima's son."

Through his long, black fringe, covering half of his face, Octavio mustered a smile that was neither really joyful nor entirely sad.

"The opinion of my friends is all that matters."

He poured what remained in a carafe into a glass and offered it to Ophelia. The light from the window filtered through the water and ended up quivering on the table.

"*En fait*, of my only friend. What can I do for you? If it's regarding that," he continued, indicating the stamp on her forehead, "the press releases from the family palace haven't yet divulged its meaning. The journal is being deluged with requests for information. I can only tell you that it concerns, almost exclusively, Goddaughters of Helen resident in Babel for less than ten years."

"Elizabeth explained that to me, yes."

Octavio's eyes began to glow red, under the effect of his family power.

"You're a little disappointed," he noted. "I can see from the way your facial muscles have gone slightly slack."

Ophelia crossed her arms in front of her stomach. She knew Octavio's vision wasn't that of a doctor but being scrutinized like this made her feel uncomfortable now. He must have noticed, since, discreetly, he looked away.

"It's not because I'm working, as an aspiring Forerunner, at the *Official Journal,* that I suddenly know everything. I'm still partly a student and am now responsible for a whole division at the Good Family. My work here consists *seulement* of checking the pertinence of the letters citizens send us, and nine times out of ten they're not reliable. The Brats of Babel don't make our task any easier by misinforming the public, thanks to their doomsaying leaflets and false rumors."

It was Ophelia's turn to look carefully at him. The sun had just disappeared behind the curtains, engulfed by a sudden tide of clouds, and that shadow reinforced the one already beneath Octavio's fringe.

"I'm not as observant as you, but I've got to know you. What's wrong?"

Ophelia suddenly realized how tense her own shoulders had become under her gown. She tried not to think about it, but she feared that, at any moment, she could be told that Anima had disappeared. She had left her family without a word of explanation, and, although she felt she hadn't really had a choice—what with her mother making all decisions and her father avoiding all responsibility—she regretted every day not to have told them how much she loved them.

Octavio glanced at the other side of the room, where the critic kept hitting the radio, doubtless exasperated by the echoes. She was paying no attention to the two of them, and even if she had, her Acoustic's ears wouldn't have been able to hear them, keen as they were.

"I don't know," he finally admitted. "As I told you, Eulalia, we're continuously receiving communiqués. Several were telegraphed to us from Totem, the ark closest to Babel. They give the impression that they, too, are experiencing difficulties, but right now it's impossible for us to check the authenticity of the source."

Ophelia took a sip from her glass. The water was as boiling hot as the air, despite the ceiling fans.

"Could the journal not send someone over there?"

"For now, all long-distance flights are suspended. The echoes are disrupting radio communications, and no one can explain why, suddenly, they are so prolific. It's not a problem for shorter journeys—I myself travelled here by birdtrain this morning—but flying over that great sea of clouds without any bearings is a different story."

"Those echoes again . . . What exactly are they?"

This query wasn't addressed to Octavio in particular, so Ophelia was surprised by his categorical answer:

"They shouldn't exist at all, and that's precisely the problem. Technically, they're not even echoes in the true sense of the word. A normal echo, for example, is when our voice comes back at us once it has rebounded off a wall. It's the return of a sound wave to the source that emitted it. These echoes behave completely differently. One doesn't hear them, one doesn't see them. Only our technological apparatuses pick them up, accidentally. No," Octavio concluded, solemnly, "those echoes don't travel on the same wavelength as ours. There's nothing *normal* about them. And even worse, they've become dangerous."

And yet, Ophelia reflected, according to Lazarus they were "the key to it all."

"Here, at the journal," Octavio continued, "we know, however, that a convoy of airships was readied last night. An initiative of the Lords of LUX. They seem to be considering leaving Babel. Maybe they've found a way to get around the echoes problem with the navigation systems? We await the official communiqués to know more."

Every time Octavio mentioned the Lords of LUX, the thought of his mother could be heard in his voice. His eyelids closed, like two candle-snuffers on the flames of his eyes, but even like that he seemed able to see through them.

"I have to check the authenticity of all the communiqués," he repeated. "All, apart from those issued by LUX, and thus from almost all of the institutions. The Lords' word is never questioned. Has the city ceased to be transparent, or is it only my vision that has changed?"

Ophelia was brought back to reality by the chiming of the table clock. Judging by the time, Thorn must have already assumed his new duties.

"I have a favor to ask you. It's both tricky for you and important to me."

She took a deep breath, searching for her words. If Octavio considered her a friend, the feeling was mutual. She would have liked to confide in him, but that wasn't possible without her mentioning the Genealogists' mission, and thereby compromising Thorn. She couldn't tell him the truth, but she didn't want to lie to him, either. She thought back to the doctor's words at her physical—she was constantly thinking of them, in fact—and decided to use them as a compromise.

"I've been advised to attend the Deviations Observatory. As a subject of study. You once spoke to me of your sister, Second. You told me that you visited her over there every Sunday. You know how that institution works better than I do. What advice can you give me?"

Octavio reopened his eyes, as if Ophelia had just thrown the rest of her glass of water in his face.

"My break is over," he declared, sharply.

As soon as they rose from the table, the silence burst like a bubble. The journalist's typewriter sounded as loud as percussion, drowning out the muffled voice from the radio:

". . . a musical feat of which only . . . of which only Romulus is capable, rivaling the fingering technique of the very greatest . . . very greatest Tactiles in the city." Octavio made straight for the main exit, the wings on his boots clicking at each stride. Ophelia followed right behind, not really knowing if their conversation was over, or not. Along the way, she bumped into a journalist hurling a pile of photographs into the wastepaper basket and shouting that they were all ruined, and that until this echo problem was resolved, he couldn't do his job anymore. Ophelia picked up a photograph that had fallen on the floor and saw that, indeed, the image was duplicated to such an extent one couldn't even make out what it was supposed to represent.

"Hugo, let's go."

Octavio had given this order to one of the automatons lined up in the large hall. He had no expression, having no face, but seemed to set off reluctantly, while his stomach let out a "No news is good news." Across his body he carried what resembled a post-bag. An aerial stood up on top of his head, and a telegraphic device had been fitted into his chest.

"Hugo gathers the communiqués I have to verify," Octavio explained, holding the door for Ophelia. "He also functions like the Public Signaling Guides to direct me to the right address. If you're not pressed for time, come with us."

His tone was curt, but less so than she had feared.

Outside, all was white. The high tide had caused an avalanche of clouds to stream between the marble facades. Ophelia exchanged a complicit wave with Ambrose, whose barely visible wheelchair remained parked in front of the steps, and then she plunged into the clouds behind Octavio and the automaton. Her glasses were instantly covered in mist. She couldn't see a thing anymore, bumping into passersby and fire hydrants. A few steps in the street were enough to drench her gown with humidity. She could almost feel her hair curling up on her head.

"I didn't see my sister growing up."

Octavio's voice, somewhere to her left, was dampened as much by bitterness as by fog. His wary steps made his wings jingle.

"I wasn't even there when she was born," he continued, speaking fast. "I was being educated at a boarding school, with Pollux's Cadets, with never a visit from my parents. To be honest with you, I didn't know my mother was pregnant. The day she announced to me that I had a little sister was also the day I discovered that our father had gone. I never even asked to see Second. It didn't really bother me that she was abnormal; I resented her for shattering our stability. When my mother did come to see me at the boarding school, to let me know that she had sent my sister to the Deviations Observatory, I just thought: "*Tant mieux*, good riddance.""

Ophelia could barely see Octavio, whose midnight-blue uniform, blanked out by the surrounding whiteness, was speeding ahead in front of her. Hugo himself was struggling to follow him, repeating in a metallic voice: "FOLLOW THE GUIDE, PLEASE!" Ambrose's wheelchair accompanied them at a distance, with its unmistakable mechanical clickety-clack.

"It took me some time to want to meet her," continued Octavio. "I finally visited her at the observatory, without my mother knowing. I, who claimed to know everything, realized that I knew nothing about this girl who shares my blood. I returned there, again and again, but she remains an enigma to me. She ceased to belong to my world the day she entered that observatory."

Like two headlights, Octavio's eyes suddenly turned on Ophelia.

"Don't go there."

"I've no intention of staying more than—"

"You don't understand," Octavio interrupted her. "Entering there is easy, getting out, far less so. Once you are part of their system, you are automatically placed under their guardianship. You give up your freedom of movement, and your right to communicate with the outside world, apart from visits, and they are *strictement* controlled. In short, you belong to them."

Ophelia's whole body stiffened. Infiltrating the observatory would force her to sacrifice what little free will she had garnered over the years.

"I deplored the city's lack of transparency," Octavio continued, sternly, "but there's no comparison with the obfuscation that reigns over there."

In contrast to these words, a burst of sunlight flooded the bridge they were just crossing. There were fewer people here than on the main avenues. This unexpected light, between two waves of clouds, made the humid grass sprouting between the cobblestones sparkle; it had no effect on Octavio's dark skin, hair, and uniform.

Ophelia didn't want to cause him any trouble. Yet she couldn't hold back her question:

"Have you ever heard of the Horn of Plenty?"

Taken aback, Octavio frowned.

"*Bien sûr!* It's a mythological reference. The Horn of Plenty varies from one ark to another, sometimes a plate, sometimes a bowl, sometimes a conch, but the principle remains the same: it confers abundance on whoever possesses it. What's that got to do with what we were talking about?"

"You say it varies from one ark to another. I'd like to know what exactly it represents here, in Babel."

Octavio stopped so suddenly in the middle of the bridge that Hugo crashed into him, spouting: "A FRIEND IS A PATH, AN ENEMY A WALL." Octavio met Ophelia's gaze through her glasses. She knew he was using his family power to decipher the fluttering of her eyelashes, steadiness of her irises, dilation of her pupils.

"Here, the Horn of Plenty is closely linked to all that is forbidden. According to one version of the legend, from before the Rupture, men and women coveted it so much that they . . . they caused harm to one another."

In Babel, no term belonging to the lexicon of violence was to be uttered in public. Even the word "crime" was a crime.

"The Horn of Plenty deemed them to be unworthy of it, and so buried itself where no one would be able to find it," concluded Octavio. "It awaits the time when humanity will finally show itself to be deserving of its blessings. The last time you asked me such ludicrous questions, it almost ended very badly. Is there something I should know?"

His mouth demanded the truth, his eyes were scared.

"No," said Ophelia.

She had no idea what she was entering into; she had no right to drag Octavio along with her, once again.

In the meantime, she still couldn't see what this Horn of Plenty had to do with the story. However, if Eulalia Gonde had worked on a project named after it, if the Other was linked to that, and if the Deviations Observatory was in the midst of conducting the same experiments at this precise moment, then Ophelia had to get herself over there as fast as possible, and too bad if that meant her temporarily becoming its prisoner.

"From the very first day, I found that there was something disturbing about you," Octavio said to her, screwing up his eyes. "I've finally grasped what it was. Whatever your objectives, you were always determined to reach them. As for me, I adapted so willingly to the path set by my mother that I don't know what I really want. I envy you. *Maintenant*, if you don't mind, I have a little job to do."

Indeed, Hugo had stopped outside the entrance to a

windmill, on the other side of the bridge, and was tapping the ground impatiently with his articulated foot. If automatons were capable of developing a personality, Ophelia would have been inclined to think that this one was bad-tempered. From a distance, she signaled again in the direction of Ambrose's wheelchair; he seemed to be hesitating between coming closer and keeping his distance. She herself wasn't too sure what she was supposed to do now. Looking professional, Octavio knocked on the door, with no longer a thought for her.

"Good day, my lady," he said, when an elderly miller's wife came to the door. "I have come about this."

Octavio showed her the telegram that Hugo had extracted with a metallic grunt.

"No, thanks," said the miller's wife.

She closed the door. Octavio shot a furious glance at Ophelia, defying her to laugh, and then knocked until the old lady reopened to him.

"I must insist, my lady. I am here on behalf of the *Official Journal*. You sent this telegram to us yesterday."

The miller's wife frowned, producing an impressive eddy of wrinkles. She put on large pince-nez and took a look at the telegram.

"*Désolée*. I took you for another of those 'Brats,' as they call themselves. They've already been here twice this morning with their leaflets. Have you taken a good look at me, young man? Celebrating the end of the world? At my age?"

"You stated that you had witnessed the landslide," said Octavio, unperturbed. "I will need some details."

"It wasn't a landslide."

Ophelia was struck by the miller's wife's confidence in asserting that. She also noticed the impressive length of her tongue, an indication that she belonged to the genealogical branch of the Gustatories. As for Octavio, he was focusing on the most microscopic changes in her expression. He was assessing her sincerity.

"Wasn't your telegram about the landslide that swept away the northwestern district of the city?"

"Yes, yes, young man. I was at the spice market, for my curry-flavored bread, when it happened. What's more, it was pouring with rain. Except it wasn't a landslide."

"What was it, then, in your opinion?"

"Well, I haven't the faintest idea. It's your job to tell me, isn't it?"

"You will make that easier for me, my lady, by giving me more details."

"What do you want me to tell you? One moment the ground was there, the next it wasn't. It barely shook my bones. Not like it had cracked, little by little, before giving way. More like it . . . like an invisible mouth had swallowed it all up in one go," said the miller's wife, miming a snapping of jaws. *En tout cas*, there was nothing natural about it."

If Octavio seemed skeptical, Ophelia was shivering all over, despite the heat. An invisible mouth. The Other's mouth? Could a reflection possess such a mouth?

"Did you notice someone or something?" she couldn't help but interject. "Anything that might have struck you as unusual?"

"Nothing at all," replied the miller's wife. "Everything was exactly as it usually is. You don't believe me because of that?" she asked, indignantly, tapping a lens of her pince-nez. "I may not be a Visionary, but I saw what I'm telling you as clear as I see the light on your forehead, *là*."

She pointed her finger straight at Ophelia, who blinked without understanding. Octavio's pupils constricted as soon as he, in turn, stared at her and was dazzled.

"Eulalia, your stamp . . . it's turned white."

THE CHOSEN ONES

Ophelia examined her reflection in the nearest window. The Alchemist ink on her forehead hadn't just changed from black to white. It was glowing like a full moon. Even when she placed her hand over it, light escaped between her gloved fingers.

"What is . . ."

Her question was drowned out by a trumpet-loud voice:

"Public announcement! This is to inform our fellow citizens that residents who are foreign . . . foreign bearing a white stamp are requested to go forthwith . . . forthwith to the municipal amphitheater. Public announcement!"

While the instruction and its echoes boomed out incessantly across the district, Ophelia turned her glasses in all directions. People had emerged from dwellings and stationary vehicles to gather around the post of every loudspeaker. Although this crowd of the curious formed a blurred mass amidst the sea of clouds, Ophelia did pick out a panicking man whose forehead was as luminous as her own.

Octavio took her aside, to be heard above the blare of the loudspeakers.

"Don't you worry. It's a mere formality."

"I don't want to go there."

"You have to. Civil disobedience would mean breaking the

law. I'm sure it's *vraiment* nothing serious. Not that long ago, you were still an apprentice virtuoso. I'll come with you."

Octavio pushed back his black curtain of hair to look straight at Ophelia. She wondered why his eyes had turned purple, then realized it was her own glasses that had turned blue. He may have wanted to reassure her, but he had himself totally forgotten the miller's wife outside the windmill, who was asking if she could get back to her work. And he paid no more attention to Hugo, whose chest telegraph had been churning out a relentless stream of communiqués since that first public announcement.

Ophelia searched for Ambrose, but couldn't locate him in the midst of all that chaos. She didn't, however, miss any of the patrols posted on every street, who, on seeing her forehead, ordered her to go straight to the assembly point. Some Zephyrs had even been employed to disperse, with their great gusts of wind, the clouds obscuring any nooks and crannies in which possible rebels could be hiding.

Octavio could say what he liked, Ophelia wasn't remotely reassured. She had promised Thorn she would find a way of joining him at the Deviations Observatory; she had no time to waste on any more administrative procedures. She would have passed through the first mirror to appear, if there had been any on her path.

Before long, she spotted, above the highest roofs, the towering structure of the municipal amphitheater. Its hundreds of arcades were a skillful alliance of stone, metal, glass, and vegetation. The colorful birds that flocked to nest there were like bees swarming around a hive. As the radio announcements continued to reverberate through the air, those being summoned poured from the four corners of the city and surged through the entrances to the amphitheater. Ophelia was amazed at their number. Among them were citizens from almost every ark, wearing the traditional garb imposed by the dress code: peplos, ribbons, boleros, feathers, veils, tartans, doublets, kimonos . . . Despite their differences, each one of them bore the same stamp and shared the same anxiety.

Ophelia's uneasiness intensified when it was her turn to pass through the doors. The family guard, whose noses resembled actual lions' muzzles, sniffed her from head to toe. Why had Olfactories been posted at the entryways?

"They are just taking precautions," Octavio commented.

All the same, Ophelia noticed that his circumflex eyebrows were now a frown. He presented himself as representing the *Official Journal*, and was greeted with the formal salutations generally reserved for the Lords of LUX. Even his automaton was entitled to more respect than Ophelia, who was obliged to turn out the pockets of her gown and show their contents.

Next, they had to climb a maze of dark stairs, where the foreheads of the summoned glowed like a procession of lanterns. Even if Ambrose had followed them up to there, his wheelchair wouldn't have been able to tackle all those steps.

Ophelia squinted when, after a final set of stairs, she emerged into the sunlight. The tiers were all open-air. The amphitheater seemed even more imposing from the inside. It had the capacity to accommodate many more people than all those who had been summoned there today, and that was really saying something.

"Take your seats quietly, *mesdames et messieurs*!" the loud-speakers exhorted at regular intervals.

Ophelia had no desire to obey them. She had just noticed the airships moored in the arena, like dormant whales. They were of a kind exclusive to Babel, combining technological innovation and interfamilial know-how. The LUX sun emblem glinted like gold on their fuselages.

"The long-distance airships," murmured Octavio. "*Pourquoi ici*? I don't understand a thing anymore."

"Mademoiselle Eulalia?"

Ophelia shaded her eyes from the sun. She had barely sat down on the scorching stone of a tier when a silhouette against the light had leant over her shoulder. It had black, watery eyes, a large pointed nose, and shaggy hair. The "assistant" badge shone out on its Memorialist's uniform.

"Blaise!"

"I thought I'd recognized your smell in the crowd."

Of all the Olfactories that Ophelia had met up to now, Blaise was definitely the only one whose acute sense of smell didn't irritate her.

"What are you doing here?" she asked in surprise, looking, in vain, for a stamp on his forehead. "You're a Son of Pollux. Don't tell me that you, too, have been summoned?"

Blaise's smile became even more bashful.

"*En fait*, I'm accompanying my . . . er . . . my friend."

If Ophelia hadn't expected to meet Blaise in this amphitheater, she was even more surprised to see Professor Wolf there, as indicated by Blaise, standing behind him. Black suit, black gloves, black glasses, black goatee; his hat, also black, was tilted in such a way as to block the glow of his stamp. He was the only Animist that Ophelia had encountered in Babel; unlike her, he was born there. His spectacles slid, on their own, down his nose to allow him to scrutinize both her and Octavio.

"Well, well," he grunted. "And there was I, hoping never to have anything to do with you ever again."

This statement didn't stop him from sitting down to the left of Hugo, whose stomach let out a "LOVE THY NEIGHBOR, BUT DON'T DISPENSE WITH THY FENCE." Wolf's rigidity, accentuated by his wooden neck brace, rivaled that of the automaton.

"Professor, your summons must be a mistake," Octavio said to him. "You may not be a descendant of Pollux, but you are still a native of Babel. According to our information, at the *Official Journal*, only recent arrivals are affected by these measures."

"They carried out a search of my home and fell on my collection of arm—"

"*Of forbidden items*," corrected Blaise, beside him, with an anxious glance at the neighboring tiers.

Mockingly, Professor Wolf raised his hat, to dazzle him with his forehead.

"What, you fear I'm going to be informed against, again? Let me remind you that my landlady has already taken care of that. It's what's brewing here, today, that doesn't smell too good."

Just as he was grunting these words, bird excrement plopped right on top of his luminous stamp. Convinced that he was responsible for this latest sign of bad luck, Blaise apologized profusely and helped Wolf to clean himself up, knocking his dark glasses sideways with an accidental jab of the elbow. When, with a sigh, Wolf put his hat back on, Ophelia noticed that his face had lost some of its hardness.

The last time she had spoken to him, he was hiding up on the roofs in the neighborhood of the powerless. At the time, he was running from what he feared most in the world, and, as Ophelia now understood, that wasn't just the old sweeper of the Memorial, who had come right into his home to terrify him. Here, in the middle of this crowd, swelling by the minute along the tiers, he seemed to be battling an acute attack of misanthropy that only Blaise's presence could soothe.

Ophelia found herself envying the pair of them. She also had a bad feeling about what awaited them, but whatever that might be, she would have to face up to it without Thorn. Maybe he wasn't even aware of this public summons at the opposite end of Babel.

"Your attention, *s'il vous plaît.*"

This voice, amplified by the loudspeakers in the amphitheater, sounded unpleasantly familiar to Ophelia's ears. Octavio's hands tightened on his knees. The anxious whispering fell silent, from tier to tier. The face of a woman, enlarged, had just been projected on to the fuselage of each airship floating above the arena. Her eyes, with their impressive acuity, seemed to probe every soul.

Lady Septima. She was at once Octavio's mother, an exceptional Visionary, and an influential member of LUX. For Ophelia, she had, above all, been a formidable teacher, who had exploited her object-reading talents while continually belittling them.

"Thank you, to each one of you, for having responded to the summons," she boomed. "Thank you, also, to Sir Pollux and Lady Helen, here present, for the trust . . . trust they have placed in us, the Lords of LUX, most humble servants of the city."

Ophelia turned to look in the same direction as everyone else. The twin family spirits were sitting, enthroned, high up in a stand, sheltered beneath a crimson canopy. They were too far away for her to see them clearly, but she did pick up flashes from the multiple lenses of Helen's optical appliance. She could have sworn that they hadn't really been given the choice to attend, either.

"As you know," continued Lady Septima's enormous mouth on the fuselage of each airship, "Babel is going through a crisis. The recent landslide in the northwest of the city, and the disappearance of six minor arks, has greatly distressed . . . distressed all of us. Nothing indicates to us that such a catastrophe could reoccur, but it remains no less terrible a tragedy, and the outskirts of the city will, temporarily, be designated an uninhabitable zone. I invite you all to observe a minute's silence . . . silence in memory of those we have lost, but also for those who have had to abandon their homes."

During this minute of silence, each summoned person was surely far more preoccupied with their own fate. Ophelia put it to good use by discreetly turning her glasses toward the stairwell they had arrived by. A security shutter had been lowered over it. A few glances around told her that all entrances to the tiers were closed.

If they wanted to turn back, it was too late.

"Today, the city needs you," Lady Septima continued, solemnly. "Our fellow citizens must regain some stability. The stamps you all bear on your foreheads make you the chosen ones. You have been designated, from among so many others . . . so many others due to your great capacity for autonomy."

Feeling increasingly tense, Ophelia rubbed her forehead, which was casting a halo of light on the lenses of her glasses. She noticed that several of those summoned were, like her and Wolf, accompanied by people who didn't bear the administrative stamp.

"*En effet*, none of you is currently detained in the city by any obligation," Lady Septima explained, articulating each syllable, "whether of a professional, conjugal, or parental nature. Babel has long sheltered you in its bosom, but it no longer has the space to harbor you. Thus, you are all requested to leave our ark as from today . . . as from today. Your possessions and properties have already been requisitioned by the city, and will be fairly redistributed among our fellow citizens. We do not doubt that you will be welcomed with open arms by your native arks. Your families will ensure that you are lacking in

115

nothing once you're there. Thank you to each one of you for thereby acting in the general interest. Would you now . . . now proceed to the aircraft by following the instructions you are given. Your stamps will be erased once you have boarded. On behalf of all the Lords of LUX, of Lady Helen and Lord Pollux, go in peace!"

Lady Septima's faces disappeared from the airships. The end of her speech was followed by such complete silence, you could hear everyone's skin heating up in the sun. When the initial protests rose up, the loudspeakers released a piercing whistle that forced everyone to cover their ears:

"*Mesdames et messieurs*, let everyone proceed quietly. The lower rows first. Those accompanying the travelers . . . travelers are requested to remain in their seats until the complete evacuation of the amphitheater."

The announcement was immediately replaced by background music, but turned up to full volume and distorted by the echoes, drowning out all voices. No one could speak to anyone anymore. The family guard circulated in the lower tiers, directing the men and women seated there to make their way to the convoy of airships. Each queue was methodically formed, subdivided, reoriented. A few people did attempt to show their distress. They shook their heads, beat their chests, pointed up at the sky, beyond the amphitheater's walls, and their whole bodies seemed to scream, "home!" "friends!" "work!" The guards, resplendent in their armor, remained resolute. There were others who attempted to raise the security shutters on the exits, or even to pass for those accompanying by tying a scarf around their forehead; they were dispatched to the airship arena as a priority. From being hesitant, the movement of the crowd became resigned. So efficient was the organization that a first airship, already full, was soon taking off with a whirring of propellers.

Seated in the higher tiers, Ophelia had watched all this while thinking at full speed.

She turned to Octavio, who looked distraught, and then to Blaise, whose mouth had twisted into a tormented combination of incredulity and guilt, and finally to Wolf, who, behind a stoical front, had turned so pale that the white ink of his stamp blended into his skin.

"No," she said to all three of them.

She didn't need to make herself heard by them—her face spoke for her. No, she would not obey. She had already been forcibly repatriated to Anima once before; she wouldn't be a second time. Her place was at the Deviations Observatory, by Thorn's side, where the answers were to be found.

She darted in the opposite direction to the procession already being marshaled by the family guard in this part of the amphitheater. She slipped between the summoned, into every gap her diminutive size allowed. She wouldn't go unnoticed for long. If there had been someone there to call out to her, she wouldn't have heard them anyway: the repeated instructions and musical interludes from the loudspeakers drowned out every sound.

Tier after tier, Ophelia kept her eyes fixed on the great crimson canopy, billowing like a sail. She couldn't see whether Helen and Pollux were still there, in its shade, but they alone could put an end to these expulsions.

She was just about to reach the VIP stand when she was stopped in her tracks. A steel gauntlet had just gripped her arm. A guard. With a jerk of his chin, he silently commanded her to rejoin the nearest line. He was carrying no weapon—merely saying that word constituted an offense—but his grip was firm. Ophelia looked straight into his eyes and was surprised to detect suffering in them. His Acoustic's ears were flattened, almost like an animal's, to protect him from the loudspeakers' cacophony. And yet his pain seemed to reside elsewhere. It was obeying his orders that grieved him. Ophelia then realized, like a punch in the stomach, that the Lords of LUX were endangering them all by making them board the airships.

She hardened every muscle in her face to make herself clear to the guard through her flesh:

"No."

One sandal after the other, she edged toward the stand, pulling with all her might on her steel-clamped arm. Violence was forbidden in Babel; that applied to this guard, too. If he didn't release his grip, he would dislocate her shoulder.

He gave in.

Ophelia dived into the stand. Before her, the two family spirits, as massive as the pillars holding up the canopy, were passively watching the evacuation.

"Stop these embarkations!"

She had drawn on all the breath left in her lungs to scream these words, and yet she couldn't distinguish her own voice from those of the loudspeakers.

Pollux turned from the arena. He had heard her. With his acute senses, statuesque physique, and paternal benevolence, he had the makings of a king. And yet the golden eyes he directed down at Ophelia expressed only powerlessness. He was incapable of the slightest initiative.

She ignored him to address Helen, and only her:

"Stop these embarkations," she repeated, articulating each syllable. "The echoes are dangerous. They disrupt the navigation controls."

With a mechanical slowness, Helen rotated on the casters of her crinoline dress until she, in turn, was facing Ophelia. The optical appliance fixed to her elephantine nose began to raise certain lenses and lower others, adjusting her vision until she could make out Ophelia. The giant was herself somewhat painful to look at. So narrow was her wasp waist, between her more than ample hips and bust, she seemed about to snap at any moment.

All that these twin family spirits had in common was the book they each carried, attached to their belt: two Books with pages as dark as their own skin.

The guard, who had followed Ophelia into the stand and was visibly torn between what he should or shouldn't do, sought to intervene. With a spiderlike movement, Helen gestured to him to leave her alone. Had she grasped the seriousness of the situation? Her enhanced hearing, which already struggled with the slam of a door or a loudly blown nose, was here being assailed from all directions.

Ophelia pointed at the second airship as it was taking off.

"Do you really agree with this? You are entitled to have your say, you are our godmother. I was myself one of your pupils."

Helen's huge mouth articulated a response that didn't reach Ophelia, but she guessed, from the querying curl of her lips, that it was more of a question. She couldn't remember her. Like all the family spirits whose Books had been mutilated by Eulalia Gonde, Helen was condemned to forget everything all of the time. Why would she give more credence to a little stranger than to the Lords of LUX?

Ophelia unfolded the page that she kept preciously among her false papers.

COME AND SEE ME SOMETIME, YOUR HANDS AND YOU.

"You have already trusted me once."

She raised herself up on tiptoe and handed the message to Helen, whose optical appliance was immediately set in motion on her nose to enable her to read. She would at least recognize her own handwriting. It may not have been possible to see her eyes, due to the layers of lenses, but it was quite clear that Ophelia now had her full attention.

"Help us."

Helen's long fingers closed around Ophelia's wrists like crabs' claws. The paper tore.

"The echoes aren't dangerous, young lady."

Ophelia felt Helen's voice vibrating against her cheeks, spreading right across her skin, besieging her eardrums to the detriment of all that wasn't her. Neither loudspeakers nor amphitheater were there anymore.

"The echoes speak to whoever knows how to listen to them. You are all, including my brother, blind and deaf."

Helen's mouth was an abyss bristling with teeth, so close that Ophelia could have counted them if there hadn't been so many.

"The echoes are everywhere now. They are in the very air you are breathing."

Helen finally released Ophelia's wrists, on which her fingernails had left their mark. Very carefully, she removed the optical appliance, which she was never without, and without which she saw the world as but galaxies of atoms. Her pupils, exceedingly dilated, took over her eyes. They were like her mouth: wells that devoured the light. That devoured Ophelia.

"They are everywhere, young lady, and around you even more than anywhere else. You attract the echoes like flies. They expect the unexpected from you."

Ophelia was stunned.

"But the airshi—"

"Shut up and listen."

The enormous pupils saw, heard, touched things that were completely beyond Ophelia.

"You should go beyond the cage. Turn back. Really turn back. There, and only there, you will understand. You may even be able to make yourself useful. You claim that I afforded you my trust, to your hands and to you, but when the time is over, will you have enough fingers?"

All that Ophelia had grasped in this tangle of words was that Helen wouldn't be stopping the expulsions. She was like a radio receiver tuned to a different frequency from her own. The frequency of the echoes? The very second Helen went quiet, the sensory barrier that her power had surrounded her with shattered.

Ophelia was engulfed in noise, and it was no longer just the loudspeakers. What was taking place now, right around the stand, led her to think that maybe she had made the situation worse.

The Fabrication

As the family guard lost control, men and women surged forward to hold out their arms, imploringly, to the family spirits. They pointed at Ophelia, indicating that they, too, wanted the right to plead their cause. The canopy's shade intensified the luminous ink on their foreheads. Their cries were so desperate, in some cases, so indignant in others, they could be heard despite the sirens.

All were repeating the same words:

"Give us a job!"

Because her optical appliance was in her hand, Helen watched them without seeing them, listened to them without hearing them. As for Pollux, he smiled at them, hesitantly. Far from diminishing, the cries just got louder.

Never had Ophelia witnessed such an uprising in a public place in Babel. All of these people, whom they wanted to send back to their families of origin, had started building new lives for themselves here. How many of them would see their homes inhabited by others? How many were being thrown out when they had nowhere else to go? How many nuisances like Wolf were being got rid of at the same time? Overcome by their distress, Ophelia didn't dare to imagine how they would all feel if they discovered that this one-way flight might not even reach its destination.

It was just then that she spotted, among all the faces, the only person not to have one. Hugo, the automaton, was cleaving his way through the crowd to reach the stand, scattering telegram tapes as he went. Octavio was sitting up on his shoulders. Ophelia understood why when he disconnected the loudspeaker from the nearest post, making its siren stop. Encouraged by his initiative, others did the same, from one tier to the next.

"I am a Son of Pollux."

Perched on the automaton, Octavio didn't have to raise his voice. His declaration captured the attention of all those who had besieged the stand. He wasn't big, but he had a charisma that wasn't just down to his virtuoso's uniform. Ophelia herself was hanging on his every word.

"*En fait*, I am the son of Lady Septima. The future successor of those who want to send you away from Babel. And yet," he continued, unperturbed by the sounds of disapproval that were already rising, "I share your outrage. The way you have been treated today is unjustifiable. As a representative of the *Official Journal*, I will make that known to our entire ark. So, I beg you, keep calm. We can find a solution as long as we seek it together, with Lady Helen and Sir Pollux."

A few seconds of silence followed, during which Ophelia, transfixed by Octavio's red eyes, was convinced that order would be restored.

But neither Helen nor Pollux reacted, the former having retreated to her echoes, the latter prisoner of his own indecision.

"Me, my lord, I've got a solution!" someone exclaimed. "Employ me instead of your automaton!"

"Real work for real people!" added someone else.

The crowd immediately began to jostle Hugo while chanting, in unison, "Job stealer! Job stealer!" no longer concerned with Octavio, who clung to the automaton's telegraph aerial to keep his balance. When the metal belly growled, "Laziness is the mother of all vices," the collective anger turned to rage, to boos, to blows. A violence that had been repressed for years erupted against the machine. Trapped up on Hugo's shoulders, Octavio had to struggle against those grabbing at his boots to tear off his Forerunner's wings.

He fell.

As Ophelia entered the fray to assist him, a pathetic attempt to help, an explosion rocked them all. Thick, acrid smoke spread like volcanic gas. All those who had tried to destroy Hugo stared wide-eyed with astonishment, the whites of their eyes standing out against their soot-covered skin.

All that remained of the automaton was a heap of dust. Had he exploded?

At first there was shock, then panic. The commotion in the amphitheater turned into anarchy. Some screamed, "Murder!" others, "Assassination!"—and too bad that those were forbidden words. Despite their gigantic size, Helen and Pollux were swept up in this human torrent. The family guard had lost control.

Lady Septima's authoritarian voice rang out through the last loudspeakers to remain connected:

"Those summoned who leave the confines of the amphitheater other than by airship will be deemed outlaws. I repeat . . . repeat: those summoned who leave the confines of the amphitheater other than by airship will be deemed outlaws."

There was no one left to listen to her. The real danger, right now, was the crowd. In the middle of the crush, Ophelia spotted a crouched form on the ground, covered in Hugo's dust.

"Octavio!"

She had to endure much pushing and shoving before reaching him. He was being trampled underfoot.

Ophelia called out his name again, tried to help him up, was pushed over on top of him. She curled into a ball to protect herself from the knees striking her from all directions. They were going to end up with broken bones.

They needed help.

Ophelia sensed a power, lurking deep inside her like a wild beast, that awoke to her call. The Dragons' claws. Never before had she been so acutely aware of their existence, their parameters, their impetus, of the way they extended her nerves to adopt the form and intensity she might want. Ophelia was so amazed to have this much control of her claws, after three years of putting up with them, that, fleetingly, she almost forgot about the crowd. Prompted by a primal instinct, she felt her consciousness extend beyond her bodily limitations; she connected to a web of neural networks that weren't her own. Her claws allowed her to see a multitude of frenzied legs far more clearly than her other senses did.

Don't hurt.

Exerting her power, Ophelia cast away all but herself and Octavio, triggering an avalanche of bodies and expletives all around them.

This break gave them just enough time to stand up before the next surge of feet. Beneath the layer of soot covering him, Octavio seemed unscathed. Or almost. He blinked with eyes that no longer glowed at all, and uttered five almost inaudible words:

"I can't see a thing."

Ophelia took his hand. Octavio had come to this amphitheater for her; she would leave it with him. She led him to one of the stairwell security shutters, toward which bodies were charging while barging into each other. A few joined forces to try to raise the barrier. Ophelia used her Animism to contaminate the shutter with her determination, but it wouldn't budge. The claws were of no use here, either: they only affected living beings.

"There!" someone shouted.

On the other side of the shutter was a crank connected to some gears. Beyond reach. All arms plunged between the slats, stretching toward the mechanism. A Vesperal Phantom managed to extend its own arm further by partially turning it into vapor. Reaching the crank and turning it demanded a supreme effort but combined with the exertions of those pushing up the shutter, it succeeded in unblocking the exit.

Everyone surged down the stairs in a flood of footsteps.

Pushed along by the current, Ophelia scrambled down the steps. She clung onto Octavio so as not to lose him in the chaos. Every turn in the stairs flung them against the wall.

The echoes of Lady Septima became increasingly distant: "Outlaws . . . laws . . . law . . ."

At the turn of one final spiral, they were engulfed in fog. The exit, at last. Ophelia just kept running. Her sandals skidded on the damp cobbles. She was aware only of the mist on her glasses and Octavio's hand in hers.

Some arms enfolded them, pulling them backwards. It was Blaise and Wolf. With index fingers pressed to lips, they pointed out the figures moving around in the haze. The family guard was carrying out mass arrests. A few steps more, and Ophelia would have fallen right into their trap.

She turned in all directions. Where to escape? Octavio was still wide-eyed but sightless. His family power couldn't be counted on, and they were surrounded by shadowy forms. Which of them were guards? Which civilians?

One of them was standing close to Ophelia. Too close.

Anonymous, motionless, and silent.

Ophelia couldn't make out its face, but she recognized it instantly. It was the mysterious figure in the fog she had encountered at the edge of the void, the previous day. The same silhouette, the same strange bearing, hypervigilant, as though waiting for something.

Slowly, the shadow in the fog took a few steps to distance itself—steps that were soundless on the cobbles—and then stopped. Waiting, once again.

It was there for them.

Whether it was friend or foe, Ophelia decided that she couldn't afford to dither. If they remained here, they would get caught. She tightened her fingers around Octavio's, and signaled to Blaise and Wolf to follow her.

Satisfied, the shadow set off again. They walked, blindly, behind it, through successive layers of cloud. All that now reached them of the sun was a twilight glow. The world around them was reduced to indistinct figures crying out, coming together, separating, in a kind of mass hysteria. It was an uprising the likes of which Babel hadn't known for centuries. Some people took advantage of it by taking to the streets to fling leaflets and cobblestones around, which appeared as dark streaks against a white backdrop. Laughter was their response to the family guard's whistleblowing.

"Celebrate the end of the world in style! Join the Brats of Babel!"

Ophelia, Octavio, Blaise, and Wolf made it through this chaos without encountering projectiles, or patrols, or political agitators. The shadow was guiding them through what now seemed to be the district of the power exchanges. It remained close enough not to be lost sight of, far enough not to be identified. Not once did it emit the slightest sound.

Who are you? Ophelia repeated to herself. Where are you taking us?

The more she tried to make out its contours, the more tense she felt. It wasn't the silhouette of a woman, but that meant nothing. Eulalia Gonde no longer had a fixed appearance; maybe the same went for her reflection. It was impossible to guess what form the latter had adopted when it had left the mirror. And Ophelia had already crossed the path of this stranger twice now, since the landslide. She ruled out a coincidence, but from that to deducing that it was the Other . . . Why would someone whose favorite pastime consisted of destroying arks suddenly care about the fate of a few humans?

Ophelia held her breath. The stranger had stopped in the middle of the fog. It uttered not a word, but, like some mime artist, started making absurd gestures, pointing at the sky with its left hand, the ground with its right hand, then at the sky with its right hand and at the ground with its left hand.

"A lunatic," muttered Professor Wolf.

Evening closed in, and the stranger's shadow became absorbed into those of that neighborhood. Ophelia moved forward to the spot where it had stopped. She banged into the gates of a factory, topped by a huge pediment, all brickwork and wrought iron.

FABRICATION OF AUTOMATONS
LAZARUS & SON

Once again, this couldn't be a coincidence.

"What now?" asked an anxious voice.

Ophelia noticed several glowing spots in the fog. It was the foreheads of some of the summoned who, overtaken by events, had just followed them at a distance. They didn't know one another, but they were all outlaws from now on.

Ophelia pushed at the gate. It wasn't locked.

Together, they made their way into the factory. A strange

mechanical dog with several heads stood up, with a great clickety-clack, as they approached. It didn't sound the alarm. They then discovered a large, barely lit hangar in which rows of faceless figures were working on production lines, all along the conveyor belts. They were all automatons. They were cutting out, filing down, piercing, linking, and screwing parts that seemed straight out of a clockmaker's shop. As they concentrated on their repetitive tasks, they showed no reaction to the visitors' arrival. For a moment, Ophelia expected to see Lazarus in the midst of all this activity, before recalling that he was on his travels. The automatons had clearly been designed for constructing other automatons. The factory functioned autonomously during its owner's absences.

Ophelia still couldn't find the stranger who had saved them from the patrols. In an adjoining garage, on the other hand, she found a wheelchair. Empty.

"Ambrose?" she called out.

The door of a wagon with propellers immediately opened. The adolescent leaned out, awkwardly, to take a puzzled look at Ophelia and all those accompanying her. The scarf wound around his hair was now standing up in the form of a question mark.

"*Mademoiselle*? I was coming to your rescue! *C'est à dire*, I would have if I'd managed to get this heliwagon started. It's a touch trickier than my whaxi. How did you know where to find me?"

"I didn't. Someone led us here, but has disappeared before the introductions. Do you have a pharmacy in the factory? My friend needs some treatment."

No sooner had Ophelia made this request than Octavio let go of her hand to rub his soot-blackened eyelids.

"Water will be fine."

"*Bien sûr!*" exclaimed Ambrose, extracting his legs, first

one then the other, from the heliwagon. "There's a tap in the maintenance area, beside the stairs."

He staggered over to his wheelchair, hampered by his inverted feet. His struggle became so grotesque, the outlaws looked away.

"You are Lazarus's son?" grunted Professor Wolf. "One of your automatons has just caused complete mayhem. It exploded."

As he settled into his wheelchair, Ambrose seemed more contrite than surprised.

"Imploded," he corrected. "Someone tried to take it apart, I presume?"

"A whole mob."

"*Diable!* Father incorporated a self-destructive mechanism in all his inventions, to protect his trade secrets. It's spectacular, but harmless."

"Harmless!" Wolf scoffed. "It sparked everything off. Couldn't Lazarus have just filed for a patent like everyone else? Already, back when he taught at my college, he always had to be different."

Ophelia turned her attention to the group of outlaws, who were passing around industrial sandpaper to rub against their foreheads. But however hard they rubbed, the luminous ink remained. She could read on their faces the same internal questions. What now? What to do? Where to go?

Ophelia felt sorry for them. With her glove, she stroked the lettering on the side of the heliwagon: "DELIVERY OF AUTOMATONS." For herself, she knew *what*, she knew *where*, and she knew *how*. Whoever the stranger in the fog might be, they had done her a serious favor.

"Come," she said to Octavio, whose red eyes were flickering like defective lightbulbs.

She led him to the maintenance area and ran some water

for him at the sink. Silently, he filled his cupped hands with it, plunged his face into it, and then did the same, again and again, until abruptly stopping. He remained standing there, fingers pressed to eyelids, as if wishing he never had to reopen them ever again.

"Are you still determined to enter the observatory?"

"Yes."

"I wanted to discourage you. Forget that. Everyone should have the right to go wherever they want."

"Octavio—"

"What my mother said today in that amphitheater . . ." he interrupted her, his voice tight. "I am so ashamed."

Ophelia watched the gray water trickling through his fingers. She herself had a real taste of ashes in her mouth.

"Would you like to—"

". . . be alone. Yes. *S'il te plaît.*"

Octavio curled his hands into fists against his eyes, and then added, falteringly:

"Tomorrow, I will return to the journal. I will return to the Good Family. I will change things from the inside. I promise you. But this evening, don't look at me."

Ophelia backed away.

"What you said today in that amphitheater . . ." she said, quietly, before closing the door. "I'm so proud."

Without the slightest idea what she was doing, and without the slightest hesitation, either, Ophelia clambered up the factory's small staircase. She emerged onto a roof that had been turned into a terrace, wedged between two brick chimney stacks. The factory cleaved the sea of clouds like an ocean liner.

Ophelia gripped the wrought-iron guardrail to control her shaking. The whistleblowing of arrests being made still rose up from the town center.

It isn't my fault, she repeated to herself, several times.

It wasn't her fault if there were landslides. It wasn't her fault if there were expulsions.

She raised her glasses from the fog to direct them into the distance, above the sea of clouds, toward the artificial lights merging into the stars. Babel's minor arks. With ease, Ophelia located the dome of the Memorial, bright as a beacon, and the more discreet lamps of the Good Family. The sight of them filled her with nostalgia. These places had been hers for a while. Having been treated as an undesirable had wounded her.

How many people today had been dispatched far away against their will? How many would arrive safe and sound, despite the echoes?

"They are everywhere, and around you even more than anywhere else," Helen had said.

"Look closely into the echoes. They're the key to it all," Lazarus had said.

Ophelia was trying to understand, she really was trying. An invisible thread seemed to connect Eulalia Gonde, the Other, the landslides, and the echoes, but it was full of knots.

An exterior light went out just as Blaise came to lean on his elbows, to her left, up on the roof. His profile, with its long, pointed nose, was barely discernible in the dark.

"Whatever you've got on your mind, Mademoiselle Eulalia, you're going to have to be *très* careful. The family guard has memorized your smell, as it has that of all those who were over there. They are first-class Olfactories, they will track you down relentlessly."

"I'm not staying in town. But what will become of the others?"

Professor Wolf leaned on his elbows to the right of Ophelia. The glow from his forehead replaced the light that had gone out. He had lost his dark glasses and hat. Judging by the way he was clutching his neck brace, that race across the city had severely tested his vertebrae.

"Lazarus's kid is going to put us up until things settle down. He's got guts. If we go down, he'll go down with us."

Blaise ruffled his hair, making it stick up even more.

"It would seem that life in Babel is about to get even more complicated for us."

Elbow to elbow with these two men, whom the whole world prohibited from touching each other, Ophelia felt the urgent desire to protect them growing inside her. If a single landslide had divided an entire city, what would happen if it were ever to occur again? Wherever the Other was, whatever its appearance and its intentions, Ophelia knew at least this much: it would strike again if she didn't stop it first.

She looked even further away, toward the most distant points of light. Over there, at this precise moment, somewhere behind certain walls, Babelians were working on the Cornucopianism project, just as Eulalia Gonde had before becoming God. Was Thorn right in thinking that what was done could be undone? Was it possible to bring Eulalia Gonde back to her human state, send the Other back into the mirror, and repair what was still repairable? And what if the only remedy for the void was plenty? But what would be the role of the echoes in all that?

Ophelia felt duty bound to find the answers at the Deviations Observatory. With Thorn.

"No one takes themselves voluntarily to that kind of institution without having a very good reason," he had warned her.

What she found wonderfully ironic in this whole situation was that the Lords of LUX had just provided her with what she had lacked.

In the Wings

He wanders the streets of Babel. Cries, whistles. Pollux's family guard arresting anything that moves. Anything but him, obviously. He could dance under their very noses, and they wouldn't arrest him.

No one ever arrests him.

A couple of steps, and he reaches the summit of the highest pyramid. There he sits down and watches Babel sinking into the fog. The aging Babel. A city far too old for their tiny little memories.

History is going to repeat itself. He's seen to that.

It would have been premature for Ophelia to leave Babel today. She has something else to accomplish here, within the archipelago's borders, at the Deviations Observatory.

Oh yes, history is going to repeat itself. Like that, it will finally be able to end itself.

THE TRAP

The automatons' inanimate bodies were harnessed to the heliwagon's roof. Every jolt shook their limbs, making a bone-rattling sound. Plunged in darkness, Ophelia felt as if she were surrounded by skeletons. She leaned against one of them when she sensed the heliwagon was losing altitude. Yet another aerial check? The rear doors half-opened. The beam of a torch lit up the faceless head of an automaton beside Ophelia, then the doors closed and the hum of the heliwagon's propellers started up again.

"Sir Octavio and Sir Ambrose say we shouldn't encounter any more patrols."

Ophelia could just make out a shaggy-haired figure among the automatons, elbowing his way through with difficulty to join her at the back. As soon as she lifted the turban hiding her forehead, her stamp cast a lunar glow on Blaise, and shadows between the worry lines on his skin. Noticing them, Ophelia regretted having told him of her intention to enter the Deviations Observatory; ever since, he had been determined to escort her.

"You should have stayed at the factory with the other outlaws," she said, sighing. "If I get caught . . ."

"They will deport me, too? Between you and me, Mademoiselle Eulalia, I won't remain on an ark that doesn't want people who are dear to me. And also, I wanted to discuss something with you, but . . . *eh bien* . . . not in front of Wolf."

Sheepishly, Blaise rolled up the sleeve of his Memorialist uniform to uncover his arm. By the light of her forehead, Ophelia could make out a tattoo. An interlaced "A" and "P."

"It stands for 'Alternative Program,'" explained Blaise.

It took a certain time before Ophelia understood.

"You have been part of the Deviations Observatory?"

"I don't know why it's so important to you to get in there, *mademoiselle*. What I do know is how hard it was for me to get out of there. My parents had sent me there for me to be . . . you know . . . *corrected*." Blaise smiled sadly as he said the word. "I was still only an adolescent, but they had already understood the path I was taking. I remained at the observatory until I came of age, and even after that, I wasn't allowed to quit the program."

Squashed by the automatons and shaken by the jolts, Ophelia gazed at the two letters tattooed on Blaise's arm. Marked for life.

"What is it, the Alternative Program?"

"The other side of the picture. The Deviations Observatory is renowned for achieving excellent results in . . . in cases such as mine, among others. But when they examined me, they assured my parents that my condition didn't fall within the standard program, that I was an invert of a *très* particular sort, that they were prepared to take me on entirely at their expense in order to study me. I got board and lodgings and laundry for years. Every month, I asked to go home, and every month I was told that it wasn't my decision. And then, from one day to the next, they returned me to my parents, with no explanation. As if I was no longer of the slightest interest to them. I have only confused memories of what went on over there, of what I did there, of what I witnessed there. But if I can be sure of one thing, *mademoiselle*, it's that the observatory was far less interested in my romantic preferences than in my bad luck."

Blaise had declared this while shoving Ophelia to one side. An automaton's harness had come undone just behind her, threatening to bring several pounds of metal crashing down on her head.

"Your bad luck," she repeated. "Why?"

"They didn't tell me. They never say anything. They observe."

"But you," Ophelia insisted, "did you observe anything special over there?"

"Everything's special over there, *mademoiselle*. I was surrounded by inverts. Inverted minds. Inverted bodies. Inverted powers."

Ophelia hesitated. She wouldn't get another chance to ask questions to someone who had known the observatory that intimately, even if it was long ago.

"Did you hear any mention of the 'Cornucopianism project'?"

Blaise's forehead wrinkled even more as his eyebrows shot up.

"Never."

"Of the Horn of Plenty, maybe?"

He shook his head.

"It wasn't mentioned in front of me at the observatory, but I repeat to you: they never say anything."

Ophelia looked at the dislocated body at her feet. When not wound up, an automaton really was like a skeleton. She remembered the conversation they had once had, she and Blaise, in the city's catacombs. "Some humans are objects while they're alive."

"What they did to you . . . What they're going to do to me," she said, in a voice she wished sounded braver. "Am I going to suffer?"

Blaise's face stretched like rubber, and then he clumsily grabbed her shoulders.

"Not in the sense that . . . that you mean it. It's just . . . just that . . . *Zut!*"

Blaise had never found expressing himself that easy, but the more he spoke of the observatory, the worse his stammer became, as if he himself were suddenly full of echoes. His fingers gripped Ophelia's shoulders. His dark, moist eyes widened.

"Within each of us there exists a boundary, Mademoiselle Eulalia. Something that is . . . is necessary, something that limits us, something that . . . that contains us inside ourselves. They . . . they will try to make you cross that boundary. Whatever they say to you, *mademoiselle*, the decision will be yours."

From the way her feet seemed to want to leave the floor, Ophelia sensed that the heliwagon was just landing. They were arriving. *She was arriving.* Thorn was expecting her. It mattered little what this observatory had in store for her, she wouldn't be alone. Even here, in this heliwagon, she wasn't alone.

"Thank you, Blaise. Take care of yourself. And of Professor Wolf."

Blaise's hands let go of Ophelia's shoulders to clasp her face. He pressed his forehead against hers, blocking out the light on it.

"He avoided me for fifteen years," he whispered to her, so quietly he seemed to want her to be the only one in the world to hear him. "Fifteen long years during which I thought he was protecting himself from me, when in fact it was me he was protecting from himself. Until the collapse of the northwestern district. Because *you* had advised him to speak to me. I don't know if you're aware," said Blaise, searching for Ophelia's eyes in the depths of her glasses, "of the loneliness you rescued me from that day you spoke to me for the first time in that birdtrain."

Their foreheads knocked together when the heliwagon came to a halt. After a few moments, the rear doors opened. It was Octavio.

"No one in sight. Hurry up."

Ophelia pulled her turban down over her forehead before slipping out. The dawn was a tepid pink. Palm trees shivered in the vicinity of the void. The heliwagon had landed on a delivery terrace at the top of a tower. Octavio was right, the place was deserted.

Ophelia went closer to the edge. She wanted to see the observatory from above before experiencing it from the inside. It was spread out before her, an inextricable tangle of pagodas and railroad tracks, gardens and factories, old stones and metal structures. It had something of both the ancient imperial city and the industrial park about it. And yet Ophelia soon clocked a system within this seeming chaos: the observatory was divided into sectors separated by gigantic red doors, themselves incorporated within fortifications. A calculated partitioning.

The institute was dominated, at its center, by a colossal statue: a giant whose head had several faces. "I see everything, I know everything!" it silently proclaimed.

"In that case, let's talk a little," Ophelia whispered to it. "That's what I've come for."

She returned to the heliwagon's controls, where Ambrose held an inverted hand out to her, through the opening in the door.

"*Bonne chance, mademoiselle*. I envy you a little, I'm so curious to know what they study here! My father told me that, of all his clients, the Deviations Observatory was the one that ordered the most unusual items from him. I wouldn't be surprised if you came across some pretty disconcerting automatons in there."

Ophelia didn't find this prospect particularly encouraging. She couldn't stop herself from reaching toward the scarf, rolled into a ball on the adolescent's head, but all she got was a stirring of sulky wool. This new separation she was imposing on both of them didn't bode well for a reconciliation.

"*Désolé*," said Ambrose, looking embarrassed.

Ophelia shook his hand as awkwardly as he did hers.

"There's an Animist proverb: 'Like master, like object.' You give my scarf the feeling you gave me from our first encounter, and that you're giving many people today. That of sanctuary."

Octavio had observed their exchange through the gap in his fringe. His tired eyes hadn't yet recovered their brilliance, but they were scrutinizing Ambrose with an indecipherable expression. He indicated a hangar, made up of thousands of panes of glass, at the other end of the delivery terrace.

"There must be a tradesmen's entrance there. I'll accompany her and then be back," he told Ambrose and Blaise.

Inside the hangar, Ophelia and Octavio saw only pyramids of crates and stationary small trucks. True, it was still early, but after the hysteria that had swept the rest of Babel, this calm was unnerving.

They descended the tower's numerous stories in a service elevator.

"Is that Ambrose really the son of Professor Lazarus?" Octavio asked, abruptly. "He doesn't look like him. *En fait*," he added, not allowing Ophelia the chance to reply, "he looks like no one. I sat beside him throughout the flight. His body really is very strange."

Ophelia refrained from retorting that her own body was no

less strange, and that she intended to use that fact to infiltrate this place. Even if that thought made her stomach shudder.

"Will you return to the *Official Journal* after this?"

"First to the Good Family. I'm responsible for the division of Pollux's apprentice Forerunners. If I don't clock in every day, it would be considered a dereliction of duty."

Ophelia raised her eyebrows.

"After all that's happened? After the collapse of the northwestern district? After the riots in the city center?"

"Especially after all that. It's order versus chaos, from now on."

The service elevator eventually opened onto a corridor, which led to another corridor, which led to a reception. They found no one there, either. Some forms were provided on the counter. You had to fill one in yourself, slip it through the slot of a tube, and lower the lever to propel the pneumatic dispatch. Ophelia had already been through this procedure once before, to see Mediana. Today, instead of ticking the box "VISIT," she ticked the box "ADMISSION."

She didn't even have time to make for the waiting room before a polite voice called out to her:

"Mademoiselle Eulalia?"

A woman was walking steadily toward her. It wasn't the young girl Ophelia had dealt with on her first visit, but she was wearing the same yellow-silk sari, the same dark-lensed pince-nez, and the same long leather gloves. On her shoulder she had a mechanical beetle, and under her arm, a document-holder on which was clipped the form Ophelia had only just filled in. As if she'd been lying in wait for her for days.

"This way, *s'il vous plaît*," she said, opening a pretty glass door to her. "Not you, my lord."

The woman had directed a stiff smile at Octavio, who was already following on. She showed no regard for his virtuoso's uniform and didn't ask him for his name. She already knew perfectly well who he was.

Ophelia exchanged a final look with him. An intense look.

"Changing the world," she murmured to him.

The corners of Octavio's mouth quivered. He jerked up his head so his whole fringe was flung back, laying bare the scars on his nose and eyebrow where, previously, he wore his gold chain.

"From the inside," he said in reply.

He left with a resolute clicking of his heels, instilling courage in Ophelia. She followed the woman across a room that might have resembled a medical office had there not been beetles on all the shelves. They shone like precious stones in the morning light from the windows.

"You have requested admission to our observatory," the woman declared, ensconcing herself in an armchair and placing her document-holder in front of her. "I'm listening to you."

Once seated, Ophelia first ensured that she could see her interviewer's reflection in the windowpane. She was neither Eulalia Gonde nor the Other, as far as that test could be trusted. Fine. She took off the turban concealing the administrative stamp on her forehead.

"I'll be brief. A doctor advised me to join your program. I know you already hold a file in my name. I don't really understand why, but one thing of which I am certain is that this observatory is my last resort to avoid being deported from Babel."

Ophelia didn't have to try hard to seem desperate. Her fear was real. Beyond the ground beneath her feet, here and now, the rest of the world had become a giant question mark.

The woman flicked through the pages clipped to the document holder. Ophelia would have liked to be perched on her shoulder, instead of the beetle, to read the information the observatory held on her.

"In other words, Mademoiselle Eulalia, it's a request for sanctuary?"

"I'm volunteering for whatever you might find interesting about me."

The woman tilted her head so she could maintain her focus through the dark lenses of her pince-nez. She handed her a blank piece of paper and a fountain pen.

"Must I sign somewhere?"

"No, Mademoiselle Eulalia. Please just write: 'But this well was no more real than a rabbit of Odin.'"

"Sorry?"

Ophelia was taken aback. What well? What rabbit? And above all, why Odin? Wasn't that Farouk's old name?

"'But this well was no more real than a rabbit of Odin,'" the woman repeated, with a fixed smile. "Write, *s'il vous plaît*."

Ophelia obeyed. The woman immediately took her page, in exchange for a blank one.

"*Parfait*. Rewrite that sentence, but with your other hand this time."

"I can't write with the other hand."

"Of course you can," the woman calmly assured. "We are not asking you to write well. Merely to write."

Ophelia obeyed once again. The words came out hideously through the metal nib. Even when concentrating, she inverted most of the letters. The woman paid no attention to the result. It was Ophelia, and only Ophelia, that she was observing with polite attention through the dark prism of her pince-nez. She didn't have the eyes of a Visionary. What was her family power? Was she using it at this very moment?

"*Parfait*."

The leather of her gloves creaked when she added the two

pages to her document-holder. Each of her gestures was excessively methodical, as if handling highly toxic chemicals. She stood up and put the turban back on Ophelia's head. She pushed it down so hard, in order to cover the stamp, that it felt uncomfortable. She then made her enter a closet that was as narrow as it was dark, and closed the door. The darkness was so intense and so hot, it took Ophelia's breath away. She could no longer see the glasses on her own nose. This explained the turban: darkness was seemingly part of this experiment.

"Don't move, *s'il vous plaît.*"

There was a flash of light, sudden as lightning. Then a second one. Then yet another one. Was the woman taking a photograph of her? Ophelia was so dazzled that she didn't immediately notice that the closet door had been reopened.

With a smile, the woman indicated the desk to her, on which, this time, a little lacquer box awaited her.

"You are an Animist, Mademoiselle Eulalia."

It wasn't a question.

"To the eighth degree," Ophelia lied.

"Specialized in the reading of objects."

Once again, it wasn't a question. If the Deviations Observatory had had access to Ophelia's file from her admission to the Good Family, there was nothing new she could tell them. And yet the woman seemed to be waiting for confirmation from her.

"I am indeed a reader."

"Would you mind awfully giving a little demonstration?"

Still half-blinded from the flashes in the dark closet, Ophelia approached the box.

"There is a sample inside," the woman explained.

Ophelia slid back the panel on the box. A tiny lead ball sat on a red cushion. Her blood instantly started to throb beneath the entire surface of her face. An organic din hammered her ears.

"Might we proceed with your reading, Mademoiselle Eulalia?" the woman inquired, politely.

She seemed to be struggling to limit her smile to professional proportions.

Ophelia unbuttoned her gloves, one after the other. Until this moment, she had felt in control of the situation. She had come here by choice. She was submitting to this observatory's tests because she was willing to do so. She was showing them only what she had decided to show them of herself.

That was how things had been supposed to happen.

"I have to ask you the question," she said, in a tone she hoped was detached. "Is this object the property of the observatory?"

"Absolutely, Mademoiselle Eulalia."

A lie.

Ophelia breathed in to prevent anger from darkening her glasses. Don't shake. Don't give yourself away. She focused entirely on the ball of lead in the box. The projectile from a cartridge. She knew that what lay before her eyes was impossible—it should have been—but, stunned as she was, there was one domain in which she couldn't be deceived. She knew personally every item in the collection of Anima's Museum of Primitive History. And this one in particular.

She seized the lead ball with her bare hands. Nausea seared her throat. It wasn't her own nausea but that of the last person to have handled this exhibit without protection. A pathetic simpleton, in a bowler hat, who wanted to know about the wars of the old world, whom Ophelia had wanted to teach a good lesson. That was four years ago; it felt like forty to her. As she went back further and further in time, passing from reader's hands to reader's hands, from nausea to nausea, she prepared herself for the impact that was inevitably coming. The pain, abstract but genuine, hit her straight in the stomach.

The agony of the soldier whose internal organs had been punctured by this cartridge, several centuries ago, became her agony. This time, it was her own nausea that overcame her, so violently that she almost vomited over the desk.

She placed the projectile back on its cushion, closed the box, and pressed her fist against her trembling lips. A tear spilled onto her cheek. How could she have inflicted that on someone else?

No, she corrected herself, once the powerful surge of empathy had subsided. Why had that been inflicted on her? By what improbable combination of circumstances had the Deviations Observatory obtained this exhibit from the museum in which she, Ophelia, *not Eulalia*, had once worked?

"Would you care for some water, *mademoiselle*?"

The woman's eyes hadn't left her, before, during or after her reading. They shone behind the dark lenses of her pince-nez, a gleam heightened by curiosity.

"Would you like my evaluation?" Ophelia asked her, coldly.

"No, Mademoiselle Eulalia, that wasn't the purpose of the exercise."

"What was it, then?"

The woman took out an inch-thick document from the desk drawer. Ophelia put her gloves back on before taking hold of it. *Agreement between the subject and the Deviations Observatory: consent to the act of studying protocols I to III of the alternative program and relative confidentiality clause.* The title on its own made one dizzy.

"The Lords of LUX lay down the laws," declared the beetle woman, "but none is above the medical secrecy that we have applied here for several generations. For as long as you remain within our walls, you will no longer be accountable to the outside world."

Ophelia didn't understand a single line of the dozens of

pages that made up the agreement. This jargon required serious legal expertise.

It was no longer of any importance. She signed.

The woman's smile had almost imperceptibly increased as Ophelia returned the document to her. The future would determine which one of them had fallen into the other one's trap.

The Glasses

Ophelia stifled a shriek. Her eyes widened behind the hair streaming over both eyebrows. From boiling, the water had turned to freezing, before stopping just as suddenly, leaving her gasping and hugging a body reddened by such extreme temperatures. The steam cleared, evacuated by the ventilation, revealing the yellow-sari-clad figure that had just released the shower pull-chain. Even without glasses, Ophelia saw the smile. This beetle woman made no attempt to respect her modesty. She watched her awkwardly getting out of the tub, skidding on the tiled floor, and then rubbing herself down fastidiously.

"Where are my clothes?"

Ophelia found none of the belongings she had left on the bench. Instead, what awaited her were neatly folded, pocketless sarouel trousers and a sleeveless tunic. The observatory definitely wanted her to have nothing to hide. They had even confiscated her sandals.

"My gloves," she requested.

The woman politely shook her head to say no.

"I need them, and you know it."

Another shake of the head. Ophelia didn't understand. No they wouldn't return her gloves, or no she wouldn't need them?

She got dressed, grimacing each time her hands, involuntarily, read the fabric. She visualized a humble workshop deep in a souk, a second-rate sewing machine, the casual whistling of a dyer: at least no one had ever worn these garments before her.

"My glasses?"

Yet another shake of the head. Ophelia felt her breathing quicken, and forced it to slow down. She had prepared herself for the likelihood that nothing would be easy here; above all, she mustn't let them get the upper hand.

On the woman's shoulder, the mechanical beetle opened out a mirror. It was so tiny that it only reflected fragments of Ophelia's face. She at least had the satisfaction of seeing that her forehead was finally cleansed of its stamp. The luminous ink had dissolved under the shower; maybe this water had alchemical properties.

"And now?"

With a courteous gesture, the woman invited her to follow her. As soon as she moved off, she lost definition, merging confusingly with the decor. Ophelia had better quickly get used to walking in a blur, without gloves or shoes. Playing at spies was going to prove harder than anticipated, but if the observatory really was determined to make her task harder, she would get her own back at it.

As they passed through a series of corridors, Ophelia was struck by the electric lightbulbs: they all crackled and flickered, without exception.

Finally, she emerged into the fresh air, where the morning sun dried her hair instantly. The flagstones roasted her toes. The woman led her through fragrant jungles, shady galleries, and an endless succession of doors.

Although all Ophelia could see of the world was colorful pointillist painting, she could hear its sounds very clearly. She picked up the buzzing of an insect here, a mechanical whirring there, and, passing a window, the brassy tones of a trumpet. She heard, too, children's laughter and parents' anxious questions—"Is he making progress?", "Is she safe here?"—and sensible voices assuring that progress was excellent and security guaranteed; that young and less young alike flourished at the observatory more than anywhere else; that the standard program had always worked wonders, but everyone was clearly free to go home whenever they wished to.

Were Eulalia Gonde's secrets to be found somewhere here, within earshot?

Ophelia never took her myopic eyes off the woman, whose silk sari undulated before her. She couldn't shake off the nausea triggered by her reading of the exhibit from the museum in Anima. When and how had that woman got hold of it? The Genealogists were right about one thing: this observatory was way ahead of her. But to what extent? What did they know about her? Of her past? Of her abilities? Of her intentions?

And what about Thorn, she wondered, digging her fingernails into her now uncovered palms.

Thirty-one months. Thirty-one months during which Ophelia had lived under the watchful eye of the Doyennes, unable to set foot outside her parents' house without their Rapporteur being hot on her heels. Thirty-one months during which she had stopped herself from going in search of Thorn because of them, for fear of putting him in jeopardy. If Archibald hadn't succeeded in slipping through the net to get her out of there, she would still be on Anima. But what if she had been mistaken? If, during all this time in Babel, where she had believed herself free of Eulalia Gonde's surveillance, she had in fact remained a prisoner of it? If Eulalia Gonde had led her straight to Thorn?

Basically, Ophelia had no idea who was really in charge of

this observatory. Maybe it wasn't Eulalia Gonde. Maybe it was someone else. Someone who knew her very well.

Whoever this person might be, did they know that Sir Henry was in fact an escaped prisoner? Was Thorn in danger within these walls, as the Genealogists' previous informer had been? And what if Ophelia had got there too late? If they had made him disappear, too?

She screwed up her eyes. The woman had just passed under an ornamental porch, on which was carved, in large letters:

OBSERVATION

The porch led to a hall of such immaculate whiteness that it was painful. Ophelia couldn't make out the architectural details, but if she went by the smooth chill beneath her feet, it was a veritable marble palace. The casement windows flooded the interior with sunlight.

The beetle woman joined the ranks of what Ophelia noticed, as she got closer, was a pretty impressive assembly. Figures draped in yellow silk and clutching clipboards peered at her through their pince-nez. Observers. Finding herself the focus of all these eyes, exposed in the brightest of light, couldn't have felt more uncomfortable. With her bare arms, calves, and feet, and her bedraggled curls, Ophelia looked like a street urchin.

A young girl whispered:

"You requested to be present at each arrival and each departure. The inverted person here present is a rather particular case, *monsieur*. Her deviation falls within the remit of the alternative program."

By way of response, there was just a resonant tap-tap. Ophelia did her best not to show the relief that made her every muscle relax. One by one, she released her fingernails from her palms. Thorn was here. He was well. She tried, above all, not to search for his face among those, sketchy and anonymous, surrounding him.

No one bothered with introductions.

A man made Ophelia sit down on what resembled a piano stool, as white and as cold as the floor. He adjusted the height so Ophelia's feet were properly flat on the ground. Without ceremony, he applied a stamp to her forearm; the ink of the interlaced "A" and "P" glistened. And that was it. She had just swapped one stamp for another.

Next, the man started measuring her: her head with cephalic calipers, then her right middle finger and her left foot with a tape measure. So total was the silence, the clicking of the instruments echoed around the hall. The man's eyes were hidden behind the dark lenses of his pince-nez, and although he didn't really smile, a persistent dimple hovered at the corner of his mouth, which Ophelia found disturbing. On his shoulder he carried an automaton in the form of a lizard.

Quite affably, the man asked her to stand up, and then sit back down on the stool at a different angle, which didn't make things easier. She was now directly facing Thorn, whose characteristic silhouette stood out from the rest of the assembly. In the end, she was grateful to have been deprived of her glasses. Like that, she couldn't be tempted either to meet or avoid his gaze. What little she could make out of his face was full of shadows, despite the brightness of the place. He had been seated in a separate armchair, positioned to one side of the front row, so he could watch proceedings while remaining on the sidelines. He had crossed his arms in a detached way that suited his new role of chief family inspector.

He was observing the observatory.

A young girl stood near him, with, on her shoulder, what

appeared to be a mechanical monkey. Ophelia thought she recognized the Babelian who had received her on her first visit to the observatory. She was holding out a tray of refreshments for Thorn, and everything about her demeanor suggested the utmost respect.

In fact, he was even very well.

The lizard man had finished taking Ophelia's measurements; now he was silently giving her a checkup. He made her close one eye while raising the opposite arm, and then the reverse. There followed a very lengthy series of similar movements that, although apparently innocuous, made Ophelia feel increasingly uncomfortable. Perhaps because she was not wearing her corrective lenses, she began to feel a migraine rumbling deep inside her head. From being required to keep switching from right side to left side, she ended up unable to tell the one from the other. All around her, everyone assembled was religiously taking notes, amid a constant rustling of paper, exchanging comments in hushed voices, as though attending some rare performance.

Ophelia found the situation completely ridiculous. She was just hoping not to become even more so herself when the lizard man slapped her in the face.

It was such an unexpected slap that, for a fraction of a second, Ophelia was unable to think. With head flung toward shoulder and cheek on fire, she couldn't fathom what had just happened.

What she was very swiftly aware of, on the other hand, was the grating of metal echoing around the hall. Thorn had stood up.

"*Ne vous inquiétez pas*, Sir Henry," the monkey girl whispered. "The procedure must surprise you, but it is in accordance with the first protocol. The invert present here is consenting, no city rule has been infringed."

Ophelia's mind immediately starting working again. She had no idea what the procedure expected of her, but she wouldn't allow Thorn to compromise his cover to defend her.

She returned the man's slap.

"You gave me no instructions," she explained in a steady voice. "It seemed the most logical reaction to me."

The entire assembly scribbled away in a frenzy of fountain pens. The lizard man picked up the pince-nez that had fallen from his face. The moment he put them back in place, his dimple disappeared. Ophelia noticed, from the slight shift in his gaze, that he had just discovered *something* that extended beyond her. Something that was invisible to her.

The man halted his manipulation of her, made no comment, and returned to the ranks of the assembly.

It's like Gail's monocle, Ophelia realized, with a jolt of surprise. The pince-nez of each of these observers functioned according to the same principle. But what mysteries did they reveal to their eyes? What had they all discovered about Ophelia that she didn't know herself?

Thorn sat back down in his seat with intentional slowness, and didn't cross his arms again. He, too, had understood. Ophelia needed neither to see him nor hear him to know that they were sharing the same thought at the same time. We need those lenses.

The beetle woman came out from the assembled ranks and, with gestures of exaggerated politeness, invited Ophelia to follow her.

"The invert will now be taken to the containment zone, *monsieur*," commented the monkey girl, leaning over Thorn's chair. "It's important that subjects of the alternative program are not put in contact with those of the standard program."

"I will need to inspect that zone, too."

Thorn's voice resonated as far as Ophelia's stomach.

"*Bien sûr, monsieur!* We will show you all that you wish to see, within the limits of medical secrecy."

As she followed her guide across the hall, leaving the assembly behind her, Ophelia could feel the moist footprints her bare feet left on the marble at every step.

The limits of medical secrecy . . .

The woman made her leave through a different porch, opposite the other one, on which this time were carved the letters:

EXPLORATION

No sooner had Ophelia walked through than the double doors, painted red and several meters high, closed behind her. Here there were no children laughing or anxious parents. Ophelia had to go through three more doors, each separated from the next by a vast esplanade.

She thought of the stranger in the fog who, twice already, had contrived to cross her path. She doubted they would manage a third time here, and didn't know whether that was a good or a bad thing. Would she see them again one day?

She arrived at the feet of the giant she had gazed at from the landing tower. He was even more overpowering seen from below. Without glasses, Ophelia thought he resembled a mountain. A railway tunnel had been cut through his base; it was the only means of accessing the part of the observatory on which the statue turned his back.

The migraine was getting worse by the second, as if it were inside her own skull that Ophelia was now walking. She had no idea what had been done to her, but she felt like locking herself in a bedroom, blacking out every window, and burying her head in a black pillow.

The beetle woman indicated to her to climb aboard a small

wagon, fit for a fairground carousel, but didn't join her. She grabbed hold of a lever. Just before lowering it, she deigned finally to crack a smile.

"If you really want to understand the other, first find your own."

"What did you say?"

Ophelia's question was swallowed up at the same time as she was by the darkness of the tunnel. She gazed at the circle of light shrinking behind her as the wagon sped along the track. In front of her, like an opposite image, the tunnel's exit gradually went from the size of a spark to that of a sun. She kept her hands clenched so as not to touch anything, less out of duty than out of fear of being distracted by an involuntary reading. What that woman had just said to her, was it a philosophical concept, or was she actually talking about the Other? Ophelia would have liked to shut her migraine up, even for just a few seconds, to think about it. Those exercises had done her head in.

The sides of the tunnel started to react strangely to the daylight as it grew and grew and grew the closer the wagon got to it. They started sending out thousands of multicolored geometrical shapes. Ophelia understood, too late, that this tunnel had been designed like a giant kaleidoscope. An infinity of fractal combinations penetrated her eyes in a flash. The migraine turned into a howl. Ophelia closed her eyes to stop anything else from entering them.

The wagon slowed down, and then stopped. The migraine stopped with it.

Ophelia reopened her eyes. A building site spread out before her, as far as the eye could see and in the minutest detail, as if she were once again wearing glasses.

She was wearing a pair.

Except they weren't her glasses.

They were Eulalia Gonde's glasses.

THE ATTRACTION

"The mess grub's disgusting, but you'll get used to it. At least we don't die of hunger, like in town. Have to know where to go, over there. You ever been to a real restaurant, Officer God?"

The sergeant gives Eulalia a look intended to be uncouth, without really being so. She instantly spots the mole, quivering slightly, at the corner of his eye. She is younger and slighter than him, but it's clear to her that she intimidates him. She often has that effect on people—she already had it on her teachers.

She smiles at him, indulgently.

"Just a tingle sime . . . single time. And if you'll allow me to correct you, my name is pronounced *Gonde*."

The sergeant now walks in silence, as the rubble crunches under his military boots. Eulalia understands that he's humiliated. She spoke to him like a child, not like a man, and even less like a soldier.

Gripping the handle of her small case, she looks around the building site they are both crossing. Clouds of sand scour her glasses. Army excavators are destroying what was once the forbidden city of the last emperor of Babel—soon to become a truly unique observatory.

Eulalia's eyes linger on the recumbent carcasses of ancient

157

trees. Yet more history uprooted forever. It doesn't upset her. She has no attachment to the past; all that counts is the future that will rewrite itself upon these ruins. She can already imagine it, this new world. It throbs beneath her feet like the heart of a baby waiting to be born. It's the reason she volunteered for the Project and devoted her adolescence to preparing for it.

It's the reason she exists.

They enter a dilapidated stairwell. Step by step, the sounds of the building site fade and disappear. The descent seems endless. The sergeant keeps glancing at her, over his shoulder. His mole increasingly quivers.

"Only survivor of your whole family, eh? Condolences."

"Everyone loses someone during a war."

"But people who lose everyone, they're thinner on the ground. Is that why they chose you?"

His lips twist on the word "that." Eulalia intrigues and annoys him all at once. That, too, is something she's used to. She wonders what exactly he knows about the Project. Probably no more than she does, maybe even less.

"In part, sergeant."

Eulalia can't quite see herself explaining the other part to him, the most essential part. They didn't choose her. It was she who made sure she was chosen, out of hundreds of orphans. She always knew that she was called to save the world.

The army has found *something*, here, in this ancient city, that's going to assist her with that. *Something* that has the power to put a stop to the war, to all wars. Despite military secrecy, the rumors circulated in town, and Eulalia knows they are well-founded. She has always thought that, if humanity is this aggressive and bellicose, it's not so much out of hatred of others as of fear of one's own frailty. If each person in the world were capable of performing miracles, they would stop fearing their neighbor.

Miracles, that's what they all need.

"What've you got inside that? It's within the rules, at least?"

This time, the sergeant is indicating the small case she's holding. The mole, at the corner of his eye, flutters like an anxious little bird. Eulalia imagines—she imagines endlessly—the child he was, that he still is, and she suddenly feels overcome with affection. If the sergeant hadn't been her superior, she would have tweaked his cheek, just as she was doing only yesterday to the new arrivals at the orphanage.

"My writetyper . . . I mean my typewriter. They gave me permission to take it with me."

"For the reports?"

"For my stories. Stories without war."

"Oh yeah. A cellar, that sure inspires peace."

Eulalia stops on the bottom step of the stairs and contemplates the basement in which she knows she will be spending a lot of time. She has to admit, she's disconcerted. She has been through intensive training on the army's most sophisticated cryptanalysis machines.

All that's here is a simple telephone.

And suddenly, it's the fall in reverse. A dizzying, baffling sensation of falling upwards. The telephone seen from the ceiling, then the ascent of the stairs, then the flight above the building site, the imperial city, the continent, the entire Earth. A round planet, all in one piece, with no arks and no void.

The old world.

Ophelia sat up in bed, shaken and clammy, a scream stuck in her throat. This had happened upon waking ever since she had confronted that Memorial sweeper. And as always, she needed a moment to collect her thoughts.

She had, once again, been visited by the memory of Eulalia Gonde. It even went beyond that. She had embodied her from within, in her flesh, in her name, with a degree of precision and clarity she had never attained before.

Just as a "why?" was forming in her mind, Ophelia became aware that she didn't recognize her bed. It was strangely tilted, and when she shifted position, it rocked from one leg to another. All around there were just cushions, of every shape and color. Even the pajamas she had on rang no bells.

She had no memory whatsoever of having gone to bed here—of having gone to bed, period.

Ophelia searched around for her glasses, before recalling that the observatory had confiscated them from her. As it had her gloves. And yet she hadn't read either the sheets or the pillows in her sleep. A shiver coursed through her as she stroked all this silent silk. She really had to concentrate to get any distant impressions from it, and they were too vague to interpret. Touching objects without being flooded with visions hadn't happened to her since gaining her family power. She raised her hands into a ray of light, slipping between the slats of a shutter. How pale they were, compared with her suntanned arms . . . It felt like wearing gloves of a new kind.

Ophelia cleared a path through all the cushions. No sooner had she stepped down from the bed than she knocked over a pile of books. Putting them back in place, she saw they were all blank, with no title or text. The rest of the room followed suit. Empty frames and handless clocks littered the walls. Light switches had no effect on bulbs, which continued to flicker infuriatingly from the ceiling. The radio set Ophelia dived on to hear the news didn't even honor her with a crackle.

As for the door, it was locked.

Ophelia was reading almost nothing of all that she touched in this bedroom. Had the observatory dulled her family power within a single night? The thought was alarming.

"No problem."

She would wrench this place's secrets from it, with or without hands.

She couldn't find a handle for the shutter at the window. She pressed her face to the slats to see outside, but the sun blinded her. Her hopes were further dashed when she came across some mirrors in the bathroom: they were all the distorting kind, making Ophelia's reflection twisted and grotesque. To consider passing through a mirror, she needed a stable reflection.

This proliferation of uselessness was suffocating.

Ophelia banged on the faucets until they spluttered some water, and had a wash. Her dream—her *recollection*—continued to grip her from within. It was a feeling hard to define, halfway between joy and sorrow.

She looked her reflection in the eye, in the puddle at the bottom of the sink. There was no trace of the Other in that particular past, no allusion to some rebellious reflection, not even the merest thought, as if at this stage, it wasn't yet part of the story.

Ophelia had to pull the chain several times to flush the toilet. At least she had confirmation that Eulalia Gonde had been to the Deviations Observatory, even if the place wasn't called that yet, after leaving the military orphanage. This project for which she had volunteered, it must have been the Project Cornucopianism mentioned by the Genealogists, but Ophelia had seen no Horn of Plenty in her recollection, either.

Just a cellar and a telephone.

The sound of a key drew her myopic eyes back to the door, which opened theatrically onto the silhouette of a woman. She had the shape of a carboy, topped by a giant bun.

"Mommy?"

The word had just popped out. It was but a second later that Ophelia knew that was impossible. This woman wasn't her mother. In fact, it wasn't even really a woman. It was an automaton.

From under its apron, on which was embroidered the word "nanny," an inhuman voice rang out:

"GOOD MORNING, *CHÉRIE*. DID WE HAVE LOVELY BYE-BYES . . . BYE-BYES?"

Ophelia had never seen an automaton like this one before. It had a realistic face, with wide-open eyes, a snub nose, and a mouth stretched into an excessive smile. But its body was like that of an articulated doll. It had been got up in a puffed dress and light-auburn wig, filling Ophelia with confusion. After the exhibit from the Anima museum, it certainly couldn't be a coincidence anymore: the observatory knew who she was and where she came from. And it was using that to unnerve her.

"What time is it? What happened to me after the tunnel? I slept right through, since yesterday?"

The automaton unbuttoned Ophelia's pajamas without asking her first or replying to her questions.

"I WILL BE YOUR NANNY THROUGHOUT . . . OUT YOUR STAY HERE, *CHÉRIE*. I WILL TAKE GREAT CARE OF YOU. LET'S DRESS YOU QUICKLY, WE HAVE A BIG DAY AHEAD!"

"I'll dress myself."

A nanny really was the last thing in the world she wanted on her back. Her annoyance increased as she put her clothes on. Only yesterday, she couldn't brush against them without unintentionally going back in time; today, they were virtually unreadable to her.

While Ophelia was struggling into her sarouel trousers, the nanny-automaton brushed her hair so vigorously, it turned into a cloud of static. Not for a second did she try to find her some shoes. So it was barefoot that Ophelia proceeded along a vast corridor that proved even more cluttered with knickknacks than the bedroom, if that were possible: the vases, furniture, display china all had obvious manufacturing defects, rendering them unusable for anything but decoration.

All along the corridor, other doors opened on to other bedrooms, from which other sleepy individuals emerged. From what Ophelia's eyes allowed her to see of them, they were men and women of all generations and complexions, each escorted by a nanny-automaton disguised in a different way. They wore the same clothes, leaving arms and calves bare, and the same dark tattoo on the shoulder.

Were they, then, all inverts? Some showed deformities, others didn't. There were about fifteen of them, at most. Not one of them returned Ophelia's "good morning." In fact, no one spoke to anyone.

She followed the others down a staircase, its steps cluttered with cardboard boxes. This residence was like some giant junk room. To her great annoyance, her nanny-automaton never left her. Uncovering the secrets of Project Cornucopianism with such an escort promised to be tricky.

Once on the ground floor, Ophelia looked for the cellar with the telephone from her dream. Instead she found a refectory. Here, a lavish buffet was spread out, offering a profusion of cakes, spices, custards, pies, cookies, sweet and savory pancakes, sweetmeats, jams, and so much more.

It was excessive, indecently excessive for so few residents.

Ophelia felt her heart race like a spinning top. She saw the residence's deluge of objects under a new light. That Horn of Plenty, which, until then, had been just an old, somewhat abstract legend, suddenly seemed very real to her. Was it to be found somewhere here, right under her nose, in the guise of a bowl or plate?

Of course not. The observatory had hidden it from view, but that didn't stop Ophelia from feeling very close to what she had come looking for.

She took a hearty bite from a pastry. She almost spat it right out; it tasted revolting. The same thing happened with everything she helped herself to. There was a startling contrast between the appetizing appearance of the food and its appalling taste. Even the tea proved barely drinkable.

This buffet was in the image of the whole residence. Ophelia's disappointment was equal to her excitement. Was that really *all* the Horn of Plenty was? An abundance of faulty goods? How could she and Thorn use that to counter Eulalia, the Other, and the landslides?

In the refectory, the inverts chewed away in silence, each in his or her corner. Ophelia couldn't swallow a thing.

She frowned when a fat brioche rolled toward her, on the tablecloth. The gift came from a young man sitting on the other side of the table, close enough for her to see his slanting eyes and big rosy cheeks. His half-smile revealed the whitest teeth. He, too, had the Alternative Program stamp on his shoulder. His were the first eyes Ophelia's had met. She wondered what his inversion consisted of, since he seemed so ordinary. Having said that, hers didn't show, either, at first glance. Blaise had told her that there existed all kinds of inversions: those of the body, those of the mind, and those of the powers.

Thorn would have advised her not to touch the gift of a stranger, but what food could really be trusted here? She bit into the brioche and found it edible.

"Thank you."

Discreetly, the young man pressed a finger to his lips to encourage her to be silent, and then pointed at their nanny-automatons, miming, by rotating his index finger, the turning of a gramophone record. Right. The automatons were fitted with a recording device. If Ophelia couldn't ask a question without the risk of being recorded, investigating was going to prove quite a challenge.

A gong rang out.

"IT'S TIME, *CHÉRIS!*" announced all the nanny-automatons, in unison.

Everyone went through a door and into a cloister. There, too, boxes bursting with knickknacks got in the way. The sand-colored columns, eroded over the centuries, clearly dated back to the time of the imperial city. Ophelia brushed her fingers over them without managing to penetrate their history. Without glasses, it was hard for her see the vast courtyard stretching beyond the jagged shade of the arcades. It didn't look like a garden, more like some industrial structures. So that's where the containment zone was situated.

A morose silence prevailed among the inverts. The nanny-automatons ensured that they each kept their distance from the rest. Their line passed a procession of individuals in monks' habits, concealed under gray hoods. They, apparently, were neither automatons nor inverts. One of them turned discreetly as Ophelia went by but said nothing to her and kept walking.

After a succession of galleries and boxes, the inverts were finally led to the large inner courtyard, already baking from the sun. The industrial structures at last became clearer to Ophelia's eyes: rusty carousels, empty fairground stands, a stalled big wheel, and, wherever possible, heaps of scrap. An old amusement park? Was that what the Alternative Program consisted of?

Ophelia had the unpleasant sensation of moving away from what she had glimpsed in a dream.

She was taken into an oppressively dark big top. Several rickety chairs faced a screen onto which, through a beam twinkling with dust, a projector cast jerky images. In the middle of the big top, a record player was blaring dissonant music.

Each invert sat at a distance from his or her neighbors.

Ophelia was put in the front row. The young man of the brioche sat two chairs away from her.

The nanny-automatons had posted themselves at the entrance to the big top, waiting for the end of the screening. Ophelia hoped the show wouldn't last long. On the screen in front of her, geometrical shapes kept endlessly forming and distorting, giving her both a splitting headache and nausea.

"Don't stare at them too much."

The whisper had come from the young man of the brioche. He sat nonchalantly in his place, arms and legs crossed, head raised at the screen, but his slanted eyes were turned toward Ophelia. They glinted with curiosity in the darkness of the big top.

"Don't stare at me too much, either. Do what I do. Pretend."

Ophelia gazed at the screen without really looking at it. Here, in the cacophony from the record player, away from the nanny-automatons, they could at last talk.

"I'm Cosmos."

Ophelia liked the sound of his voice, his slightly oriental accent, his hint of derision. Listening to him, she felt very small once again. It was how Eulalia Gonde had felt in front of that sergeant and his quivering mole. But what was it?

"Have you been on the program for long, Cosmos?"

"Long enough to advise you not to stare at these images. Every day, they start with the screening. It conditions us, like the larval towel . . . I mean, like the arrival tunnel. Apparently, you fainted? You're not the first to pass out. I myself threw up."

Ophelia clenched her toes on the carpet. She looked around for a reflective surface, in vain.

"And then?" she asked. "What do they have in store for us?"

"Exams. Interviews. Workshops. You'll soon understand. Or rather, no, you'll understand nothing. They're all a bit loony here. You, you seem like a sensible person. You're like me."

There was a cough behind them. Over her shoulder, beyond the rows of chairs and the projector, Ophelia could make out some figures in gray habits standing at the back of the big top.

"Don't look at them," Cosmos whispered, a little more quietly. "They're collaborators. Recruited by the observatory to dusty us . . . to study us."

Ophelia took a long, deep breath. One slip of the tongue could be a coincidence; two prompted caution. If she'd had a pocket mirror, she could have checked that this boy really was who he claimed to be. This thought had barely crossed her mind when Cosmos changed place, to sit a chair further away.

"You suddenly mistrusted me. Why?"

His voice, which Ophelia found harder to hear due to the distance and the music, had lost any trace of humor. This young man was an Empathetic. At least, he seemed to be. His family power allowed him to feel, to a degree, whatever Ophelia felt.

She decided to speak frankly to him:

"You express yourself like someone I know. And it's not a friend."

Cosmos couldn't resist an astonished glance at Ophelia, prompting another disapproving cough from the wings.

"My electrocution poem . . . elocution problem? I've had it since I've been here. They heal nothing in this place. They unhinge us even more. It shows up in either speech or movement. It'll get you sooner or later, too."

Ophelia's toes unclenched on the carpet. Were Eulalia Gonde's slips of the tongue due to what she had been through for Project Cornucopianism? Was that why she herself was experiencing object-reading problems? Had a single journey through that strange tunnel sufficed to make her hands illiterate?

Cosmos lowered his voice even more, making it almost inaudible:

"Unless one escapes first. Alone, it's impossible. If one teams up, one chairs a dance . . . one has a chance."

"I volunteered to come here. I have no intention of escaping."

"If we don't escape, *mademoiselle*, they'll make us disappear."

"Disappear how?"

"There are three protocols. Now, we're right in the first. Don't know where those transferred to the second go; they're seen sometimes from afar. But as soon as they're fan stirred . . . I mean, as soon as they're transferred to the third protocol, they're never heard of again."

Ophelia clung to what Blaise had told her in the heliwagon.

"Maybe they were simply sent home?"

"We're not all lucky enough to have a home," replied Cosmos. "In my case, no one is waiting for me outside. And you," he added, somewhat mischievously, "I bet you're here because you've got nowhere else to go."

A distant gong rang out again, bringing an end to the screening, and to their conversation.

"The Deviations Observatory has its own necropolis," Cosmos whispered to her as he stood up. "Don't know about you, but personally, I don't fancy ending up there."

With these words, he rejoined his nanny-automaton. Ophelia was led by hers to an individual tent, more modest in size than the big top, where some collaborators made her go through all manner of absurd motions: bend the elbow, close one eye, hop forward, swivel the head, and so on, to the point of dizziness. At no time did any of them show their face or say a word to her. Were they wearing dark-lensed pince-nez under their hoods?

They then made her sit down in the darkness of a photographic booth. Ophelia was so dazzled by the flashes that she let her nanny-automaton guide her by the shoulder to the next stage of the protocol. This took place on the platform of a steam-powered carousel, unlike any she had seen before. Instead of seats there stood easels, like those normally found in artists' studios. Each invert was standing. As soon as Ophelia was installed in front of her easel, the carousel began to turn.

"YOUR LEFT!"

Some started to do calligraphy, others to draw, all using their left hand.

"YOUR RIGHT!"

As one, all the inverts swapped hands. The carousel switched direction to a ghastly chorus of creaks. One woman's breakfast came up.

Cosmos was right. They were all a bit loony here.

Ophelia peered at her blank page, not knowing what to do with it. In fact, all she could think of was their conversation under the big top, forced to admit that it had troubled her. She wasn't afraid for herself, not yet anyway. She was afraid for Thorn. The Genealogists were the most powerful Lords of Babel, and yet they hadn't managed to protect their previous informer. Had he taken part in the third protocol? Ophelia knew that the best way to help Thorn was to be his eyes and ears wherever the observatory wouldn't let him inspect, but she would have liked to put him on his guard.

She jumped when the nanny-automaton spanked her.

"YOU WON'T GET OFF THIS CAROUSEL AS LONG AS . . . LONG AS YOU HAVEN'T DONE YOUR EXERCISE LIKE A GOOD GIRL, *CHÉRIE*."

Ophelia observed her nearest neighbors. An old man kept halting his calligraphy to hit one of his ears while muttering "must go up down below . . . must go up down below." Despite her myopia, Ophelia could see the shadows under his eyes, which were as black as the ink he was spattering over his face.

She felt sorry for him.

When she turned to the other side, she felt even sorrier upon seeing the profile of a young girl, who was busily coloring. Her cheek bore the pimples of early puberty. Ophelia hadn't noticed her at the residence. Curiously, of all the inverts on this carousel, she alone had no nanny-automaton. She was, on the other hand, being closely studied by a team of collaborators.

"YOUR EXERCISE, *CHÉRIE*," repeated the nanny-automaton.

Ophelia grabbed a bent pencil, as unreadable as all she'd touched since waking, and wrote the same sentence several times: "But this well was no more real than a rabbit of Odin." She still didn't have the slightest idea what these words meant, this way she would save herself from the humiliation of a public spanking on a steam-powered carousel. The rotating, first one way, then the other, turned her words into scribbles.

She couldn't stop herself from snatching furtive glances at the profile of the young girl beside her. The more attention Ophelia paid to her, the more that strange impression left by her dream resurfaced. It was bittersweet, it appealed to her and hurt her at the same time. What was it all about, in the end?

The carousel stopped when the gong rang out in the distance. The young girl made a beeline for Ophelia with a big smile, her drawing clutched to her stomach. Now that she was facing her, hair tucked behind ears, her face revealed all its peculiarity. It was completely dissymmetrical. Ears, eyebrows, nostrils, teeth, even the contours of her forehead and jaw: nothing matched up, as if half of two different people had been combined. One of her eyes didn't even have an iris, and its disturbing whiteness was directed at Ophelia.

A gold chain linked the arch of her eyebrow to her nostril.

"Second," murmured Ophelia.

Octavio's sister. Lady Septima's daughter. Neither half of

this face resembled them. Without the chain, it would have been impossible to tell that the three of them were related.

"The pecked assails the hay."

"Sorry?"

Ophelia couldn't understand. Second frowned with her different eyebrows and became insistent.

"Gravitate by the iron and hang the mountains."

Ophelia shook her head, increasingly confused. This gibberish was worse than those slips of the tongue. Second sighed. She handed her drawing to Ophelia and jumped off the carousel.

It was a strange but remarkable picture, skillfully drawn, down to the smallest detail, as if the jolting of the carousel hadn't affected her pencil stroke at all. It depicted a boy who looked a lot like Octavio: he was crying, surrounded, at his feet, by papers torn to shreds.

All the nearby collaborators immediately surrounded Ophelia to confiscate the drawing and pass it around among themselves, taking notes all the while. She paid no attention to them. She had just understood the nature of that feeling of pressure on her stomach she'd had since waking. It was what Eulalia Gonde had felt toward the sergeant, toward the orphans, and that she would feel much later toward the family spirits. A visceral emotion that had permeated every fiber of Ophelia's being.

The maternal instinct.

COMMUNION

The clouds unraveled like wool across the sky. Victoria felt as if she were made of the same stuff. She couldn't feel the wind making the grass shiver or smell the orange trees' aroma. She weighed nothing, had no form anymore. She was sinking into the bathtub. She was missing the Other-Victoria's weight, which had so often exasperated her. Of course, her child's mind couldn't string together such tricky words to express all these thoughts.

"Do you find this world peaceful, little girl?"

Victoria turned her attention to the Fake-Ginger-Fellow. He was sitting right beside her, but the sound of his voice was as distant as that of the river, on the bank of which they had stopped.

"Peace has a price. If your right hand causes you to fall, cut it off and throw it far away from you. That's what I did, you know? When we change ourselves, little girl, we change the entire universe. Because what is outside is like what sins aside . . . what is inside."

He picked out a stone in the grass, threw it awkwardly, and then showed Victoria the rings spreading in the water.

"That's what you are."

The Fake-Ginger-Fellow's eyes searched for Victoria under

the orange trees, without managing to focus at length on her. She needed him. Or, more exactly, although she couldn't have put it in such terms, she needed to feel she existed thanks to him. As long as he was conscious of her presence, she would be able to keep herself afloat in the bathtub. The giant whirlpool of last time had terrified her; what would she do if it tried once more to sweep her away?

"You are doubtless too young to understand what I'm going to say to you, but I must say it to you precisely because you are too young. The use you make of your power is range as dose . . . dangerous. Every rupture worsens that of the world."

With his big, muscular hand, the Fake-Ginger-Fellow stroked the swarm of shadows that were mingling with those of the orange trees surrounding him. Victoria had learned not to be afraid of them anymore, but she didn't get too close to them, all the same.

"I also have another me. I've given him my joys, my sorrows, my experiences, my desires, my fears, all those contradictions that were impeding me. The more I gave him, the more the Other in turn gave me. And the more he asked for, too. He always asked for more. I had no choice but to give him up, in the interest of the world."

The Fake-Ginger-Fellow's eyes alighted on Victoria, as if just finding her, finally, among the butterflies. Eyes full of emptiness. A part of her vaguely sensed that he needed her a little, too.

"Your second you, who remained back there, in the Pole, with your parents, she gave you up, too. You're the one who dimpled her . . . who impeded her. You probably don't understand what I'm trying to explain to you, little girl, but it's important. She's not the other. You are."

No, Victoria didn't understand a thing. And yet she started to feel a sadness she couldn't express with either cries or tears.

"I have nothing against you and can do nothing for you," the Fake-Ginger-Fellow then said to her as, stiffly, he got to his feet. "As long as you're happy to remain a shadow among shadows, you're a problem only to yourself. The real danger begins when a reflection leaves its mirror. And, while remaining hidden, takes down what has taken centuries to build."

With ludicrous contortions, the Fake-Ginger-Fellow got rid of the bits of twig stuck to his clothes. The river water reflected the entire landscape apart from him—him and Victoria.

"This body, that of a powerless person, has its limitations, but be patient . . . Of all my children, Janus has always been the most unpredictable and the least cooperative. If he finds me at his place before I have found his Needlers, we'll have to start from scratch again. And I no longer have time to do that. We mustn't rush things, little girl. At some moment there'll be loophole. There's hopefully a swallow . . . always a loophole."

On a sign from him, Victoria followed the Fake-Ginger-Fellow through the orange trees. He moved strangely when they were alone, as if it was more natural for him to twist his legs. He forced himself to walk normally as soon as he pushed open the gate to the usual public garden. It was really torture for Victoria to see all these roundabouts and rocking horses and not be able to play on them. There were never any children here. Once, Victoria had glimpsed a few laughing in the distance, but as soon as the Fake-Ginger-Fellow had arrived at the gate, the children had disappeared.

The Funny-Eyed-Lady was sitting on one of the swings and digging deep furrows in the sand by dragging her shoes. The slanted light of the setting sun made her dark hair appear almost blond. She was gripping the chains while watching Twit, meowing and weaving endlessly between her calves. The cat darted away as soon as the Fake-Ginger-Fellow came and sat down on the neighboring swing. Twit didn't like them much, him and Victoria.

As for the Funny-Eyed-Lady, she barely raised her head.

"Anything doing on your side?"

"Nothing."

Victoria had noticed that the Fake-Ginger-Fellow spoke very little once they were no longer alone. She also noticed that the Funny-Eyed-Lady's lips were all scratched from being bitten so much.

"Nothing on mine, either. Walls without doors and deserted gardens wherever I went. As if all of LandmArk's architecture had folded into itself. My Nihilism's a dead loss here. Canceling only the family power of Farouk's descendants, eh? Some talent."

The Funny-Eyed-Lady's voice had thickened so much, she seemed to be stifling it from within. Victoria had often seen her angry, but never to this extent. Her fingers were strangling the chains of her swing as she bent over even more, showing the roots of her hair: it wasn't a trick of the light, it was growing back blond. The Fake-Ginger-Fellow remained silent.

To Victoria's surprise, the Funny-Eyed-Lady finally burst out laughing.

"It's the pits! If we can't leave this ark anymore, or have dealings with any Arkadian, I'm soon going to run out of cigarettes!"

The garden's gate creaked when it was Godfather's turn to arrive. He was whistling a chirpy little tune. Victoria ran up to him. Even if he was unaware of her presence, even if his smile remained elusive, Godfather made her feel less sad. Every morning they all split up, and every evening they all met up again in this garden, where they all spent the night together. It was like a game with no loser or winner.

"So?" grunted the Funny-Eyed-Lady. "Has our situation evolved, ex-ambassador?"

Godfather kicked up a ball lying in the sand, and made it bounce higher and higher.

"Perhaps."

"Perhaps?"

Only the ball bouncing on Godfather's foot replied to the question. The Funny-Eyed-Lady got up so suddenly that her swing rocked to and fro.

"While waiting for that 'perhaps' to become a 'yes,' I'm off to answer a call of nature."

She headed to the back of the garden, to a little tiled building that Victoria knew to be the restroom. She had once accompanied Godfather there out of curiosity. She hadn't done so twice.

The last bounce of the ball sent it spinning so high in the air that it didn't come down; it got stuck in the branches of a tree. Godfather watched the leaves twirling around in the sunset's rays. He caught one in midair, and turned it this way and that, between his fingers, with fascination, as if trying to fathom the mysteries of the universe through it. Victoria adored this way Godfather had of studying everything in minutest detail, touching everything within his reach, tasting everything that could be popped into the mouth. It was a bit like he was experiencing the world in her place.

"I'm certainly no expert in monogamy," he finally declared, "but I know a lonely woman when I see one."

Still perched on his swing, the Fake-Ginger-Fellow glanced at the restroom at the back of the garden. The sun, increasingly low in the sky, was stretching all the shadows, apart from those that were tightening like brambles under his soles.

"I'll speak to her."

"And what if, instead, we spoke, you and I?" Godfather suggested. "A man-to-man talk."

With his usual smile, he leaned over the Fake-Ginger-Fellow, who slowly, very slowly, raised his bushy eyebrows. Godfather focused on him in much the same way as he had, a moment before, focused on the leaf he'd caught as it fell. A shadow, such as Victoria had never seen before in him, started to fall from his eyes—how could such light eyes produce such darkness?—and penetrate those of the Fake-Ginger-Fellow.

"Or should I say," whispered Godfather, "man-to-god?"

Victoria was fascinated and scared and excited; she was too many things at once and had no words to describe them. Godfather's shadow just kept spilling out until it had enshrouded the body of the Fake-Ginger-Fellow, despite it being sturdier than his own. The latter was caught in this black trap without even attempting to struggle. The rocking of his swing gradually came to a stop. His jaws opened, but he uttered not the slightest sound. Nothing else seemed to exist for him, beyond the implacable eyes of Godfather, who kept leaning further in, mingling their gold and flame locks.

"What is it like? How does it feel when one possesses thousands of identities and is drowning in the consciousness of a single man?"

Godfather's voice was soft as silk. Nevertheless, Victoria felt an entirely new respectful fear of him.

There then occurred something astonishing. The Fake-Ginger-Fellow's face went all soft and changed shape, as if his flesh were made of modeling clay. His features became finer, his hair lightened, and in mere moments, he looked like Godfather. He had his beauty, his untrimmed beard, his gaping hat, even the black tear on his forehead. He had his eyes. With a single look, he projected onto Godfather all the shadows that shot out from under his feet like countless tentacles.

"And you, my child, how do yodel full . . . do you feel?"

Victoria's first shock was seeing Godfather collapsing to the ground. Her second was when the Funny-Eyed-Lady threw herself onto the Fake-Godfather, making him fall off his swing. Crouching over him, armed with a monkey wrench, she hit him again and again and again and again.

"You really believed it, you cylinder-head gasket?" she screamed. "Thought you'd fool us for a long time? What've you done with Fox?"

Horrified, Victoria saw that Fake-Godfather's skull kept losing its shape and then reforming under the blows.

"Are you done, my girl?" he asked, wearily. "Calmer now?"

"I . . . am . . . not . . . your . . . girl!" screamed the Funny-Eyed-Lady, bringing her monkey wrench down between each word. "God or not . . . I'll take you apart . . . piece by piece!"

"That won't be necessary," a voice interrupted.

It was the man-woman from the last time. Victoria realized that he was in the middle of the garden, then she realized that there was no more garden. They were all now in a very large room. It was even more fancily decorated than Mommy's boudoir.

Stretched out in the middle of a rug, Godfather lifted himself up onto his elbows. His first gesture was toward his hat, which had fallen with him.

"Really, Don Janus, we almost waited for you. I was starting to think you hadn't received my message."

"Your message, *niño*? The one that consists of knocking on the walls of all the houses and repeating 'God is here'? I've known subtler ways. I must, however, admit that you did honor your part of the deal. You proved to me that LandmArk was implicated in your little affairs."

The man-woman indicated to the Funny-Eyed-Lady to move back, and then he bowed his gigantic body toward the Fake-Godfather.

"Señora Gonde. It's been a long time."

The Fake-Godfather changed shape until he was back to

being the Bespectacled-Little-Lady whom Victoria had briefly met on the bridge, between two Fake-Ginger-Fellows. She seemed fragile and tiny compared with the man-woman but didn't seem at all intimidated.

"I truffled the pine . . . preferred the time when you called me 'mother.'"

"A mother capable of reproducing identically anyone she meets in the street, but not her own creatures. Pretty ironic, isn't it."

The Bespectacled-Little-Lady raised a hand toward the man-woman towering over her, but he disappeared and then reappeared at the other end of the rug.

"You'll understand if I don't let you get too close to us, my Book and me, Señora Gonde. I've grown attached to my intact memory."

Godfather tried to stand up, but couldn't. Half a smile lingered at the corner of his mouth, but Victoria could see clearly that he was shaking. He stared at the Bespectacled-Little-Lady with a mocking curiosity.

"What are we going to do with her, Don Janus?"

The man-woman wrapped a finger in the curl of his moustache.

"Nothing."

"What do you mean, nothing?" whispered the Funny-Eyed-Lady, tightening her grip on her monkey wrench.

"Nothing," repeated the man-woman. "You find yourselves here in a non-place of my making. Even the most gifted of Arkadians couldn't leave it unless I decided so. That applies equally to Señora Gonde, powerful as she may be. I committed myself to us—what was the expression you used, again?—us 'all giving her a real tongue-lashing.' Consider it done. You have proved to me that my ark was implicated in your affairs, but it was through your own fault. It's you who brought Señora

Gonde to me. So it's you who will keep her company here and stop disrupting the world."

"Janus. Give me an Arkadian."

The Bespectacled-Little-Lady pushed her brown hair back over her shoulders, and it now hung down to her waist.

"Give me a Needler."

Victoria had once heard Mommy use that tone. Her necklace had broken, and beads had rained down, all over the sitting room. They were so sparkly! More tempting than all the treats in the candy jar. Victoria had crawled under the armchair to retrieve one and had put it to her mouth, curious to know how it tasted. Mommy had then knelt down, dress rustling, held out her wide-open palm, and, in the blue of her eyes, Victoria had seen a storm that had terrified her. "Give it to me."

Like the Bespectacled-Little-Lady now.

A smile lifted the man-woman's moustache.

"There was a time when I would have been unable to do anything but obey you, Señora Gonde. You just had to demand, and my brothers and sisters would submit to you on everything. That time has passed. It ceased once you, yourself, ceased to be yourself."

The Bespectacled-Little-Lady frowned.

"You've got the wrong enemy, Janus. You've all got the wrong enemy. It's not me who disrupts the world; it's the Other. If you don't quickly help me to find him and stop him, it billow rotate . . . it will be too late."

The man-woman let out a sigh that made his ruff quiver.

"The centuries go by, and it's always the same refrain. And my response will always be the same: no, I do not authorize you to approach my Arkadians and to assimilate their powers. You are not worthy of this talent that you yourself bestowed on me. If you were, you would already possess it. Take no offense, Señora Gonde, but the Other never existed anywhere, except in your uncontrollable imagination. I hope, at least, that this last will prove useful to you making the evenings drag less in my non-place."

With these words, the man-woman disappeared, leaving a large space on the rug, on which Twit was already sharpening his claws. Victoria looked at the Funny-Eyed-Lady, who looked at the Bespectacled-Little-Lady, who looked at Godfather.

"Alright," he said, still lying on the floor. "I admit it—*that* I hadn't seen coming."

THE DEVIATION

Ophelia was sleeping badly. Her nights now merely amounted to a fitful drowsiness in which the old world and the new were confused. She always awoke with a start, dazzled by the flickering lightbulbs, gripped by a vague fear, as if there were still an old sweeper ready to terrify her, to keep her away from Eulalia Gonde's secrets. And when it wasn't the nightmares, it was her thoughts that churned like the drum of a washing machine. The rickety bed didn't help with thinking straight.

She was obsessed with the Other more than ever.

He had caused the death of thousands of individuals, without ever coming out of the shadows, but she was haunted by what, first, he had killed in her. Having or not having children was a decision that should have been down to them, her and Thorn. The Other had lumbered her with a memory she hadn't wanted and deprived her of her very first adult choice. Ophelia wasn't even certain anymore of her own feelings: did this indignation come from her, or from what Eulalia Gonde would have felt in her situation?

Every time she fell on her warped image in the bathroom's distorting mirrors, she thought of that long-ago night when, despite herself, she had released the Other. Despite herself, really? She tried with all her might to remember what had set things off. She saw once again her bedroom on Anima. She saw once again the wall mirror. She saw herself once again in her dressing gown. She thought she saw once again that presence, barely perceptible, behind her own reflection.

Release me.

There must have been something else. As young as she was, Ophelia would never have given in, without a reason, to the whim of an unknown reflection. She couldn't have decided, on a mere impulse, that the best thing to do was to pass through the mirror to clear the way for him. And then, once again, what had happened next? While she was stuck between her bedroom and the home of her great-aunt, what had become of the Other? From where did he exit? In what form? What had he been doing for all these years?

Ophelia sometimes thought back to that glazing-and-mirror store, where she had seen herself covered in blood, in front of Eulalia, the Other, and the void. It was infuriating to be plagued with strange visions, and yet not be able to remember something that really did happen to her during her own childhood!

Just like her repetitive thoughts, for Ophelia, each day at the observatory was an exact replica of the day before. The nanny-automaton took her to the projection room, where geometrical shapes formed and distorted on the screen; accompanied her into a tent where Ophelia went through the same crazy movements before being photographed; led her from one carousel to another, on which there were absurd workshops; sat in on both her medical consultations and her meals; and then locked her into her bedroom until the following day.

The only disruptions to this ritual were the very frequent power cuts, which stopped the carousels mid-circuit and put out the refectory lights mid-supper. Since arriving, Ophelia hadn't seen a single lightbulb working properly.

She had lost all notion of time. She had also lost the only person she could really talk to. Cosmos, whose attempt at conversation hadn't gone unnoticed, was no longer allowed to sit beside her in the projection room. And there weren't many places one could talk that were free of a nanny's recording device, or away from the collaborators. Ophelia had had no further dealings either with the beetle woman or the lizard man or an observer since joining the Alternative Program. As for the directors of the Deviations Observatory, she had picked up the odd whisperings about them, but hadn't encountered them once since arriving.

She hadn't seen Thorn again, either, and, of all the privations, that was the hardest. Was he managing, on his side, to investigate without arousing suspicions?

While waiting to be able to talk to him, finally, she watched, listened to, touched everything she possibly could within the containment zone. She had found nothing vaguely resembling a Horn of Plenty—her image of one, at any rate. On the other hand, she noticed that every day there were more useless knickknacks around the corridors, and more wasted food in the trash. She hadn't had another revelation about Eulalia Gonde's old life, so she made do with endlessly revisiting, in her mind, her last memory, trying, in vain, to establish connections between the cellar with the telephone, Project Cornucopianism, Eulalia's metamorphosis, the advent of the Other, the collapse of the arks, and the inverts' carousel rides.

And yet she knew there was a link.

Maybe Ophelia had already reached the limits of the first protocol of the Alternative Program. Maybe it was in the second protocol that things finally made some sense. According to Cosmos, it was from the third protocol that no one ever returned, but she wasn't there yet. When she had announced to her nanny-automaton that she felt ready to move on to the next stage, the latter had let out such a guffaw that it sent shivers down Ophelia's spine.

Ophelia peered up at the blurry statue of the colossus, standing in the middle of the observatory like a stone mountain, his head with its several faces looking down on the world. "I see everything, I know everything!" How he annoyed her . . .

In short, time was passing, and Ophelia hadn't got any further. She couldn't see any logic to all that the observatory made her do, her and the other inverts. The only thing that was blatantly obvious to her was how right Blaise had been. The Alternative Program didn't seek to heal inversions; it made them worse.

Every day it became harder for Ophelia to read objects in the residence, despite there being so many of them. On the other hand, she did find herself animating them, without meaning to, increasingly frequently, and always at her own expense. Cushions bounced on her while she slept. Chairs trod on her feet, furniture pushed her around. Once, during supper, a fork had stabbed her in the arm.

Things began to get worse when, one morning, Ophelia put her tunic on back to front. Much as she kept trying, it proved impossible for her to put it on the right way round without the help of her nanny-automaton. Next it was the turn of the handles. Door handles, drawer handles, faucet handles: they all became insuperable obstacles to Ophelia. It was no longer just her Animism that was awry, it was her. Left and right, up and down, they all got mixed up in her hands. Getting out of the restroom became a daily challenge. She would have found it easier to keep making slips of the tongue, like Cosmos . . . She didn't know whether it was the gymnastics she was made to do, the screenings she had to attend, those carousels she had to suffer from morning to night, or a combination of all that, but for her, nothing seemed to go smoothly. It had taken her years to curb her clumsiness, since the disastrous mirror passage that had released the Other and messed up her organs; barely a few days here had sufficed to make her relapse.

And yet, she wasn't the worst off. In at least one of the three morning screenings, a woman on the program had an epileptic fit. An insomniac started screaming like a lunatic just as he was dozing off. The old man who would hit his ear kept muttering the same phrase, "must go up down below . . . must go up down below . . . must go up down below . . .", as if repeating the words an invisible crowd was shouting down his earhole. Cosmos himself, who seemed one of the least unstable, would sometimes isolate himself in a corner, motionless, for hours.

And then there was Second.

The intriguing, the fascinating Second, with her two-sided face. She looked like no other invert and benefited from a special regime. She didn't sleep at the residence, didn't have her meals with the community, only took part in workshops that appealed to her, and could speak to whomever she liked without being chastised. Sometimes she would stare into space for ages, her iris-free eye wide open, and then she would start to draw. It was almost compulsive.

If she received visits from Octavio or Lady Septima, it was all very discreet. Ophelia noticed that she sometimes left in the middle of a carousel circuit, led away by an observer, and reappeared an hour later. What was astonishing, not to say worrying, was her presence within the first protocol. According to Octavio, his sister had been interned since early childhood; she was now entering puberty. A long time for a single stage of the program. Second was never accompanied by a nanny-automaton, but the collaborators did follow her extremely closely. They took notes and exchanged whispers from the shadow of their gray hoods as soon as she took out her pencil. Every drawing she did was systematically requisitioned by them. Ophelia would have found them ridiculous had she not been herself equally disturbed.

She didn't know whether it was down to her being a new arrival, but Second sought tirelessly to communicate with her, more than with anyone else. She rushed toward her as soon as she spotted her, gripped her by the wrist, and cheerily spouted nonsense at her: "Bristle the taste buds!"; "The umbrella wrecks everything"; "Are shovels without mess needed?" Even when she tried to write her thoughts down, it was the same gibberish. One time, she had launched into an endless speech featuring the weather's tactlessness, crushed prawns, lunar axes, distracted missiles, a falcon reported missing, and dental hairiness. Despite trying her utmost, Ophelia understood absolutely nothing, to the great frustration of Second, who ended up giving her a drawing with an annoyed flourish.

Unlike her language, her sketches were strikingly realistic. Those she did for Ophelia always featured Octavio, from different angles, but all had in common that he looked dreadfully tormented. The collaborators confiscated all of them, without exception. Ophelia didn't know what to think of it. Was Octavio aware of these drawings? She hoped not. They would give the impression that his little sister yearned to see him suffer.

Ophelia revised her opinion somewhat when, one afternoon, she caught Second giving a drawing to another invert on the Alternative Program. It depicted a simple nail, but Second redrew it several times and handed it, always insistently, to the same person. A few days later, that invert trod on a rusty old nail when climbing aboard a carousel, and had to be taken urgently to the infirmary. Ophelia was surprised to see, once again, on Second's dissymmetrical face, the annoyance she showed every time she hadn't made herself understood. Had she really anticipated the accident? Ophelia had lived with some Seers during her apprenticeship at the Good Family; none of them would have been able to foresee something so specific so far ahead.

It suddenly struck her that perhaps Second, despite her communication difficulties, had the answers to her questions. And answers were something Ophelia desperately needed. She had no intention of continually reliving the same day, week after week, month after month, when the Other could cause a new collapse at any moment.

One morning, however, something happened that broke the routine of the protocol. Instead of leading her to the screening room, with the others, as usual, the nanny-automaton said to her:

"NOT TODAY, *CHÉRIE*."

They walked together between the carousels, rusted and faded by time, and invaded by weeds moaning in the drafts from the cloister. Here, a circuit of aerial tracks with no train. There, a mechanical planetarium with frozen orbs. The park's only amusement was in its name. Its very gravel burnt the soles of the feet.

The nanny-automaton went over to a carousel that Ophelia had never seen working. It was entirely separate, almost concealed behind heaps of defective objects, and so dilapidated that it creaked as soon as they climbed onto its platform.

"SIT DOWN, *CHÉRIE*."

"This carousel . . . is it the second protocol?"

"IT'S JUST A LITTLE GAME."

Only one seat remained in the middle of the carousel; it didn't look that much fun. Ophelia had barely sat down before the nanny-automaton strapped her in tight enough to wind her.

"That's too tight. It's hurting me."

"EVERYTHING IS PERFECTLY PERFECT, *CHÉRIE*."

The nanny-automaton pulled a key from her cleavage and put it into a lock on the carousel. The circular platform remained immobile, but the seat sank under it. Turning like a screw, it made a ghastly racket of steel and wood as it descended deeper and deeper into the ground. Ophelia was plunged into stifling darkness. Her heart pounded, constricted by the strapping. She tore her fingernails trying to unstrap herself. She was still going down.

Her eyes flickered when lightbulbs started flashing all around her. The seat had finally come to a stop. She couldn't undo the strap, but in any case, the only way out was the very well she'd been forced down. The air itself smelt of stone. She found herself sitting in the middle of a subterranean room, facing a table.

Upon the table, a telephone.

Ophelia instantly forgot her fear. It was the cellar of Eulalia Gonde's memory. Despite her myopia, she recognized the walls, the dimensions, the height of the ceiling, as if she personally had resided in it. Did this telephone harbor all the secrets of the old world, and have all the solutions for the new one? Could it be the Horn of Plenty?

Ophelia forced herself to make a cool assessment of the situation. Yes, she finally found herself where Eulalia Gonde had worked on the Project centuries ago, but it wasn't the same telephone. The one in front of her, like all objects in the observatory, had a manufacturing fault that made it almost unusable: the numbers on the dial were so distorted, they were illegible. This certainly wasn't the Horn of Plenty.

It started ringing before Ophelia had time to wonder what to do with it. Restrained by the straps of her chair, she had to make several attempts to pick up the receiver.

"Hello?"

"*Hello.*"

It was just an echo, which wasn't surprising. But might there be someone at the other end of the line?

Of course there was.

There could be no doubt that, for this particular experiment, whatever its nature, Ophelia was being listened to. After all, "observing" was the very purpose of this institute.

Her fingers tightened around the receiver. No longer being able to read objects made her feel deaf to everything. Other hands had inevitably touched this telephone before her, but she detected no thought, no emotion.

And her? What was she expected to feel? What was she supposed to do?

It was then that she noticed, on the table, just behind the telephone, in the flickering light of the lamps, a stand on which was placed not a musical score, but a booklet. On the page was an uninterrupted string of words and numbers even more nonsensical than Second's utterances. They were printed large enough for Ophelia to make them out without glasses. She knew she wouldn't be brought back up as long as this experiment wasn't concluded.

She read out loud, but was immediately bombarded with echoes from the telephone. To those echoes were added those of the cellar itself, acting like an echo chamber. There were so many of them! It was virtually impossible to remain focused on the text. When Ophelia reached the end of the page, a mechanical device turned it so she could carry on reading. What was there followed suit: nothing but words and numbers. Just a little game, eh?

Time passed, the pages turned. Ophelia's throat and ears were starting to ache.

This experiment was unfathomable. And yet she was convinced that all the absurd things she had been made to do since her arrival at the observatory—the screenings, the gymnastics, the workshops—were simply aimed at preparing her for this. They had reproduced exactly Eulalia Gonde's work conditions for Project Cornucopianism. But what, then, did it consist of, that work? What was supposed to happen here, with this telephone?

Ophelia would have given anything for there to be, at the other end of the line, someone finally to give her an explana . . .

She stopped abruptly in the middle of her reading. For a few long seconds she heard nothing but her jerky breathing against the receiver. A sharp pain whistled in her ears. It wasn't coming from the telephone but from inside her own head. Ophelia cracked like an eggshell to allow a new memory to hatch. She could . . . yes, she could now recall what had happened in this cellar.

She, Eulalia Gonde, sits in the same place. Exhausted. Excited. Her whole arm aches from holding the telephone receiver. Months in a cellar voicing a succession of words forwards, and then backwards, with no result.

Until now.

"You are impossible."

"*Impossible?*"

The voice in the receiver is as cracked as her own. Anyone would have thought it an ordinary echo, but Eulalia isn't just anyone. She has prepared herself for years in expectation of this moment. She spent her childhood at the orphanage with an arm tied behind her back, one heel higher than the other, an eye patch, wax in one ear and cotton wool in one nostril, totally deforming herself so that her left side would become overdeveloped. She was born for this.

That echo well and truly deviated; she's certain of it.

"Unlikely, if you prefer."

The sudden silence in the receiver worries her. She hasn't halted the call for one moment since yesterday evening, not even to eat or go to the restroom. Above all, she mustn't lose him. Not him. Not after her entire family.

"Are you still there?"

"Still there."

She breathes a sigh of relief.

"Good. I feel a little lonely."

"A little?"

"A lot in fact."

Eulalia smiles through her tears. Crying isn't professional, but she can't stop herself anymore. She's overflowing with joy and sadness, hope and fear. She remembers, as if it were yesterday, the first time she heard mention of the phenomenon. She had just arrived at the military orphanage. Often, after lights out, in the darkness of the dormitory, there would be talk of the army's experiments on the echoes. "To scramble enemy radio communications," explained the supervisors. And then some information leaked out. The impossible had happened. An echo, it was said, had deviated on contact with a left-handed person. It had only lasted a few seconds, the echo hadn't stabilized, but Eulalia had immediately known, with all the wisdom of youth, that *that* was what she had to do.

Befriend an echo. And, from this first miracle, generate new miracles.

Forgotten in her cellar, she has just succeeded where all her predecessors failed.

"My spurriers . . . superiors . . . " she says, " they don't often come down to see me. I haven't yet told them about you."

"About you?"

"No, not about me. About you."

"About me."

"Exactly. I don't know if they'll handstand you when . . . if they'll understand you. Even me, I'm not really sure I understand you. I find it hard enough to understand myself."

With the receiver wedged in the hollow of her shoulder, Eulalia unfolds a handkerchief and blows into it. She glances at her typewriter, gathering dust in a corner of the cellar. It's been weeks since she last eked a sentence out of it. Her current typescript, *The Era of Miracles*, remains unfinished. Eulalia is forced to admit that she almost had doubts about her stories. About her own story.

This echo, this . . . *other*, whoever it might be, had given her back all her convictions.

"You've not yet told me your name."

"*Not yet.*"

"And yet I think we're sparking. . . starting to know each other well. Me, I am Eulalia."

"*I am me.*"

Eulalia wipes the tears that won't stop running down. The deviation is becoming more pronounced. This echo learns fast.

"That's an interesting response. Where do you transmit from?"

Silence once again in the receiver.

"Alright, my question was a bit complicated. Where are you, right now?"

"*Here.*"

Oh yes, it learns very fast.

"Where's here?"

"*Behind.*"

"Behind? But behind what?"

"*Behind behind.*"

Ophelia gazed at the telephone before her, as though finally seeing it. Her migraine had stopped at the same time as the memory. It had lasted but a heartbeat, a tiny fragment of time during which everything, absolutely everything had become obvious to her. But, already, that impression was weakening.

The only certainty left to her was that neither the cellar nor the telephone was really important. They were just the conditions necessary for an exceptional encounter. That was how the Other had burst into Eulalia Gonde's life. He wasn't her reflection. He was much more than that: he was an echo, one of a kind.

Intelligent.

Helen had been right, back in that amphitheater stand. All that had happened, all that was happening, and all that would happen was directly linked to the echoes. One of them had, in the past, communicated with Eulalia Gonde, and it was from this contact that everything had followed. She had conveyed to it what was most personal to her—her desires, her memories, her humanity—and she had received something in return, something that had enabled her to create the family spirits, change identity at will, turn her stories into reality.

The Other had revealed the secret of plenty to her.

So this was what the Deviations Observatory wanted. To reestablish a dialogue with the Other. They needed him. Their Horn of Plenty was dysfunctional, as the boxes of faulty objects cluttering every corner made clear.

That is what Project Cornucopianism was. Or that, at any rate, was its starting point, the threshold of a far more extensive experiment.

Ophelia started to shake feverishly. She had often wondered why the Other, once released from the mirror, hadn't stepped out through the one in her bedroom, on Anima, in front of her whole family. What if Octavio was right? What if the echoes evolved on a different frequency? What if the Other had, all this time, been right there, beside her, without her being able to see him?

She stared at the stand, where the mechanical device was tapping the page with an oppressive clatter to make her continue her reading. She knew she was being listened to, but maybe she had a unique opportunity here, in this cellar, to communicate with the Other, just like Eulalia long before her.

"You used me to leave the space between the mirrors," she said into the receiver, "so you owe me one. I don't know whether this message will reach you, but it's time that we met again. Show yourself. Speak to me. Come and find . . ."

A click and a dial tone indicated to Ophelia that the line had suddenly been cut off.

Her seat starting rising, forcing her to let go of the receiver. The sun hit her in the face once she reached the surface, back on the carousel. The nanny-automaton unstrapped her. The disturbing face, a bad caricature of her mother's, gave her a fake smile.

"THE LITTLE GAME IS OVER, *CHÉRIE*."

THE MEETING

"Send me down again."

Ophelia tugged as hard as she could on the dress of her nanny-automaton, but the latter continued to cross the amusement park with dogged little steps, distancing them ever further from the carousel, and the cellar, and the telephone.

"Let me continue the experiment!"

The nanny-automaton didn't even deign to respond. Totally indifferent, she ploughed on, while her stomach churned out an insufferable ditty. She alone held the key that allowed access to the secret room.

Ophelia couldn't stand the idea of returning to her routine as if nothing had happened, while the Other was perhaps reachable by telephone. If the observatory wanted to communicate with him, so did she, so why not let her do so?

The heat bearing down on the cloister was stifling. As if the air had created a thick curtain behind which all truths had retreated. The inverts had finished their morning workshops and were just starting their lunch break. All Ophelia could see of them was some pathetic figures. They were scattered across the amusement park, each in their corner, shaded by stalls, munching the vile rice the nannies served them every day at this time.

Eulalia Gonde had been one of them long before their

birth. She had trained hard to become an invert herself, as if that were indispensable to enter into dialogue with the Other.

Ophelia had had enough of this solitude, imposed on them the better to exploit them. By squinting, she spotted Cosmos. He was sitting on the edge of a carousel that had sinister wooden tigers instead of horses. His nanny-automaton watched over him from a distance.

Ophelia went straight to him. Her own nanny would soon notice that she was no longer following her; she only had a few spare seconds.

"We must talk. Fast."

Cosmos immediately looked away from her. Going by the smell, he was munching a lentil fritter. He must have contacts among the cooks always to get food for himself that was worthy of the name.

"Calm down," was all he said.

"You've been at the observatory longer than me, and you said yourself that we had to help one another. I need to know now all that you know."

"Calm down," repeated Cosmos.

His voice had become imperious. He was no longer the lively young man who had given her his brioche on the first day. Ophelia had come to realize that his inversion resided in his bipolarity. In other circumstances, she would have left him alone, but she was burning with impatience.

"They put you through the telephone experiment, too, didn't they?" she insisted. "Can you at least tell me if you heard something? Maybe an echo that wasn't norma—"

Cosmos hurled himself at Ophelia so violently, they fell together onto the gravel. He gripped her shoulders to keep her face a breath away from his own. His slanting eyes bulged, his breathing was rapid, his lips curled back on teeth full of lentils.

"Calm down!"

Ophelia wasn't sure anymore whether this order was directed at her, or at himself. She was totally flummoxed. She tried to push away this body crushing her own, but the more she struggled, the more Cosmos dug his fingernails into her shoulders. He was shaking her so vehemently that she was stunned by the impact every time her head hit the ground.

"Calm down!" he roared. "Calm down!"

She slapped a hand on Cosmos's chin to push him away, but in vain. Trapped under him, she looked around for help. Some collaborators—to her, merely gray figures—were watching the scene while still taking notes. The inverts had gathered around in alarm; among them, Second was manically drawing, as if she feared Ophelia and Cosmos breaking the pose. As for the nanny-automatons, they made very sure not to move, as if this situation wasn't part of their remit. Wasn't one of them going to intervene?

Instinctively, Ophelia turned her claws on Cosmos, just as she had on the crowd in the amphitheater, but despite how close they were, she missed him. That power was as off-kilter as her Animism. She yelped when Cosmos bit her hand. He seemed compelled to tear her to pieces.

Ophelia stared, wide-eyed. They were going to let him get on with it. They were going to let him kill her.

Cosmos's teeth and fingernails finally let go. A collaborator had grabbed him at the waist.

"Move away, Eulalia."

A female voice. Ophelia didn't wait to be told a second time. She dragged herself on the ground, her wounded hand pressed to her stomach.

The woman collaborator restrained Cosmos's raging body as best she could, while he screamed and foamed at the mouth. An elbow in the face knocked back her hood.

It was Elizabeth.

Ophelia had completely forgotten her being employed by the observatory. She was bleeding at the mouth. The blow had split her lips, maybe even broken a tooth, and yet she kept her cool. She gripped her arms around the middle of Cosmos, whose movements were gradually losing their violence, and whose features were slackening one by one. His empathy was absorbing Elizabeth's calmness like a sponge. The anger gradually faded from his eyes, leaving just vacancy.

Finally, he let himself fall, limply, forehead to the ground.

"Sorry," he stammered. "Sorry . . . Sorry . . . Rosy . . . Sorry . . ."

Elizabeth released him, gently. Her weary gaze, weighed down by heavy eyelids, turned to Ophelia, ignoring the collaborators, who had stayed back and were coughing like stern judges.

"You're not looking too presentable."

Ophelia pointed at the spatters of blood mixed in with her freckles. Even without glasses, she could see that much.

"You're not looking too great, either."

They exchanged a smile lasting but a twitch of the lips. The nanny-automaton pulled Ophelia by the ear. Fighting against a machine, even a dolled-up one, was a lost cause. Ophelia could only stumble through an endless maze of carousels, galleries, and stairs to her bedroom, in which she was locked up.

"YOU HAVE BEEN DISOBEDIENT, *CHÉRIE*. YOU WILL BE DEPRIVED OF GAMES AND MEALS UNTIL . . . UNTIL TOMORROW."

Once alone, Ophelia spent a considerable time barging into the room's rickety furniture, pacing feverishly up and down, wrestling with all her questions, listening to the gong on every hour of the afternoon, and then, battle-weary, she sank into the suds of a bath. Her shoulders were covered in scratches, her hand was swelling around the bite, and, from the mirrors' distorted reflection, the mechanical fingers of the nanny-automaton had left a pinch-mark on her ear. It was the back of her head that hurt most: among all the gravel she kept finding in her hair, she could feel the contour of a massive bump.

Fine.

Entire days without event, and now, in a matter of minutes, she had discovered the true nature of the Other, and triggered Cosmos's fit of rage, along with the displeasure of the observatory.

Now that she considered the situation with some hindsight, she understood that her biggest mistake was what she had said into that telephone receiver. She had asked the Other to meet with her again. What if the message really had reached him? If he took her at her word, decided to accept her invitation, and turned up at her room, devastating everything on the way? She might know more about him now, but she still hadn't a clue how to go about defeating an echo capable of destroying entire arks.

Ophelia was just putting her pajama top on back to front for the fifth time, patently incapable of telling left from right, when she heard a scraping noise. Hurried steps could already be heard, disappearing down the corridor.

A folded piece of paper had been slipped under the door.

As soon as Ophelia opened it up, dried fruit rained down onto the floor. She had to bring the page right up to her eyes to decipher the minuscule handwriting.

So sorry.

Now you know why no one's waiting for me outside.

But someone is waiting for you this evening.

A doodle accompanied the note; it vaguely resembled the statue of the colossus. Ophelia's pulse started racing. Thorn! Had he used Cosmos to arrange a meeting with her? How? The observatory had kept him apart from the inverts from the start.

She screwed the message into a ball and disposed of it in the toilet. A sunset blazed between the slats of the shutter. And her? How would she get herself out there this evening? Thorn was doubtless counting on her Animism to unlock the door of her room, as at Berenilde's on the night of her getaway. What he didn't know was that her family power was no longer working normally. The handless clocks in her room spat their parts in her face whenever she went past, and she had abandoned propping her bed up with books, since these just had fun pulling away in the middle of the night.

"Eulalia?"

Ophelia quickly pressed her ear to the door. That voice . . .

"Elizabeth?"

"Not so loud."

The whisper from the other side was beyond quiet. She had to bend down to the keyhole to hear it properly.

"I'm not allowed to be here. I wasn't allowed to intervene earlier on, either. No interaction with the subjects, that's the rule for all collaborators."

Behind the calm tone, some emotion was discernible. Ophelia knew Elizabeth well enough to be aware of how important hierarchy was to her. That she had broken the rules, first to come to her aid, then to visit her, was totally unexpected.

Ophelia gazed at the scattered dry fruit she had forgotten at the foot of the door.

"How is Cosmos?" she asked, anxiously.

"Better. He's having his meal in the refectory right now. His empathy suffers from a rare deviation. He doesn't merely pick up the emotions of others. He feels them and amplifies them, like a resonant chord, until it becomes a chain reaction. Next time you're in a bad mood, avoid him."

Ophelia pressed her forehead to the door. Today she had lost control, and, worse, she had made Cosmos lose it. This was basically what the observatory hoped for. They were infantilized, isolated, and deconstructed, to be reshaped at will.

She had let this place get the upper hand. And she hated that thought.

"Elizabeth, can you open the door to me?"

"Sure."

Ophelia's relief was brief.

"I'm kidding. I've disobeyed enough for you, Eulalia. Do you know that, right now, Sir Henry is carrying out an inspection of the observatory?" she continued, to stop Ophelia from insisting. "The incident between you and Cosmos reached even his ears. Normally, he isn't authorized to infringe medical secrecy, but they agreed to make an exception, given the seriousness of the situation. Sir Henry asked to question Cosmos himself, following your . . ."

Elizabeth searched at length for a term that wouldn't contravene the Index.

"Our fight," Ophelia said, impatiently.

"Your *disagreement*," Elizabeth corrected, reprovingly.

So that was how Thorn had been able to convey his message. For that alone, Ophelia didn't regret having got herself a bit roughed up. She stared at the blackness within the keyhole. But what about her? Could she use Elizabeth to communicate with Thorn, without the observatory knowing? Up to what point did the two of them mutually trust each other? Beyond their apprenticeship at the Good Family, they had nothing in common.

"Elizabeth, why are you here?"

"You know that, don't you? You saw me signing that contract with the Genealogists. It's rather I who should be asking you that question. Finding you in this observatory, among the inverts, was pretty surprising."

Ophelia remembered the procession of collaborators she

had encountered on the first day: one of them hadn't been able to resist turning around as she passed.

"I meant now, outside my room."

"Ah."

A slight jolt indicated that Elizabeth had leant against the door.

"One day you asked my advice, Eulalia. Do you remember what I replied to you?"

"Yes."

Remain neutral. Observe without judging. Obey without arguing. Learn without taking a stand. Take an interest without becoming attached. Fulfill your duty without expecting anything in return. That's the only way not to suffer. The less one suffers, the more efficient one is. The more efficient one is, the better one serves the city.

Ophelia had learnt this advice by heart. It was some of the worst advice she had ever been given.

There was hesitation in Elizabeth's breathing, through the keyhole, and then the words tumbled out, whispered reluctantly:

"I can't cope anymore. I can't tell you about the work I'm doing here. I don't even have permission to talk to other collaborators about it—the containment principle applies to us, too. We've all sworn allegiance to the observatory. But equally, I've sworn allegiance to the Genealogists. They . . . they expect me to inform them as soon as I've managed to decode everything. They tell me it's my duty as a Forerunner. Hierarchically, they're my superiors, but professionally, the observatory is my employer. Whom must I obey, Eulalia?"

Ophelia was overcome by profound pity. She couldn't see Elizabeth right now, but it was almost possible for her to imagine her long, flat body pressed to this door like that of a child. She was the same age as her, was more intelligent than her, but making her own choices terrified her to the point of asking her, a virtual stranger, to make a decision for her.

"You must find the answer to that question yourself. What do you, Elizabeth, want?"

"To make myself worthy of the helping hand Lady Helen offered to me when I was in the street. I have never felt more able to help her than here."

This time, there had been no hesitation. Ophelia was puzzled. In what way did Elizabeth think she could pay her debt to the family spirit?

When the latter spoke again, her voice had recovered its seeming composure:

"The Genealogists are Lords of LUX, and Lords of LUX know better than anyone what is in the general interest. So I'll leave it up them to decide, as I always have. I shouldn't have lowered myself to doubting them; I'll confess my sin to them next time we meet. This observatory shouldn't have anything to hide from them, either. Thank you for your advice. I'm now going to return to the collaborators' quarters."

Ophelia frowned. Thank you for her advice? Elizabeth hadn't understood a thing she had tried to tell her. Once again, a missed opportunity between them.

"Thank you for intervening despite the rules," she said, with a sigh. "I appreciated that side of you."

"Violence is prohibited in Babel, and, protocol notwithstanding, you didn't seem to be particularly consenting."

Ophelia picked up the rustle of a habit on the other side. A hood pulled down. The signal of departure. She might not get a second chance to broach the subject.

"Elizabeth."

"Hmm?"

"I know about Project Cornucopianism. Have you seen it yourself, this Horn of Plenty?"

Such was the silence through the keyhole, Ophelia thought Elizabeth had gone. But her reply finally came, more weary than annoyed.

"I repeat to you: I can't say anything. Not only because I don't want to, but also because we, the collaborators, have no overall view of the project. I devote myself to the task I have been assigned, period. You should do the same. Ah, before I forget."

A sound of paper under the door. Ophelia squinted at the sheet. She immediately recognized Second's style; it was probably what she was drawing during Cosmos's attack, but it wasn't a new version of Octavio. She had done a self-portrait that faithfully, and somewhat cruelly, depicted the disproportions of her face, with its unequal eyebrows, deformed nose, first pimples, irregular lips, mismatched ears, and that eye devoid of its iris. She had added, for some reason, a big scratching-out in red pencil, covering half of her face.

Ophelia turned the sheet over and was surprised to find another drawing. She stared, wide-eyed. This one depicted her, for the first time; a tiny her in the middle of the white paper. Two characters stood beside her: a very old lady to her right, and an unidentifiable, monstrous creature to her left. That wasn't all. Second had wielded her red pencil on Ophelia's small body, so that it virtually disappeared. Blood.

"Second was determined to give it to me," said Elizabeth, behind the door. "I think she wanted me to pass it on to you. I'm counting on you, obviously, to hand it over to the collaborators tomorrow. Don't ask me why, but the observatory keeps all of Second's drawings in its archives. I must leave you now. Knowledge serves peace."

With this parting shot, spoken with renewed fervor, Elizabeth went off, steps fading away at the end of the corridor. Ophelia couldn't help but feel disappointed in her. Octavio had gone through the same crisis of conscience, but, unlike him, she had made the choice not to choose.

Having said that, she had divulged more to Ophelia about her work than she thought she had. The use of the verb "to decode" wasn't insignificant. This Forerunner had transformed the Memorial's database thanks to the single language, from concave to convex, of punched holes. If she had been capable of inventing her own code, she was surely capable of breaking someone else's.

Furthermore, she seemed convinced that her work would be of service to Helen. But what could a family spirit desire most if not understanding her own Book? The observatory expected of Elizabeth the same thing that Farouk had expected of Ophelia, and that no one had, to this day, managed to accomplish: deciphering the language used by Eulalia Gonde to create the family spirits.

Ophelia still didn't know why or how, but that, too, was an integral part of Project Cornucopianism. She had so much to say to Thorn . . .

Pensively, she watched the light fading between the slats of the shutter. Night really had fallen, and she still didn't have a clue how to meet him at the designated place. She had been unable to bring herself to make Elizabeth her messenger. She was far too indoctrinated a citizen; she could have given herself up, straight after helping her.

She would have to manage on her own.

Ophelia stopped herself from looking at Second's gift, in the bulbs' flickering light, from again seeing herself covered in blood. She refused to think about the nail incident. No, this drawing had nothing to do with her vision at the glazing-and-mirror store. That old woman didn't represent Eulalia Gonde, that monster didn't represent the Other, that white expanse of paper didn't represent the void that would swallow them all.

That certainly wasn't the hidden meaning of the story.

Ophelia tore up the drawing and threw it into the toilet—too bad for the archives! She pressed her ear to the door's keyhole. First, a succession of soft thuds: the bare feet of the inverts, each returning to their room. Then a metallic clicking: the nanny-automatons locking all the doors before leaving the residence.

Once all was silent, Ophelia went over to the shutter. She slid all her fingers between the slats, for the strongest grip. She pulled hard, again and again. All objects in this place had flaws. She hadn't found that of the door, but she would find that of the window. One hinge gave way, then a second. A final tug threw Ophelia back on to the bed, shutter in hands.

She leant out into the night. The warm wind lifted her hair. It was the first time she had a view of the back of the residence. Its façade was sheer as a cliff. Ophelia could just make out, a few meters from her window, the shutters of the neighboring rooms. Out of reach. She looked up at the higher stories of the residence. Inaccessible. She then peered down, toward the ground, to gauge the distance. She couldn't see it. She squinted, hoping to dispel this myopia that turned the stars into a vague froth of lights. Down below, there were neither cobbles nor grass nor roofs.

There was nothing there.

The window of her room looked out onto the void.

Ophelia walked slowly backwards, as if the rug, the floorboards, the bricks were about to disintegrate beneath her feet. She huddled in a corner of the room, as far as possible from this square of night, and the draft it had created. The feeling of vertigo made her spin within her own body.

She would never be able to climb down this wall, not with the certainty of the void if she fell, not with two hands that were clumsier than ever. She would not be able to join Thorn, not tonight, not ever.

This place was stronger than her. Stronger than them.

Ophelia pinched the bite mark left by Cosmos. The pain felt like a welcome release. She surely wasn't going to give up so fast, when Thorn had gone to such trouble to arrange a meeting with her. She had to get a grip on herself, and think. Reason like a Babelian. The city was made up of many minor arks; being next to the void had been part of daily life for so long that the architecture was adapted to it. The observatory would never have risked lodging study subjects so close to mortal danger.

Ophelia pushed her vertigo to the back of her mind. She grabbed a cushion from her bed and threw it outside. It fell right onto the façade, just below the window, defying the gravity that should have sent it hurtling down.

A transcendium.

Taking a deep breath, she hoisted herself onto the edge of her window. She did her best to ignore the din her blood was making. All her instincts screamed that she would fall, and the night already seemed to be pulling on the foot she dared to stick outside.

It was a transcendium. A transcendium. A transcendium.

Ophelia's knee leant against the stone. She focused only on the cushion lying on the façade, not far from there. Just forget what was up and what down. The only law that existed, here and now, was the one that kept that cushion in place.

After endless maneuvering, Ophelia found herself kneeling on the wall.

No, not a wall, she told herself with conviction. Ground.

Resolutely, she turned her back on the void—the *horizon*—and went up—*walked*—along the façade. She had taken transcendiums hundreds of times at the Memorial, and at the Good Family, but none had made her feel as thoroughly unnerved as this one. What if the observatory building also had some manufacturing fault? What if just one misstep could cancel the effect of this artificial gravity?

Ophelia felt the rough texture of each brick on the bare skin of her feet. She finally reached the cornice of a roof. She was almost there. She had to wriggle around to go from vertical facade to horizontal roof, and once she had made it, she remained for a moment, flat on her back, gazing at the stars, legs shaking. Her pajamas were drenched in sweat. She thought of those sections of arks that had fallen away, and of the airships sent into the sky regardless of the danger. It was much more, even, than a thought. It was something etched onto her body, from now on.

The stepped roof descended toward the cloister, terrace after terrace. Ophelia twisted her ankle several times, but finally landed on the flagging of a gallery. Returning to her room would be another challenge; she'd think about it when the time came.

She ran through the labyrinthine shadows of the cloister. She didn't care about either the small stones under her feet or the mosquito bites on her arms. She didn't stop running until she had reached the feet of the colossus, at the entrance of the tunnel that cut through the statue's base.

A shadow among the shadows welcomed her there with the click of a watch.

"We have six hours and forty-seven minutes before the first gong of the morning."

Ophelia advanced slowly. The moment Thorn's arms closed around her, up, down, left, and right returned to their rightful places. She had found anchorage, at last.

THE SHADOW

Inside the kaleidoscopic tunnel, it was total darkness. Despite the walls being crazed with countless mirrors, they reflected nothing of the two figures feeling their way along. Although Ophelia kept tripping on the tracks, she preferred the dark. The last time she had been through this tunnel in daylight, the flashing of all the mirrors had made her black out. To keep going, she relied on the mechanical grating ahead of her. Thorn's leg didn't lend itself to being discreet. If he had needed to tackle the maze of the containment zone to reach Ophelia's room, the whole observatory would have heard him coming.

Still, he walked jolly fast, regardless of his disability! Ophelia followed him without asking any questions, at a reasonable distance from his claws, but she wouldn't have minded a longer rest. Thorn's hug had lasted five seconds, watch in hand, before they had set off.

He came to a halt right in the middle of the tunnel. Electric light bounced off the surrounding mirrors. It had burst through a door set into the wall, a door so low, Thorn had to bend double to get through it. Ophelia hadn't noticed it on her journey in the wagon. She, in turn, entered a side corridor, closing the door behind her.

Just as she was straining her eyes to get the measure of the place, in the flickering light of the bulbs, a weight on her nose made her jump. Leaning toward her, Thorn's face suddenly appeared to her in minutest detail. The steeliness of his eyes. The scars cutting into his skin. The stern furrow across his forehead. And, underlying all this severity, an indefinable raw energy that affected Ophelia to her very bones. By restoring her glasses to her, Thorn had restored her sight, and so much more.

He also returned her reader's gloves to her.

"They will have to be hidden. They were in a cabinet in the admissions office. I replaced them with substitutes that should fool them. And talking of substitutes . . ."

Thorn held out his fob watch. At first, Ophelia thought he was showing her the time, then she realized it was about their reflections on its face.

"Always check that your interlocutor has one. Don't drop your guard, even for me. Eulalia Gonde and the Other will assume any face to deceive you."

With this advice given, he continued along the corridor at a hurried pace. He couldn't stand fully upright without banging his head on the ceiling.

"Let's not waste time. There's one thing that I must show you."

Getting her fingers into each glove was a tricky exercise for Ophelia, but she was keen to put them on to conceal Cosmos's bite. Thorn knew what had happened; he didn't need to see it. But would she ever, one day, be able to use her family power again? She hadn't read another object since that exhibit from Anima's Museum of Primitive History.

"There's one thing I must say to you, right now. They know who I am. Who I was. They may know about you, too."

If Thorn was surprised or bothered by this, he didn't show

it. Quickly pointing his finger, he indicated to Ophelia to watch where she put her feet. The corridor had just opened out onto an underground pool in which water, green with algae, stagnated. One more step and Ophelia would have fallen in.

"If that is the case," he replied, "they haven't used it against me up to now. They are going all out to impress me, opening all doors to their departments, but keeping me well away from what's essential on a pretext of medical secrecy."

Thorn made them skirt the pool along a border that seemed thousands of years old. His leg brace vibrated against the ancient carved stone.

"However, the observers are not as well informed as they would have us think. They have no real decision-making power. It's clear that each person working here only has a partial view of everything, unaware of what his or her neighbor is doing. The young girl observer who is my assigned guide is either the most ignorant of them all, or a better actress than my aunt. She reveres the very uniform I wear, bores me with praise, and never answers questions. In fact," Thorn said, catching Ophelia as she skidded on the border, "I am scarcely more informed than I was at the start of my inspection. I don't even know what's going on beyond these walls. The radio sets no longer work, and the *Official Journal* is out of date when it reaches us."

"I have a lot to tell you."

Which Ophelia immediately did, as they entered a security passage with multiple doors that each had to be opened, and then closed.

The summons to the amphitheater. The forced expulsions. The implosion of the automaton. The general rioting. The frantic escape with Octavio, Blaise, and Wolf. The unknown figure in the fog. Sanctuary at Lazarus's factory. Arrival at the observatory, thanks to Ambrose. The admission test. The faulty

212

objects. Cosmos's secrets. Second, and her strange drawings. The telephone in the cellar. Elizabeth's decoding work.

It was a hasty, breathless, but pretty complete account of events. Thorn hadn't stopped walking—he only slowed down when Ophelia described her visions of Eulalia Gonde's past—but she knew he had registered each sentence as surely as a nanny-automaton's recording spool.

They now emerged onto a gangway overlooking a basement, where impressive machines steamed away like stationary locomotives. The temperature here was extreme. Ophelia was still in her pajamas, but she wondered how Thorn managed not to roast under all the gold decorations of his uniform.

"Is this what you wanted to show me?"

"No. I'm making the most of a detour to check something."

Thorn lifted the cover of a container of meters, at the edge of the gangway. Despite his patent disgust at the grease and dust, even covering his nose with a handkerchief to examine the dials up close, he nodded with satisfaction. Taking a phial from his pocket, he disinfected his hands.

"I'm done here. Let's go up."

At the end of the gangway, a stone stairway was sunk into the rock. Lightbulbs flickered, almost giving up the ghost, just as they did all over the observatory. The walls were veined with interlacing pipes and roots.

Ophelia started to climb the steps, not taking her eyes off her feet to keep them synchronized. Spiral stairways were the worst. And her toes, no longer very clean.

"Are we still inside the statue?"

"Yes. The observatory was built on the ruins of an ancient city. Several secret passages remain from it that are no longer used. I memorized all the plans."

Thorn's voice sounded even lower in the stairway. He was holding the handrail firmly, only letting go to release the articulation of his leg brace, which sometimes seized up. Ophelia thought to herself that for him, too, going up couldn't be easy. She sensed he was tense. She had already sensed it when in his arms. His claws were buzzing all around him like a swarm of wasps.

After numerous spirals of stairs, and then a final secret door, they reached an anteroom with gleaming tiles. An elegant elevator allowed official access to it, certainly more comfortable than the stairs they had just come up. The anteroom led to a large ebony door with no handle, on which a golden plaque declared:

DIRECTORS' APARTMENTS
VISITORS PROHIBITED

Ophelia hadn't expected to visit the homes of the directors of the observatory. Didn't they risk coming across them? She had never met them, but wasn't particularly keen on making their acquaintance that night.

Thorn went over to a wall mirror in the anteroom.

"Wait for me here."

Ophelia was struck by the uncompromising look, entirely devoid of pride, he gave his reflection before plunging into it. It was the first time he was resorting to his mirror-visiting ability in her presence. This power demanded confronting one's true self. Thorn managed to do so, but didn't appreciate what he saw, for all that.

The door to the apartments opened onto him. Although it had no handle on the outside, but it did have one on the inside. Ophelia anxiously scanned the furthest reaches of what seemed to be an enormous library—barely visible due to the weak nightlights. The ceiling was so high as to disappear. All aspects of the décor were as refined as they were practical:

clearly labeled shelves, aligned furniture, old-master paintings, clocks that purred, perfectly balanced busts on their pedestals, and not a frill pointlessly to overload such elegance. The exact opposite of the containment zone, with its deluge of faulty objects. But were the apartments unoccupied?

"There's no one here," Thorn assured, closing the door.

"What if the directors return?"

"There are no directors. These apartments are used as a façade, and for storing archives. The real brains behind the observatory remain in the shadows."

Ophelia blinked. The collaborators were working for observers who worked for nonexistent directors?

"What if Eulalia Gonde were the brains?"

"I have considered that, so similar is this opaque, pyramidal system to her own, but I strongly doubt that she knows what is going on here. It is not in her interest that others should know how to replicate what she once did."

With these words, spoken harshly, Thorn opened one cabinet among the many making up the library. He handled everything with precision. Expertise. He would leave not a trace of his visit behind him. Ophelia noticed a fine standing mirror, which reflected back to her a little woman in mis-buttoned pajamas, and with curls sticking out in all directions. So it was through this mirror he had gained entry. It wasn't the first time he had come here.

While Thorn methodically examined the cabinet, Ophelia stood right up to one of the vast rose windows. What she saw through the stained glass took her breath away. She was looking down on the esplanades and pagodas of the entire observatory. They weren't just rose windows; they were the eyes of the colossus. From here, now she had her glasses back, Ophelia could even distinguish the stars from the lights of the city. The minor arks formed a constellation all of their own, in which she spotted the Memorial's beacon, the more discreet lighting of the Good Family, and, in the distance, a sea of clouds absorbing Babel's brilliance.

What had become of Blaise and Professor Wolf? And the scarf? Were they still staying with Ambrose? Had the hunt for outlaws continued? Had Octavio managed to tell the citizens what had taken place?

Ophelia suddenly realized the degree to which the observatory shut them away, inside a kind of parenthesis.

"It's curious," she murmured, against the window. "Never a high tide here. The sea of clouds keeps its distance. As if we're forever in the eye of a cyclone."

When, pensively, she focused back on the observatory, she noticed an enclosure. Were those monoliths she could make out in the dark? They were tombs. Cosmos was right: the institution had its own necropolis. Ophelia couldn't help but suddenly think of the third protocol from which, according to him, no one had ever returned.

She turned away from the window and inspected the frames arranged on the large desk. The photographs in them were old, faded by time. She noticed one in particular. Former inverts, recognizable in some cases by their malformations, were posing in front of a carousel. What had caught Ophelia's eye was the hole in the middle of the photograph. A whole silhouette had been cut out, erased from the group. Along with it had gone an arm, wrapped in a friendly way around its shoulders, belonging to a young boy who himself seemed somehow familiar. Who were they?

"Here."

So absorbed was Ophelia in the photograph, she hadn't heard Thorn approaching. He handed her a file.

"What's this?"

"Medical images. They concern you."

Ophelia's hands shook inside their gloves as they opened the file. It was noticeably thick. Inside, there were envelopes containing photographs, some enlarged. Ophelia featured in each one, in profile, from the front, and from the back.

The photographs taken in the dark closet.

Did they reveal what Ophelia hadn't yet admitted to Thorn? Did they make clear that anomaly that would prevent her from being a mother, him from being a father? The thought of him finding out in that way, rather than directly from her, weighed on her.

Ophelia examined the photographs beside a nightlight. She was so surprised, she forgot all her previous thoughts.

A shadow.

Blurred due to the flashes, it spilt from her body like ill-defined smoke, varying from one picture to the next. It was more extensive around Ophelia's hands. Even more peculiar: the shadow seemed slightly out of line with the edge of her body, as if they didn't quite match. Could that be linked to her inversion?

"Those pictures were taken on the day you were admitted," Thorn commented. "Now look at this one," he said, indicating another photograph. "It was taken the following day."

The shadow was still there, but the mismatch had increased. In the space of just one day, a real separation had occurred between Ophelia's pale body and her dark aura. Was that down to all those dissymmetrical movements she had been asked to do? On each new photograph, day after day, the separation increased.

"I don't know what they are doing to you," said Thorn, "but it is changing you. A little more than that, even."

His voice had become leaden. His tension was contained there, in these photographs.

He began a gesture to stop Ophelia, but she was already

making straight for the cabinet. He had taken infinite care to extract the file without disturbing, by even a millimeter, those beside it. Ophelia was incapable of doing this. She emptied the shelves, one after the other, scattering half of the files on the way, under Thorn's frozen gaze.

She absolutely had to see for herself how things were for the other subjects of the observatory.

Each photograph had a shadow, but it was thinner among the powerless (as specified in their files), and only separated from the body among the inverts on the alternative program. It differed from one individual to another—more extensive around the ears of this person, around the chest of that one, around the throat of another one. Why these differences? Why was Ophelia's shadow concentrated around the hands?

"These shadows reflect our family powers," she said, finally understanding. "That's why my Animism and my claws are disordered. Because of the separation."

"That's not all," said Thorn, who, file after file, shelf after shelf, was trying to restore order where she had created chaos. "The Deviations Observatory holds a whole arsenal of measuring instruments, more or less concealed, in order to count the echoes. Not only those perceptible to eye and ear, but also, and especially, those that elude our senses. I studied these statistics closely."

Between tidying two files, Thorn handed Ophelia a piece of paper, traced with his compact, nervy handwriting. It featured mainly graphs, drawn with precision.

"First notable fact: the echoes have multiplied since the collapse of the northwestern district."

Ophelia nodded. Yes, she had realized that.

"Second notable fact: their number varies according to certain conditions."

"I noticed that in the cellar. I was almost deafened."

"Third notable fact," continued Thorn, as if he hadn't been interrupted, "their number also varies according to people. The echoes' frequency observed in the immediate vicinity of the powerless is weak. That frequency increases close to people related to a family spirit—and consequently, a family power. It increases considerably close to inverts. I would go even further: the greater the inversion, the more echoes there are."

Over the drawer pulled out before him, Thorn suddenly directed a steely look down at Ophelia.

"Fourth and final notable fact: you hold the record. Of all the inverts on the Alternative Program currently assessed, you are the one who induces the most echoes."

Ophelia thought of Helen, in that stand at the amphitheater. Of what the giantess had seen. Of what she had said to her. "They are everywhere, young lady, and around you even more than anywhere else." At least that made more sense than the cage, the turning back, and the fingers she had mentioned to her.

"I'll recap," she said. "We all possess a shadow that we can't see. With inverts, this shadow is mismatched, and the worse the inversion, the greater the mismatch. This particularity attracts the echoes, for some reason. The Other is himself an echo—a very rare echo, capable of thinking for itself. The observatory thus uses inverts to lure him, to obtain from him the secret of the Horn of Plenty that he, formerly, would have delivered to Eulalia Gonde. Have I missed anything?"

Ophelia was about to clean her glasses, hoping that would give her more clarity of thought, when she noticed that they had never been cleaner. Thorn's fastidiousness had something to do with that.

"I had to limit my research to the last five years," he said. "The archives older than that have either been moved, or destroyed."

Ophelia opened a random file that Thorn had only just returned to the correct place in its cabinet. It belonged to a subject from the standard program, whose shadow perfectly surrounded their entire body. So what was it made of? Why wasn't it visible to the naked eye?

"The black lenses," whispered Ophelia. "So that's what they use them for. To make our shadows visible. Perhaps even the echoes, too."

She thought back to that slap the lizard man had given her on the day she was admitted. He had then seen "something" surrounding her. Had he seen her claws instinctively reacting to such aggression? Ophelia was starting to think that he had even deliberately sought to provoke them, the better to observe them. Nothing seemed to be left to chance here; it was alarming.

As she was going through all the photographs in the file, searching for new evidence, she was suddenly struck by the subject's smile on each one. Attached were more traditional portraits, in which they posed sometimes with a musical instrument, sometimes with a piece of pottery. She came across a group photograph, of the other subjects of the standard program, in which they were all having fun making faces for the camera. Even the members of the observation team, with their dark pince-nez and yellow-silk saris, joined in with their laughter. There were no collaborators in habits, or nanny-automatons there. Only radiant faces.

Ophelia thought of Cosmos's fit of rage. She thought of the old man who kept hitting his ear. She thought of Second confined to her gibberish. This observatory had the means to help them, but preferred to exacerbate their deviations, the better to use them.

"And meanwhile," she muttered, feeling her anger rise, "they watch us struggling within our own bodies."

"One word."

Thorn hadn't spoken loudly, but something in his tone made Ophelia switch her attention from the photographs to him. He was veering toward her, fist leaning on a table, eyes intently searching her own. Had she the ability to see the shadows, she would have seen the one, bristling with claws, growing all around him. He was probably unaware of it, and she didn't have the heart to tell him, but he was hurting her.

"Just one word from you," he said, "and I will get you out of this observatory this very night. We don't have much time left, but it is still feasible. We will find a place where you won't have to fear either being deported or even located."

"You want me to go? To run away?"

Thorn's expression became hard to read, due to the nightlights.

"What matters is what you, yourself, want. You have, and will always have, the choice."

The dice of my own existence, thought Ophelia.

"The Pole . . . do you miss it sometimes?"

Thorn seemed thrown by the question, but his fingers tightened instinctively around the fob watch. A present from Berenilde; Ophelia knew that from when she had accidentally read the dice he'd owned as a child.

"I left several items of unfinished business back there. None has priority over the one I am dealing with here and now."

This response was devoid of sentimentality, but Ophelia felt moved. Of course Thorn feared, as she did, never seeing his family again. Except that he no longer had the choice. He couldn't return home without first reporting to the Genealogists in Babel, and then the law courts of the Pole. He had sacrificed his dice a long time ago.

And he never complained.

Ophelia wouldn't complain, either.

"Same here. I want to finish what I have started."

The ambivalence became even more marked on Thorn's half-lit face.

"I can tell you, now: I was hoping that you would make that choice."

"Really?"

There was a pounding inside Ophelia's chest. She calmed down as soon as Thorn placed in her hands a plan of the observatory, and pointed to a particular location.

"A visit to the collaborators' quarter would be highly instructive. I wager we will find more than one answer there: the true nature of the shadows and the echoes, along with their link to Eulalia Gonde, the Other, the landslides, the Horn of Plenty, and the decoding of the Books. I don't have the right to inspect any of that work. I am not even authorized to set foot in those laboratories, due to so-called medical secrecy. We will find a way for you to go there instead of me."

Ophelia examined the plan close up. She wasn't particularly sentimental, but that was, by far, the least passionate declaration Thorn had ever made to her.

"When?"

The long, bony finger slid across the paper.

"I have taken in the schedules of all the collaborators. I know where they are at all times. There is just one gap in the timetable when they are all occupied outside of their quarter: between the third and fifth afternoon gong."

"I managed to get out secretly tonight, but it will be less easy in daylight."

"I will help you with that," Thorn assured, calmly. "Tomorrow, I'll go on the offensive. The electricity meters I checked earlier don't tally with the readings that were supplied to me. In other words, there is something within the containment zone demanding a considerable consumption of energy. Something extremely well hidden."

Ophelia thought of the lamps always only half-working, and the carousels breaking down.

"The Horn of Plenty?"

"Precisely. I'm going to use that discrepancy to proceed with a more rigorous inspection of the containment zone. The observatory may not be run by the Lords of LUX, but it owes its smooth operating to their subsidies. Those in charge will just have to submit to my technical checks. In short," Thorn concluded, folding up the plan, "I will draw the general attention to myself for the two hours when the collaborators' quarter is empty. You will be able to go there without worrying."

The more Ophelia listened to Thorn, the more she realized how much he was still the Treasurer of old. In fact, it was the entire North that he carried within him. He even looked so little like a Babelian, with his sun-resistant pallor and polar-bear manner, it was a wonder he was seen as an authentic Lord of LUX. The Genealogists really must have influence to expose him to the public like this without it ever raising any questions.

"What if they send me down to the cellar before then, what should I do?"

"Get yourself out of it. I don't know if that experiment really is to establish contact with the Other, but if so, we must, at all costs, avoid attracting his attention. Whether we are talking about him or Eulalia Gonde, we are not yet ready to stand up to them."

Ophelia hoped it wasn't too late, after her stupid act of bravado on the telephone. She forced herself, above all, not to think of what she had seen, *thought she had seen*, at the glazing-and-mirror store.

"Fine. Tomorrow, between the third and fifth gong, I'll go

to the collaborators' quarter. With a bit of luck, the Horn of Plenty is to be found there."

Thorn's lips flinched slightly.

"The most important thing is to understand the principle. If we discover how Eulalia Gonde freed herself from her human condition, and how the Other freed himself from his condition of being an echo, then we will, in turn, be able to liberate ourselves from them."

Ophelia suddenly felt as if she could breathe easier. Thorn sometimes had the manners of a paper-knife, but his lack of doubts swept her own away. She banished from her mind the glazing-and-mirror store, Second's drawing, the blood, and the void. The only reality now was him, was her, was them.

Thorn pulled on the chain of his watch, which opened and then closed with a wink of its cover.

"Right," he said, sounding businesslike. "Since you have chosen to remain, we are left with time to spare."

"Time for what?"

Ophelia feared the outlining of a new mission. She was already uncertain of fulfilling the one for the following day without getting caught—with the disastrous consequences that would ensue. She realized, after the event, that her question had had an unexpected effect on Thorn. His whole face had hardened, from the tension lines on his forehead to the muscles in his jaw.

"For us."

Ophelia raised her eyebrows. In those two commanding words, there had been possessiveness; and then, a second later, in the hastily lowered eyes, shame. As if Thorn had disappointed himself. It wasn't the first time Ophelia encountered contradictory emotions in him.

She felt herself being drawn to him by an irresistible impulse. Thorn kept her carefully within his field of vision.

His eyes were like ice: cold and burning at the same time. Ophelia would have so loved to soften that intransigence . . .

She sensed the claws' galvanic current on her skin, making her a live wire. She raised herself up on tiptoe and, with fumbling but determined movements, tried to undo the golden buttons of his uniform. To release him from this false skin. To return him to himself, if only for one night.

Thorn's attention had become all-consuming. Usually so reluctant to eat, he suddenly seemed ravenous.

As he enfolded her with his entire body, Ophelia made herself a new promise.

She would change the way Thorn looked at himself in the mirror.

THE COLLABORATORS

The day began normally, as far as the Alternative Program was concerned. Feeling groggy from being up all night, Ophelia struggled to get her foul breakfast down; feigned interest in the screened ballet of geometrical shapes in the big top; did the routine gymnastics in front of the team of collaborators; and endured the endless photographic session, which, she now knew, would highlight the increased gap between her body and her shadow. Next, the usual carousel circuits. Ophelia had to write with both hands on a revolving stand, and then run backwards on a treadmill. She finally dozed off while staring at a toy windmill attached to the handlebars of her velocipede.

The cellar with the telephone no longer featured at all.

Ophelia dodged Second whenever she was approaching her, with her white eye wide open and a new drawing. She found it hard to ignore her crestfallen expression, but she couldn't face seeing herself covered in red pencil again. As for Cosmos, it was he who kept his distance from Ophelia, even if, several times, she caught him looking at the bite mark he had left on her hand.

The third strike of the gong cut through the stifling heat of the afternoon.

Wiping the sweat from her neck, between two carousels,

Ophelia glanced anxiously at the hazy gray figures ambling languidly across the cloister. All the collaborators had left their quarter as expected, but still no sign of Thorn. If she tried anything at all right now, she would be noticed before doing ten steps. She was starting to think the diversion had failed when, finally, something stirred among everyone around her. The same murmur—"Sir Henry's here!"—flew from mouth to mouth, crossing the containment zone like a paper dart.

The nanny-automatons stopped all the activities and led the inverts back to the residence, apart from Second, who remained alone on her carousel horse. The rest they locked in their rooms with a tray meal.

"IT'S JUST AN INSPECTION OF THE ELECRICAL FITTINGS. WE'LL GET BACK TO THE GAMES TOMORROW, *CHÉRIS*."

As soon as the key had turned in its lock, Ophelia didn't waste a second. She put on the gloves and glasses she had hidden under her bed, and then removed the shutter, now hanging on just one hinge. Her first escape had gone unnoticed; she hoped that luck would again be on her side.

She slid through the window. Walking on that wall at night was one thing; doing it in broad daylight with an unrestricted view of the void and a searing wind in one's face quite another. When she reached it, the roof of the residence burnt her feet.

Thorn's surprise inspection in the containment zone was having the desired effect. Like miniature figurines, the gray-clad figures were all gravitating around his dazzling uniform.

Ophelia descended, terrace by terrace, until, with some acrobatics and almost as many bruises, she landed in an orchard. If she had got the itinerary right, she had reached the collaborators' quarter. The hardest was still to come. She had barely more than an hour to extract this place's secrets. She went through an infirmary, a scriptorium, a library, and a kitchen that smelt shamefully good—clearly not where the inverts' meals were concocted. All of the quarter's rooms had no windows, as on the plan Thorn had made her memorize. This could work in her favor. The flickering light from the bulbs made the shadows shudder. At least the diversion had worked: Ophelia met no one on the way.

That was true up until the hub of the quarter. She hid just in time, in a blind spot: two collaborators were on guard. Ophelia risked a quick flash of her glasses at them. They were pacing along a corridor toward one another, habits brushing as they passed, gray hoods pulled over faces, completely silent. One was going forward, the other going back. After several steps, they wordlessly switched roles. The one going back started to go forward, and vice versa.

On the opposite side of the corridor, there was a small closed door. For it to be guarded like this, it must allow access to the laboratories. Ophelia couldn't reach it without being seen, for the moment at least. She and Thorn had envisaged this scenario. Crouching in the dark, she waited, hoping it wouldn't take much longer. Every minute spent here was eating into what little time she had.

At last, all the lightbulbs went out. The power outage promised by Thorn. The windowless quarter was plunged into darkness. There was the sound of bodies colliding, and then two weary whispers:

"Another power outage?"

"Another power outage."

Ophelia darted into the corridor, on tiptoe, hugging the wall to avoid any contact with the pair of collaborators. Having located the door to the laboratories, she felt her way to open it. Quick, hurry up before the light returns! Her hands fumbled around the handle, confusing left and right—the simplest of actions had become exasperatingly difficult.

Finally, a click. She slipped through the half-opened door and closed it behind her, centimeter by centimeter, so the wood didn't creak.

She had made it to the other side.

Leaning against the door, she took in the darkness in front of her, with her eyes, with her ears, with all her senses. What if Thorn had got it wrong? If some collaborators had remained in the laboratories? If the return of light betrayed Ophelia's presence among them?

The lightbulbs came back on all at once. There was no one there.

The room was vast, divided into compartments separated by thick partitions, like the cells of a beehive. The ceiling fans restarted with the electricity. The air was more breathable. On the walls, unused pegs clearly awaited the collaborators' hoods.

Here, as in the entire containment zone, there were piles of boxes overflowing with faulty objects. Combs without teeth, fake jewelry, pots with holes, bent spoons, wasted food, and still nothing remotely resembling a Horn of Plenty. It was so frustrating never to find anywhere a cause, the effects of which were clear everywhere.

At the bottom of a trash can, Ophelia found some pince-nez, in a pitiful state. A collaborator must have accidentally sat on them. The only lens still dangling from the frame was cracked. And black.

Ophelia stuck it over one eye, under her glasses. Her perception of the world instantly changed. Every partition, every lamp, every object was surrounded by the finest white vapor, endlessly disappearing and then reappearing around it. The fans, like propellers on a boat, projected theirs far and wide, in great concentric circles.

"What the . . ."

As soon as this muttering left Ophelia's lips, it, too, turned into mist and dispersed.

She tried snatching at it. Her own hand instantly appeared to her in duplicate. One was as black and solid as the lens stuck to her eye; the other white and vaporous, overlapping the first.

Ophelia had more surprises to come.

With every gesture she made, and even those she didn't, she projected a little of her shadow all around her. And sometimes, before completely dispersing, it would come back to her diminished, like a returning wave, so slight it was barely detectable, despite the special lens.

It wasn't just the shadows Ophelia was seeing. She was also seeing the echoes.

The pince-nez worn by the observers worked like a photographic negative, revealing what couldn't be seen with the naked eye. The shadows and echoes disappeared as soon as Ophelia removed the lens. She would have gladly taken it away with her, but the damaged glass broke up in her hands.

So, everything had a shadow. Even better, the shadows and the echoes were different manifestations of one and the same phenomenon.

It was a good start.

Ophelia visited the laboratories, one by one, in search of answers. In them she found turned-off stills, slates scrawled with equations, scales like those used for post, and a number of other measuring instruments. Her increased clumsiness and Cosmos's bite didn't make the task of opening every drawer any easier for her. The scientific notebooks were unfathomable.

Two words kept cropping up: "aerargyrum" and "crystallization." She had no idea what their significance was, but she fell on a photograph of Cosmos inside a report. She leafed through it. Every line corresponded to a date, but the comment written was always the same:

"Subject unsuitable for crystallization and not reclaimed by family. Kept in protocol I."

Ophelia looked at the appendices. They featured a few photographs similar to those she had found in the directors' apartments. On each one, she could see a shadow separating from Cosmos's body, as if another version of him had stepped a little to one side. Attached to the photographs were dozens of drawings in which she recognized, not without surprise, Second's signature style. They were actually sketches rather than drawings, and all depicted the same dark silhouette. At the base of each image, a collaborator had recorded the date.

Did Second see people's shadows, then? Supposing that were the case, in what way were her drawings important? After all, the Deviations Observatory already knew how to capture the shadows in photographs.

Ophelia hurriedly searched for her own report. She found it in a separate cabinet. It was less voluminous than Cosmos's, given her recent arrival on the Alternative Program. At first, it was same daily appraisal:

"Subject unsuitable for crystallization and not reclaimed by family. Kept in protocol I."

However, Ophelia got a shock when she saw that the comment had changed recently:

"Subject suitable for crystallization and not reclaimed by family. Kept provisionally in protocol I. Soon forecasted for protocols II and III."

She checked the appendices. The photographs were, nevertheless, the same as those she had already seen, showing a separation between her body and her shadow. Nothing new. At first it was the same with Second's sketches, but the most recent ones had become totally different. Hastily scribbled, the shadow was starting to split up, as if scissors had been viciously applied to its shoulder area, and its arm was about to come off.

Ophelia had never seen anything like that through the lens. Was Second foreseeing what the photographs and the pince-nez didn't yet show?

Ophelia thought of that nail. She thought of that picture of her covered in red crayon, she thought of that old woman, and she thought of that monster.

A sudden change in the lightbulbs' output reminded her to be vigilant. She would have to take advantage of the next power cut to leave the laboratories without being seen. Time was short.

As she went back to investigating, a desk caught her eye, due to the state it was in. Dozens, hundreds of notes were scrawled across every centimeter of slate and partition. The cubicle's owner had even written straight onto the precious-wood counter. To which the maintenance staff had reacted, on a memo left nearby: "So paper's just for marsupials, is it?"

Ophelia examined the notes close up. In places, she recognized the writing so characteristic of the Books. Arrows and circles had been drawn in chalk in an attempt to find meaning in all these arabesques, without great success, judging by all the crossings out.

Elizabeth's decoding work.

The Genealogists had manipulated her specifically for this task, but why were the Books of such interest to them? Because they held the secret to the family spirits' immortality? And what about the Deviations Observatory? What exactly did it expect from this decoding? What did it have to do with the shadows and echoes? What did it have to do with the Horn of Plenty?

At this rate, Ophelia wouldn't have found a real answer between now and the fifth strike of the gong. She felt as if her mind was as partitioned as the laboratories: she could still see only the parts, never the machinery.

Enough.

Eulalia Gonde had passed her memory on to the Other, who had, in turn, passed it on to Ophelia. The time had come for her to put it to good use. She took a chair and sat before a blackboard that Elizabeth had covered in code. A language formerly invented by Eulalia.

A language invented by *me*, Ophelia corrected, taking a deep breath.

She was going to use it to trigger a new vision. She stared doggedly at the writing, forcing herself not to think anymore of the time passing, or her own impatience, or the future, or the past. Only of the chalk marks facing her. It was no different from reading an object.

Forgetting oneself the better to remember.

A flash tore through her head. This migraine, which had never really left her since entering the observatory, was suddenly hitting the high notes. Ophelia had the paradoxical sensation of rising up from her chair while falling from high above. The chalk on the blackboard turned into a stratosphere, then into a scattering of clouds, then into an old world, then into a city scarred by bombardments, then into an old district being rebuilt, then into a little pedestal table on which two porcelain cups shine out.

Eulalia grips hers with her thinner hands. She holds the gaze of the caretaker on the other side of the table. Tortoiseshell glasses against steel spectacles. He has seriously aged since the last time. The scarf end of his turban still hides his jaw—what's left of it, at least. His face, like Babel itself, is ravaged by war.

"Your first blasted leave in four years," he growled into his scarf. "And it's me you want to see?"

Eulalia nodded.

"You're looking rough. Like you're my age."

Eulalia nodded again. Yes, she must have lost at least half of her life expectancy. You only get out what you put in. She regrets nothing.

"I heard about the orphanage."

"There's nothing left to say about it. A blasted bomb killed the kids. Everyone quit the island. Including me. A caretaker without a school, makes no blasted sense."

Eulalia understands him, inside out. She feels as if her family has been snatched away from her for the second time.

"We'll reopen it," she promises him. "Just you and me."

The caretaker sits with military stillness, but his hands shake on either side of his cup.

"I'll have snuffed it before they let you return to civilian life."

He glances furtively at the soldiers standing to attention outside, beside the bar's door. Since Eulalia has been working at the observatory, for the Project, she can't go anywhere without having them hot on her heels. It's not her life they're protecting, contrary to her superiors' claim, but what she might divulge.

"We're going to reopen the school," she insisted. "A completely different school for . . . for completely different children. But I must know: are you with me?"

The caretaker watches her drinking her tea without touching his own.

"How can I say no? You've always been my blasted favorite."

Eulalia knows it. At the orphanage, all the kids were scared of him, except her. While the others played at war, she visited him in his lodge to talk about universal peace, and tell him stories in which the deserters were heroes.

Eulalia ignores the soldiers, who keep shooting nervous looks at her from the bar's entrance. All that counts is her friend. An old man who, like her, has nothing left to lose.

"I don't have . . . I don't have the permission, and I don't intend, to tell you about the Project. I'll never tell you what I've seen, what I've . . . what I've heard, what I've been part of, all that the Project has changed in me. What I can tell you is that they're on the wrong . . . wrong track at the observatory."

Her residual stammer makes the caretaker frown. She knows it would take her weeks, maybe even months of therapy to get the better of it, and the doctors warned her she could never be totally free of making slips of the tongue. A small price to pay, there, too.

She tilts her glasses up at the small patch of sky above them. The bar's roof is being repaired. The workmen's hammers aren't ideal for conversation, but they're not ideal for eavesdroppers, either.

"My superiors think only of peace for the city, a peace entailing new . . . new wars. One must think bigger. Much bigger. I have a plan."

The caretaker says nothing, but Eulalia knows he is listening to her very seriously. He has always listened to her. It's for that reason, too, that she has chosen him.

"We won't be alone. I've . . . Let's say that I've sort of met someone. An extraordinary person. Who has transformed my vision of the world. Transformed me. Taught me that there exists . . . that there exists *something other*, that's even more extraordinary. It goes beyond anything you can imagine, anything I, myself, imagined, and yet I've never been short on imagination."

Eulalia can feel herself quivering with elation merely from evoking the Other. He has become so close to her that she detects his presence on every reflective surface around—the bar's copperware, the tea in her cup, even the lenses of her own glasses. He is her, and she is him. They are singular and plural.

"So what is it, this plan?"

There's no irony in the caretaker's question. Eulalia's fervor is such that she's ignited a spark in his eyes. He's known her since her very first day at the orphanage, but she knows he's never really considered her a child. Today, he looks at her as if she were his mother, as if she were the mother of all humanity.

Eulalia likes this look.

"To save the world. And this time, I know how."

At the door of the bar, a soldier indicates the clock to her. Her leave is already over. She will have to return to the observatory and obey orders, but not for much longer. Oh no, not for much longer.

As she's laying a banknote on the table, she takes the chance to lean forward discreetly:

"I need only three small things: echoes, words, and some compensation."

The caretaker's surprised face goes back to being chalk on the blackboard. Ophelia blinks, no longer daring to breathe, still immersed in Eulalia Gonde's memory. Ramifications and new connections multiply in her migraine-afflicted mind, opening doors to inner rooms she had no idea even existed.

She could see the mechanics.

Ophelia knew she had to leave this place right now, get back to her room, and wait for nightfall to meet up with Thorn again in the directors' apartments, as agreed. First, she wanted to make sure of one last thing. She borrowed a magnifying glass from a collaborator's drawer, and randomly picked one of the faulty objects in boxes. A pan that, from its nauseating smell, had contained one of the gross tarts they served them daily in the refectory. She examined it from every angle. She had to strain her eyes, on top of the magnifying glass, finally to find what she was looking for: microscopic characters inlaid in the metal, almost like those in the Books.

Yes, Ophelia could finally see them, those mechanics.

The Horn of Plenty produced nothing.

It converted echoes into matter.

And it did so thanks to a code.

Ophelia put the tart pan and the magnifying glass back where she had found them. She was starting to collect the pieces of the puzzle, but she would sort them out once she was far from here. First she had to think of a way to distract the attention of the two collaborators in the corridor, in case she couldn't count on another power cut.

She didn't get the chance.

The small door she had arrived through had just opened, letting in a crowd of collaborators. They all unbuttoned their gray hoods to hang them on the pegs. Stumbling, Ophelia hid behind a cubicle. Why were they already back? Had Thorn's inspection been completed sooner than planned?

They were as silent among themselves as they were toward the inverts. Only their sandals made the polished floorboards squeak. For once, Ophelia felt lucky to be barefoot as she ran from one cubicle to the next to avoid being seen. Each collaborator returned to their personal laboratory.

As steps approached, Ophelia darted into the nearest cubicle and crouched under a workbench. The collaborator she was actually trying to avoid walked in himself. She had gone and trapped herself. Crouching deep in her hiding place, she watched the gray habit's silky folds caress the floor. A hand, also gloved in gray, grabbed the stool, but instead of putting it in front of the workbench, it placed it beside a partition.

"It was no accident," whispered the collaborator. "I don't understand what happened, but it was *certainement* no accident."

He had the refined tone of a scholar. Ophelia was wondering whether he was talking to himself, when a muffled whisper replied to him from the other side of the partition:

"It's none of our business."

"Lady Septima's daughter, she's everyone's business."

Ophelia almost banged her head on the workbench. Had something happened to Second?

"Let's hope, above all, that she hasn't been too damaged," said the other voice. "We need her. At least that incident cut short Sir Henry's inspection. I found that intrusion *très* disagreeable."

The collaborator's habit stirred. Bent double under the workbench, Ophelia edged forward very carefully to see him better. He was perched on his stool, with one ear pressed to the partition. His bald pate shone with sweat. If he could just stay in that position, Ophelia might be able to get out without being noticed.

"Damaged?" he muttered, sadly, just as she was leaving her hiding place. "She's still but a child."

"You are *vraiment* naïve, dear colleague," replied the voice from the neighboring cubicle. "We will speak of it again in a few months' time. Or rather, we won't speak about it again. Speak to me again and, unfortunately, I will find myself obliged to denounce you to the management."

Ophelia dashed out of the laboratory. She hadn't been discreet, the collaborator must have seen her. He would raise the alarm.

There was no alarm, no shouting.

Her relief was short-lived. Even if all the lightbulbs went out now, Ophelia would never be able to get out through the door without bumping into a whole group of collaborators. She needed another exit.

At the back of the room, she spotted a yellow drape, above

which was written, in big letters: OBSERVERS ONLY. She couldn't recall having seen an entrance here on Thorn's plan, but at least she shouldn't find any collaborators on the other side.

She slid along the partitions, ducking each time she passed in front of a workbench.

A female collaborator was busy unloading a cart, on rails, that had just delivered a load of objects. It was the same junk that cluttered up all the trash cans, but the woman was handling it as if dealing with precious stones, and noting everything down, item by item, in an inventory register.

Ophelia slipped behind her and dived behind the drape. She found a maze of badly lit steps, which she climbed up, came down, and stumbled back up again. Where had all these stairways come from? They didn't feature on the plan.

Finally, she emerged into a corridor.

It was, in fact, much more than a corridor. It stretched so far, its end couldn't be seen, and its vault of lancet arches soared up tens of meters from the ground. Incense sticks produced a perfumed haze, pierced here and there by blades of light escaping through the stained-glass windows on high. A nave, all stone and glass.

Ophelia found herself shivering.

She passed a basin, resting on the shoulders of a buckling and grimacing statue. Was it an authentic font?

She walked for a long time straight ahead, never glimpsing the end of the nave. It couldn't be infinite, surely . . . The side aisles were punctuated by chapels, closed off by as many doors. An observer could be lurking behind each one of them. As, indeed, could the Horn of Plenty.

The flagging was inlaid with giant golden letters.

One step. EXPIATION.

One step. CRYSTALLIZATION.

One step. REDEMPTION.

This place made Ophelia feel extremely uncomfortable. She was considering turning back when a voice froze her to the spot.

"*Benvenuta* to the second protocol."

THE MISTAKE

The words ricocheted for a long time around the sculpted stone of the nave. Ophelia searched for their source through the swirls of incense. She found it on one of the kneeling stools in the side aisles. A slight figure, deep in contemplation, was so totally still that it seemed at one with the wood and the velvet. Its profile, inlaid with illuminations, glimmered in the light from the stained-glass windows.

Mediana.

Ophelia's first reflex was to check that Mediana was properly reflected in the sheen of the flagstones. That done, she still didn't feel reassured. Although she had known that Mediana was also at the Deviations Observatory, put there by Lady Septima herself, she hadn't thought of her once since being there. All this time, she had presumed she was a charge of some other department, with no connection to her own.

"Is this it, the second protocol?" Ophelia asked, astonished, her eyes sweeping around the nave. "What are you doing here?"

Mediana didn't answer. She didn't need to be either Eulalia Gonde or the Other to represent a threat. During their mutual apprenticeship at the Good Family, this Seer had imposed her own rules on Ophelia. She had used her power to intrude forcefully on her memories, and to blackmail her, seriously jeopardizing both herself and Thorn. The last time Ophelia had seen her had been right here, at the observatory, in the visitors' conservatory, shortly before the landslide. At the time, Mediana had been so traumatized by her encounter with the Memorial sweeper that she had been incapable of holding a conversation. Slumped on the elbow ledge of the kneeling stool, her posture conveyed the very same apathy. Her pajamas still floated around her like baggy skin.

And yet, Ophelia sensed that she was completely different.

"What are you doing here?" she insisted. "Are you also part of the Alternative Program? Unlike me, you're no invert, as far as I know."

Mediana still didn't respond, but Ophelia resolutely kept her distance. She didn't trust her praying pose.

She loathed the thought of needing her.

"Could you at least indicate to me where the exit is?"

A spasm lifted the corner of Mediana's lips. Ophelia suddenly realized that she was kept on the kneeling stool by shackles around her ankles and wrists. She wasn't deep in thought; she had been chained here against her will. EXPIATION. CRYSTALLIZATION. REDEMPTION. Was that really what the second protocol consisted of? Treating the subjects like culprits?

"I made a mistake."

Mediana had spoken very quietly, but the nave's acoustics carried her voice up to the rafters. She seemed to be dehydrated. How long had she been attached to this kneeling stool?

Ophelia's glasses darted nervously from one part of the nave to another. An observer could suddenly appear from a chapel at any time. She had no desire to linger, but no one, not even Mediana, deserved such treatment.

She searched for the key to the shackles in the statue alcoves. Not finding it, she emptied a pot of incense sticks and, having rinsed it in the baptistery, filled it right up. Awkwardly, she brought it to Mediana's lips, but she just let the water run down her chin, without swallowing any. Her wide-open eyes stared straight ahead, beyond the bowl, beyond Ophelia, beyond the nave's walls. They shone with a mix of fever and fervor.

"I made a mistake," she repeated, slowly. "I spent *tutta* my life chasing after little secrets of no importance. I will soon be ready for the third protocol."

This was how Mediana had changed. Behind her lackluster appearance, she glowed with the same intensity as the illuminations inlaid in her skin.

Ophelia leaned toward her ear.

"Have you, yourself, seen the Horn of Plenty?"

Mediana didn't seem remotely interested in the question. Her gaze became even more distant, as though lost in search of inner horizons.

"I can't release you," said Ophelia, sighing, "but I can try to alert your cousins, if they're still in Babel."

"Why?"

"Because what you're being made to suffer here is unacceptable."

"I'm expiating."

"And because no one has returned from the third protocol."

Mediana's mouth twitched provocatively, revealing something of the former queen of the Forerunners.

"I won't make the same mistake again. No more little secrets. The only one worth pursuing now is the one the observatory has promised me. But first, I must crystallize. Only then will I know redemption."

Mediana's linked hands shook with conviction as she spoke words that made no sense to Ophelia. At least one thing was crystal-clear to her: she must quit the program before ending up like this. In one of the laboratory files, someone had written that she was suitable for crystallization and forecasted for protocols II and III. All because Second had drawn a split in the shoulder of her shadow.

"What is crystallization? What use is it to them?"

Mediana licked her dry lips. Ophelia suspected her of taking a certain pleasure in knowing something that she herself didn't, as if even here their rivalry was back in force.

"To them? They didn't tell me. To me, crystallization will be of use to obtain what I have always desired. Genuine knowledge! An *assolutamente* new perspective on our reality."

Ophelia pushed her glasses up on her nose. Eulalia Gonde had come out with the same thing after her encounter with the Other on the telephone in the cellar. That echo had, one way or another, completely changed her vision of the world. Was crystallization the phenomenon that allowed one to invoke the Other? The Deviations Observatory seemed desperately in need of him, and of his knowledge.

Mediana must have taken Ophelia's silence for disdain. Despite her physical exhaustion and bleary eyes, she was jubilant.

"So you reckon only inverts like you have that privilege, *signorina*? That's missing the essential."

"So what is the essential?" asked Ophelia, impatiently.

She couldn't linger much longer. If she got caught here, when she should have been locked in her room like all the inverts, she, too, would end up shackled to a kneeling stool.

"Renunciation."

Mediana's reply was swallowed up by a rumble of thunder across the nave. Steps approaching. Such was the resonance here, impossible to know which side they were coming from.

With a vague flicker of her eyelids, Mediana indicated a confessional, a few flagstones along, to Ophelia. The sound of steps was getting louder, second by second. There were several of them. Ophelia couldn't afford to hesitate any longer. She hid behind the yellow curtain of the confessional stall just as Mediana was addressing those arriving:

"Show me the path to crystallization. *Per favore.*"

By moving the curtain slightly, Ophelia saw a gathering of observers around Mediana's kneeling stool. It was the first time she was seeing any of them since entering the containment zone. They were recognizable by their yellow garb, shoulder automatons, and black-lensed pince-nez.

They said nothing. They merely looked at Mediana.

As Ophelia edged back into the stall's darkness, she noticed a movement beside her. Where the grille separating confessor and confessant should have been—according to the religious-history handbooks she had studied, in any case—there was a mirror.

Here, at last, was the way out she was looking for. To which destination? As far as she knew, the only mirrors in the observatory that weren't distorting were in the directors' apartments, and she wasn't supposed to go there until nightfall. The directors may not exist, but someone looked after the medical files that were stored there. Going there during the day was too risky.

In her mind, Ophelia pictured the Memorial. And inside the Memorial, the Secretarium. And inside the Secretarium, the hanging mirror. Over there, in Eulalia Gonde's secret room, she would finally be able to think, away from prying eyes.

She plunged deep into her reflection, slipping into the in-between as though suddenly thin as a sheet of paper, and then emerged into broad daylight.

She found herself face to face with a flabbergasted old lady. Wearing an academic gown, she held a book in one hand and a magnifying glass in the other. No less taken aback, Ophelia wondered what a professor was doing here, before realizing that is was she herself who was not in the right place. She had just burst out of an alcove mirror, straight into the Memorial's libraries, bang in the middle of a public consulting room. All those using the facilities had interrupted their reading to peer at this barefoot intruder, who was breaking the most basic rules of the dress code. There were fewer of them than before the landslide, but enough for Ophelia not to be able to go unnoticed among them.

She tilted her glasses up at the terrestrial globe of the Secretarium, floating weightlessly at the center of the atrium. On two occasions, she had landed over there unintentionally, and now that she deliberately wanted to get there, she'd bungled it?

The separation of her shadow.

It affected not only her ability to read and animate objects, but also to pass through mirrors. Right, how was she going to get back to the observatory? Already, some Memorialists had alerted security, while the good citizens were pointing accusatory fingers at her.

A Necromancer made straight for her.

"This way, *mademoiselle*, if you please," he called out to her. "I must proceed with checking your papers."

Obviously, Ophelia didn't have them. They had remained in a cabinet, kilometers away from here, and the "AP" tattoo on her arm would be no substitute. Beyond the observatory walls, she was now nothing but an outlaw. If she allowed herself to be apprehended, it would mean immediate and definitive expulsion from Babel.

She swiveled round to face the mirror through which she had accidentally arrived. Separated shadow or not, she had to get away. Now.

"*Mademoiselle*," the Necromancer called, more firmly.

Already, Ophelia's body temperature was starting to fall. She knew that this man wouldn't hesitate to freeze her on the spot if he suspected her of running away.

"*Mademoiselle!*"

Suddenly, Ophelia felt herself slowing down. The mirror was just a breath away, but hers was already turning into condensation. Her lungs were hurting her. She saw her own face turn wan behind her glasses. In the background, the Necromancer's uniform kept getting bigger behind her back, his hand reaching out to stop her.

She. Was. Almost. There.

Ophelia let herself fall, like a block of ice, into her reflection, which instantly absorbed her. What little presence of mind she had left said: "Observatory." She crossed the in-between in a trice, and then a change of lighting indicated to her that she had emerged. She couldn't do anything but continue her fall where she had interrupted it.

Carpet.

Curled up on the floor, Ophelia shook with uncontrollable shivers. She could neither stand up nor speak anymore. Breathing was torture.

A figure, lit from a window, leaned over her.

"Cold."

That was the only word Ophelia managed to get out, between her teeth. Darkness fell on her, so suddenly she thought she had gone blind, before understanding that she had been wrapped in a bedspread. She snuggled up in it. Little by little, degree by degree, her body temperature went back up. Her numb skin began to burn as feeling returned. Violence might be prohibited in Babel, but a clubbing wouldn't have been less painful.

She felt around for her glasses, which had fallen with her onto the carpet. When she put them back on her nose, she discovered a bedroom. Sitting on the bed, a man was humming a lullaby. A stranger bursting through his mirrored wardrobe didn't seem to have greatly disturbed him.

Ophelia gave him back the bedspread he had covered her with.

"Thank you."

He held the bedspread limply and, not knowing what to do with it, put it around himself, while still humming.

Ophelia lifted the mosquito screen from the window. The gardens were flooded with the intense light of late afternoon. In the distance, the giant statue of the colossus eclipsed the sun. Ophelia suspected as much: she had again veered off course. She had aimed for the directors' apartments, and landed instead in a Standard Program bedroom. The fact that she had never seen her reflection here had made no difference. At least her host had proved very cooperative. He asked no questions, and, when Ophelia, finger pressed to lips, sneaked out of his room, he just let her go quietly. Like a bird one has nursed and then allows to fly away.

Ophelia sped through the many stories of the residence. Sounds reached her from different rooms, music practice here, children's laughter there. The Deviations Observatory's gilded façade.

But me, she thought, I've seen the other side of the picture. The spectacle of Mediana, chained to that kneeling stool, remained imprinted on her glasses.

Ophelia only just avoided some nurses and some supervisors. No one here was hiding under a gray hood, but they all had whistles hanging from their necks. After some more detours, she went along a gangway that, if she could trust the signposts, led to the directors' apartments. The gangway did, indeed, disappear into the side of the colossus, where the gate of a lift gleamed. Ophelia made a discreet about-turn as soon as she spotted that this approach was secured by two figures standing guard.

She would have to get round the problem—once again.

She ended up finding a service stairway, so old that it almost fell apart under her weight. It allowed her to go back down to the statue's base. The tunnel, finally! Ophelia dived in, making sure, above all, not to stare at the thousands of kaleidoscopic surfaces flashing the light of the sunset back and forth along the walls. She found the hidden door Thorn had taken her through the previous day. She only felt really safe once she was up above, right at the top of the statue. She took cover in the secret passage adjoining the antechamber of the directors' apartments, concealed behind the tapestry. She collapsed onto a step, out of breath and legs, and didn't move again. For a long while, in the flickering light of the bulbs, all she heard was the stifled hiccup of her breathing.

She had made it.

Despite all the mistakes along the way, she had managed to get back from the collaborators' quarter, and be at the agreed place—and early, too.

It was only at that moment that she finally felt it, so intensely that she had to hug her chest to ease the pounding. Fear. It wasn't just from almost falling into the hands of the observers, or ending up frozen by a Necromancer. No, this panic rose from the depths of her being. Ophelia knew only a tiny fraction of Eulalia Gonde's secrets, but she seemed to glimpse a far greater truth, lurking in a recess of memory, with such crushing implications that it all made her feel like uncharted territory to herself.

How had Thorn managed, all these years, to bear the weight of the memory passed on to him by his mother? He had known from childhood that their world was but a giant web, woven century after century by a self-proclaimed God, and had made it his duty, without seeking anyone else's opinion, to put an end to it.

Huddled on the step, Ophelia rested her head on her knees. She was longing for him to be there, to draw a little on his steadfastness . . .

She must have dozed off without realizing as, suddenly, she was woken by the sound of the lift. Someone had just entered the antechamber. Ophelia recognized, from her side of the tapestry, the grating of steel that had become so familiar to her.

"I will wait alone."

The Babel accent was one of the most melodious in the world; from Thorn's mouth, it sounded more like a dirge.

"Will you allow me to keep you company, *monsieur*? The directors are always *extrêmement* busy. I myself have still never met them. I know you are determined to give them your report this evening, but you may have to wait a long while before they open to you."

It was the young monkey girl who escorted Thorn everywhere. If she really did believe in the existence of the directors, she was very seriously misinformed. Ophelia picked up a shrill note in her voice that made her feel uncomfortable. There was far more than politeness and ignorance behind her words.

"I will wait alone."

Thorn had articulated each syllable as an automaton would. Ophelia immediately regretted her fleeting jealousy. So lacking was he in indulgence toward himself that it was inconceivable to him to be considered attractive.

Astonishingly, the young monkey girl was undaunted.

"Perhaps . . . perhaps you should change your clothes, *monsieur*? I can drop your uniform off at our laundry if you . . . *eh bien*, if you trust me with it."

Ophelia felt this conversation was taking a most curious turn.

She could almost see, through this tapestry separating them, the pretty figure in a yellow sari, automaton on shoulder, nervously pressing a document file against her chest. She even seemed to see the eyes, dark and bright at the same time, she was turning up at Thorn, while still maintaining a respectful distance.

"About Mademoiselle Second," the young girl went on, "the doctor said that the wound was shocking, but not concerning."

Ophelia's astonishment just kept growing. The voice on the other side of the tapestry, conversely, shrank to the level of a whisper.

"I'm not allowed to speak of it, *monsieur*, but these black lenses I wear enable me to see certain things. Contrary to appearances, what happened wasn't your responsibility. Mademoiselle Second shouldn't have thrown herself on you like that. She is sometimes so impulsive with her drawings. The fault was hers. It doesn't matter who you have been in the past, you are *maintenant* a Lord of LUX!" she said, louder, quivering with adulation. "The Lords of LUX are untouchable and they never make any mista—"

"I will wait alone."

Thorn's response was unchanged, but imbued with a hostility that deterred the young girl from persisting.

"Good night, *monsieur*."

With a rustle of silk, she left. As soon as the lift carried her off, Ophelia pushed aside the tapestry and stepped forward onto the tiled floor of the antechamber.

Thorn was standing in the light from the lamps. He was staring, sternly, at the ebony door of the directors' apartments before him. Not that he was seriously contemplating it opening, rather, he seemed mainly to be avoiding his reflection on the shiny surfaces in the room. He only consented to turn his attention from the door and onto Ophelia once he became aware that she was approaching. He showed neither surprise nor anger. What emotion there was in his eyes was turned against himself. He was standing resolutely with his back to the wall, as if wanting to keep all of space within his field of vision. With his fingers, he was screwing up a sheet of paper. The gold of his uniform was spattered with blood.

Seeing him like this devastated Ophelia.

"All that for a drawing."

Thorn had made this statement without a hint of feeling. And yet, barely had he made it before his rigidity broke down. The hard lines of his face gave way, one by one. The brace on his leg bent as if no longer able to bear the weight of this body that had become intolerably heavy.

With a clatter of steel, Thorn let himself fall to his knees.

He clung with both hands to Ophelia, so hard she almost lost her balance. She stood firm. Here, now, as shaken as she was inside, it was up to her to be solid for them both. Thorn continued to collapse in on himself, head drooping, shoulders tense enough to snap. He was clasping Ophelia as if he wanted both to hang onto her, and keep her apart.

To stop his claws from creating a new victim.

The abyss he was sinking into was like the void between the arks. An endless fall from which none returned.

Ophelia would not allow it.

She gripped Thorn as hard as he was gripping her. She closed her eyes, the better to visualize their claws, which were throbbing to a chaotic rhythm. Her own, warped by the observatory; Thorn's, sharp as thorns. They weren't harmful in themselves. They were him, they were her. Using an instinct that came to her from an unknown family power, Ophelia tried to connect her nerve impulse to Thorn's, to defuse it. She had to make several attempts, due to that gap between her and her shadow, but she did, finally, succeed. She felt Thorn shuddering against her, and the muscles of his shoulders tightening even more. She thought for a moment that he was going to pull away, furious, but then his shoulders finally relaxed. That permanent tension besetting his big, bony body fell away for good. He had stopped fighting against himself.

He didn't move anymore, kneeling on the tiled floor, his forehead buried in Ophelia's stomach, which was in knots. He was sobbing.

Second's crumpled drawing lay on the floor.

A rabbit leaping from a well.

Bloodred.

(Parenthesis)

Eleven months, four days, nine hours, twenty-seven minutes, thirteen seconds earlier.

Thorn was sitting on a gilded chair. Eighty-four centimeters high, forty-eight wide, forty-two deep, excluding decimal places and the level of the actual seat. He didn't calculate deliberately. Measurements just came to him, unbidden, intruding whenever he engaged with his surroundings. They were there, in the mesh of the mosquito screens on the gilded windows, in the gap between the legs of the gilded furniture, in the volume of liquid in the gilded carafe, in the geometrical patterns on the golden carpets.

They were particularly there in the hands, also gold, of the lounge's clock.

Thorn had been waiting on this chair, on the first floor of the Genealogy Club, for two thousand three hundred and eighteen seconds. These people showed no respect for punctuality. It was worse than rude; it was illogical. While he was wasting time, they were, too. He could have used these two thousand three hundred and eighteen seconds (thirty-eight by now) to continue with the mission they had themselves given him.

He wasn't naïve. He knew full well that the waiting was part of the game. Of their game.

One thousand six hundred and sixty-eight seconds had been added to those that came before when, finally, the Genealogist couple entered the lounge. The first time Thorn had met them, he was but a filthy fugitive, racked with fever, dragging a shattered leg. They presented themselves to him just as they did at all their meetings, forever wrapped in their golden cloaks.

"*Bienvenue*, Sir Henry," they said, as one.

It was they who had given him this name. Thorn still didn't know their own names, but he didn't need to, to know who they were. He had known that even before arriving in Babel, before escaping from the Pole. He had memorized the political intricacies of all the arks, and had kept abreast of interfamilial news for years. Yes, well before meeting them, he had understood that, of all God's servants, these two served only themselves. No need to be a great psychologist to realize that.

The man and woman settled on a sofa, so close that any space between them was impossible to quantify. Thorn turned his attention instead to the anteroposterior, transverse, and epiotic diameters of their craniums. He could take all their measurements at a glance, but he couldn't have translated these figures into any aesthetic evaluation. Were they beautiful? He found them repulsive. A little more than that, even.

"I come here as agreed."

His hurried words delighted them. With studied slowness, the man took the carafe from the pedestal table and tilted it to his wife's lips, without taking his eyes off Thorn. Provocative. A strong smell of wine hung in the air. Alcohol was forbidden in Babel, just as tobacco, obscenity, gambling, noise music, and violent novels were. All of that could be found at the Genealogy Club, but who would go and denounce the city's highest representatives?

Unimpressed, Thorn checked the lounge's clock (four

thousand three hundred and sixty-two seconds). He had seen far worse at the Pole's embassy.

"Ask me the question."

The Genealogists pretended to hesitate, and then said, in unison:

"Have you succeeded?"

There were only two replies to this question. "Not yet," "soon," or "almost" didn't feature.

"No," he replied.

His failures were their failures, but they both nodded their heads with undisguised satisfaction. And yet they sought, as much as he did, if not for the same reasons, to discover what had allowed God to become God. The mission remained unchanged since their very first encounter, when Thorn had spontaneously presented himself to them, right here, in this lounge. They gave him the means, he put them into practice; they opened doors to him, it was up to him to go through them. They used him just as he used them. And if, one day, Thorn should push on one door too many, one that closed on him without possible retreat, then the Genealogists would get rid of him as fast as they had hired him. They would take back his name, disown him, deny ever having had any dealings with him, and hand him over to God like worthy, virtuous children.

That was the rule of the game. One of the rules, at any rate.

"Come closer, *cher ami*."

Thorn brought his chair forward by two hundred and sixty-seven centimeters, and sat back down, with a grating of metal. He was now very close to them.

The woman slid forward, all rippling hair and fabric. If Thorn had even a modicum of imagination, he would have thought her made of liquid gold. She held her arms out to him in invitation. The first time she had done this, he had been unable to interpret it. Today, he knew exactly what she expected of him, just as he knew he couldn't get out of it. He held his own hands out to her. As soon as the woman's golden fingers combined with his, he felt his stomach heave. Physical contact disgusted him. There was just one exception to this rule, but he certainly didn't want to think about that—not here, not now.

"It's not important," whispered the woman. "*Ce n'est pas grave*. We know you're doing your best."

Ensconced among the sofa's cushions, the man was observing the scene with a certain relish. Beneath the gold tint, their skin was covered in goose pimples, visible to the naked eye.

Thorn asked himself the question very seriously: had he done his best? It seemed to him that, since escaping from prison, his existence had amounted to just repeated improvisations. He had resorted to his new family power to pass through the reflective surface of his cell, with no guarantee of it working. From there he had reemerged through the mirror in the library of his aunt, whose manor house had been uninhabited for weeks. Had he calculated that he would find provisional sanctuary and a reliable telephone line there? Absolutely not. It was animal instinct that had made him return to what, for him, came closest to a home. When he had contacted Vladislava, had he been convinced that the Invisible would help him to leave the Pole, in exchange for the services he had rendered her clan? A hundred times he had thought she would betray him. Indeed, he still struggled to believe that she hadn't. As for his choice of destination, he owed it simply to the unblocking of Farouk's unpredictable memory, which had been passed on to him.

The more Thorn considered the question, the more he felt that, no, he definitely hadn't done his best. He had been content, at most, to massage the statistics.

"We know that you are a highly resourceful man," the woman continued, tightening her fingers' grip. "You have already proved that to us, you will prove it to us again."

Thorn felt the first effects of the family power. It was as if needles were pricking into every pore on his hands. He forced the muscles of his face not to tense up. Not to show any discomfort. He must keep the woman and the man within his field of vision. Lie to his own family power.

"Dragon through your paternal line. You are, *sans doute*, thinking right now that this (the woman barely tightened her grip on his hands) is but an appetizer compared with the claws of your family."

Thorn thought nothing of the sort. There was no possible comparison between the pain inflicted by a Dragon, and that by a Tactile. The former comprised false information conveyed to the brain that the body then made manifest. The latter was an actual impulse transmitted from epidermis to epidermis, without anything showing on the surface.

The sensation in his hands intensified as it spread along his arms. It was no longer needles, it was nails. Rough, white-hot nails. Thorn focused all his concentration on the lounge clock (four thousand eight hundred and fifty-nine seconds), trying to persuade his claws that nothing special was happening, that this aggression was consented to, that he accepted this abuse of his body.

The woman studied his face avidly, searching for a crack in his impassive mask. She knew that Thorn couldn't use his claws against her, and, above all, that he needed them both too much in order to attain his objective.

"They say that Sir Farouk's daughter has really grown," commented the man, from the sofa cushions.

"Rare are the chosen few who have had the privilege of seeing your young cousin," added the woman.

"Dame Berenilde hides her from the world like her most precious treasure," they said, in unison.

For two seconds, a single tick and a single tock from the clock, Thorn's concentration slipped. Two seconds during which the pain penetrated deeper into his skin. He had to use all his cerebral control to stop the memory process that would take him back to the time when he was the indispensable pillar on which his aunt had rebuilt herself. He had been replaced, that was in the natural order of things. No one was waiting for him in the Pole anymore.

"Ask me the other question," he said.

The woman broke into an ambiguous smile. The pressure of her fingers became firmer around Thorn's. It was as though stinging nettles were growing beneath the skin of his entire body.

"Will you see your mission through?" asked the Genealogists.

"Yes."

"*Gentil garçon.*"

The woman released his hands and, as ever, Thorn couldn't help being disconcerted that his skin remained unblemished. The Tactiles' touch never left the slightest trace. After a final look at the clock (five thousand six hundred and two seconds), he turned his back on the two bodies entwined on the sofa, no longer paying any attention to him.

Their combined voices reached him one last time, just as he was closing the lounge door:

"We eagerly await your next visit."

Alone in the middle of the corridor, Thorn methodically unscrewed the stopper of his phial and disinfected his hands. Once. Twice. Thrice. The dirt was invisible, but he felt it in his very nerves, in his very claws, which quivered with contained hatred all around him.

No, no one was waiting for him in the Pole anymore, and that suited him.

As long as one particular person would be waiting for him elsewhere, that would suit him.

THE CONJURING TRICK

The parched lawn crunched under Ophelia's feet. As she made her way between the tombs and the fireflies, her pupils were as dilated as the moon in the sky. She had visited the cemetery in Anima in the past, and each time, upon entering, a great silence had descended on her. It was neither really serenity nor anxiety. It was more like the concentration of the tightrope walker, advancing on a wire between two absolutes.

What she felt here, in the observatory's necropolis in the middle of the night, was even less definable. She was almost forgetting to breathe. It was a very old military cemetery; indeed, the grid layout of the gravestones recalled the ranks of an army. Given that all those words were forbidden in Babel, Ophelia thought it couldn't be easy mentioning a place like this. No doubt it was never mentioned. It was enough to tolerate its presence, in a distant corner of the ark, like a neighbor one can't get rid of.

And yet, even here, the paths were cluttered with unusable objects, as if the Deviations Observatory was flooded by an excess of which it was itself the source.

Fascinating as the place was, Ophelia's eyes kept returning irresistibly to Thorn, who was leading the way in front of her. He had uttered not a word since they had left the antechamber. After descending the secret stairway of the colossus in silence, he had skirted the carousels in the old amusement park, crossed the rose gardens, away from the windows, and then pushed open the gate of the necropolis. He was now advancing with long strides, obliging Ophelia to double her own.

She was avoiding thinking about the blood that had stained his uniform, on the side Second had rushed at to give him her drawing. Thorn had been pretty laconic when telling her the circumstances of the accident, but Ophelia knew the essentials. Second had triggered the claws without him realizing it, and, although her life wasn't in danger, she would be permanently scarred. As would Thorn. Witnesses to the scene couldn't understand what had happened. No one would hold him responsible, but Ophelia knew him well enough to sense that he would have preferred to be. He saw himself being burdened with a guilt he could never clear himself of.

Changing how he saw himself, after that, was going to be trickier than ever.

They scaled a high wall that served as a barrier between the land and the void. Up there, on the sentry path, the wind was blowing wildly. Ophelia felt it slapping against the bare skin of her cheeks, arms, and calves. She didn't miss her long hair, or her old skirts. But she did miss her shoes: after all that running around, her feet were burning.

"Oh!" she blurted out.

She was struck by the view of the Good Family beyond the crenellations. Never had the minor ark seemed so close as from this observation point. One could see clearly the contours of the two twin islands, the one reserved for the Sons of Pollux, the other assigned to the Godchildren of Helen, linked by a highly symbolic bridge. The windows of the domes, the amphitheaters, and the gymnasium all reflected the moon.

Octavio must be sleeping somewhere, beneath all that

brightness. Unless he was tossing in his bed, wondering how to change the world from the inside. How would he react when he saw his little sister wounded? Ophelia's heart sank at the thought. Octavio's friendship was the best thing she had taken away from her time at the Good Family. How aware was he of Second's role at the Deviations Observatory? The inverts' fate depended on her next pencil mark, determining who remained in the first protocol and who left for the second, who would spin on carousels to the end of their days, and who would end up chained to a kneeling stool. Second was an accomplice of this place—whether voluntarily or not was another story. Was Lady Septima aware of this? Had she knowingly placed her daughter here, or had she lost control from the moment she rejected her?

In front of Ophelia, Thorn pointed at their destination: a pagoda that served as a corner tower to the wall. It fitted in so well, one barely noticed it. Wreathed in moonlight, it seemed surprisingly ordinary compared with the excessively florid architecture of the rest of the observatory. And yet, upon closer inspection, a very faint light was filtering through the shutters of its stacked stories. The light felt bright when Thorn slid open a door; Ophelia felt as if she were entering a lantern with him.

"It's here," he finally declared.

They were standing at the center of an octagonal room that formed the base of the pagoda. The light was coming from nightlights placed in cavities in the walls. Each one lit up an urn bearing a photograph. There were a considerable number of them.

A columbarium.

"All these ashes," continued Thorn, "belong to subjects who died at the observatory. They have never been claimed by any family."

Ophelia felt herself freezing up, as if necromancy were still having its effect on her. She had already experienced the dungeons in the Pole, but what surrounded her here was even more sordid. Were these urns where those who moved to the third protocol ended up? There were so many of them! The alcoves rose up over several stories, right up to the top of the pagoda, with dozens of stairways to reach them.

"Are we looking for . . . someone?"

"Something," replied Thorn, with a snap of his watch. "But first, let us pool our findings."

He'd certainly reverted to public-official mode. Ophelia was right about that. There was a newfound modesty to the way he shrank from her glasses as soon as their focus became too intense.

She decided to go first.

"We were right. The observers' black lenses allow them to visualize our family powers. But that's not all."

She swallowed. Eulalia Gonde's memory had enabled her to interpret the research she'd read in the collaborators' quarter. Now she had to translate all that into her own words. And doing so in this columbarium, surrounded by funerary urns, gave her a very peculiar feeling.

"Those shadows that encircle us, they are . . ." Ophelia searched for the right word. ". . . *projections* of our selves. When our shadows don't quite match, I think our projections likewise don't quite match, and end up returning to us in the form of echoes. A bit like an . . . a . . ."

Ophelia mimed the sweeping movement of a yo-yo.

"A gyroscopic precession," translated Thorn.

"Precisely. And due to a ricochet effect, the inverts' shadows affect the shadows of all that surrounds them, which generates even more echoes. When an ark collapses, it produces an even greater disturbance. In the end, it matters little whether we call that 'shadow,' 'projection,' 'propagation,' or 'echo,' it's one and the same thing. Aerargyrum."

"Aerargyrum," repeated Thorn, seemingly annoyed not to hold that word in his memory's library.

"At any rate, that's the name given to it by the observatory. It's a matter so fine, it's indiscernible to the naked eye. It can . . . how can I put it . . . be *converted* into solid matter if certain circumstances are combined. That's what Eulalia Gonde succeeded in doing by creating the family spirits. That's what the observatory wants to reproduce today within the framework of Project Cornucopianism. An authentic Horn of Plenty," whispered Ophelia, her voice trembling, "that would produce limitless resources. Except they can't manage to do that. Everything they produce is faulty, because they are missing what Eulalia Gonde had: they're missing the Other."

Ophelia clenched her hands, which the observatory had made even clumsier and more wayward than ever.

"The inverts attract the echoes. And the observatory exacerbates our inversions so that one of us invokes the most powerful echo of them all."

She lowered her eyes, without closing them entirely, the better to probe that second memory she was harboring.

"The Horn of Plenty needs echoes to function. These echoes respond to their own laws and logic, and only an echo could explain them to us, had it only the gift of speech. From the moment Eulalia Gonde established a dialogue with her own echo, the Other, she developed a better understanding of the world in general, and the echoes in particular. It's this understanding that allowed her to use the Horn of Plenty to its full potential. And it's this understanding that the observatory covets."

Ophelia screwed up her eyes even more. What were the

only three things Eulalia Gonde had needed, again? *Words, echoes, and some compensation.*

"The faulty objects, like the family spirits, are echoes converted into matter. They have in common the need for a code to be embodied. On a tart pan, I discovered writing similar to that inside the Books. Elizabeth thinks she has been hired to decipher the Books and help out the family spirits. In reality, the observatory wants to create an equivalent code for its own use. As long as this code isn't itself perfect, their Horn of Plenty will produce only faulty goods."

Ophelia then mentioned the files she had looked through; the split that Second had drawn in the shoulder of her shadow; the vision of Eulalia Gonde she had succeeded in triggering; her unexpected visit to the nave of the second protocol; and Mediana's forced expiation in order to "crystallize."

When she opened her eyes wide, once she had finished, she realized that Thorn was staring intensely at her, in the hypnotic glow of the nightlights. His eyes glinted with some turmoil that, yes, looked almost like envy.

"Good work."

Ophelia blushed right up to her glasses. A compliment, coming from Thorn, was quite something.

"There are still many questions without answers," she said. "I feel that this Horn of Plenty is itself just the surface of something subterranean, something much bigger, and that's what scares me. We know practically nothing about this aerargyrum that surrounds us. And then there's this 'crystallization' that seems indispensable to the Project. It's the whole point of the second protocol, but I haven't grasped at all what it consists of. Might it have something to do with that split that Second detected on my shadow?" Ophelia murmured, massaging her shoulder in search of some invisible fracture. "Since she drew one on me, I'm forecast for transfer."

Thorn dismissed this with a flick of the hand, as if these were but minor details.

"Our objective was to find out how Eulalia Gonde turned herself into God, and her reflection into an apocalypse. We now know that the very function of the Horn of Plenty is to convert. *To convert*," he repeated, punctuating the three syllables with his index finger, "not to *create*."

Ophelia agreed. There was an infectious energy in Thorn's every sentence. It was hard to speak of enthusiasm when it came to him, but it was surprisingly close.

"Eulalia wasn't content merely to convert echoes into family spirits," he continued. "She seems to have reversed the experiment. She converted herself. She gave herself all the characteristics of an echo in order to reproduce any face and any power."

"That conversion could have affected the Other at the same time," said Ophelia, feeling her excitement rise. "It may be that conversion that took place in the walled-in room at the Memorial. And it may be that conversion that triggered the Rupture. The one conversion too many."

"If we know how Eulalia Gonde did it, we will know how to undo it," Thorn reminded her. "For now, she and the Other remain discreet, but for how much longer? Our next step, here and now, is to find the Horn of Plenty."

Ophelia gazed at the urns in their alcoves, lining the entire pagoda.

"In this columbarium?"

An appalling screech made her jump. Thorn's leg brace had jammed again, as he negotiated some stairs.

"Forty years ago," he explained, while releasing his leg, "this observatory underwent extensive renovation work. The setting up of the Alternative Program, and its three protocols, goes back to that period. As do the electrical installations. I explained to you that the observatory's meters didn't tally with the readings I had been given. During my surprise inspection, no member of staff could, or would, tell me where the surplus electricity went. All I got, repeatedly, was, *'Désolé.'*"

The higher Thorn climbed, the deeper his voice got. The pagoda's varnished wood turned him into a double bass.

Ophelia tried to follow him from one set of stairs to the next, but tiredness and lack of sleep made her feet increasingly uncoordinated. She ended up losing sight of him. The countless rows of urns had the deceptively labyrinthine logic of a library. A macabre library.

"What led you to this columbarium?"

"Lady Septima's daughter," replied Thorn's distant voice, from a corridor. "Indirectly, at least. After throwing herself into my claws, she was taken urgently to the Alternative Program's infirmary. I accompanied her. At a distance," he specified, after a pause. "I was keen to make sure . . . you know."

His sentences became stilted. Ophelia felt her stomach lurch. Thorn had never hidden his aversion to children, but having harmed one today weighed heavy on him. Maybe a part of him didn't entirely reject the notion of having some one day?

His voice moved with him around the pagoda:

"I found myself in a waiting room, along with an automaton in charge of maintenance. An old model. It wore me out with its endless sayings. One of them, however, got my full attention."

Ophelia, trying to follow him by ear, went from one stairway to the next.

"What did it say?"

Thorn's voice, wherever he was, went down another octave.

"'THERE ARE PEOPLE WHOM THE PUBLIC THINK DEAD BUT WHO AREN'T.'"

Ophelia frowned. Certainly, Lazarus had implanted all sorts

of dubious proverbs into his automatons, but that one was unlike any she'd heard before.

"It was repeating something it must have heard here, in the observatory," continued Thorn. "When I asked it for details, it was unable to give them, instead offering me a recipe for eggplant caviar. I thought back to what you told me about the third protocol: those transferred to it never return. And I had memorized this columbarium from the plan."

Suddenly, Ophelia felt as if she were being judged by the portraits of the deceased, lit by the nightlights, all around her. *People whom the public think dead but who aren't.*

"Would these funerary urns be empty, then?"

Somewhere, the click of a watch cover, followed by a matter-of-fact answer:

"Evidently not. But I wouldn't affirm, for all that, that these ashes derive from human bodies."

"If the people in these photographs aren't dead," muttered Ophelia, "what has become of them?"

Thorn's metallic steps stopped.

"Does nothing strike you?" he asked, after a moment's silence.

Ophelia felt that everything here struck her. A potentially phony columbarium. The faces of men, women, and children who had just vanished into thin air. Lives conjured away.

"The bulbs," she said, finally understanding.

Here, there was a whole network of nightlights, and none was flickering, none crackling. This little pagoda, forgotten in a corner of the ark, on the very edge of the void, was better supplied with electricity than the entire observatory.

"I am firmly convinced that the Horn of Plenty is close by," commented Thorn. "If it converts the echoes into matter, it requires a large source of energy."

Ophelia agreed, but it was one thing having this knowledge,

quite another making use of it. Was the Horn of Plenty part of these funerary urns? It must be immeasurably bigger. And all these people whom the observatory made out to be dead . . . could they be the compensation Eulalia Gonde had spoken of?

The idea was terrifying.

Ophelia half-opened the inside shutter of a window. Behind the glass, the neighboring ark of the Good Family appeared clearer to her from here than from the wall. No, it was the night that was less dark: the stars were fading, dawn was arriving. Ophelia absolutely had to be in her bed when the nanny-automaton came to wake her.

"We don't lead the life of a conventional couple."

Thorn had said this as a statement of the obvious, just as Ophelia had finally located him on the top story of the pagoda. He was carefully disinfecting his hands, doubtless due to all the urns he had opened and closed to check their contents. His eyes were now following the course of an electricity cable along the beams.

"I like us not being conventional," she assured him.

She noticed, not without surprise, that Second's blood had vanished from his uniform. Thorn's fussy animism was already working, ensuring there was never a stain on, or crease in, any of his clothes. Ophelia, on the other hand, was battling with the caprices of her animism. Ever since she had got her glasses back, they had kept scarpering, obliging her to keep perching them back on her nose.

Thorn frowned as he lost track of his cable when it entered the ceiling, and then turned his stern eyes onto Ophelia.

"Earlier on, in the antechamber, you used your claws on mine. I would rather you didn't do that again."

"Did I hurt you?"

"No."

Thorn's tone had become harsh. Somewhat embarrassed, too.

"No," he repeated, less harshly. "In fact, I didn't know that Dragons' claws could be used for anything but wounding. But you won't always be by my side to regulate my power. It's for me to regain control of it. There are some problems we can only solve alone."

Ophelia knew that he was right, that she had been unwise to combine her deviant power with Thorn's uncontrollable one. Her less rational side, however, resisted the notion that their "we" wasn't enough to overcome all adversity.

"Up there," she said.

Barely visible, a crack in the ceiling indicated the existence of a trapdoor. There was no pole around to open it from the ground, but Thorn merely had to stretch his arm. With a look of annoyance, he pulled down a foldaway ladder.

"It's impossible for me to go up on that."

Ophelia didn't need persuading to climb up the rungs, even if coordinating her left side with her right proved even trickier than on stairs. Thorn had just stated that some problems could only be solved alone. She felt the need—a little childishly, admittedly—to prove to him that others could only be solved together.

She felt her way to pull the cord of a ceiling bulb, which, once on, projected a weak halo of light under the rafters. More funerary urns! There was nothing there, at first sight at any rate, resembling a Horn of Plenty.

"I'm going to take a closer look," she said. "Keep looking down there."

"Ophelia."

Inquiringly, she poked her head back through the trapdoor. Thorn's chiseled face looked up at her with a strangely solemn rigidity.

"Me, too," he said, after clearing his throat. "I like us not being conventional. A little more than that, even."

It was with an entirely inappropriate smile that Ophelia ventured among all the funerary objects. The urns and photographs appeared much older than those on display in the columbarium. Had they been stored up here due to a lack of space? The floorboards weren't polished, either, causing Ophelia to grimace every time she got a splinter in a toe.

Here, surrounded by ashes that may never have belonged to anyone, she thought again of the Other. The deeper she delved into the Deviations Observatory's and Eulalia Gonde's secrets, the less she was able figure him out. In her mind, he had no particular face. He was that voice that had asked her to release him from the mirror. He was that stranger that had messed up her insides. He was that mouth that gobbled up pieces of ark. He was that silence down the telephone that hadn't answered her call.

How could such a discreet creature have such a dramatic effect on the world? Since exiting the mirror, had the Other kept his ethereal, aerargyrum substance, or had he found a lasting bodily form for himself? And if the Horn of Plenty could convert echoes into matter, could it also reverse the process, as Thorn supposed? Would they, thanks to the Horn, be able to return the Other to his condition of echo, and Eulalia to hers of human? And above all, would they do it in time? And on their side, had Archibald, Gail, and Fox succeeded in finding the elusive LandmArk? Would they manage to persuade Janus and the Arkadians to join forces with them? Mastering space, that meant locating anyone and hiding anywhere; in short, it meant having a decisive advantage over an adversary. But what if that power ended up in Eulalia Gonde's hands? Then they would have to confront not only an apocalyptic echo, but also an omnipotent megalomaniac . . .

In the middle of all her questions, Ophelia stopped dead in front of one of the urns gathering dust. Shocked. With her glove, she wiped the old photograph that was on it, revealing a young man with gentle, antelope eyes.

Ambrose.

His arms and legs weren't reversed, he was standing perfectly upright, and yet, despite all these contradictions, Ophelia felt absolutely sure this was Ambrose. The name itself featured clearly on the urn's plaque, with a date of death going back forty years.

There are people whom the public think dead but who aren't.

Ophelia's breathing quickened. It was him, the invert who had been cut out of the old photograph in the directors' apartments. One could just see an arm, around his shoulders: the arm of the young man posing with him and the other inverts, in front of a carousel. Ophelia now understood why he had seemed so familiar to her. It was Lazarus, forty years younger.

Father and son at the same place and at the same age.

Ophelia was mired in confusion when, suddenly, she saw something move. She spun around on her bare feet, searching the loft's every nook and cranny. It wasn't an optical illusion. Someone was there, just a few steps away, where the light from the bulb didn't reach. Ophelia could make out only the outline.

The silhouette moved slowly. It didn't move around, but made silent sweeping gestures, like a mime artist. It pointed at the ceiling with its right hand and at the floor with its left, then at the floor with its right hand and at the ceiling with its left. Sky and earth, earth and sky, sky and earth . . .

It was the stranger in the fog.

As unbelievable as it seemed, it had found Ophelia again.

"Who are you?"

Determined, finally, to see its face, Ophelia plunged into the dark recess of the loft. The stranger dodged her with a simple somersault, gave a playful bow, and then disappeared, with a single leap, through the trapdoor. It moved so fast!

Ophelia scrambled down the loft's ladder. The corridor on that story was deserted. There were only urns there. She met the disconcerted gaze of Thorn, who had come to the bottom of the nearest stairway, alerted by the racket she had made.

"There's someone here," she whispered to him.

"I've seen no one."

If the intruder hadn't gone down, they couldn't, humanly, be far away. Had they gone up onto the roof?

Ophelia pulled open a shutter and awkwardly tried to slide open the window, searching through the glass for a shadow among all those that lurked as night ended.

She stiffened on noticing her own reflection. The reflection of someone dying. She was covered in blood. Even the scarf around her neck—a scarf she knew she wasn't wearing right now—was spattered with it. There was no longer either a window or a pagoda or urns, only nothingness. A nothingness that had swept everything away apart from her, Eulalia Gonde, and the Other.

Thorn's hand on her shoulder brought her back to reality.

"What's going on?"

Ophelia hadn't the slightest idea. The vision had vanished like a dream, but the nausea wouldn't go away. She had the inexplicable feeling that all her senses had detected some huge anomaly, out there, that she hadn't been able to assimilate.

Thorn looked out of the window himself. His steely eyes instantly froze, as if magnetized by a point in the sky. Except that, right there, there was nothing. Only then did Ophelia understand the signal her senses had sent her.

The Good Family had disappeared.

Just then, the emergency sirens blared across the entire observatory.

In the Wings

On top of the columbarium pagoda, on the highest of its stacked roofs, perched on the pinnacle like a heron, he listens to the sirens. An explosion of echoes. At once a song and a cry. One less bit of world, one!

He smiles at the dawning day.

Poor Ophelia, what a face she must be pulling . . . Can't say she wasn't warned.

VERSO

THE UNSPEAKABLE

The plummeting of the ark into the sea of clouds had triggered an upsurge such as Ophelia had never witnessed before. It was an almost static tornado, roaring with thunder and lightning, dense as a volcanic eruption, that formed a chasm of darkness against the pale light of morning. The very temperature of the air had fallen by several degrees.

Collaborators, inverts, and automatons were all jostling to evacuate the buildings. They were charging in all directions, screaming under the sirens, issuing contradictory orders—in short, panicking. The Deviations Observatory, until then all hushed voices and closed doors, had turned into one almighty din.

"I underestimated the Other," Thorn admitted.

Ophelia tore herself from the apocalyptic spectacle to turn to him, squeezed into their hiding place. They had hurriedly left the columbarium and necropolis, fearful of being discovered over there, and, especially, of being discovered together. They had then found themselves stuck in the middle of the old amusement park, where a group of collaborators had gathered to gaze at the column of clouds cleaving the sky. They had had no choice but to hide in the stand known as "the Fakir's Game."

"Until today, Eulalia Gonde was, for me, our most toxic enemy. I shall consider revising my priorities."

Thorn's sangfroid impressed Ophelia. She, on the other hand, was shaking all over with a mix of fear, exhaustion, and rage. Particularly rage. An internalized anger that darkened her glasses, hummed like a hive under her skin, and covered up what, above all, she didn't want to feel.

"That intruder I saw at the columbarium, he's been hovering around me since the first landslide. He always knows where to find me, and then promptly disappears. I'm really wondering whether it isn't . . ."

Her throat tightened so much, the end of her sentence got stuck there. The loathing she felt for the Other constricted her lungs. Her trapped breath screamed, like the sirens, inside her, clamored for justice, demanded vengeance, despite Ophelia banishing from her thoughts the very origin of this pain.

He was alive. *He* had to be. As long as his name wasn't spoken, *he* would continue to be.

"Certainly," said Thorn, "'that intruder' seems to be taking a close interest in our investigation. Maybe he, too, is searching for the Horn of Plenty. Whoever he may be, and whatever he may want, it's up to us to find him before the next landslide."

Ophelia couldn't help thinking they had wasted too much time. They should have already sent the Other back into a mirror and put a stop to his crimes.

She also couldn't help thinking of that reflection in the window. Of the blood. Of the final reunion. Of the void everywhere, all around, within. What if some echoes really did come from the future? Should she speak to Thorn about this?

He was just unfolding the plan of the observatory, which he had kept with him. Too big for the restricted dimensions of the stand, he was struggling to avoid the nail-covered planks surrounding them. The first light of day filtering into the tent made his scars, and ascetic emaciation, more prominent, as though he were the Fakir himself.

"The columbarium was our best lead," he said, pointing at the pagoda on the plan. "We explored every level and saw nothing noteworthy. Nothing," he added, his voice leaden, "apart from the funerary urn of a kid who manifestly is no kid."

Ophelia nodded. It had been a shock, falling on that forty-year-old photograph. Ambrose was also linked, one way or another, to Project Cornucopianism. Lazarus likewise. She would have a few questions to ask them, once she was out of this confounded observatory.

She peered through a gap in the tent. Those evacuated were all gathering near the tiger carousel, but the sirens prevented her from hearing them. Someone would end up noticing that Ophelia was absent at roll call. She must decide quickly. Once the sirens stopped, everything would return to how it was: the programs, the protocols, the screenings, the photographs, the carousel circuits, the adulterated food, the silence, the secrets, the solitude . . . The whole world could collapse, but the Deviations Observatory would continue its quest for the absolute to the end. It alone contained the solution to the problems, but Ophelia seriously doubted that their motives were the same.

"The second protocol," she declared. "I'm going to return there and find out what they are doing to Mediana. I can't see her among those evacuated, she must still be in the nave. The observatory wants to use her for the Horn of Plenty; I need to understand how and why."

To her great surprise, Thorn agreed without even attempting to dissuade her. At that moment, she felt a boundless gratitude toward him. She was grateful to him for being so steady in front of her, so present among those absent, so alive, above all.

"From the second to the third protocol, there is merely a step," he reminded her, all the same. "We don't know what became of the 'people whom the public think dead but who aren't.'"

"I have no intention of allowing myself to be indoctrinated," Ophelia assured him. "I'll return to the first protocol, wait until this evening, and from tonight, go over the wall. Literally," she added, with an apprehensive thought for the transcendium bordering the void. "I'll meet with you again before dawn, in the directors' apartments. With a bit of luck, I will finally have discovered how to put an end to . . . to all this."

With her chin, she indicated the black clouds endlessly accumulating in the sky. A stormy gale, similar to the one rumbling inside her, began to lift the flaps of the tent.

Thorn studied Ophelia more attentively, as if he sensed that what was essential hadn't been expressed.

"Where is the second protocol located?" he asked, handing her the plan.

Try as she might to lighten the glasses on her nose, it was no good.

"I can't locate it," she said, pointing at an empty area beside the collaborators' quarter. "It should be just there. There were endless stairways, and then the nave. I walked along it for tens of meters without even glimpsing the end of it . . . Could it be a distortion of space, like Mother Hildegarde used to do? I know she once lived in Babel, but I wasn't expecting to find one of her doings here."

The shadow between Thorn's eyebrows increased, but he folded away his plan with the same care he took with everything.

"Whatever happens, I won't be far away. I am going to take advantage of recent events to prolong my on-site inspection. Proceed with an inventory of fixtures, check the state of the ark, those kinds of duties."

The sirens went quiet. The silence was almost a blow.

"I must rejoin the others," muttered Ophelia.

"And I must leave right away," declared Thorn, with a snap of his watch. "I'm not supposed to be in the containment zone."

Contrary to his own words, he didn't move a muscle. He frowned at his large, inert feet that refused to obey orders. Yet again, there they were: two conflicting forces pitted ruthlessly against each other, making Thorn's attitude to everything strangely subdued. The muscles in his neck had tightened once again around what he didn't want to say.

Seeing him like this, Ophelia felt her legs, shoulders, eyelids, everywhere go weak, as the same unspoken words gripped her inside. Let's run away. Now. You and me.

She pulled off her gloves, removed her glasses, which finally became clear again, and gave them back to Thorn.

"Before dawn," she repeated.

"I won't be far away," he repeated.

They separated. Ophelia gripped the ground with all her toes, determined not to give this ark a single reason to weaken like the others, and then she ran off to join those assembled. Now that the sirens had stopped, the air hummed with answerless questions. What was the extent of the latest landslide? What had caused it? Who had been affected by the catastrophe? Was the Deviations Observatory still a safe place? Should one stay or leave? None of them dared raise their voice anymore.

Ophelia had to elbow her way between the collaborators, all whispering so quietly among themselves that it was impossible to hear what they were saying. Some were in pajamas instead of the formal habit, but they had all found time to pull on their hoods during the evacuation of the quarter, professional to the end. At least Ophelia was able to slip among the inverts on the Alternative Program without attracting any attention.

Only Cosmos turned his almond-shaped eyes toward her, as if watching out for her. He approached her, while still keeping a distance; he was weighed down enough with his own anxiety, without having to take on that of all the others.

"Where were you? They triggered the automatic opening of the doors for the evacuation. When I went to rind you in your fume . . . find you in your room, you'd disappeared."

"I was here," Ophelia replied, evasively. "Do we know who was . . . over there?"

She couldn't detach herself from the hypnotic escalation of the clouds, darkening the sky and seeming about to crash down on the observatory like a tidal wave. She tried not to put into precise words what had caused this phenomenon; to banish images of the ark—for a time, her home—that had vanished; above all, not to name those—the one—who had been swept away by the sinking of the Good Family.

"No, *mademoiselle*. No one's saying anything. Apart from him."

"Him" was the old man on the Alternative Program. He was standing a few steps away, very calm in the midst of the general bustle. His white hair danced in the wind and fell onto his craggy face. It was the first time Ophelia was seeing him not hitting his left ear. On the contrary, he appeared to be listening, with total serenity, to the whole of space behind the whispers, and kept repeating, at regular intervals, the same sentence:

"They went up down below."

As for the nanny-automatons, they just stood around, swinging their arms and awaiting instructions. They made an incongruous spectacle, with their broad, fake smiles surrounded by terrified faces. They were so full of echoes that all that came out of them was "CHÉ . . . CHÉ . . . CHÉ . . . CHÉ," never reaching the ". . . RIS . . . RIS . . . RIS . . . RIS."

Their recording mechanisms had probably stopped working, which was no bad thing in itself.

As discreetly as possible, Cosmos rubbed some soil between his hands and smeared enough on his shoulder to cover the "AP" tattoo.

"Time to pack the bags, *mademoiselle.*"

He indicated a small segment of sky that was still blue, behind the giant head of the colossus. By screwing up her eyes, Ophelia could make out a strangely glinting dotted line. Airships. An entire fleet of airships.

"The spoilt brats on the standard program will be fermented by their calories . . . collected by their families. It'll be chaos, all doors flung open. Won't get a chance like that again. You with me on this?"

"No."

Ophelia had replied without hostility, but also without hesitation. Her objective was to melt into the background until the following night. This definitely wasn't the right moment to get involved in an escape attempt.

Cosmos came closer, despite the risk of emotional contamination.

"The observatory is in crisis, *mademoiselle.* They're going to accelerate everything. I'm not the ideal friend, but I'm still less dangerous than war that rotates you leer . . . all that awaits you here."

Ophelia didn't need her glasses to notice the guilt making his ink-black eyes shine. It was right here, beside this carousel, that he had attacked and bitten her. Did he think she was angry with him?

"You told me you had nowhere else to go," she whispered to him. "If one day you get the chance to visit Anima, a door there will always be open to you."

Cosmos gave a faint smile that briefly uncovered his white

teeth and put a little color back in his cheeks. Then he left the assembly walking backwards, one step after another so as not to be noticed, becoming increasingly blurred in Ophelia's eyes, until he had disappeared completely. He was gone.

In the distance, the first airships were preparing to land. One could almost hear from there all the most prestigious families of Babel charging around the corridors of the observatory to get their children back home. Now was no longer the time for re-education. Territories were collapsing, one after the other; all families wanted was to stay together and never be apart again.

Ophelia focused all her attention on her bare feet in the middle of the gravel. Don't think about Thorn. Don't think about mother, father, sisters, brother, great-uncle, Aunt Rosaline, Berenilde, little Victoria, Archibald, Fox, Gail, Blaise, the scarf, Ambrose, whoever he really was—about all the people she desperately wanted to be close to right now.

Don't think about *him*.

There was another long wait, during which several rumblings of thunder crazed the sky, and then, finally, someone appeared. What, to Ophelia, was just a vague yellow figure had just climbed onto the platform of the carousel and now stood among the wooden tigers, looking down on everyone. Seeing this, the whispering, guiltily, stopped.

"I have two statements to make to you all."

It was the voice of the beetle woman. Ophelia hadn't heard from her since she had given her that strange advice that she still couldn't fathom: "If you really want to understand the other, first find your own."

"The first is a reminder," the woman continued. "All of you here present, both subjects and collaborators, are contractually bound to the Deviations Observatory. You will therefore remain within this containment zone for as long as the Alternative Program continues. *D'accord?*"

Ophelia couldn't see her face clearly, partly due to the pince-nez, but her voice seemed to have lost its confidence. The mass intrusion of families into the Standard Program wing probably had something to do with it. Cosmos was right, the observatory was in crisis. But if the directors didn't exist, who was managing this crisis?

"The second is an announcement. We have just received a visit from an official representative of Sir Pollux. He is not authorized to enter the containment zone to speak to you all, but, given the exceptional nature of the situation, I have agreed to be his spokesperson. I have the painful duty to inform you that a climatic event, of as yet indeterminate origin, has swept away the Good Family ark. Along with all the students who resided there," the woman added, after a pause. "Our beautiful city has lost not only its future virtuosos, but the very place that allowed them to achieve such excellence. It is an immense loss to us all. To those who had loved ones among the victims, we convey our deepest sympathies."

The silence that followed took on the consistency of rock. Hard and dense. Barely affected by the nanny-automatons' "CHÉ . . . CHÉ . . . CHÉ . . . CHÉ"s.

Even the old man shut up, after a final, "They went up down below."

The beetle woman's black lenses were then lowered toward a particular point, and all eyes swiveled in the same direction. Squatting on the ground, face shrouded by hair, Second was drawing away, indifferent to the attention suddenly being turned on her. She was dressed in a simple infirmary shift.

Ophelia felt as if she were taking on the same consistency as the silence. It was no longer saliva she was swallowing, it was stones. Despite all her efforts not to name *him*, to give *him* a last chance to exist, Octavio had fallen into the void.

"That is not all," continued beetle woman, her tone even more ponderous. "I regret to inform you all that, *malheureusement*, Lady Helen was also on site when the tragedy occurred."

"No!"

The cry had burst out from the hood of a collaborator. It was Elizabeth. She was bent double, clutching her arms, as if she had been punched in the stomach. Her yelp of pain soared right across the amusement park, bounced off the metal frames of the carousels, and caused the panicked flight of a flock of pigeons. It shot right through Ophelia, causing her actual pain. This distress overwhelmed her, replacing the distress she wasn't able to express. And yet, as the other collaborators turned away from Elizabeth, she was the only one able to understand her.

Today, the two of them were both orphaned of someone.

The three of them.

Ophelia felt compelled to go over to Second, who was drawing feverishly. She was in her own world, as usual. There was no one to say a word to her, no one to make a gesture toward her, no one to tell her the truth.

Octavio would have hated that.

Ophelia leaned over Second.

"Your brother," she said to her.

How? How to speak the unspeakable? The clouds just wouldn't stop darkening over the world.

"He won't come back."

Second finally looked up. Under that mane of dark hair, her dissymmetry was more startling than ever. Half of her face—the half with the gold chain linking eyebrow and nostril—was convulsed with nervous tics; the other half, contrastingly still, featured a wide-open, inexpressive white eye. And bridging the two, a dressing soaked in blood ran across her nose and cheeks, from ear to ear. Merely opening her mouth must be horribly painful. Thorn's claws had left her with a scar that would be part of her from now on.

Ophelia swallowed another stone. She recalled the drawing she had thrown into the toilet. Second had done a self-portrait, scored with a long, premonitory red-pencil line across it; the same red pencil with which she had scribbled over Ophelia's body, stuck between the old woman and the monster, on the other side of the paper.

The red pencil she was holding at this precise moment. Her new drawing depicted a shadow torn in two.

She handed it to Ophelia, declaring solemnly:

"But this well was no more real than a rabbit of Odin."

There was a crunching of gravel. Collaborators, inverts, and nanny-automatons were all moving aside to let the beetle woman pass through. She came close enough for Ophelia to see clearly the metal insect gleaming on her shoulder. With a mechanical click, it held out a magnifying glass, allowing the observer to take a close look at the drawing.

She couldn't stifle a jubilant smile.

"Please follow us, Mademoiselle Eulalia. You are ready for the second protocol."

Hail fell from the sky.

The Loop

EXPIATION. CRYSTALLIZATION. REDEMPTION. Ophelia sensed the metal of the letters inlaid in the flagging under her feet, and the heady perfume from the censers all around her. She was moving between the nave's towering pillars with a feeling of extreme heaviness, rather like the hail that had almost knocked her out as a cortege of observers escorted her here. Hail that had no effect on this place. The silent stained-glass windows presented a stark contrast to the commotion outside.

This second protocol, where was it really located? Ophelia had been led here along a different route to that she had taken the first time. She had been led through an underground passage, before going back up a particularly narrow stairway. From then on, it was an endless succession of the same pillars, the same stained-glass windows, the same stoups, the same chapels.

She felt as if she were stuck in the microgroove of a record.

Since she no longer had her glasses to rely on, she prioritized her ears. The observers' clothing, drenched in rain, made a continuous drip-dripping sound that combined with the slap-slapping of their sandals. They formed a moving wall, all around her, pushing her relentlessly forward without touching her or speaking to her. There were many of them—too many for her to use her claws on them.

Ophelia had got herself into another fine mess. She wondered whether she would be taking Mediana's place on the kneeling stool, but she couldn't see her anywhere. Had the Seer been transferred to the third protocol? Would her fake funerary urn soon be joining all those lining the columbarium?

Ophelia should have been scared. The trap she had been so determined to avoid had just closed on her, and Thorn probably had no idea.

The cortege of observers stopped. All together, they formed an unavoidable yellow corridor leading to the door of one of the chapels. Their faces, alert behind their pince-nez, remained inscrutable; their arms, in their long leather gloves, made not the slightest movement. Ophelia had only a door handle to turn, but she had a lengthy struggle between right and left hand before managing to do so. No sooner had she gone through the door than it was closed behind her and locked with a key. That was it. No one had told her what was expected of her, just like for the first protocol.

Ophelia blinked repeatedly, trying to clear away the flood of colors catching in her lashes. Lit through the stained glass of an oculus, the chapel's cupola was composed entirely of reflectors that changed position every second, with a discreet mechanical hum. Ophelia immediately looked away from it. It was the same principle as the kaleidoscopic tunnel and the screenings: looking at it would mean further distorting her family power. Or even worse. She tensed her shoulders, hoping to prevent the split in her shadow predicted by Second's pencil. She hated the idea that the future could be told in advance, just as she hated the bloodied reflection that had imposed itself on her twice already, like a promise of imminent death. She couldn't see the "aerargyrum" made up of the shadows and echoes, but if it really was possible to convert it into matter, then she would shape the future *her* way.

The chapel was empty. No chairs, no tables, no cupboards, nothing.

Ophelia touched all the surrounding marble, looking for some crack as a way out, something to grip to hoist herself up toward the cupola. She succeeded only in breaking her fingernails. The only object she found, stored in a stone recess at floor level, was a chamber pot. Lurking inside it was a fetid liquid she preferred not to know too much about.

Evidently, she would be here for a while.

She noticed a strange relief, on the surface of the stone, right in the center of the flagging and under the light from the oculus. A figure lying on its back. A recumbent effigy? She approached cautiously to see it more clearly. The sculpture depicted a fleshless corpse, ribs in the air. It wasn't an effigy, it was a transfixed skeleton. Its hollow eye sockets stared at the play of the reflectors above, as if showing the example to follow: lying down and looking to the end of time.

There was an inscription carved into the flagstone its skull rested on:

"TRUTH IS A LIE THAT LISTENS TO ITSELF."

It was only then that Ophelia emerged from the torpor she had sunk into since the beetle woman's announcement. She suddenly became aware of the water dripping from her hair, of her tunic stuck to her skin, of her legs shaking, as if her own body were finally reminding her of its existence.

She was terrified. She had never ceased to be, but had become too estranged from herself to realize it, until now.

Before her, the hideous figure was bathed in the changing, clashing colors from the cupola. Ophelia closed her eyes. Instead of the transfixed skeleton, she saw the walkways, dormitories, corridors, and laboratories of the Good Family. She saw hundreds of students plummeting into the perpetual storms of the great void, where no one had ever been before.

She saw the conservatoire giving way to extreme pressure, she saw the gymnasium windows exploding, she saw furniture and bodies smashed to pieces.

She saw Octavio thrown against the ceiling of his room while sleeping. Chewed up by the invisible mouth of the Other.

Ophelia reopened her eyes to gaze at the slack jaw of the skeleton, depicted by the sculptor with a morbid realism. Was that stranger she had pursued in the columbarium really responsible for all those deaths, as she was starting to believe? If she had caught him in time, could she have prevented a new landslide? She hadn't managed to see his face once, and yet, at every encounter, he gave her an indefinable sense of familiarity.

"Who are you?" she muttered, as if he could hear her from here.

"WHO ARE YOU?"

Ophelia felt her stomach lurch: it was the distorted sound of her own voice. She hadn't noticed it, but the skeleton clutched a tiny automaton in its bony hands. A parrot. It had seemingly been designed to reproduce the first phrase it recorded.

"WHO ARE YOU?" it repeated in Ophelia's distorted voice. "WHO ARE YOU? WHO ARE YOU?"

Right. The recording was stuck on a continuous echo. Ophelia hit the parrot to stop it, but only succeeded in hurting herself. The echo was ricocheting against all the cupola's reflectors, combining its cacophony with that of the colors. This chapel was just like Eulalia's cellar: a place designed to be an echo chamber.

"WHO ARE YOU? WHO ARE YOU? WHO ARE YOU? WHO ARE YOU? WHO ARE YOU? WHO ARE YOU? WHO ARE YOU? WHO ARE YOU?"

It was hellish. Ophelia now fully understood what Ambrose

had meant when telling her that, of all Lazarus's clients, the Deviations Observatory placed the strangest orders with him. That, at least, wasn't a lie.

She hammered on the door of the chapel for a long while before finally hearing some sandals approaching. A spyhole opened onto a small grille at eye level—for someone of average height, at least. Ophelia had to stand on tiptoe to glimpse the black pince-nez of an observer.

"Let me out," she demanded.

No reply.

"WHO ARE YOU? WHO ARE YOU? WHO ARE YOU?"

"Make this machine shut up, then."

Silence, again.

Ophelia decided to lay her cards on the table.

"Alright," she said, loudly, to be heard over the parrot. "You have a Horn of Plenty that doesn't work. You need the Other, and, to draw him here, you need me. But why? What are your intentions? What will you do next? Just in case you haven't noticed, it's the fate of all the arks that's at stake, out there."

The observer again refused to respond. And yet, rather than simply ignoring Ophelia and closing the spyhole, he just stayed there, waiting. Waiting for what?

EXPIATION.

Was that what they wanted to obtain from Ophelia? Repentance? A confession? Renunciation? Did she, like Mediana, have to ask for forgiveness for all her mistakes? For all her transgressions since turning her back on her family, and on Eulalia Gonde's plans?

"One moment, please," she said.

She moved away, returned, and threw the contents of the chamber pot at the pince-nez. The spyhole closed with a furious slam.

"WHO ARE YOU? WHO ARE YOU? WHO ARE YOU?"

Ophelia sat against a wall, closed her eyes, and put her hands over her ears. Once again, anger was stronger than fear. She had wanted to return to the second protocol; now she was here, even if not in the way she had planned, she would finish what she had started. She would give them nothing more without getting some explanations.

Silence for silence, words for words.

Take it or leave it.

She takes it.

The sun. The fresh air. The open sea, above all.

Eulalia rose early this morning with the need to escape from her study. Yesterday, she finished her latest story. The typewriter keys hadn't even cooled down before she had thrown it all into the wastepaper basket, without even rereading what she'd written. It's the second typescript she's thrown away.

Where had this sudden dissatisfaction come from, then? Since her encounter with the Other, she has never stopped feeling inspired, about everything. Never. So, what is it?

Eulalia sniffs.

Feet in the sand, hands in pockets, and eyes on the ocean, she breathes in the sea air, painfully. The fault surely lies with those sinusitis attacks. It's hard to remain optimistic when one spends every night gasping for breath. Eulalia is still young, but she feels prematurely aged. She has offered half of her life to the Other.

"Blasted brat!" screams a voice.

Eulalia turns toward the peace school, which occupies nearly the whole island. *Her* school. She looks around for the caretaker, who is cursing louder and louder in Babelian; she finds him about five meters above the mimosa trees, in a state of levitation, hands gripping his turban so as not to lose it. He promises Ouranos the thrashing of the century if he doesn't bring him down immediately.

Their school. They have grown so fast . . . too fast. Already, they have all overtaken Eulalia in height, but they are still only children. Helen can't go anywhere without her roller skates. Belisama accidentally made a eucalyptus sprout up in his bed. Midas turned all the silverware in the kitchen into zebra dung. Venus secretly bred boa constrictors in the fourth-floor bathroom. Artemis made an identical replacement head for the statue of the soldier outside the school, only to decapitate it once again. The lighthouse is under repair since Djinn, Gaia, and Lucifer conspired to invent some new meteorological phenomenon. Janus . . . Where has he disappeared to again, that one?

Eulalia sniffs.

She blows her nose, without managing to clear it. This dissatisfaction, whatever its cause, seems greater as soon as her attention turns to the school. She gazes at the sea, and, in the distance, glowing red in the sunset, the mainland still, and forever, being rebuilt. The war is not far away. Wherever one goes, the war is never far away.

Eulalia reflects that they will need a guard to protect the school. A scarecrow. She'll catch the boat shortly to return to the observatory. Everyone's dead over there, since the great bombardment, just as the Other had predicted to her. The Horn of Plenty is hidden somewhere under the ruins, in a place known only to Eulalia from now on. She had promised herself not to convert anything else, but the children will need protection until they're fully mature. The caretaker, who's still cursing above the mimosas, is no spring chicken anymore.

As for Eulalia, she may have lost half of her life expectancy, but time will soon be stopping for her. Her entire reality will be changing.

She notices, while taking her walk, a large sandcastle; probably one of Pollux's, judging by the aesthetic finesse of its construction. She then realizes, somewhat disconcertingly, that she's tempted to give it a good kick.

"Gonde?"

Eulalia looks up at Odin. She hadn't heard him coming. He is standing back a little, looking sideways, shoulders hunched, as if he felt he was taking up too much space, his large body a splash of white on the red beach. He is splendid . . . and so imperfect. Eulalia feels like both shooing him away and hugging him; she does neither.

"I would like to submit something to you."

He expresses himself in Eulalia's mother tongue, the language her deported parents spoke, that of a family that has disappeared, and of a distant land she can barely remember anymore. That language, if all goes according to her plans, will one day become the language of all humanity. Because war is when we stop understanding each other.

"With your permission," adds Odin, faced with her silence.

Eulalia sniffs.

This child is as quick to seek her opinion as he is to question it. When will he finally learn to hold his own, independently of her?

"Submit it to me," she replies.

Odin slowly straightens up, making himself even taller, his translucent eyes screwed up in concentration, like a piano pupil preparing to play a piece to his teacher he's practiced a hundred times. Between Odin's almost joined hands, a mist gradually gains substance until it's a tangible object. A box. He tries not to show it, but Eulalia notices, from the slight relaxing of his eyebrows, that he is relieved.

She takes the box from his fingers, tests its solidity, turns it over, then opens it. It's empty, of course.

"And? That's it?"

Odin seems taken aback by Eulalia's reaction. To tell the truth, she is as taken aback herself. It's the first time he's managed to stabilize an illusion; he must have practiced a lot to push the limits of his poor imagination this far.

She must encourage him, he's on the right path.

"Pass me your Book," she says, instead.

Odin's face dissolves like snow, but already he's pulling out, from under his jacket lapel, the work he's never without. He tries, in vain, to control this gesture with his other hand, subject to an internal struggle that's lost in advance. Like his brothers and sisters, he is programmed to obey its orders. Eulalia is well placed to know that, since it is she herself who created this line of instruction in each Book.

She pulls her faithful fountain pen out of her pocket and unscrews the cap with her teeth.

"Are you angry, Gonde?"

In Odin's eyes, which he is careful to keep averted, Eulalia detects a glint of hatred and love combined. He is unhappy that he disappointed her, as much as disappointed himself by her.

She turns the pages of the Book, conscious that she is touching Odin's most personal possession. She knows by heart each of the myriad symbols that make up the code she invented. One section controls Odin's motivity, another his ability to analyze, and yet another his perception of colors. She makes her choice, and stabs the metal nib into the flesh of the Book, ignoring Odin's stifled cry, accepting the pain she is inflicting on her own child. She crosses out a line of code, making sure she marks only what she wants to.

"You will eat without enjoyment," she said, returning his Book to him. "No caress will seem sweet to you. I have deprived you of your right to feel pleasure."

Odin hugs his censored Book to his chest. The sea breeze lifts his long, Polar locks. His wide-open eyes are filled with both disgust and adoration, but he is careful not to look straight at Eulalia. Despite what she has done to him, he doesn't want to hurt her with this power that he can't control.

"It's ordinary ink," Eulalia comments, while screwing the cap of her fountain pen back on. "It will fade with time. Use it to help me save the world."

Odin runs off, leaving behind him the imprint of his shoes in the sand.

Eulalia sniffs.

She takes off her glasses, more dissatisfied than ever, without understanding why. As she puffs on the lenses to wipe them, the setting sun is reflected in them, and, suddenly, she sees it: the reflection gives her a knowing wink.

Soon, says the Other.

Eulalia hurls her glasses as far away as she can. Her temples are throbbing madly. Her sinuses are hurting. Her head is going to explode. What is she becoming? Through taking herself for God, is she losing sight of herself?

It's not her study she's escaping from. It's the mirror that hangs in it.

"Soon," she murmurs, her voice shaking. "But not yet."

Ophelia sniffs.

She had woken with a start, breathless as if she had been running, gripped by a sudden feeling of falling upwards. For one moment, she thought the observatory itself was now collapsing. She sat up, numb from having dozed off on the flagstones. She couldn't feel her feet anymore.

"WHO ARE YOU? WHO ARE YOU? WHO ARE YOU?" the parrot continued to churn out.

The chapel was still there, immutable, its door stubbornly

shut. The same delicate light was filtering through the stained glass of the oculus, as if the sun had stood still. The only variations in the lighting were down to the cupola's mechanical reflectors, which Ophelia made sure not to look at. She felt headachy and thirsty. She had only a vague memory of her dream, but she had emerged from it with a stinking cold.

"You don't have a handkerchief, I suppose?" she asked the skeleton.

How long had she been locked up in this chapel? She had fought sleep, before being knocked out by it.

And there was Thorn, waiting for her return . . .

A sound of hinges drew her attention to the bottom of the door. A gloved hand was just sneaking through a flap to place a bowl on the floor. Ophelia rushed over to block the hatch with her thumb before it was reclosed. She hadn't been subtle about it, but there was no complaint, and already the slapping of sandals was moving off. Ophelia counted to a hundred, and then lifted the flap with as little clumsiness as possible. The opening was astonishingly wide for a food hatch. She contorted herself to stick her head through it, and quickly looked up and down the nave: it was deserted, as far as she could see.

She wriggled through the hatch, centimeter by centimeter. Had she been less slight, it would have been impossible. And yet she wasn't entirely shapeless. She heard her clothes ripping. Each time she got stuck, she emptied her lungs to gain a little space. The nave's acoustics were such that the hatch's hinges were making an awful racket.

Just don't sneeze right now.

Ophelia was almost surprised to find herself on the other side of the door without having attracted the attention of any observers. She had grazed her skin, but she had succeeded.

And now, which direction to go in?

To the left? Columns, chapels, rose windows.

To the right? Columns, chapels, rose windows.

Left, Ophelia decided. She ran through the smoky haze rising from the censers, with the feeling of losing herself in an eternity of marble and glass. Her myopia didn't do her any favors. If she did come across any observers, she would only see them at the last moment. She couldn't find the stairway she'd been forcibly escorted up. On the other hand, after endlessly running, she recognized a piece of her tunic, caught in the hatch of a chapel door. The muffled sound of her own voice was escaping through it:

"WHO ARE YOU? WHO ARE YOU? WHO ARE YOU?"

She had gone straight ahead, hadn't turned any corners, and, defying all logic, was back to where she had started. This nave was contained in a spatial loop. There could be no doubting it anymore: such architectural mischief could only be the work of Mother Hildegarde.

Ophelia set off in the other direction, determined to find the opening. There had to be one, to allow the initiated to come and go as they pleased. She flattened herself against a pillar that was sturdy as a tree, just to catch her breath. Her eyes then fell on a structure, tucked into a side aisle between two chapels, with yellow curtains.

A confessional. If she could just get to the mirror inside, like last time, she would be saved.

She rushed forward, no longer caring whether she was heard. Speed, not discretion, was of the essence right now. She banged her knee on a kneeling stool and fell into, rather than entered, the confessional.

She looked for her reflection, but instead of a mirror there was a grille. And behind the grille, a profile.

An adolescent was calmly leafing through a comic book.

"Really, miss," he said, stifling a yawn. "I had reckoned on it taking you less time."

He turned his bottle-bottom glasses, and his face tattooed with a big black cross, to Ophelia.

THE ROLE

Ophelia had last seen the Knight three years ago, at Farouk's court. He had been judged, mutilated, and then forcibly sent to Helheim, an establishment with a sinister reputation where the Pole's miscreants ended up.

"I'm not there anymore."

The adolescent had preempted the question, while licking his fingers to turn the page of his comic book. Ophelia didn't recognize his voice, it had broken so much. She had only a partial view of him due to the grille between them, but he seemed considerably taller to her. Blond curls spilled over his shoulders. Despite the black cross and thick glasses across his face, Ophelia could make out the bone structure that had replaced his childish chubbiness. She was able to check that he was indeed reflected in the varnished wood of the confessional, proving that he was neither Eulalia Gonde nor the Other.

The Knight shouldn't have been there. His presence in this nave, in this observatory, in this part of the world was, quite simply, impossible.

"It was you," whispered Ophelia. "All those setups—the exhibit from the museum, the automaton disguised as my mother . . . You handed my past to them on a plate."

The Knight's smile revealed braces.

"Of course. I promised it to them."

"To whom?"

Ophelia's ears were ringing. She was no longer conscious of her runny nose, or her swelling knee. The Knight had been deprived of his family power, he could no longer impose his poisonous illusions on her, but he was no less toxic for that. She should have run from this confessional as fast as she could.

"Who?" she insisted, sternly. "Who made you leave Helheim? Who is really running this observatory?"

The Knight closed his comic book, took his glasses off, and pressed his face to the grille, so hard that the lattice dug into his skin. He stared with eyes as pale as his cross was dark.

"Those, miss, who see the infinitely bigger picture! They spoke to me as no adult had ever spoken to me before. They gave me the second chance my own clan refused me."

Ophelia backed away when the Knight's fingers came through the grille to grip it.

"I waited such a long time . . . I counted every day in that horrendous establishment. Do you have any idea of just *how* cold I was, over there? I thought that she, at least, would visit me."

Coming from the Knight, "she" could only mean Berenilde. Ophelia noticed that his fingernails were bitten to the quick. His obsession with Berenilde hadn't abated with time.

"She did not come," he said, flattening his smile against the grille. "She abandoned me, but I, her knight, I will never abandon her. The day approaches when I will be able to fulfill all of her needs. They promised me plenty! We have at least that in common, miss, don't we? A loved one to protect."

Ophelia appreciated less and less the turn this conversation was taking—if it could be called a conversation. The Knight excelled at monologues; in that, too, he hadn't changed.

She lifted the curtain of her compartment and saw, with no

great surprise, that the confessional was circled by yellow figures. How stupid she had been! She had played her role to perfection. They had anticipated all of it, from her escape through the hatch to her hiding in the confessional. The message was clear: whatever she did, the observatory would always be one step ahead of her. One echo ahead, in fact. Second's premonitory drawings probably had something to do with that.

The Knight put his glasses back on and, with them, regained a little restraint.

"All of this is clearly part of the Project," he explained, with excessive politeness. "You have been participating in it for longer than you think. You are special to them—even though you remain, in my humble opinion, desperately ordinary. They were already very well informed about you, you would be amazed! All they expected from me were some details that were more . . . let's say more *significant* about your past. The value of Anima's museum in your eyes, your last day of work there, your complicated relationship with your mother, those kinds of little things."

Bothered by the stifling heat in the confessional, the Knight fanned himself with the comic book. Ophelia glimpsed some pink puppy dogs on the cover. She did her best not to show how sullied she felt.

"I have never confided in you."

"But you did confide in your great-uncle. I read every letter you wrote to him when you were in the Pole. What I know isn't very important," assured the Knight, as Ophelia's jaws clenched. "What matters is what *they* know. They knew, for example, that you would come to the observatory on your own initiative. It was just a matter of time, they said, all we have to do is wait. It needed to be *your* decision, do you understand, miss? The whole experiment depended on it. Just as it depends on what you're going to decide now. Either you're a good girl and return to your chapel, or we cause harm to Mr. Thorn. Or Sir Henry, whichever. My lady hardly reacted well to my decimating her clan; I would rather not harm her nephew."

Ophelia felt as if every drop of her blood was frozen. The Knight's words drilled into her chest. She should have run away with Thorn when they still could.

"I want to speak to him."

"That's impossible, miss. They have committed to no harm being done to him for as long as you show goodwill. They always keep their promises. Cross my heart!"

With his thumb, the Knight had traced the vertical and horizontal lines that darkened his face.

"Goodwill for what?"

"For expiating, for crystallizing, and for obtaining redemption. They say that you're *nearly* there, miss, but we can't complete that work on your behalf."

"I have no crime to expiate, no idea what crystallization is, and you can keep your redemption."

Ophelia's voice was as parched as she was. Anger was burning up what little moisture remained in her body.

The Knight's response gave nothing away:

"They say that you will discover all that for yourself."

"And Mediana? I know that she was here," said Ophelia, losing patience and throwing caution to the wind. "Has she crystallized? Has she found redemption? What have you done with her?"

The Knight shook his blond curls, looking annoyed.

"Your questions are devoid of interest. Personally, I can see only one that merits being asked. 'Miss Ophelia,' 'Artemis's girl,' 'Mrs. Thorn,' 'Mademoiselle Eulalia'," he listed, with an ever broadening smile, "that's a lot of roles for just one person. Without them, who are you really?"

He knocked three times on the wood of the confessional. A glove immediately lifted the curtain of Ophelia's section; the interview was over. The Knight had already dived back into his comic book, while gnawing at what remained of his fingernails.

Ophelia was returned, under escort, to her chapel. Her swollen knee made her limp, but she made it a point of honor to walk tall. She wouldn't let them see how shaken she was; absolutely not, she wouldn't allow them that satisfaction.

Once the door had been locked, she remained standing in the swirling colors of the chapel, as still as the transfixed skeleton, answering the parrot's "WHO ARE YOU?"s with stubborn silence. She had already lived through all kinds of experiences that had bruised her ego. She had been belittled by the Doyennes of Anima, humiliated by the courtiers of the Pole, rejected by the city of Babel . . .

Never had she felt ridiculed to this degree.

Down by the hatch, the bowl still awaited her. Rice broth, now cold. Ophelia had to lift the bowl with both hands, she was shaking so much. She would have liked to throw it through the spyhole; she drank it. She would have liked to scream loud enough for Thorn to hear her; she kept quiet.

She turned over the empty bowl. The meal had been as ghastly as all those in the first protocol. If she'd had a magnifying glass, she might have seen microscopic letters printed on the porcelain. With each mouthful, she had swallowed a former echo converted into matter. Her stomach was protesting. This Horn of Plenty was definitely far from perfect.

What if the observers ended up achieving it, that perfection? If they proved capable of producing endless edible food, drinkable water, working objects, or even lands that didn't collapse? If they decided to turn themselves into new gods?

They would then be as powerful as Eulalia and the Other. As dangerous, too.

But who really was the brains behind them, in the end?

"WHO ARE YOU? WHO ARE YOU? WHO ARE YOU?"

The bowl slipped from Ophelia's fingers and broke into pieces at her feet. It instantly evaporated, returning to being aerargyrum, now that its code was shattered—just like with the old sweeper of the Memorial when the hunting rifle's bullet punctured the plate on his forehead. Ophelia felt hungry and thirsty again, as if she'd never had any broth. She rubbed her tongue on her palate, but the unpleasant taste had disappeared.

She gazed at the flagging, and the iridescent colors dancing on it. She now understood that this chapel was an improved version of the cellar with the telephone. What had taken Eulalia Gonde months would be accelerated here. The moment Ophelia looked up at the mechanical reflectors, she would be condemning her shadow. Would she survive that?

She suddenly remembered that strange vapor that had left the Knight's body when Farouk had withdrawn his family power. Had she seen aerargyrum at the time without realizing it? Was that what crystallizing was? Relinquishing part of oneself? How would that enable the perfecting of the Horn of Plenty? Until now, Ophelia had thought the observatory used the inverts to attract the Other by recreating the conditions of his encounter with Eulalia Gonde, but there was no cellar or telephone here.

Nothing but a parrot, she mused, glancing at the automaton soldered to the skeleton's hands. A machine condemned to repeat, idiotically, the same echo.

"WHO ARE YOU? WHO ARE YOU? WHO ARE YOU?"

Ophelia lay down on the flagging, beside the skeleton. She was so close to it, she could see the stone maggots coming out of its nasal cavities. The last time she had been forced to confront herself was in the isolation chamber at the Good Family. She had had to face up to the guilt and cowardice that were preventing her from going forward. She had no desire to live through that a second time.

Ophelia turned from the cupola in a final act of resistance, but then she thought of Thorn.

They always keep their promises.

She opened her eyes wide and stared straight at the giant kaleidoscope above her. The optical shock made her back arch. Her myopia turned the geometrical shapes into a mire of colors. It was as if a rainbow were being pushed through her pupils, and then pushed further, deep into her skull.

"WHO ARE YOU? WHO ARE YOU? WHO ARE YOU?"

Had any broth remained in Ophelia's stomach, she would have vomited it. She spat out acidic bile instead. She breathed deeply and, once the spasms had subsided, lay flat on her back. Above her, thousands of fragmented mirrors amplified the stained-glass window of the oculus, reinventing new rose windows, again and again and again. It was like confronting a galaxy gone mad.

It was the start of a very long spectacle, at once sublime and terrible. Ophelia spent hours lying on the flagging, irradiated with colors. She would sit up whenever the migraine became too intense, her nose started bleeding, or she felt dizzy, but she always ended up lying down again. And so her ordeal carried on where she had left off.

Contrary to what the Knight had told her, the decision as to whether to continue or to stop was in no way hers to make. Not if Thorn depended on it.

Night never fell in the chapel; Ophelia soon lost all notion of time. She quickly gave up counting the parrot's countless "WHO ARE YOU?"s. Instead, she made do with counting the bowls they kept sliding through the hatch for her, but their increasing number did nothing to reassure her.

How she smelt didn't, either. How long had it been since she'd washed?

She allowed herself breaks that were as brief as physically feasible, to sleep and eat a little. She believed that the longer she exposed herself to the kaleidoscope, the sooner she would have completed her side of the deal.

How could she know if she was on the right track? She heard the clicking of the spyhole, from time to time, telling her that she was being constantly observed, but she was never spoken to. No directions, no encouragement, nothing.

And yet, Ophelia did notice some changes. And they weren't pleasant.

Such as realizing that the flagstones were inexplicably crumbling under her body, where she had taken to lying. Next, it was the bowls that disintegrated, moments after she held them in her hands, forcing her to gulp down her broth fast, before it disappeared. Her animism was no longer merely disrupted, it had become destructive. Using the chamber pot was nightmarish.

Ophelia's exasperation was at its height when her Dragon power started turning against her. Little by little, her arms and calves became covered in scratches, as if she were struggling through invisible brambles.

Expiation.

She was outraged at the thought. What was she being punished for? Everything was going from bad to worse, and it was the fault of Eulalia and the Other. A pretentious human and an insatiable echo. They had sacrificed one part of the world under the pretext of saving another; had come to their little agreement between themselves, unbeknownst to everyone else; and they were changing clauses of it today.

No, it wasn't Ophelia's fault that the Other had used her, that she resembled Eulalia, that the arks were collapsing, and that Octavio had lost his life. It wasn't her fault that she'd had to abandon her family. It wasn't her fault that she couldn't start her own.

It's not my fault.

Ophelia was split wide open. Just then, what was that? She had felt dissociated from her own thoughts. New fractals were forming every second across the chapel's cupola. Each combination caused her a jolt of pain, but she could no longer blink, or turn her head away.

"WHO ARE YOU? WHO ARE YOU? WHO ARE YOU?"

I am not them and they are not me.

The lights, colors, and shapes were dancing. They weren't only up there anymore. They were forming and re-forming in every molecule of Ophelia's body.

"WHO ARE YOU?"

I am no longer an Animist.

"WHO ARE YOU?"

I am not the daughter Mommy wanted.

"WHO ARE YOU?"

I will never be a mother myself.

"WHO ARE YOU?"

With Thorn, I was "we." Without him, I am just "I."

"WHO ARE YOU?"

Who is I?

Swept up in the kaleidoscopic whirlwind, Ophelia had turned into a spectator of thoughts. She was acutely aware of the crumbling stones under her back, of the space around her and within her. The more hollow she became, the more she sensed herself existing in a different way.

They say that you're nearly there.

Understanding dawned. The inverts in the alternative

program were made to suffer by the Observatory, but not to break down their family powers and split their shadows. Those were just the side effects of a much more profound separation. Mediana's renunciation. Eulalia's compensation.

CRYSTALLIZATION.

No, Ophelia wasn't, in fact, really Artemis's girl, or Mrs. Thorn, or Eulalia, or the Other, or even Ophelia. Because she was all that at once, and much more besides.

Within each of us there exists a boundary, Blaise had warned her. *They will try to make you cross that boundary. Whatever they say to you, the decision will be yours.*

My decision.
Our decision.

There are no more colors.

They have all combined to make white, paper-white, the page of a book in which Ophelia now takes up just seven letters.

Just a name fading away.

A simple role.

And the page tears.

REDEMPTION.

The Platform

"WHO IS I? WHO IS I? WHO IS I?"

Slowly, Ophelia moved her toes. She was so numb, she felt as if she were part of the floor. Had she lost consciousness? She eased open one eyelid. Up there, the kaleidoscope's mechanical reflectors had stopped moving. She turned her eyes to the transfixed skeleton, lying to her right. The skull, instead of looking up at the cupola, now stared at Ophelia with its empty sockets.

The sculpture had changed position. Right.

"WHO IS I? WHO IS I? WHO IS I?"

Ophelia hitched herself up onto her elbows. All around her, the chapel was transformed. From the flagstones, giant mineral petals had emerged, overlapping each other in a blossoming of amazing complexity, as if the kaleidoscope projections had replicated themselves down below.

It took a moment for Ophelia to realize that it was she, and she alone, who was responsible for this. Her animism, which was barely able to make a vase shake, had just stopped a mechanism from a distance, remodeled an ancient statue, and molded several cubic meters of stone as if it were modeling clay.

Ophelia's eyes slid along the skeleton's exposed ribs to locate the metal parrot, between the now wide-open hands.

"WHO IS I? WHO IS I? WHO IS I?"

This new echo, on the other hand, wasn't down to animism.

It was then that she noticed the shadow in the middle of the flowering flagging. The stranger in the fog, the intruder at the columbarium, was standing right in front of her. A shudder coursed through Ophelia. Although she looked for a face, she didn't find one. He was made of black matter, as if the natural light from the oculus had no effect on him.

The shadow was what it had always appeared to be: a shadow.

Ophelia tried to get up, without success.

"Are you the Other?"

The Shadow shook its head—or what served as one. *No*, it replied, silently, *I am not the Other*. Stuck on the floor, Ophelia stared long and hard at it. She wasn't inclined to believe the Shadow, not only because she had encountered it at every landslide, but also because it was such an obvious culprit. It's exhausting, hating someone who is never in front of you. No, Ophelia really wasn't inclined to believe the Shadow at all. And yet, she did believe it. Its familiarity to her had nothing to do with her distant, childhood memory, with that presence behind the mirror in her bedroom, with "Release me."

"Fine. Are you the echo of someone I know?"

The Shadow hesitated, and then shrugged its shoulders in what was neither really a yes nor altogether a no.

"But you, do you know the Other?"

The Shadow pointed a shadowy finger, somewhat mischievously, at Ophelia.

"Me, I know the Other?"

The Shadow nodded.

"Have I met him?"

The Shadow nodded.

"Since I released him from the mirror?"

The Shadow nodded. Several times.

"I saw the Other and didn't recognize him?"

The Shadow nodded. Ophelia was increasingly disconcerted.

"What does the Other look like?"

The Shadow again pointed at Ophelia. Someone that looked like her. Not a great help.

"But you," she insisted, "who are you? Another Other?"

The Shadow shook its head. This time, its finger slid in the direction of the parrot.

"WHO IS I? WHO IS I? WHO IS I?"

Ophelia listened to the continuous echo more attentively. It was her voice, and yet it was no longer really hers. The dissociation she had experienced, that rupturing that had split her in two, the feeling of deliverance that had followed, all that had resulted in a deviation. The awakening of an unknown consciousness. An intelligent echo.

Eulalia Gonde hadn't met the Other; she had *generated* him, exactly as Ophelia had just done.

"I've created another Other?" she muttered, flabbergasted.

The Shadow put both thumbs up to indicate approval. The next instant, it had dissolved into the light from the stained-glass window.

"Stay!"

Ophelia rushed to where the Shadow had disappeared. Suddenly dizzy, she fell to her knees. She felt so weak and so vibrant at the same time! She would have felt no different if, after a lifetime with scoliosis, her bones had all been straightened in one go.

Meanwhile, whoever it was, the Shadow had gone. Again.

"WHO IS I? WHO IS I? WHO IS I?"

Ophelia pulled a flagstone, broken between two stone flowerings, up from the floor. She lifted it above the parrot. She had come here to repair Eulalia's mistakes, certainly not to repeat them. This little automaton, so like a child's toy, had become a time bomb. It must be destroyed before the echo could further free itself.

"WHO IS I? WHO IS I? WHO IS I?"

Ophelia's fingers started to shake around the slab of stone. It was too heavy for her, and yet she couldn't let go of it. This echo was but a burble of consciousness, but a consciousness all the same, one born from her own consciousness, from which it had freed itself. The shaking now took over Ophelia's whole body. An emotion, more imperative than any moral dilemma, was churning her insides.

She couldn't.

Some leather gloves gently took the flagstone from her hands. Ophelia was in such turmoil, she hadn't noticed that the chapel had been invaded by observers. They calmly moved her aside, gathered around the parrot, took notes, and deployed an array of instruments. Some even prostrated themselves on the floor.

Ophelia was led out of the chapel, far away from the echo. From her echo. She put up a struggle, but had no strength; she felt like a rag doll. Unknown arms were restraining her as much as supporting her. She thought she saw, fleetingly, amid the yellow flurry of observers, the Knight's braced smile. She found herself, somehow, going down a stairway, then another one, and then yet another one. She had been brought out of the nave. The men and women escorting her held her with half-pressing, half-protective hands. Each contact with their gloves triggered feelings in Ophelia that weren't her own. Febrility, exaltation, hope: she was able to read objects again.

After a dizzying number of stairs, she was brought to a crypt and forcibly plunged into an immersion font full of boiling-hot water. She was soaped, rinsed, dried, oiled, massaged, perfumed, and fed by an anonymous crowd, who then silently withdrew, leaving her naked and dazed, surrounded by mosaics.

A gate closed, with a clanging of iron. Ophelia had just been transferred from one prison to another.

There was some clothing, carefully laid out on a cushion. It was her own, confiscated on the day she was admitted, along with a change of underwear. Ophelia saw, among it, the replacement glasses and gloves that Thorn had left in her file.

Thorn. How many nights had he waited for her in the directors' apartments? He could be putting himself in danger right now to find her.

She got dressed as fast as her dizziness allowed. Fastening the gown and the sandals came surprisingly easy to her. Her left hand and right hand were no longer at war: despite shaking, one was completing the actions of the other in disconcerting harmony. In fact, as far back as she remembered, they had never been so nimble. Ophelia was, however, convinced that she was missing something very important. What had this observatory done to her?

She got her answer when she caught her reflection in a splendid cheval mirror. It was her face, it was her body, but she felt as if she were looking at a stranger.

She was no longer a mirror visitor.

Ophelia knew it with every fiber of her being, before even touching the surface of the mirror and feeling all that resistance. She had already experienced a blockage, or a disruption, but what she was feeling right now bore no comparison. It was like noticing the sudden absence of an arm under a shirtsleeve.

They had mutilated her.

"*Merci.*"

Ophelia had thought she was alone in the crypt. The beetle woman sat solemnly on a stone bench.

"Let's talk a little, *mademoiselle*."

She smoothed the yellow silk of her sari, and, in a way that was no longer officious, indicated to her to sit down beside her. To Ophelia, it felt as if the foundations of the entire observatory were swaying beneath her sandals, but she remained standing. The beetle woman didn't seem offended. The little automaton shimmering on her shoulder gave the disturbing impression that, of the two of them, it was the real observer.

"From our first meeting, I knew we would have this conversation, you and me. A real conversation, I mean, without constraint or pretense."

"After weeks of secrets," snapped Ophelia.

"We had to interfere as little as possible in your inner journey. That's the procedure on the Alternative Program. You would have known that, had you read the agreement you signed more carefully, *mademoiselle*."

"And what you put me through in that chapel? That wasn't interference? You have amputated my family power."

"Only a part of it. It could have been worse. It could have been a part of your life. And, without wishing to offend you, the final decision, to give up that part of yourself, was yours. We are *très* grateful to you."

Ophelia felt her pulse racing. Had the echo dissociated itself from her by taking part of her shadow with it? She might, then, still have a chance of getting her power back.

"You should also be grateful," the woman remarked. "You have never been so much yourself as right now! Thanks to us, you have finally realigned yourself. Any lingering discrepancies will gradually fade away. After all, you have lived with serious dissymmetry for years."

As she listened to these words, Ophelia stopped herself from instinctively clutching her stomach. Her first thought had only been for that particular malformation, although it was hardly a priority.

"*Desolée*," said the beetle woman. "You will never be able to give birth. Your body hasn't changed, only your perception has. The Other marked you in your youth, didn't he?" she continued, with intense curiosity. "He made you, as it were, a reflection of God, in your own right. Of Eulalia Gonde, if you prefer," she corrected, seeing Ophelia frown. "It was a suitable starting point, but if you had come to us too soon, the experiment would have failed. It had to be your choice, your expiation, and your redemption. Aren't you going to put them back on?"

The woman indicated the glasses and gloves left on the cushion. Ophelia forced herself to put them on, even though these accessories were suitable neither for her sight nor for her hands. Thorn alone had the originals. The observers knew enough about them already; they didn't need to know, too, that he and Ophelia had met up, secretly, to rifle through their drawers.

"Have you kept your promise? You have caused him no harm?"

"What are you referring to?"

Sitting bolt upright on her bench, the woman was smiling. Was it her way of indicating that Sir Henry's secret was safe, or was she unaware of the substance of the Knight's threat? It was terribly frustrating, but Ophelia wasn't going to risk compromising Thorn's cover if it was still protecting him. She let it go.

"What are you going to do with the echo?"

"Come now, *mademoiselle*. You know that we know that you know."

Ophelia now felt her heart racing. Yes, she knew the observers would try to establish a dialogue with this echo, as Eulalia Gonde had once established with the Other. She knew they would study it until they understood it, inside out; learn the language of echoes from it; and, finally, achieve a viable conversion. She also knew, even if it pained her, that Thorn and she also needed a Horn of Plenty in perfect working order.

She knew all that, but that wasn't her question.

"I'll rephrase it. What are you going to do with the Horn of Plenty?"

The beetle woman let out an indulgent sigh.

"You have achieved a miracle, *mademoiselle*. No candidate before you had achieved crystallization. We will make sure that your miracle goes on to achieve new miracles."

"What new miracles?"

"It's not within our remit to decide."

"Who, then? Who really decides here? Who thinks for you?"

"It's not part of our remit to tell you."

Ophelia's heart was no longer racing. It was pounding.

"A God who dominates the world, and an Other who destroys it, wasn't that enough for you?"

The woman took off her pince-nez. Only then did Ophelia notice all the lines fanning out from her tired eyes. She was no longer an observer, but a simple Babelian, marked by the sun, and by life. Had she herself lost a loved one during the last two landslides?

"Destroyed, or purified, *mademoiselle*, it all depends on one's point of view. The old world was a hell blighted by war," she murmured, lowering her voice for the last word, as if the Index held as much sway here as anywhere else. "Thanks to the Other, Eulalia Gonde created a new humanity, directed by outstanding guardians, and they all endeavor, together, to purge our souls of vice, generation after generation. In all honesty, I don't know why the Other deviated from the original plan today. Perhaps he reckons the new world isn't yet worthy of being saved? That's why it's our duty to push the quest for perfection further," the woman continued, with increased fervor. "As for you, you have already fulfilled your duty."

There we are. It was precisely as Ophelia had feared. Whoever the brains behind the Deviations Observatory might be, they were following in Eulalia Gonde's footsteps, treading deeper, even. Their intention wasn't to release men and women from a subterranean dictatorship, but to bring the lost sheep back onto the straight and narrow. It was still all about imposing on them a way of seeing, a way of doing, a manual for life. A perpetual childhood, in short.

Ophelia didn't believe for a second that this was what the Other was waiting for from humanity, to end his apocalypse.

"This world's real problem," continued the woman, sensing Ophelia's misgivings, "is that it remains desperately incomplete. We are all incomplete, *en fait*, and some even more than others."

Ophelia wasn't in the mood for more philosophical musings. She insisted on the concrete.

"What are the shadows? What are the echoes? What are the Others? What are they, really?"

The woman hesitated, and then her expression turned dreamy.

"The air you breathe, *mademoiselle*, is not the only air there is. There's another air mixed in with it, right here, all around you, at this very moment. Odorless. Undetectable. We call it aerargyrum, literally 'air-silver.' You imprint your whole body on it, along with your family power, if you have one. This air is sufficiently dense in places for you to glimpse it, armed with the right instruments. You propagate your every action in it, your every word, and sometimes, when this air is disturbed by certain, particular circumstances—a major landslide, a minor discrepancy—it sends them back to you in a return wave."

Ophelia instinctively blocked her lungs. When she had seen the laboratories through the prism of the lens, she had thought that only shadows and echoes were composed of aerargyrum. She now realized her misapprehension. The aerargyrum was everywhere. What she had visualized represented merely the spume of an invisible ocean.

"Imagine now," the woman continued, her tone cloying, "that one of these return waves starts to reflect for itself. To reflect . . . A verb that, in this case, is *parfaitement* appropriate. Imagine it, then: this double of yourself, entirely made of aerargyrum, that suddenly becomes conscious of itself, that crystallizes itself around that thought, that appropriates your language, and just wants to speak to you about all that clouds your perception. That's what an Other is."

Ophelia thought of the Shadow, that had visited her in the chapel without the observatory knowing, and had gone to great lengths to make itself understood by her. A condensation of aerargyrum without a body, but with a will, but which, nevertheless, claimed not to be the Other.

No, quite clearly, the essential was still slipping through her fingers.

"Your aerargyrum," said Ophelia, "where does it come from?"

With her pince-nez, the beetle woman indicated a stone archway, right at the back of the crypt. The flickering light from the bulbs did nothing to dispel the shadows lurking there.

"If you want to know, *mademoiselle*, go through the last door."

Until now, it had been hard for Ophelia to concentrate fully on the conversation. The strange glasses hurt her eyes, and her fingers were picking up the past of her fake reader's gloves, imposing visions on her of their previous owner—a certain "Gigi," from the Standard Program, who suffered from an obsession with cigarette lighters and yogurt.

This business of the door got her full attention.

She walked, with measured steps, toward the impressive ornate archway looming in the darkness. Fine letters, similar to those on the OBSERVATION and EXPLORATION doors Ophelia had passed on the day of her admission, were carved into the stone:

COMPREHENSION

They definitely had a thing about capital letters here.

Ophelia screwed up her eyes to peer into the shadows under the archway. After a few moments, she could see two parallel lines. Tracks. What the observer called a door was in fact an underground platform. The tracks disappeared at the far end of a tunnel that descended into the bowels of the earth.

"Is that the third protocol?"

"Yes."

The woman had joined her at the edge of the platform. She cupped her ear to encourage Ophelia to listen. Ophelia could hear the tracks humming. Headlights dazzled her. A hot gust made her gown slap against her thighs. A train of just one carriage drew to a halt and an automatic door opened in front of her.

"Each candidate admitted to the second protocol has had the privilege of going through the final door," declared the woman, crossing herself. "It doesn't matter that none of them crystallized before you did, they helped us to perfect the Alternative Program. So we weren't ungrateful. As we're speaking now, they have penetrated the final secrets of the universe. Bless them."

Pensively, Ophelia considered the stationary train.

"They are all dead."

"No one is dead."

"So why do they never return?"

"Yes, *mademoiselle*. Why?"

Ophelia held the woman's disturbing gaze. Was she insinuating that they had *chosen* not to return? It was hard to believe.

Inside the carriage, the elegant seats were covered in velvet. The lampshades gave out a mellow light. There was no one in the carriage, not even a driver. The step at the door seemed to be waiting for Ophelia.

"Am I supposed to board this train?"

"*Bien sûr.*"

Ophelia turned her glasses back to the closed gate of the crypt. Maybe it was from having eaten a real meal, or maybe the feeling of being in danger, but her strength returned, and with it her two family powers. She was no longer a mirror visitor, and she doubted she could repeat the wonders her animism had achieved in the chapel, under the effects of crystallization. However, she could feel the juddering of the mosaics beneath her feet, and the nervous system of the woman opposite her.

The observer put her pince-nez back on, with a smile.

"Your shadow is visibly bristling," she said, with amusement, tapping her fingernail against one of her black lenses. "Are you thinking of using your animism and your claws against me to escape?"

"Give me just one reason not to."

This woman seemed dauntingly confident. Ophelia wondered, once again, what her family power was.

"In your opinion, *mademoiselle*, what does the third protocol consist of?"

Ophelia held her breath. According to the Babelian legend Octavio had told her, the Horn of Plenty had judged humans to be unworthy of it, and had buried itself where no one could find it. Buried. Thorn and Ophelia had searched for it on every story of the columbarium; it was *under* the building that it was buried. And this underground train led directly to it.

The woman studied her reaction with sympathy.

"Curiosity is gnawing at you, isn't it? You have that in common with all the other candidates. It's that curiosity that made you such a talented reader of objects, that put you in Anima's Museum of Primitive History, that led you to Babel's Memorial, and that finally drew you to this crypt. As long as you don't know the whole truth, you will never feel whole yourself. This train leads to all your answers."

These words made Ophelia feel a mix of exasperation and agitation.

"All those who have approached the Horn of Plenty have looked truth in the face!" the woman insisted, with unfeigned fervor. "A truth that not only changed their conception of reality, but also changed them, themselves, profoundly. I have seen men and women setting off on the train so many times . . . I've lost count! It has always returned empty. No one chose to get back on it."

"Do you mean to say that you, personally, have never seen the Horn of Plenty?"

Ophelia was amazed.

"I don't have the right to do so, *mademoiselle*. Not yet. We, the observers, still have work to finish here, aboveground. But the day is approaching, yes, when it will be our turn to take the train."

The woman's eyes shone behind their black lenses. The beetle on her shoulder used an articulated stalk to tap on her cheek.

"*Quoi*? Oh, yes, I was supposed to give you this from Mademoiselle Second."

The woman pulled out a piece of paper she had kept in a fold of her sari. Unsurprisingly, it was a drawing: a portrait of

Octavio similar to all those Second churned out, depicting him surrounded by torn-up papers. His eyes—always that horrid red pencil—expressed unspeakable distress. A cry for help that Ophelia hadn't managed to hear. She felt herself shaking, down to her stomach. Second had foreseen what would befall the Good Family, she had, time and again, tried to warn them, and once again, hadn't made herself understood in time.

"Sometimes," murmured the beetle woman, "an echo reaches us before the source that caused it. Those echoes escape our lenses, but never escape Mademoiselle Second. That girl has a keen eye, if I may put it like that. She also asked me to repeat the following to you: 'But this well was no more real than a rabbit of Odin.'"

"What on earth does that mean?"

"I haven't the slightest idea," the woman assured, with a bigger smile. "Mademoiselle Second said those words just before your arrival at the Deviations Observatory, and repeated them several times since, which is pretty unusual. I presumed they would mean something to you."

Absolutely nothing, thought Ophelia. And, not content to repeat this absurd sentence, Second had illustrated it in a drawing that she had been determined, at all costs, to give to Thorn. She would bear the scar for life.

"You are using her."

The beetle woman rubbed her chin, as if giving serious thought to this accusation.

"I can't pretend I understand her, but I think Mademoiselle Second uses herself, all on her own. She is essential to us," she still, willingly, admitted. "She sees when crystallization is latent in an individual. The first protocol allows us to separate, as far as possible, a subject from their shadow, inverts being particularly prone to such separation, but the splitting is a spontaneous phenomenon. Mademoiselle Second can see in advance when a shadow is about to split. At the time when she wasn't yet among us, when we could only rely on our lenses, our detecting was tardy: during the time it took to transfer the subject to the second protocol, the shadow separated of its own accord, without any control, or any receptacle, and the echo produced would be lost without crystallizing. Likewise, if we proceeded with a premature transfer, and neither the subject nor their shadow was prepared for the next stage, the outcome was fatal to them. All those stillborn echoes, all those minds afflicted with madness . . . a dreadful waste. Oh, yes, Mademoiselle Second was *vraiment* a blessing to us. Certainly, we have still had one failure after another since her arrival, many abortive crystallizations, but that way we could gradually correct our protocols, so that, on the day you entered my office, *mademoiselle*, we were finally ready!"

Ophelia looked more carefully at the stationary train in front of her, its open door, with step pulled out, its velvet seats inside, the soft light from its lampshades, which didn't penetrate the darkness of the tunnel.

"What you say is contradictory. How can one phenomenon be both spontaneous and foreseeable?"

The beetle woman managed a sibylline smile, annoying Ophelia even more, and then indicated the portrait of Octavio, getting increasingly crumpled between her fingers.

"Our mastery of crystallization is still not great, but we have at least grasped one thing about it. Loss plays a crucial part in it. It's what we call 'the compensation effect.'"

Ophelia would have produced a conscious echo to fill the void left by Octavio? And Second would have been aware of that? She would have understood that the appearance of a new Other was conditional on the death of her own brother?

Ophelia tore up the drawing. Today, more than ever, the idea of predestination was repulsive to her. What was the point of drawing shadows, splits, brothers, nails, old women, and monsters, if nothing was down to chance?

"You have so many questions!" the beetle woman said, sympathetically, as she studied Ophelia's face with an almost jealous interest. "Allow me to put one more to you. What would you give to see the world through the eyes of the Other?"

Ophelia gazed at the torn drawing in her hands, just like her shadow had been. Eulalia had experienced a momentous revelation when she had conceived of the Other down that telephone line. Her vision of the world had been changed forever by it. As for Ophelia, she felt just as ignorant as before. She thought of the parrot, and again it made her feel uncomfortable. WHO IS I?

The woman's eyebrows twitched, mischievously, while her beetle waved its articulated arm toward the train, as an invitation to board.

"When you have the answer to that, *mademoiselle*, you will have all the answers."

With these words, to Ophelia's great alarm, the woman moved calmly away, signed herself as she passed the baptismal font, opened the iron gate, and climbed the stairs, without closing the gate behind her.

No intimidation, no threat. Ophelia had only one decision to make: the train or the stairs.

"It can't be that easy!"

Ophelia's protest got lost among the religious statues. The woman and her beetle were already far away.

On the platform, the door was still open. To Ophelia, boarding this train meant finally finding the Horn of Plenty, but also, perhaps, no longer being able—or no longer wanting, crazy as the idea seemed—to return. Going back up the stairs meant seeing Thorn again, who had been waiting for her for days; or, more likely, being stuck forever in some new spatial loop. Each choice contained both the promise of a reward and the risk of being condemned.

The train, or the stairs?

Ophelia was dying for some yogurt.

She took off Gigi's gloves, since she didn't need to pretend anymore. She did, on the other hand, keep the glasses: suitable or not, they were always better than seeing nothing at all. She breathed out to empty herself, and, without boarding the train, seized the handle on the door with her bare hand.

She ceased to be herself in order to slip into another skin, inlaid with gems, thin and dehydrated, the skin of a loser, the skin of defeat, a skin that hasn't managed to obtain redemption, but so what, *signorina*, since I'm ahead of you. This last-chance train, I'm catching it first. Will you succeed where I failed? I don't give a damn since I will discover the truth before you, and that, *signorina*, is the only thing, down here, that really counts!

Ophelia felt a jubilant smile coming to her lips that wasn't her own. It was the first time someone had deliberately left a thought on an object as a way of addressing a personal message to her. Mediana had boarded the train of her own free will, and was making sure she knew it. Ophelia would have had so many things to ask her, but she immediately felt herself being carried by the tide of time in reverse, going back further and further into the past of all the women and men who had grabbed this handle to climb the step. A crowd of souls, some impatient, others terrified, but all equally unsure of what might await them at the end of the tunnel, while still burning with curiosity.

Ophelia let go of the handle and looked deep into the tunnel. Black. The blackest of blacks. All those people were convinced that this train would take them to the answers. Had the previous informer of the Genealogists been one of them?

As long as you don't know the whole truth, you will never feel whole yourself. It was true. Ophelia longed to give meaning to what had none, to find the one who had torn apart the world—her world—and finally get her revenge on them. Thorn also needed to do that. There remained too many questions without answers, too many victims without the culprit.

She climbed the step and took a seat in the train. The door immediately closed with a mechanical bang. Ophelia's heart was making pretty much the same noise. She took a deep breath, ready to face the mysterious terminus of this train. She vowed not to leave Thorn a fake funerary urn in lieu of her. She would return with the Horn of Plenty. She would get back her echo and her mirror-visiting power. Together, they would overcome all their adversaries.

She was thrown forward as the train set off.

It wasn't going down. It was bringing her back up to the surface.

THE RENUNCIATION

Ophelia understood nothing about anything anymore. The train was going back into the bowels of the observatory at breathtaking speed, taking her further away, by the second, from her destination, from the Horn of Plenty, and from all the answers. Then it slammed the brakes on. Thrown back into her seat, she felt her lungs empty of air. The shades on every lamp in the carriage shook.

The door opened. The step came out. Ophelia had arrived.

She waited a while, in case the train decided to set off again, in the right direction this time, but finally accepted that it wouldn't. She alighted onto a platform as dark as the tunnel she had left. She was still in the vaults of the ancient imperial city.

The train left as it had arrived. Absurdly.

Ophelia felt her way along a labyrinth of stairways. She felt increasingly disorientated. To this was added a new challenge: learning to walk again. After years of bad coordination, suddenly, no thinking was needed anymore, no wondering which leg to put forward first, when to bend which knee, and how to keep her balance. Moving ahead had become disarmingly simple. Ophelia had so little confidence in her own feet, she couldn't just blindly trust them, but as soon as she sought to correct them, she unfailingly tripped.

A sense of deep foreboding gripped her. It increased when, arriving at a crossroads, she finally found a source of light. All the bulbs were spent apart from one, which, flickering, showed the path to follow. The same thing happened at each intersection, each junction: one stairway was lit up, the others dark.

After never-ending steps, Ophelia finally glimpsed the light of day. Of evening, in fact. A stormy dusk, fiery as a furnace, filtered through the barred windows of a cellar. The chirring of crickets combined with a whiff of damp vegetation.

Freedom seemed too near, too possible. If that train led to all the answers, why, then, had it brought Ophelia back to where she started? Why had she been guided up to the surface, bulb by bulb? She knew far too much, the observatory would prevent her from rejoining civilization. She certainly wouldn't be allowed to speak to Thorn.

She would never be allowed to see him again.

Ophelia blinked, dazzled by the sunset. The last stairway she had just, breathlessly, climbed had opened onto a splendid verandah, its glass panes shrouded by sulfurous clouds. Among the potted lemon trees, three figures, silhouetted against the light, sat at the end of a very long table. All had turned to Ophelia, but she only noticed the tallest of them.

From the way Thorn had straightened up, he was as surprised as she was.

"Take a seat," said a man, indicating a chair at the other end of the table.

Ophelia sat down in a trance. She recognized the observer from the mechanical lizard he carried on his shoulder: it was he who had slapped her in front of everyone, on the first day. His dimple had turned into an unpleasant furrow. He seemed neither satisfied nor surprised to see her here.

"It's not her."

Ophelia tried to see whom this voice, at the other end of

the table, was coming from. A combination of concentration, apprehension, and decidedly revived animism meant that the substitute glasses, after some refocusing, allowed her to recognize Lady Septima, installed in the seat of honor. Her eyes, redder than ever, were dissecting her at a distance, from under her fringe. The resemblance was so striking, it hit Ophelia like a punch to the stomach. Never had she missed Octavio more than at this table. On his mother's face, hatred and grief were in harrowing conflict, as though she found it intolerable that this little stranger hadn't fallen into the void instead of her son.

"It's not her, *en effet*," said the observer, "but she can be seen as good compensation. She was your pupil, after all."

"What compensation?" asked Ophelia.

She had to force herself not to turn to Thorn, whom she could just see in the corner of her glasses, sitting back a little. If she looked at him right now, she would be incapable of pretense, and would betray the true nature of their relationship.

"My pupil?" hissed Lady Septima. "She never would have been if Lady Helen, God rest her soul, hadn't imposed her on me. In any case, that's beside the point. I was tasked by Sir Pollux, in person, to get all of his descendants to safety in the center of town. The minor arks are no longer safe, we must proceed with the evacuation of our citizens."

The lizard man agreed, while wiping his pince-nez on his gown.

"Families who expressed the desire to do so could leave with our hosts, this very day."

"Not all of them."

"Mademoiselle Second is a special case."

Ophelia tried to follow this conversation that she had interrupted. So, Lady Septima had suddenly just remembered that she had a daughter. It seemed to her, however, that it wasn't really the mother speaking here through her. More like an owner.

"We offer you all our sympathy, my lady," said the observer, sounding understanding, "but Mademoiselle Second belongs in the Alternative Program. You can see her within the framework of authorized visits."

Lady Septima pursed her lips. Dazzling in the LUX uniform, and haughty in her chair, she was acting the mistress of the house. But Ophelia sensed that, of the two, it was the lizard man who had the advantage. As for her, she found them just as daunting as each other. Despite the relief she had felt on seeing Thorn, the deep foreboding hadn't left her. Maybe it was the aroma of the lemon trees, but the atmosphere on this verandah was as bitter as you can get.

And there was something else. Shards of windowpane glinted on the floor, as if they had just lain there since the hail following the last landslide. When Ophelia glanced through the cracked panes, she saw paths that were still damp, despite the sweltering heat of the evening. The windows of the elegant Standard Program buildings were almost all broken, and yet, like those of the verandah, their shards had still not been cleared away. She spotted a swarm of airships moving off in the sky. The only airship still moored in the gardens was under the watch of the family guard, and bore the LUX sun emblem.

Ophelia clasped her hands together, as much to calm herself as to stop reading her own gown. Was it possible that what, to her, had seemed to last days, in the depths of the second protocol, was actually just a few hours here? Did time pass differently in a spatial loop? Had the Good Family only fallen this morning?

Her attention was brought back into the verandah when Lady Septima clicked her tongue with impatience.

"The circumstances have changed; Second's place is henceforth with LUX. Don't force me to order you to go and get her."

"Notwithstanding all the respect we owe you, my lady, the Deviations Observatory no longer takes any orders from LUX."

The lizard man's voice was soft, but intransigent. Lady Septima might not be naturally pale, but Ophelia could see her blanch from the other end of the table.

"You have benefited from more than generous subsidies—"

"Subsidies duly put to good use; Sir Henry, here present, can testify to that. The observatory was recognized as being of help to families, it contributed to rectifying a great many deviations, and to forming exemplary citizens. We are irreproachable. That was not the case for you, and we lament that."

Ophelia shrank into her chair, battling more than ever the temptation to look at Thorn. She should have expected as much! The observers were going to denounce them to Lady Septima. And what if they declared to her here, now, not only that Thorn was not a lord, but also that he had disfigured her daughter? That the pupil whom she had personally trained had never given her her real name? No more Sir Henry, no more Eulalia, no more pretense. Lying was deemed a misdemeanor in Babel; theirs was serious enough to be a crime. They would end up in prison, within touching distance of Eulalia Gonde's and the Other's ultimate secret, when the world could collapse at any moment.

Why, in God's name, had that train not taken her to the Horn of Plenty?

The lizard man shook a bell. Answering his call, a collaborator waiting outside entered the verandah. In a resigned way, they removed their gray hood to reveal messy hair. Elizabeth. Her eyes were in as parlous a state as the observatory's windows, and her swollen lips still hadn't gone down since being elbowed by Cosmos. She was a pitiful sight. And yet she stood tall as she clicked her heels and brought her fist to her chest:

"Knowledge serves peace."

Lady Septima slumped in her chair. As talented as Elizabeth was, she had never found favor with her.

"Are you going to summon all my former pupils?"

"This one infringed the principle of containment and divulged confidential information," said the observer, not losing his dimple. "She did so on behalf of LUX."

Lady Septima's fingers stopped drumming the armrests. Her astonishment seemed sincere.

"That's a *très* serious accusation."

"It's a *très* justified accusation. Here are some reports we intercepted that she intended to give to you."

The man passed a file to Lady Septima, which she gingerly flicked through, as if fearing her reputation could be tarnished from this contact alone.

"Forerunner, what have you to say in your defense?"

"The accusation is deserved, my lady. I broke professional secrecy."

Ophelia stared at Elizabeth, whose freckles were fading along with the sun. Was that it? Wasn't she going to explain to them that she had done it because the Genealogists, and thus, through them, LUX, had ordered her to? This was no longer loyalty; this was stupidity.

The man's dimple deepened further, without the hint of a smile on his lips.

"You will understand that this incident damages the bond of trust between the Deviations Observatory and the Lords of LUX. Henceforth, we will expect no further subsidies from you, just as you will no longer have any right to oversee our activities. Be assured, we are the first to be very sorry about this."

It was a veritable declaration of independence. In fact, this man didn't seem at all sorry, and Ophelia realized that it was thanks to her that he felt so superior. The Deviations Observatory no longer needed either LUX's patronage or Elizabeth's services. By supplying it with a new Other, Ophelia had offered it boundless possibilities. A power far too great in hands far too unworthy.

She stood up so energetically that her chair, thanks to animism, also lifted off the ground.

"I, too, have a declaration to make."

"Ah, yes," the observer cut in, "let us return a little to the case of Mademoiselle Eulalia. She was admitted here before the new decree on residence permits for Babel reached us. We offered hospitality to an outlaw. To maintain cordial relations with LUX, despite our differences, and to prove to you that we will always cooperate to benefit the general interest, we are, today, making amends for that mistake. We are handing Mademoiselle Eulalia over to you."

Casually, he passed another file to Lady Septima. Ophelia took advantage of their brief exchange of looks to do the same, finally, with Thorn. Silently, he indicated to her to keep quiet. He himself was stiff as a board, clenching his watch in his fist, as if he feared the slightest creak of metal, the slightest click of a cover might make the situation even more catastrophic.

On his uniform, nothing remained of Second's blood, apart from a tiny stain that his animism hadn't removed. A scarlet stain that hadn't had time to fade. Crazy as it might seem, Ophelia's stay in the nave of the second protocol really had taken place in the space of a single day.

"Sir Henry," said the observer, politely offering Thorn his hand, "this also brings your inspection to a close. Do pass on all our best wishes to the Genealogists."

Lady Septima made her way to the exit, indicating herself

that the meeting was over. She clicked her fingers to make Ophelia, Elizabeth, and Thorn follow her, with no longer a word or a look in their direction. Outside, the family guard now formed a guard of honor, which promptly closed up in their wake.

Ophelia was leaving one trap for another. She felt duped, and stupid.

Beside her, Elizabeth marched on. She shed her monk's habit on the lawn, revealing the midnight-blue-and-silver frock coat of the virtuosos, which she had never stopped wearing underneath. A citizen to the tips of her boots. What did the punishment awaiting her matter, she had already accepted it.

That wasn't Ophelia's case. She was building up strategies, each more risky than the last. She thought, painfully, of her lost mirror-visiting power when she saw the sunset reflected in the puddles. Pushed by the guard, she went up the gangway of the airship and discreetly directed her glasses at Thorn's big back. Did he, himself, have a plan?

On board the airship, there were many civilians with suitcases bursting at the seams. Their conversations stopped the moment Lady Septima cast her flashing eyes over them. It was disconcerting to see such a small woman having such a big influence. She didn't need to issue orders to proceed to take-off; each member of the family guard played his part, and then returned to his position in total silence.

Thorn was the only one who dared to break it:

"Drop me off in town with your two pupils. The Genealogists will have questions to ask them, and I myself must give them my report."

Lady Septima examined the insignia pinned to his uniform, and then the tiny bloodstain to the side.

"Your appearance doesn't conform to regulations, Sir Henry."

That was her only comment. She indicated a banquette to Ophelia and Elizabeth, and then settled herself in the cockpit. She had a final look at the Deviations Observatory, with a quiver of what might be regret, and then seized the helm with controlled rage.

Ophelia pressed her face to the porthole. In the ever-extending shadow of the colossus, she glimpsed the observers who had gathered to watch takeoff. They were all smiling. Almost all. The young girl with the monkey was sending grand gestures of farewell to Thorn, who didn't notice her behind the window, so entirely focused was he on the new equation confronting him.

The last moorings were released. The airship took off in a flurry of propellers.

IN THE WINGS

Titan has lost three skyscrapers, Pharos its boating resorts, Totem its chimera farms, Leadgold its industrial district, and The Serenissima a quarter of its network of rivers. He leaps from one ark to the next (oh, Heliopolis no longer has its South Station). Wherever he goes, lands fall apart, time accelerates, space is retrieved. Many men, women, animals, and plants got sucked into the holes (farewell, Zephyr's great windmills). Those who remain don't dare to leave their homes anymore. If one's going to disappear, might as well do so convivially, with one's family, one's house, and the dog. Clearly, from his point of view, events are becoming increasingly interesting (and Vesperal's deserts increasingly deserted).

He thinks of Ophelia, of her eyes full of anger and confusion. She took him for a world destroyer, him, really, what a bizarre idea . . . She came so close to discovering everything, understanding everything! Fortunately, she failed—again. Ophelia's defeats are more decisive than her victories.

He strides across several thousand kilometers, and returns to distant Babel, to the Deviations Observatory, at the top of the colossus, inside the directors' apartments.

He arrives at just the right time. The observers have all gathered to congratulate themselves. At the center of the room stands a large glass cloche, from which the muffled sound of a small artificial parrot emerges:

"WHO IS I? WHO IS I? WHO IS I?"

Around it, hands are being shaken, shoulders patted, cups of tea being raised to the directors, who are conspicuous by their absence. Within this assembly, clad all in yellow, half don't know that the directors don't exist, and the other half still don't know who pulls the strings.

But he does. False modesty aside, very little is missing from what he knows.

He takes care to hide where no one will notice him. Without their dark-lensed pince-nez, the observers can't see further than the ends of their noses; with the pince-nez, however, they see a little too well. They would discover not only his presence, understated though it might be, but also his true appearance. He's acquired a taste for anonymity.

He notices two special young guests, sitting quietly in the midst of the observers. The Knight is swamped by his thick glasses, cross tattoo, and braces; Second has disappeared behind her crooked fringe, the enormous bandage across her face, and the sheet of paper she is drawing on.

He could almost laugh at it.

Little by little, the effusiveness dies down, the conversations dry up. Best not to stay up tonight, ladies and gentlemen, tomorrow the real work finally begins! The observers leave, one after the other, but not without a final look, full of hope, at the parrot under its glass cloche:

"WHO IS I? WHO IS I? WHO IS I?"

Soon, only the lizard man, the beetle woman, the Knight, Second, and the echo remain in the directors' apartments. And him, obviously.

The atmosphere has lost some of its joviality; this should be even more interesting. He takes the risk of stepping out of the wings a little, to get as close as possible to this reality that isn't really his own. Second almost spots him out of the corner of her eye, hesitates a moment, then returns to concentrating on her drawing. Apart from her, no one detects him.

The Knight puts his cup of tea down in a way that's meant to be aristocratic.

"Let's talk business. If this echo has deviated, it's in part thanks to me. I've fulfilled my contract, I demand my share of plenty. Here are my demands."

He hands an envelope to the beetle woman, who reads its contents.

"An entire ark?"

"That can't collapse," specifies the Knight.

"That's a pretty large territory for you alone."

"Oh, I won't live there without company. When there's nothing left of the Pole, Lady Berenilde will have privileged access. Without her daughter, preferably."

The beetle woman and lizard man exchange blank looks.

"You will have to show patience, *jeune homme*. Our echo isn't mature enough to reveal all its secrets to us. It's still short on vocabulary."

"WHO IS I? WHO IS I? WHO IS I?"

Second, silent for once, is drawing with eyes wide open, possessed by a new vision of the future.

The Knight gets up without a glance either at her or at anyone.

"I will wait a little, but not too much. I will go and fetch plenty myself, if need be. After all, I know where to find it. Good night."

There are just four of them left. The lizard man, the beetle woman, Second, and the echo. Five with him, the invisible witness, spectral spectator, Shadow among the shadows.

"Was that the right choice, dearest colleague?" the woman

observer suddenly asked. "Handing *her* over to Lady Septima? Knowing all that she could divulge to the Lords of LUX?"

"The Horn of Plenty rejected her, dearest colleague. Let its will be respected."

The lizard man's reply rings true. At that very moment, all the lamps in the apartments go out, and then come back on again. Electrical endorsement.

"Such a thing had never happened before," admits the woman. "The Horn of Plenty always accepted the candidates who boarded the train. It's certainly the first time . . . But all the same, dearest colleague," she adds, getting a grip on herself, while adjusting her pince-nez, "did you also have to hand over that collaborator? Mademoiselle Elizabeth was on the verge of decoding the Books."

"Precisely. I got rid of her before she knew too much. The last time the Genealogists sent us a spy, our mistake was to put him on the third-protocol train. He didn't deserve such an honor, and his disappearance just made the Genealogists pay more attention. Rest assured, dearest colleague, Mademoiselle Elizabeth is no longer of any importance. Her work will save us considerable time. We will merely have to wrap it up without her . . . and with it."

The lizard man places a hand, respectful and possessive, on the glass cloche containing that very echo.

"WHO IS I? WHO IS I? WHO IS I?"

The beetle woman gazes pensively at the rose windows, through which daylight is fading.

"Come, come, dearest colleague, you have nothing to fear from those young ladies. They can no longer harm us from outside our walls. Just look at Mademoiselle Second! She's been doing that drawing for hours."

The two observers lean over. He does, too. Under Second's precise pencil, a flying ship is falling from the sky.

He smiles at the sight of it. Everything's perfect. Ophelia's story, the story of them all, will finally reach its veritable conclusion. He must be ready for the grand denouement.

But before that, he has one last little thing to accomplish here.

"WHO IS I? WHO IS I? WHO IS I?"

He takes advantage of the observers' distraction to approach the large glass cloche and slip inside it, like the shadow he is. He flicks at the echo, trapped inside the automaton's mechanism. Fly off, my friend.

"WHO IS I? WHO IS . . . "

The lizard man looks aghast. The beetle woman blanches. Second stops drawing.

The parrot has fallen silent.

THE AIRSHIP

Through the porthole, the Deviations Observatory was now but an island surrounded by a stormy sea of clouds.

Ophelia was appalled. She was leaving behind a Horn of Plenty that couldn't be found, an unidentified shadow, an emancipated echo, and a terrible feeling of unfinished business. Why had the Deviations Observatory given her the illusion of choice, only to go against her decision? Why speak to her of all those things, in the crypt? Why show her the train? Why dangle before her the chance of an answer to all her questions?

So great was her frustration, she could feel it growling inside her like a caged animal. Those observers had made a fool of her, to the very end.

Outside, night fell for good. The portholes turned into mirrors. The reflection of Elizabeth, who was sitting beside her, was exasperatingly expressionless. As for Ophelia, she couldn't sit still. She turned around to stare at the passengers. Judging by their dress, there were some descendants of Pollux here, but also, surprisingly, several of the powerless.

At a sign from Lady Septima, a guard lowered a switch, turning off all the lights onboard. Ophelia understood why when, after a moment getting used to it, she saw the stars through the porthole. Because of the echoes, radio communications were no longer reliable; navigating had to be done visually. It was easier to distinguish land when not projecting light everywhere.

After a seemingly endless silence, the airship descended onto a small ark, which Ophelia recognized from having visited it twice. It was the district of the powerless, where Professor Wolf had formerly lived, and where Fearless-and-Almost-Blameless had died of terror. Ophelia had slept on one of these roofs, in an abandoned greenhouse, with Octavio. They had become friends that night.

She turned abruptly away, to stop the memory from taking hold.

She frowned on hearing muffled protests behind her, in the dark. With methodical efficiency, the family guard had lowered the gangway and made several passengers disembark. It had all happened extremely fast; the airship was already gaining altitude. Ophelia wiped away the mist her breath had left on the glass of the porthole. On the quayside the airship had stopped at, some men, women, and children looked completely distraught, in the middle of their trunks. The light from the streetlamps showed up the whiteness of their clothes. It was the powerless she had seen onboard. Lady Septima had uprooted them from the center of town to confine them to just one district—a minor ark that, according to her own admission, was more likely to collapse than inland districts. These people were born in Babel, had lived there for generations, but their mistake was not having any of Pollux's blood in their veins.

The passengers who had remained on board stifled embarrassed coughs. Ophelia felt no better than them. Her protesting spirit had got stuck in her esophagus.

At the helm, Lady Septima's wide-open eyes were incandescent. This was no longer the sign of her Visionary power, but of the volcano seething inside her. To her right, Thorn barely stood out from the surrounding darkness. He didn't move, said nothing.

They flew over the district of the Memorial. Its titanic tower, clinging to its little patch of land, jutting out into the void, was all lit up. There was probably no one left inside at this time, but the bulbs weren't designed to go out. They were illuminating the dome, allowing a glimpse, inside, of the terrestrial globe, floating in suspension.

And inside that, thought Ophelia, is Eulalia Gonde's secret room, and the hanging mirror where she conversed with the Other.

It was there that the old world had ended and the new had begun, there that Eulalia had turned herself into God, there that the Other had ceased to be an innocent little echo. It was infuriating still not to know *how*.

The illumination of the Memorial was so strong that, despite the darkness, one could see the surrounding mimosa trees, the statue of the headless soldier outside the entrance, and the age difference between the oldest half of the building and the half rebuilt after the Rupture.

Ophelia turned to Elizabeth, whose breath she could see in the half-light. Under her puffy eyelids, dull eyes. Neither the disembarkation of the powerless—of whom she was one—nor the view of the Memorial—despite it owing its modernization to her—had stirred her. She had built her life around Helen, serving her interests and seeking her recognition, but that existence was over.

The airship finally flew over Babel's town center, where the tide of clouds had reached unprecedented levels. Only the top stories of lofty buildings, the chimneys of the power exchanges, and the summit of a pyramid poked through. Lady Septima landed the airship without a hitch, despite the lack of visibility. The family guard disembarked to maneuver the airship on the ground and moor it firmly.

"Would you all leave calmly, please," directed Lady Septima, finally addressing her passengers. "A tram awaits you outside. You will be taken to your temporary accommodation. There you will be *parfaitement* safe."

"When will we be able to go back home?" one of them asked, timidly.

"You are at home, Son of Pollux. The whole of Babel is your home. What difference does it make that it be here, in the heart of the city, rather than on a little minor ark?"

No one replied. The gangway led into a fog so thick, the night was white. The civilians were swallowed up in it, one by one, with their suitcases. Once the evacuation was completed, the tram's headlights moved off, into the distance.

At a military clicking of heels, Lady Septima swiveled round to Thorn.

"Remain onboard, sir. I will escort you myself to the Genealogists, but I have a final formality to complete here. You two, with me."

This time she had addressed Elizabeth and Ophelia, who had to unstick her damp gown from the banquette.

"What are you going to do with them?"

Thorn's question had a ring of warning about it, but the only reply he got was the clatter of Lady Septima's heels down the gangway. Elizabeth followed her, obediently. Ophelia, on the other hand, instinctively recoiled, drawing the family guard, and their metal gauntlets, to her.

Thorn beat them to it by gripping her shoulder.

"I'll take care of this."

He plunged into the clouds with Ophelia. The family guard made a racket with their steel-tipped boots. They were in front, behind, everywhere. Where were they taking them to? The only clues were at ground level: cobbles, tracks, a gutter, and, here and there, trampled leaflets:

AND YOU, HOW ARE YOU GOING TO CELEBRATE THE END OF THE WORLD?

Ophelia couldn't speak to Thorn, but she could feel his fingers gripping her. She peered into the fog, hoping the Shadow would burst forth to help them escape, once again. Instead, Lady Septima's red eyes greeted them at the end of their march.

"I told you to wait onboard, sir."

Thorn's fingers tensed. Ophelia understood why when a night wind scattered the nearest clouds. They were standing on what remained of the spice market, where the first landslide had occurred. An airship, considerably bigger than the one they had just left, was moored on the edge of the void. A long-distance craft. An appalling number of hands were banging on the windows of its huge gondola.

On the ground, beside the landing stage, the guards on duty were all holding rifles with bayonets. Real rifles.

It was only at the sight of them that Elizabeth's eyelids finally deigned to lift. For the first time, doubt seemed to have stirred her. Hesitantly, she opened her mouth to speak, but it was Thorn who said the forbidden word:

"Weapons. That's illegal."

"Preventive equipment for peace. You stayed shut away in that observatory for too long, Sir Henry. As I have already said, circumstances have changed. And the laws have, too. But the Index is very much still in force."

Ophelia suddenly realized that she, personally, wasn't remotely surprised. Deep down, the moment she had seen Lady Septima on that verandah, she had known that this was how it would end. Her son was dead, she needed scapegoats. And she needed to sacrifice them as fast as possible, in the middle of the night and the fog, just a few steps away from the tram that had driven the good citizens to their new abodes.

"How many people have you crammed into that airship?" asked Thorn.

"The required number," replied Lady Septima. "And two more: Mademoiselle Eulalia, Mademoiselle Elizabeth, you dishonored the late Lady Helen, and you rendered yourselves unworthy of being her Goddaughters. I condemn you to banishment."

"I did not dishonor her."

If only with a pathetic muttering, Elizabeth had finally decided to react.

"Accuse me of any wrongdoings, but not that one," she implored. "Not that one."

"I leave you the choice, ex-virtuoso. You can go up this gangway either in an exemplary way or in a shameful way."

Elizabeth was a good head taller than Lady Septima, and yet she suddenly seemed tiny in front of her. Her bruised lips quivered. She bowed her head as a sign of surrender, held her fist to her chest in a final regulation salute, and then went up to board the airship.

Thorn's hand strengthened its hold on Ophelia. His harsh words succeeded in turning her to jelly:

"This airship wasn't designed to transport so many passengers, not to mention the radio communication problems. These people will not reach their destination, and you know it."

"What I know, Sir Henry, is that you are not an authentic Babelian."

Lady Septima had made this statement without deigning to look up at him. She was examining the brace he needed to remain upright. Around them, the moths could be heard colliding with the lanterns of the family guard.

"You are an error that infiltrated our ranks. The Genealogists offered you a chance, which you have constantly wasted, but that," Lady Septima admitted, reluctantly, "is not for me to judge. So go and fulfill your duty by giving them your report, and let me fulfill mine by entrusting Mademoiselle Eulalia's fate to me. *Maintenant*."

Ophelia gazed at the windows of the airship, pummeled by all those fists, and then the void—the unfathomable, the unimaginable void—that awaited them.

She could almost feel, through Thorn's fingers, the blood coursing under his skin to lubricate the workings of his brain. Undoubtedly, she didn't have his mastery of mathematics, but she could still tell that their adversaries were too numerous and too heavily armed. If Thorn used his claws right now, they would turn their rifles on him. Ophelia's animism wasn't up to stopping bullets.

"I'm going on," she decided.

With a determined jerk of her shoulder, she freed herself from Thorn's fingers. One of them, at least, had to get out of this situation safe and sound.

And since it wouldn't be her, she might as well have as few regrets as possible:

"You have tainted Octavio's memory."

Ophelia had articulated each syllable while gazing at the fire burning in Lady Septima's eyes. The Visionary could penetrate to the very marrow of her bones, but, for the first time, it was Ophelia who saw clearly through her, and her words had affected Lady Septima. The murderous rage consuming this woman was, first and foremost, directed against herself. She couldn't forgive herself for losing her son and abandoning her daughter, but since she was blind to her own feelings, she looked elsewhere for a culprit.

"Go on up, *petite fille*."

Ophelia made one step toward the airship; after the next step, she was sprawled on the cobbles. Her sandals had animated themselves without her knowing, tying their straps together to prevent her from leaving. She could act brave, but her animism wasn't taken in by that. Lady Septima clicked her tongue, but much as Ophelia struggled, she couldn't untie the knot, or take her sandals off. They were going to drag her onto the gangway, with the help of their bayonets.

"Return this to the Genealogists on my behalf."

It was Thorn's voice. His true voice, his Northern voice.

He had taken off his LUX insignia to hand it to Lady Septima. Then, with a grating of metal, he kneeled down beside Ophelia. The high-tension lines that electrified his face had all relaxed. There were no more conflicting currents, just a single certainty that shone from his eyes in the depths of the night.

"Together."

Awkwardly, he lifted Ophelia up in his arms, and went up to board the long-distance craft.

WHIRLWIND

Victoria had always been fascinated by the spyhole at home. How often had she found Mommy with her eye pressed to it, even if no one had just knocked on the door? How often had she, too, wanted to look out, beyond the real walls and fake trees of the house?

Today, Victoria felt as if she was on the other side of the spyhole. All she could see of the world was miniature images and minuscule sounds. She had sunk so deep in the big bathtub, full of shadows, that she couldn't move or feel anything. She wasn't scared. In fact, she was barely conscious of her own existence; she was dissolving, like those aspirins Mommy dropped into her glass of water. And she increasingly wondered who exactly were that Mommy and that house her thoughts were forever returning to. At the same time, she also wondered who that Victoria was, thinking of that Mommy and that house.

A noise, blurred by the echoes, brought her attention back to the little spyhole on the world, on the very surface of the bathtub. Not really a noise, more a voice. Godfather's voice. Who was Godfather?

Until then, Victoria had stayed between two waters—memory and forgetting, form and formlessness—but she knew that, if she used the strength she had left to go back up to the surface, the fall that would follow would drag her down to the very bottom of the bathtub, from which she would never return.

To see Godfather one last time. Before forgetting him altogether.

She focused entirely on the spyhole, on the voice escaping through it, on the colors that gained meaning as she widened her view. A man was mending the many rips in his shirt. He was badly shaved, badly combed, badly dressed, but there was an intensity to his every movement. He was singing to himself. The red thread he had picked for his sewing job stood out against the whiteness of the fabric, and when he had finished the mending and buttoned up his shirt, seeming very pleased with himself, it looked to Victoria as if his body were slashed with wounds. She seemed to remember that he was Godfather, but the less Victoria felt herself, the more her perception of him, no longer limited by her child's eyes and words, deepened. Had she found him handsome before? How had she not seen how damaged he was, behind his smile? She loved him all the more for it. This man had been a part of her ever since he had leaned over her cradle and—something inside Victoria suddenly remembered better than her—since he had whispered to her: "No one's worthy of you, but I'll try all the same."

"It's torn yurt . . . your turn, ex-ambassador."

Victoria's view widened through the spyhole to include the woman sitting opposite Godfather. The Bespectacled-Little-Lady. They were both settled on an assortment of cushions and rugs, separated by a board game. The Bespectacled-Little-Lady was waiting, in no apparent hurry, poker-faced behind her long, dark hair, but the shadows were writhing frenetically under her body.

Godfather piled up three black checkers on the board and, with a swipe of his hand, took all the white checkers.

"You're making up the rules, ex-ambassador."

"I'm adapting to my opponent, ex-*madame*."

Victoria saw them, but she also saw the emanations produced by their every movement, their every word, like so many rings in the water of the bathtub. Sometimes, a few returned as echoes.

Victoria widened her view even further. They were playing in a huge cabinet of curiosities, in which objects from the four corners of the arks were amassed: stuffed chimeras, weightless chairs, perfumed books, a vast map of the winds, clouds under cloches, electromagnetic cup-and-ball toys, an animated; she could give each of them an identity, deeper than words, as if she had always known each object intimately; as if, deep inside her, there was someone who knew much more, just waiting to be dissolved, too, in order to emerge. Her view of this place was now so complete, she could imagine it in its entirety, its smallest nooks and crannies, its connecting rooms; she could even sense, beyond its walls, the spatial distortion isolating this place from the rest of the universe.

"You never eat?"

Godfather was now calmly cutting around a can with a can-opener, but his light eyes questioned the Bespectacled-Little-Lady, on the other side of the checkerboard.

"I have not been subject to demonic perusal . . . organic disposal for centuries, ex-ambassador."

"Which doesn't stop you from being trapped here with us, ex-*madame*."

Godfather screwed up his eyes, as if doing so helped him to fathom the Bespectacled-Little-Lady, behind her round face, pink lips, long eyelashes, and strange dress with two bare knees poking out.

"I'm really struggling to get used to your true appearance. You look like our little Mrs. Thorn, to a degree that's disturbing."

"It's rather she who looks like me."

The can-opener froze in Godfather's fingers.

"How the devil did you end up stealing people's faces? Was your pretty little one no longer enough for you?"

The Bespectacled-Little-Lady limply shrugged one shoulder.

"I see," murmured Godfather, his smile returning. "You didn't choose to do so, it just happened. You played with forces that turned against you. But why does your talent for duplication not work on the family spirits? They are your personal creation, after all."

"Without their Books, the family spirits are nothing," explained the Bespectacled-Little-Lady. "And I can't take on the base of a fluke . . . face of a Book."

Godfather opened the can with a final flourish.

"I've changed my mind. You and Mrs. Thorn have nothing in common."

From a neighboring room, a torrent of expletives, gushing of water, and meowing in protest could be heard. Another woman, with hair half-dark, half-blonde, slammed the door behind her, unconcerned about the puddle of water she was spreading all around her. Anger oozed from her every pore. It was the Funny-Eyed-Lady, as Victoria vaguely recalled. The cat following her—"Twit," as Victoria also recalled—shook itself furiously.

Brandishing the can of food, Godfather let out what was at once a sigh and a smile.

"Pity's sake. Don't tell me we haven't got conveniences anymore, ex-mechanic. I can't guarantee the final outcome of this meal."

"I'm just looking for a way out, myself."

"You won't find one, either in the bathroom or anywhere else. You don't need me to tell you—the little favorite of our much missed Hildegarde—what a non-place is. I haven't managed to conjure up a single shortcut to the outside world, and even God in person," he sniggered, indicating his opponent, "hasn't managed to get out of here, despite her myriad powers! Let's be patient, my dear."

The Funny-Eyed-Lady looked down at the board game with disdain, but Victoria knew, from the way her vibrations deluged the Bespectacled-Little-Lady, that it was at her that her hatred was entirely directed.

"Carry on with your little games. I will demolish this place, brick by brick, if I have to."

"You promised me the face mate . . . same fate," the Bespectacled-Little-Lady said to her.

The Funny-Eyed-Lady grabbed a javelin from a sporting display. She stabbed it, viciously, into the nape of the Bespectacled-Little-Lady, before leaving with another slam of the door. Victoria felt neither surprise nor horror at the violence of the scene, just extreme curiosity. She would soon fall back down to the very bottom of the bathtub, where she wouldn't feel a thing anymore.

"You asked for it," said Godfather, sucking a finger smeared in pâté. "Taking Fox's place, that was a really bad idea."

The Bespectacled-Little-Lady gazed pensively at the point of the javelin sticking out of her throat. With a grotesque twisting of her arm, she seized the shaft hanging down her back, and pulled it straight out. The wound on her neck instantly closed up without any bleeding.

"It matters little whether I killed him or saved him. That poor child doesn't believe a thing that hums from my south . . . comes from my mouth. She has already tried to kill me forty-three times. You, never. Why?"

With a mischievous expression, Godfather rearranged the checkers on the board.

"Because, by shutting us up together in this non-place,

Janus made me your punishment. So I try my best to make my company as tedious as possible for you."

The Bespectacled-Little-Lady placed the javelin on the rug, beside the cushion she was sitting on. Her movements were calm, but under her body the shadows' writhing became ever more frenetic.

"You're excelling at it."

"Less than Thorn does," Godfather muttered, sliding a checker across the board with the pâté-smeared finger. "I'd like him to be here with us! No one beats him at ruining a party."

The Bespectacled-Little-Lady then moved her checker forward. Victoria, who really wasn't herself anymore, saw, rising from the board, all the echoes of the moves to come. She realized that she already knew the outcome of this game that had only just begun.

"I will repeat it to you, ex-ambassador: I dedicated my life to saving the world. Every second I lose in this non-place leaves my children outside without protection, which they need today more than ever. You've rot the gong money . . . got the wrong enemy."

Godfather's lips stretched from ear to ear.

"The Other, hmm? No thanks, ex-*madame*. A touch too abstract for me. It's because of *you* that Baron Melchior assassinated my guests. Because of *you* that old Hildegarde committed suicide. Because of *you* that my link with the Web was broken, and I was disowned by my sisters. Saving the world, you say? You have destroyed my world."

The Bespectacled-Little-Lady gazed at Godfather with a faraway look. The eyes behind her lenses—noticed Victoria, no longer missing a single detail—didn't reflect the light from the lamps. The Bespectacled-Little-Lady wasn't herself reflected, either, on the varnished checkerboard, or on the water siphon on the table. She was never reflected anywhere.

"Is that the kind of game you want to play, ex-ambassador? Very well." One by one, her checker wiped out all of Godfather's, just as Victoria had anticipated. "Baron Melchior assassinated your guests in my name, but was it not your duty to protect them? Mother Hildegarde committed suicide to deprive me of her power, but did you ever give her a reason for living? As for your sisters, did you not envisage for one moment that they just needed an excuse to turn away from such an intrusive brother? I personally believe that you steward . . . destroyed your world all on your own. You left behind you a chaotic embassy, ashamed wives, and offended husbands. You were always just an embarrassment to your family, to *our* family. When you will die, no one will miss you and you won't miss anyone."

Godfather gazed at the board, and his clear defeat. He was still smiling.

"When I will die," he repeated, in a low voice. "You know, don't you? Since when have you known?"

"I took on your face and I was you," said the Bespectacled-Little-Lady. "Not for long, but long enough to feel in my flesh the illness that's eating away at you. An illness that carried off your parents, and that's now growing in you, day by day. We both know that your nays are mumbled . . . days are numbered. And we both know that, if you avoid your sisters, it's because you tremble at the thought that theirs might be, too."

Victoria had never understood adults' conversations; right now, somewhere inside her and around her, someone understood everything. But it wasn't that someone who suddenly wanted to cry out. It was Victoria. For the first time in ages, the Bespectacled-Little-Lady turned her head toward her, squinting, as if, finally, she could detect her screaming silence.

Godfather chuckled as he rubbed the black teardrop between his eyebrows.

"My own transparency has backfired on me. I'm forced to admit that you're right, ex-*madame*, except about one thing: there is at least one person whom I will miss."

Victoria didn't hear the end of the sentence. The non-place was rocked as if by an almighty hiccup. The paintings dropped from the walls, the checkerboard tipped over, and Godfather fell into the Bespectacled-Little-Lady's arms.

"Goodness' sake," he said, extricating himself. "What has that ex-mechanic gone and broken now?"

"It wasn't me," grumbled the Funny-Eyed-Lady.

She had just come through the door she had left by a bit earlier, with a mechanical drill in each hand, and Twit hot on her heels.

"It's that."

She pointed at the hole, the size of a plate, that had appeared right in the middle of the rug. They all leaned over it. The hole looked out onto a starless darkness, but what none of them seemed to see was the vortex it had caused. A storm of echoes. Victoria felt herself being sucked down, as if a plug had been pulled and a force was dragging her not just to the bottom of the bathtub, but much further down than that.

"The landslides," said the Bespectacled-Little-Lady. "The Other is shattering space, even the non-place can't withstand it. Do you believe me now, Janus?"

She turned to the giant man-woman who was standing where, a second before, there was no one. He, too, was gazing at the hole in the middle of the rug, with one end of his long moustache coiled around his finger, looking extremely annoyed.

"I don't really have a choice. There's more and more void, and less and less land. Since you haven't left this non-place, *Señora* Gonde, it means the problem is elsewhere."

"Give me the final power I'm missing, Janus. Allow me to

find the Other again, before he hurls the whole world, your ark included, into the abyss."

"Your 'Other,' *señora*, is even more elusive than me. I asked my best Needlers to locate him. Not one of them succeeded in doing so."

"You have to know what you are looking for to be able to find it. You don't know the Other like I hoe limb . . . know him. Make me your Needler, Janus, and everything will return to order."

"Disastrous idea," said Godfather.

"Disgusting idea," said the Funny-Eyed-Lady.

Victoria didn't know what the man-woman's response was. She couldn't hear a thing anymore. The vortex was swallowing sounds and forms. The Bespectacled-Little-Lady suddenly seemed to see her, and all the shadows held down by her feet stretched their arms out to her. So many arms, and not one caught hold of Victoria. The whirlwind swept her far from the surface, to depths where no more boundaries existed between what was her and what wasn't her.

She forgot Godfather, Mommy, and the house.

She forgot Victoria.

ADRIFT

When Ophelia was doing her apprenticeship at the Good Family, there was a chore she dreaded more than any other: cleaning the drains of the showers. All that a body sheds that is least appealing sticks together in a stringy sludge that must be removed regularly from the plugholes to avoid blockages, particularly when the showers are shared by a community of men and women of all ages. The smell from the Residence's drains was unspeakable.

It was that very smell that pervaded inside the long-distance airship.

The cabins, holds, and bathrooms were overflowing with passengers. They clung tightly to the few personal belongings they had managed to take with them at the time of the roundup. One man was hugging a toaster, defying anyone to take it off him. Some people were so exhausted, they had lain down on the floor, no longer even protesting when kicked by feet stepping over them.

The heat everywhere was ferocious.

Since the embarkation door had been closed, Thorn had remained standing, rigidly, at the threshold of the airship. To him, each passenger represented an algebraic variable to be added to an increasingly complex equation. He was already, compulsively, opening his disinfectant bottle.

"Follow me," Ophelia said to him.

She had finally got the better of the recalcitrant sandals. She cleared a path for them, asking people to move aside to let them pass, earning her more than one grunt. She hadn't walked straight since waking up in the chapel, unable to stop herself from correcting movements that no longer needed to be corrected. Despite trying to avoid contact with people, she kept reading their clothes, soaking up ever more fear, ever more anger, and ever more sorrow. The family accents of almost every ark were combined here. Around the security lights, the alchemical ink glowed on the foreheads of those outlaws who had escaped from the amphitheater, and on those of many others. What remained of Babel's cosmopolitanism and diversity had been mustered here.

Stooping under the low ceilings, Thorn was doing his best not to let anyone near him. Just being tripped up would have triggered a fatal clawing.

Ophelia spotted Elizabeth, sitting at the back of a packed cloakroom, but she didn't respond to her wave. Seeming resigned, she had drawn up her long legs, like an ironing board folded up and put away in the cupboard for some time.

It was a real challenge to get to the picture windows of the rear walkway; all had been taken over by men and women pounding the reinforced glass, and cursing with no end of forbidden words. This group had no stamp on their foreheads, but their motley garish gowns certainly didn't conform to the dress code.

The Brats of Babel.

At least here, Thorn could lean against a window and keep everyone in his sight. All that could be seen through the window was part of the foggy quayside and the silhouettes of the guards on duty, deaf to the passengers' entreaties, their bayonets glinting in the lamplight.

"What are they waiting for?" asked Ophelia. "More outlaws?"

Thorn had a picked up a napkin from a sideboard. He was using it to wipe away, fastidiously, the grease left by countless fingers on the glass. He then pointed to a windsock outside. It was limp.

"Nina's Breath."

"Which is?"

"The name Babelians give to the south wind. It rises every night during the dry season."

"But why wait for it? This is an airship, not a balloon."

From a pocket, Thorn took out the gloves Ophelia had entrusted to him. He put them on her himself, first one hand, then the other, even buttoning them up at the wrists for her. A most intimate thing to do. Thorn was suddenly behaving as if the frenzied crowd was but an abstraction. It was only once he had replaced the substitute glasses with her real ones that his steely eyes looked hard into Ophelia's.

He didn't need to say a thing to her. She had understood. There would be neither pilot nor crew.

"You should have stayed on the quayside," she muttered.

Thorn's stern mouth stretched. It was a grin as brief as a snap of elastic, but Ophelia found it more comforting than any words.

"Hold onto the handrail," he told her.

The sudden pressure of the wind made the structure of the whole gondola creak. Outside, the windsock had just lifted. The family guard cast off the moorings. The few streetlamps in Babel penetrating the fog promptly disappeared. The passengers' protestations soared throughout the airship, as it was carried away, over the sea, by Nina's Breath, tossed around like a paper bag.

Adrift on the sea of clouds.

The passengers fell against each other, like dominoes. Ophelia dreaded to think what it would have been like, gripping this handrail without her gloves preventing her from reading it. She felt as if she were actually inside one of the Alternative Program's carousels.

"We must take . . . control of the airship," she managed to get out, between chattering teeth.

Thorn's leg brace was now at a disturbing angle, but he seemed far more troubled by some chewing gum stuck to the elbow of his uniform.

"I doubt Lady Septima has been so kind as to make navigation possible."

He unfolded his long arm to grab Ophelia just as she was losing her balance. The airship was tilting to one side. There was an eruption of cursing; this can't have been how the Brats had envisaged celebrating the end of the world. Just as everyone was clinging to whatever they could, Ophelia saw what she thought was a drinks trolley hurtling across the floor. It was Ambrose. His inverted hands were trying to activate the brakes on his wheelchair, without much success. All the wool of the scarf, wound around his neck, was bristling. He, on the other hand, seemed pretty calm; his face even lit up the moment his eyes met those of an astounded Ophelia.

"You, here, *mademoiselle*? How did you . . ."

The rest of his question got lost with him, as he continued his unavoidable descent of the walkway.

The airship started to rock back and forth. More cursing. At the mercy of every lurch, Ambrose was sent hurtling in the opposite direction. Thorn caught him by the scarf as his chair whizzed past them again, bringing it to an abrupt halt.

"What on earth are you doing here?"

It was almost an accusation. Disconcerted, Ambrose fluttered his long antelope lashes several times. In the midst of this nauseating furnace, his golden skin, black hair, and white clothing had retained all their silkiness.

"The outlaws I was sheltering . . . I couldn't do anything about it, *désolé*. Olfactories in the family guard had memorized their smell, and tracked them down to my father's place. On Lady Septima's orders. We were all arrested, and then separated, days ago. I don't even know if they, too, are onboard. This airship is ginormous, I haven't found them. Is it true, what's being said? The Good Family has also gone?"

Ignoring both the rocking and the shouting all around them, Thorn tightened his grip on the increasingly twitchy scarf, forcing Ambrose to look him straight in the eye. The gentleness of the one exacerbated the hardness of the other.

"What were you hiding from us, you and your father?"

"I don't understand, sir—"

"On the contrary, I think you understand perfectly well."

From their first encounter, Thorn had seen Ambrose as a potential spy for Lazarus, and, through him, for Eulalia Gonde. Discovering his funerary urn in the attic of the columbarium hadn't improved that opinion.

As for Ophelia, she no longer had an opinion. She stared at Ambrose's sheepish reflection on the window of the walkway, as she had done so often recently, to reassure herself that she wasn't in the presence of the Other, but what did it prove, really? Mirrors didn't reveal every imposture. Ophelia might not know who Ambrose really was, but she was sure of two things: the first was that the scarf trusted him; the second, that this wasn't the time for explanations.

"You're a driver," she cut in. "Would you know how to pilot this airship?"

Ambrose, half-strangled, shook his head, until Thorn deigned to release him.

"Apparently, the command bridge has been sabotaged. And

that's not the worst news, *mademoiselle*. Going by the direction and speed of Nina's Breath, we won't find any ark to land on. Father taught me cartography: there's nothing in that direction. Just clouds."

Ophelia was starting to feel decidedly nauseous. A jolt made the walkway's handrail dig into her ribs, totally winding her.

She thought again of that train refusing to take her to the third protocol. Of all the answers that remained in Babel, from which she and Thorn were moving further away by the second. Of that shattered world, where they hadn't managed to find their place, she the runaway, he the fugitive. Of the past that Eulalia Gonde had turned upside down, and the future the Other wanted to deprive them of. And of the Deviations Observatory, which, at this precise moment, was repeating the same mistakes with *her* echo.

WHO IS I?

No, Ophelia wouldn't allow it. She took in a great gulp of air, became conscious once more of the stench, the cries, the jolts, and, more vivid than all that, of Thorn's big hand holding hers. *Click click*. The fob watch was swinging hypnotically at the end of its chain, attached to his shirt, its cover opening and closing, quick as a heartbeat.

Seeing it, Ophelia was struck by a crazy idea.

"Where is it, this command bridge?"

Ambrose was really struggling to steady his wheelchair. Having half his limbs set the wrong way round didn't make things any easier for him.

"At the other end of the gondola, *mademoiselle*, but it has been sabotaged, as I told—"

"We must go there," said Ophelia.

With his back to the window, Thorn scrutinized the increasingly outrageous mayhem prevailing on the walkway. The jostling sometimes turning into fighting, sometimes into hugging. Some passengers were organizing wagers to predict the exact time of their death—the less optimistic not giving themselves more than fifteen minutes.

If a man yelled in panic, the Brats would throw themselves on him, laughing like lunatics, and stuff their leaflets into his mouth. Some musicians had got their saxophones out, launching into wild jazz improvisations; one of them cracked his teeth when a jolt knocked him over. An old lady was dancing, stark naked, on a table to the rhythm of the airship's swaying.

Thorn wrinkled his big nose. To Ambrose's astonishment, he grabbed the handles of the wheelchair and set off, pushing it straight ahead of him.

"And there was I, thinking you didn't like me, sir."

"I don't like you," grunted Thorn. "I'm using you."

Sure enough, he was maneuvering the chair like an ice-breaker, cleaving through the throngs of passengers. Ophelia followed him closely, to ensure that no one could trigger Thorn's claws from behind. It was doubtless an extension of her own Dragon power, but she could see Thorn's shadow ever more clearly, crackling like electrified barbed wire. Controlling himself in such circumstances must be a perpetual challenge.

Together, they advanced through the anarchic ebb and flow of the crowds, battling with the lurching, making their way through stinking gangways, packed dormitories, looted kitchens, trashed crew's quarters. The lights were forever going out and then coming back on. In this shifting between night and day, sobbing combined with uncontrolled laughter. It was mass hysteria.

And then there was silence.

It fell on the airship, heavy as a coffin lid, and so suddenly that Thorn slammed on the brakes of Ambrose's wheelchair in the middle of the ventilation room. Ophelia was about to ask what was up, but her question froze at the same time she did. She had felt it deep inside: the certainty of finding herself somewhere she should never have found herself.

The portholes had turned white. The airship was sinking beneath the surface of the sea of clouds.

Into the great void between the arks.

Never had Ophelia been overwhelmed by such a feeling of rejection, such a visceral need to be elsewhere. It was like when she had been locked in the incinerator room; or when Farouk had unleashed all of his psychic control on her; or when she had glimpsed oblivion when facing the Memorial's sweeper. No, it was far worse.

It was prohibited.

"Ophelia."

Thorn had let go of Ambrose's chair to lean over her. His thumbs were pressing into her cheeks and lifting her eyes up to his, which were astonishingly steady. The sweat streaming down his scars fell in big drops onto her glasses.

Ophelia should never have dragged him along with her. She didn't recognize the wheeze that came out of her own throat:

"The void . . . We shouldn't be here."

Speaking had become as challenging as breathing.

"Keep going," said Thorn. "We're nearly there."

Ophelia noticed, under the enormous copper ventilation pipes, the huddled figures of men and women. No one onboard was crying or laughing anymore. Engulfed in his oversized chair, as it veered around the room, Ambrose stared wide-eyed in horror. The scarf had curled into a ball against him.

"Planetary memory, planetary memory . . ." he kept on repeating.

Behind him, right at the end of a final gangway, gleamed the huge glass partition of the command bridge.

Thorn was right, they were nearly there.

Ophelia moved with legs of lead. She was in conflict with

her whole body, a conflict more daunting than her years of disjointedness, more disconcerting than her realignment. She felt in excess. They were all in excess. None of them had the right to be here, where formerly, before being reduced to dust, the land of the old world had stood.

On the command bridge, the instrument panels' dials had been removed, the cockpit had lost its helm and all its levers. It was even more disastrous than Ophelia had envisaged. The sea of clouds was already seeping through the cracks in the windows, spreading its fog inside the cabin. The oppressive feeling was unbearable.

"We can't do a thing here without regaining some altitude," said Thorn.

Without niceties, he pushed away a man who had frozen at a radio receiver, and took his place. He switched the radio off and pressed his mouth to the trumpet of an acoustic tube. He swallowed several times, struggling, too, with every atom of his being, and then his deep voice rang out across every part of the airship.

"Listen, everyone. We are too heavy."

Echoes piled onto his words, so he paused between each one. He pulled off his uniform jacket. His shirt was soaked, showing up the form of his spine, which he was twisting to be at the height of the trumpet. He no longer made any attempt to soften his native accent.

"We all come from different families. You're a Cyclopean? Make yourself weightless. You're a Phantom? Turn yourself into gas. You're a Colossus? Reduce your mass. If there are any Zephyrs on board, summon uplifting winds. You may no longer be citizens of Babel, but you are no less who you are. Each one of you can contribute to bringing us back up to the surface."

Once the countless echoes had faded, there was a very

long silence. The fog was thickening, second by second. The metal structure of the gondola then emitted a sinister groan. Although barely perceptible, Ophelia felt as if she weighed more. Paradoxically, the unbearable guilt weighing down on her lessened, little by little. They were rising up again.

"It's working," Thorn declared, into the trumpet. "Keep going."

Cries of relief erupted in all directions when the airship emerged into a vast starry night. Even Thorn allowed himself a sigh of relief.

Ophelia gazed at this great beanpole she had married, despite the disapproval of their two families. She felt proud of him like never before. He cleared his throat when he noticed how she was looking up at him—a throat-clearing that the echoes repeated through the sound system of the entire airship.

"It's merely a reprieve," he said, covering the end of the trumpet. "We're still in the middle of nowhere, at the mercy of the winds. What should we do?"

Thorn was naturally authoritarian; it was always he who gave instructions. For him to await her orders, with total confidence what's more, made quite an impression on Ophelia. She shook herself. She had no desire to endure another plunge into the void and lose all her faculties.

"I'm going to animate the airship."

Even to her ears, that sounded crazy. Thorn arched his eyebrows.

"Well, not the airship, strictly speaking," she corrected, "but its piloting mechanism. Lady Septima has sabotaged only the manual controls."

"Your animism can do that?"

"Of course, since I haven't a choice."

Ophelia positioned herself in front of the central stand

where the helm should have been, facing the great night-black windows, in which she could see her reflection. A tiny little woman, minus one of her powers, at the helm of a flying liner.

Not any old little woman, thought Ophelia, looking her reflection in the eye. The captain.

She anchored her feet firmly to the floor, stood erect, and placed her hands around an imaginary helm. Now was the time to make intelligent use of her realigned shadow. Every member of her family had a talent for giving a second life to damaged objects; she would prove that she wasn't bad at it, either.

She made a turning movement to the left, visualizing the interior workings and wirings as if they were her own sinews. After a moment in limbo, the airship slowly changed course. She turned in the opposite direction, to rule out a coincidence; the airship veered to the right.

Ophelia might not be a mirror visitor anymore, but she wasn't powerless, for all that.

There was enthusiastic applause behind her. Ambrose had caught up with them on the command bridge; the sound of his inverted hands clapping, knuckle against knuckle, sounded rather odd.

"You would make a *très* respectable whaxi driver, *mademoiselle*! All we need do now is pick a destination."

"It's up to you to guide us," Thorn admitted, reluctantly. "Lazarus taught you cartography. My encyclopedic knowledge has its limits."

"It's hard to determine exactly where Nina's Breath has taken us, sir. We won't find land anywhere around here. Perhaps we should make a U-turn and go back to Babel?"

"You've landed on your turban, young man!"

Ophelia raised her eyebrows. It was the growling voice of Professor Wolf. His black jacket stood out against the half-light of the gangway, as he advanced with difficulty toward them. His goatee beard was dripping sweat over his neck brace. On his back he was carrying the unconscious body of Blaise, whose long pointed nose hung over his shoulder.

"Leave it," grumbled Wolf, seeing Ophelia's obvious concern. "He passed out from the smell. Olfactory, and all that. Right now, the priority is, *above all*, not to take us back to Babel. Things are taking a very nasty turn back there, the city is on the verge of civil war. A war in which people like us," he said, hitching Blaise's inert weight up on his back, "have become the enemies to be eradicated."

"I also think we should seek sanctuary elsewhere," intervened a woman passenger who, until then, had been prostrate in a distant corner of the cabin. "Totem is the ark that's closest to Babel; we could take refuge there."

The man Thorn had pushed aside joined in the discussion, too, as he jumped out from under the radio receiver.

"Totem? That's much too far, we'll never reach it! Not with faulty communications and without a professional pilot. The wheelchair *garçon* is right, we should return to Babel."

Within moments, the command bridge was invaded by passengers who all had contradictory opinions about which direction to take. Things didn't take long to get heated. Ophelia was finding it increasingly hard to stay focused on her piloting job. Above all, she mustn't break the empathetic link she had formed with the machine, otherwise she wouldn't be piloting anyone anywhere.

Just as she was turning around to ask for some quiet, all her attention was suddenly drawn back to the window in front of her. Her reflection showed a tousled head with a questioning look. Why had she felt such an urgent need to keep looking at it?

"Switch off the lamps," she ordered. "Quickly."

Thorn didn't ask her a single question, which was just as well since she wouldn't have known how to answer him. He tore a stool up from its bolts and smashed the bulb on the ceiling, to everyone's astonishment.

The glass stopped reflecting the inside of the bridge, to reveal, just visible against the dark night sky, the spire of a belfry. The airship was heading straight for it.

THE ARK

There was no more belfry, no more airship. Ophelia had stepped out of the present. It wasn't a new page of Eulalia Gonde's past. Neither was it a vision of a bloody future. No, this time it was her own memory, her own childhood. She was gazing at herself in the wall mirror of her bedroom on Anima. Her sleepy eyes weren't yet shortsighted, her tousled hair hadn't yet turned brown. Her body wavered between childhood and adolescence. A call had got her out of bed.

A call of distress.

Release me.

"Sorry?" Ophelia whispered, very quietly.

She didn't want to wake Agatha, asleep next door. Maybe she should have. Maybe it would have been more sensible to call their parents. Ophelia was used to objects with strong personalities, but a talking mirror, that was pretty weird, all the same.

Release me.

Looking more closely, it seemed to Ophelia that there was someone behind her reflection. A silhouette whose outline slightly overlapped her own. She turned around, but there was no one behind her.

"Who are you?"

I am who I am. Release me.

"How?"

Pass through.

Ophelia rubbed her eyes, which were heavy with sleep. She hadn't yet passed through any mirror. Her father had frequently done so when young, it couldn't be hard. But was it a good idea?

"Why?"

Because it must be done.

"But why me?"

Because you are who you are.

Ophelia stifled a yawn, and her reflection did, too. The silhouette hiding behind it didn't move. Nothing of all this seemed real. In fact, Ophelia wasn't really sure she was awake.

"I can try."

If you release me, it will change us: you, me, and the world.

Ophelia hesitated. Her mother had never let her change anything at all. That's how it went on Anima. The same domesticated objects, the same little habits, the same traditions repeated from generation to generation. Ophelia's life had barely begun, and she could already predict what it would be like: decent work, a good husband, lots of children. In the world such as she knew it, nothing ever changed. And for the first time, because an unknown voice had conjugated the verb "to change" in the future tense, Ophelia felt a newfound curiosity growing within her.

"Alright."

Ophelia focused all her animism on the helm's mechanism, forcing the airship to swerve. She avoided a head-on collision with the belfry, but only just. There was some shaking, and a bell vibrating, and screams, and Thorn's arms. Ophelia sensed, by the way her stomach lurched, that they were now falling. She no longer knew what to expect—fatally crashing into the ground? Endlessly plunging into the void?—but she certainly wasn't prepared for the soft "plop" that barely jolted her jaws.

They stopped moving. It was all over.

Stupefied murmurs rose from every part of the airship. Ophelia carefully extricated herself from Thorn, whose bony frame had closed over her like a cage, while searching in the gloom for the glimmer of his eyes. He seemed as disconcerted as she was to be still alive. There were reeds brushing against the window of the command bridge.

Had they landed in the middle of a marsh?

"It's *absolument* impossible," Ambrose voice whispered. "There shouldn't be any arks in this part of the world, the maps are categorical."

Thorn sat up with a creaking of metal. With his eyes, he followed the gigantic whalelike form disappearing among the lingering stars, high above the reeds. The collision with the steeple had separated the balloon from the gondola.

"Wherever we are," he said, "we're here for a while. Let's proceed with the evacuation."

The passengers rushed out of the safety exits and found themselves knee-deep in the marshes. Some offered helping hands to others. The Brats got together to lift Ambrose's wheelchair, carrying him to dry land, while he hugged the scarf tight so it didn't fall in the water. Maybe these people felt rather ashamed of the madness that had overcome them during the flight, but what had happened onboard would stay onboard.

Not for Ophelia it wouldn't.

Standing quite still among the water lilies, she gazed at the airship, now more like a grounded clipper with its sails cut off. She wasn't really sure what had happened, in that cockpit window, but it had brought a memory back to her that was still making her temples throb.

Later. She would think later.

In front of her, Thorn was bending back reeds as tall as him, to clear a path to the bank. The belfry stood proud, like a capital letter stamped on the dawn.

"If you hadn't avoided it, we would be dead."

He had said that as a simple statement, without emotion, yet watching for Ophelia's reaction from the corner of his eye. There wasn't one. She was silently moving her sandals through the murky water. She didn't even react when Blaise, who had finally regained consciousness on Wolf's back, started endlessly apologizing, much to Wolf's exasperation.

The stranded passengers regrouped around the belfry. When they pushed on its doors, only reverberations from the bells answered their calls.

"Over there!" someone exclaimed.

Ophelia saw it, too, in the early morning light: a country road winding between vineyards. And right at the end, almost as far as the eye could see, the contours of a village stood proud on the horizon. Briefly, she turned her glasses back toward the marshes, where what remained of the airship basked, and barely much further, toward the clouds of the void that they had had such difficulty escaping from. The cliff that served as a frontier between sky and land was so vast as to seem endless.

"This," observed Thorn, "is not a minor ark."

They all set off toward the village, like a stream of refugees. The less patient among them strode ahead, but many were shattered after the eventful night, and took the time to sample some grapes. The air, increasingly warm, soon vibrated to the chirping of the first cicadas. They walked around a tractor that stood in the way. Ophelia had never seen one of this sort. It seemed in good condition, and yet its driver had left it in the middle of the road.

The road's cracked tar made Ambrose's wheelchair jump at every pothole.

"Do you think . . . we could be . . . on LandmArk?" he asked, joyously. "After all . . . it's the only ark . . . that doesn't appear . . . on any map. Father says the Arkadians . . . can't be found by anyone looking for them . . . but maybe they've made . . . an exception for us?"

Ophelia was asking herself the same questions, and many more besides. She had so many, she no longer knew which way to turn. Just the fact of walking alongside an adolescent whose date of death went back forty years was disturbing. She glanced at the scarf, curled up on Ambrose's lap. She knew they would have to have a serious talk, but at the moment, there were too many people around them, and not enough clarity in her mind.

"Mademoiselle Eulalia?"

Blaise had approached her looking apologetic, and even more so when he saw the "AP" stamped on her arm, as though he bore some responsibility for all she might have been through at the Deviations Observatory. He gripped the sleeve of his Memorialist's uniform, which covered up an experience they now had in common.

"I shouldn't be, because it means things didn't go well for you, but I'm *vraiment* pleased to see you again."

Ophelia smiled at him, conscious of not feeling what she should have felt.

Later. She would feel later.

She slowed down when she noticed that Thorn was trailing. He was limping. His leg brace had suffered from the journey, but he didn't seem particularly concerned. He was studying the surrounding vineyards with such intensity, he seemed to be converting each bunch of grapes into a bunch of statistics.

"Something's not normal," he said to Ophelia.

She agreed. She sensed it, too, without being able to define what it was exactly. It wasn't easy for her to be objective, however, since her own body no longer had anything normal about it; or perhaps, on the contrary, it had become too normal, no longer tripping on every bump, or banging into the first obstacle, or damaging objects as soon as her attention wandered. Once, picking fruit demanded her full concentration; now it had become simplicity itself. The beetle woman had told the truth on one count, at least: the disjointedness was already disappearing. The crystallization had succeeded where years of physiotherapy had failed.

The sun was at its zenith when they finally arrived at the edge of the village. There were enthusiastic cries at the sight of stone buildings, paved paths, terraces full of pots, but then the euphoria died down.

There wasn't a villager to be seen anywhere.

The Brats of Babel rang several doorbells, but no one opened to them. They proceeded to swear furiously while kicking the closed shutters of stores.

"Very smart," sniped Professor Wolf. "If the people here are hiding from us, that's bound to fill them with confidence."

He was resting on a bench, his black jacket over his arm, wiping his forehead, which the sun had turned scarlet. Sitting with his back to him, Blaise was sniffing the air with his big pointed nose. His forever anxious face creased up even more in disgust.

"There's the smell of rotting food. Everywhere."

Ophelia looked around at the streets' shop signs. They had nothing written on them, no "Haberdashery & Hosiery," or "Surgeon-Barber." A tin basket was lazily swaying above what must be the grocer's store. Ambrose went closer, as far as his chair allowed, to the folding grille protecting the shop window from intruders. He looked forlornly at the displays of decaying fruit and vegetables.

"They're not hiding," he said, with disappointment. "They've gone."

"Maybe they, too, were fleeing from the landslides?"

This hypothesis, spoken in a raucous whisper, had been put forward by Elizabeth. Ophelia had completely lost sight of her onboard the airship. And for good reason: with face gaunt with exhaustion, arms stiff against body, and hair stuck to frock coat, she had flattened herself so much that, soon, she would be nothing but a line merging into the background. In the space of one day, the model citizen had lost her best-of-all-worlds, and Ophelia hadn't the slightest idea what she could say to her to make this loss acceptable.

Later. She would express herself later.

Thorn decided to knock, methodically, on every door, even though he no longer seemed to expect to come across anyone at all. His way of walking, like a broken automaton, resounded lugubriously around the deserted streets. Ophelia silently followed him. Through some half-closed shutters, she glimpsed parlors with wilted flowers, flies swarming around forgotten plates, and furniture stripped bare. There was plenty of pottery, but no posters, no photographs, no newspapers, no plaques, no names. The villagers had left their homes, but left nothing of their past.

After a meaningful look from Thorn, Ophelia took her gloves off. She didn't like to read an object without permission, but she understood that these were exceptional circumstances. She burnt her fingers on the door handles, made white-hot by the sun. They all conveyed the same bitterness, which, if it had to be put into words, would have been something like: "I don't want to leave, I don't want to leave, I don't want to leave, I don't want to leave . . ." The door handles bore witness to nothing else, no other layer of lives lived, as if the fateful intensity of that final moment had erased all those that had come before.

Ophelia picked up a sign of denial. Thorn's eyes seemed more questioning, from under his eyebrows, but he left it at that, and decided to give up on his door-knocking.

They rejoined the others, who had all gathered on the village square, to quench their thirst at the drinking fountain, and gorge on grapes. Here, the late-afternoon light was filtered by the plane trees. Garlands of flags, left over from some celebration, danced from one roof to another. An awkward silence had descended, with each person staring warily at their neighbor. They were souls without homes among homes without a soul. As the daylight faded, a musician took out his saxophone and played a little. Voices joined in with him. Finally, a burst of laughter. More animation. Soon there was singing, waltzing, whistling: they were alive, here and now.

Sitting on the edge of the fountain, Thorn declined two invitations to dance, and consulted his watch seven times. His index finger scratched his bottom lip, which was so thin as to be almost invisible, while his forehead dropped lower and lower. All that concerned him was tomorrow.

"The villagers didn't plan to return," he muttered, between his teeth. "Not for a long while, at any rate. I'm not convinced that this ark is LandmArk. The question is: wherever we are, how do we leave here?"

Beside him, Ophelia was mindlessly chewing a grape. She looked at all the former Babelians around them who had no idea where they were, and yet were celebrating their new haven. She looked at Ambrose, whose wheelchair was spinning in the midst of the dancers. She looked at Blaise and Wolf, whose shoulders, forever weighed down by worry, were gradually lifting. She looked at Elizabeth, who had withdrawn miserably to a corner, turning her back on the party. Finally, she looked at herself, looking.

Bracing herself, she put her head under the spout of the fountain. The cold water would clear her thoughts.

This time was the right time.

"I must talk to you," she said to Thorn.

He immediately put his watch away and got up, as if he had been waiting for those five words all day. They moved away from the village, climbing up a hill covered in olive trees until the raised voices were reduced to murmurs. From the top, they discovered new expanses of grass and water, glinting even further into the distance. A road cut though them, with its worn, cracked tar. At the foot of the hill, what looked like a bus stop had been invaded by stinging nettles.

Ophelia gazed at this mysterious ark that had almost killed them, and yet had saved their lives.

"I have done two really stupid things," she announced.

She sat down in the tall grass, scorched yellow, and gazed up at the sky. It was a maelstrom of sunshine and clouds, changing appearance from one second to the next.

"I gave birth to an echo. Not only was I incapable of finding the Horn of Plenty, but, on top of that, I supplied the observatory with the final element they were missing to reproduce the same mistakes as Eulalia: a new Other. I sacrificed my mirror-visiting power there. The more I try to make my own choices, the more I'm playing their game."

Thorn shared the almost stone-like stillness of the olive tree he was leaning against. True to himself, if he was surprised or shocked, he didn't show it.

"And the second stupid thing?"

Ophelia rubbed her tongue on her palate, for the lingering sweetness of the grapes.

"I released the Other from the mirror. Deliberately. I finally remembered that confounded night. His voice, in particular, if one can call it a voice. It was so sad . . . The Other warned me that it would change me, and it would change the world. I didn't know by how much, but I still acted knowing the facts. Basically, that was what I wanted: for things to be different. If the arks are collapsing, if there were deaths, and if there are more to come, it's because I didn't want to become like my mother."

Swallowed by the clouds, the sun went out like a lamp. The vivid colors of the landscape took on a pastel softness. Ophelia was amazed at her own calmness; the wind was making the whole hill tremble, apart from her. She suddenly noticed how itchy her wet hair on her shoulders felt; hair that should have been golden, and that, from one day to the next, centimeter by centimeter, had started to grow in a much darker color that wasn't hers.

"All this time, I felt damaged by the intrusion of Eulalia's echo in my body and my mind. It was my stain. When we began to understand that it was the Horn of Plenty, I . . . Let's say that my motivation was more selfish than yours. Freeing us, me and the world, has always been your sole aspiration. You immediately thought of how this Horn of Plenty could turn Eulalia and the Other back into what they were originally. For myself, I mainly thought of how it could turn me back into the person I would have been without them. Except that now, I know that that change was my choice from the start."

She went quiet, drained of breath.

With some tricky maneuvering, Thorn shifted over beside her. If his body wasn't the right shape for most chairs, which were invariably too low, it was even less so for the ground. With an inscrutable expression, he stared at the water slowly dripping from Ophelia's hair.

"You are totally unaware of it, aren't you?" He waited until some shrill laughter from the party, carried by a gust of wind, faded. "Of our rivalry."

Ophelia stared at him, not understanding.

"I, myself, became aware of it early on," he continued, abruptly. "This determination that won't stop growing in you, and is taking up more and more space. You want your independence. Even your obsession with the past—your object readings, your museum, your reminiscences—it has always, basically, been about being better able to free yourself from it. You want your independence," he repeated, separating each syllable, "and I, myself, want to be indispensable to you."

His pupils had dilated as his speech went on, as if some inner darkness were invading him, little by little. Ophelia curled up and hugged her knees, but Thorn allowed her no time to react.

"You mentioned my aspiration to free you, and the world. I aspire to nothing whatsoever. I need you to need me, it's as basic as that. And I know full well that, in this conflict of interests between us, I'm doomed to be the loser. Because I am more possessive than you will ever be, and because there are things that I can't replace."

He took out his bottle of disinfectant and, after some tense hesitation, instead of opening it, he offered it to Ophelia, as if he were giving up using it.

"So much for my stain. If you can live with it, then I can, too."

Ophelia took the bottle without the clumsiness she had been cured of, despite herself, but aware that there were many other ways of breaking what was precious. Remaining silent for any longer was one of them.

"I can't have children."

There, she had said it. She had said it, and she still felt just as calm. She didn't even know why she had made such a big deal about it, no more than she understood why Thorn was now looking apprehensively at her.

"And it's entirely my fault," she added.

She pursed her lips to stop their inexplicable trembling, but it spread to her teeth, nostrils, eyelids, her whole body. The bottle of disinfectant slipped out of her hands and rolled on the grass, down the slope, to get lost among the stinging nettles, at the bus stop right at the bottom.

"I'm sorry."

She no longer felt at all calm, and her stomach was hurting her. Living was hurting her. Octavio, Helen, and all the others should have all also had their place on this hill, facing this sky, under these olive trees.

"I'm sorry," she stammered, not knowing what else to say. "I'm so . . ."

Her tearful voice drowned in Thorn's shirt. With a creaking of metal, he had pressed Ophelia against him, hard, as if he wanted to contain her suffering with the same force as was needed to control his claws, but the apologies kept flooding out of her, in uncontrollable sobs, again and again and again.

THE STRANGERS

Ophelia woke up surrounded by stars. Night was nearing its end. Her first thought, at the sight of all these constellations, was that she didn't know the name of one of them, but that didn't stop her from finding them amazing. She had never really approved of Artemis's interest in them. Why would a family spirit prefer stars to her descendants? She understood it better now: the secrets of the sky were less terrifying than those of her own life. Ophelia found it hard to believe that she shared the blood of a person who had originally been an echo, and even harder to believe that she had herself given birth to an echo that could well become a person, too.

Impossible lives suddenly appeared from nothingness. Others were plunged into it, or would never get out of it.

Ophelia's chest lurched with a mix of guilt, curiosity, and fear. Her tears had released her emotions, painful as splinters of glass, but necessary, too. She couldn't claim she felt well, but at least she felt.

Beyond the hill of olive trees, where she had fallen asleep, exhausted from too much crying, the voices from the party were getting more raucous. The laughter had become coarser, the songs bawdier. The Brats must have found some wine in a villager's cellar. And a firework, too: there was a whistling in the sky that exploded into a single shower of light and smoke, pretty disappointingly, it must be said, and then more laughter and songs.

"Those idiots are going to end up causing a fire."

Ophelia turned her glasses toward the figure half-leaning over her, totally still amid the swaying grasses. All she could detect of Thorn were angular contours and watchful breathing. Of course he wasn't sleeping; like his claws and his memory, he never rested.

"What are you thinking about?" she murmured.

There was no shortage of subject matter. Ophelia had told him, in great detail, all that had happened in the second protocol: the chapel, the parrot, the confessional, the Knight, the crystallization, the Shadow, her partial Mutilation, the beetle woman, that train, finally, that should have taken her to the third protocol, and that hadn't . . .

There was enough there to make one go mad.

Thorn's reply was practical:

"About how to get back to Babel. It won't be easy, even aside from the fact that we've lost all means of transport. LUX has placed the entire city under surveillance, and we wouldn't survive a second expulsion. Even more than Lady Septima, it's the Genealogists I don't trust; we'll have to avoid crossing their path at all costs. As for the Deviations Observatory, in the eventuality that, defying every statistic, we access it, I doubt they would let us get our hands on their Horn of Plenty without a fight. There, in broad outline," concluded Thorn, after this monotonous account, "is what I'm thinking abou—"

"We could stay here."

Thorn's breathing went silent. As soon as the impulsive words were out, Ophelia regretted them.

"But we mustn't," she hastily continued. "Me least of all. Now that I know that I released the Other of my own free will, I must face the consequences. If he finds us again, before we have found the Horn of Plenty, he won't give as a chance to turn him back into a mere echo."

Despite what she said, she was fully aware of how little she knew about the Other. The Shadow had revealed to her that she had already met him, several times, without ever recognizing him. Where? On Anima? In the Pole? In Babel? Was he someone she had spoken to? An echo with a new body, a new face, perhaps even a new reflection? If so, then it could be anyone. It could be Ambrose, the enigmatic Ambrose who wasn't anything he seemed to be, neither adolescent nor the son of Lazarus. No. Unimaginable. It was impossible for Ophelia to associate Ambrose with the widening void. And hadn't he himself believed, at one time, that she was the Other?

Back to square one.

Ophelia had thought of the Other as an invisible enemy, monstrous and ruthless, but the unlocking of her childhood memory had turned that upside down, too. That call for help from the mirror in her bedroom, and the sincerity of his warning, had made the Other harder to hate. Had he manipulated Ophelia, or was his distress sincere? That was no excuse. Never would she forgive him, any more than she would forgive herself, for what he had done to Octavio, and to the world. And was perhaps still doing at this very moment.

Above her, half of the stars disappeared. Thorn's huge shadow had darkened them, like the sign of a storm.

"Don't get the wrong culprit. It's not you but Eulalia who is entirely responsible. Where is she, that woman who cares so much about the fate of humanity, while her chosen ones dispose of undesirables, and her reflection tears our world apart? She's hiding on the other side of this vast chessboard she has created, on which all the pieces—LUX, Genealogists, observers—have long been playing their own game with their own rules."

Her hair tangled with grass, Ophelia stared at the huge frame looming over her in the dark, and which, like the Shadow, was faceless.

"How can one win against them, then?"

"By being aware of the game. We will find the Horn of Plenty, we will reduce Eulalia and the Other to powerlessness, and then we will smash the chessboard."

Although Thorn couldn't see Ophelia any more than she could see him, she nodded her head. The indefatigability of this man swept away her doubts, and his determination touched her. A disparity persisted between them, however. Thorn was an arrow focused on its target. Ophelia couldn't dispel the feeling that there was another target, far bigger than Eulalia and the Other, a truth far crazier and far more fundamental. The Deviations Observatory had revealed some astounding things to her, but she felt that she had missed the most important of all: a revelation she needed in order to free herself definitively from the past.

Ophelia was obsessed by that train that had almost led her to the final answers, she yearned to get back on it, with Thorn this time, but she also feared not returning from its destination unscathed. She had already lost her mirror-visiting power; would she have to make more sacrifices?

Once again, Ophelia dismissed the apocalyptic scene that had appeared to her at the glazing-and-mirror store and in the window at the columbarium, just as she dismissed Second's drawing—the old woman, the monster, and her body scrawled in red pencil.

We will smash the chessboard.

"And afterwards?" she asked. "Once it's smashed?"

They had still never spoken about it.

"Afterwards," Thorn replied, without a second's hesitation, "I will give myself up to seek justice. A true justice this time, with a real court and a real trial. I will settle my debt to our two families, and will proceed with the annulling of our marriage—its legal validity has become pretty dubious."

Ophelia had hoped for a slightly rosier picture of their future.

"And afterwards?" she insisted.

"Afterwards, that will be your decision. I will wait for you to make your request."

She let out a strangled cough. In the Chroniclers' memory, there had never, historically, been any woman in the Pole who had got down on one knee, ring in hand.

"*Our* decision," she corrected.

A particularly obscene refrain, wafting over from the village square, passed between them.

"I haven't yet said that I will accept it."

Ophelia stared wide-eyed behind her glasses. She didn't dare move, for fear of triggering an involuntary claw attack, but she would have paid a lot to see the expression on this face that she had always known to be overly serious. Was that, as she struggled to believe, an authentic attempt at humor? Was Thorn really trying to put a smile back on her face? She considered how far they had both come since that grim meeting in the rain on Anima, him with his bearskin, her with her sparrow-like voice.

"Then I'll just have to be persuasive."

Thorn descended on her, replacing all the sky's darkness with the even more intense darkness of his body. It was an awkward move, a little shaky, as if he were still embarrassed to impose his over-prominent bones on Ophelia.

"When my aunt lost her children, I wasn't enough for her."

In this abrupt confidence, there was a shift that Ophelia had already detected, on rare occasions, in Thorn. It resembled anger, but wasn't.

It was almost a challenge:

"Will I be enough for you?"

Ophelia contemplated this black hole that had swallowed up the very last stars. In reply, she gave him, unreservedly, all the tenderness she had. Thorn was, in more ways than one, an uncomfortable man, but she felt so alive with him! The Other had changed her, yes. He had made her the clumsiest of all the Animists. And it was because she was the clumsiest that she had endeavored to become the best reader of objects. And it was because she had become the best reader of objects that her path had crossed Thorn's.

She might have regrets, but that wasn't one of them.

It was, however, with some embarrassment that she emerged from the tall grasses, a little later, as the dawn was setting nature alight. There was a young girl at the foot of their hill, sitting on the bus-stop bench. Ophelia's glasses turned crimson. How long had she been there? Had she heard them? The young girl was handling, very carefully, the bottle of disinfectant that had rolled down the hill the previous evening, which she had seemingly bothered to extricate from the stinging nettles. Ophelia was pretty sure she wasn't one of the airship passengers. She was wearing soil-stained clothes and simple espadrilles, but her eyes were extraordinarily bright. They looked up at Ophelia, as soon as she discreetly straightened her gown, as though magnetized by her movement. The young girl then put the bottle down, got up from the bench, and started climbing the hill.

"Thorn. Someone's coming."

"I've seen," he grumbled, re-buttoning his shirt up to the collar, and smoothing his messy hair with his palm. "And she's not coming alone. A little more than that, even."

Indeed, men, women, children, older folk were all arriving along the road and across the fields. There were too many to count. Ophelia wondered how she hadn't noticed them, until she observed their extreme discretion. They moved without making a sound and without haste, but with total determination. They had the same soil-stained clothes and sparkling eyes as the young girl.

"Who are you?" Thorn asked them.

Despite the authoritative tone of the question, the new arrivals didn't answer him. They did, however, keep heading straight for him. The olive-tree hill would soon be swamped with people.

Ophelia knew that she and Thorn were the strangers here, but she found all these country folk very invasive.

"Let's warn the others," she muttered.

They returned to the village by going down the other side of the hill, with this human tide, swelling by the second, hot on their heels. All they found on the square were bodies dozing in the shade of the plane trees, an unreasonable quantity of empty bottles, and a nauseating smell of alcohol. A large, dark mark had been scorched into the ground from the lighting of the firework. The only person awake was Ambrose, who, since one of his wheels had got stuck between two cobblestones, had been politely calling for help for what must have been some time. The scarf was tugging, with its every fiber, on his inverted leg to try to release the chair.

He smiled with relief on seeing Ophelia and Thorn, and then his eyebrows shot up when he discovered the crowd stretching into the distance.

"Are they the villagers?"

"Let's hope not," said Ophelia, unblocking his wheel. "I can't see us explaining to them how the wine cellars were looted. We must quickly wake everyone up."

Thorn threw buckets of water over those sleeping, heedless of the howls of protest erupting all around him. More considerately, Ambrose served fresh water to Blaise, who had got sick from just one gulp of alcohol, but when he tried to do the same for Professor Wolf, his necktie, contaminated by a particularly cantankerous animism, just slapped him.

As for Ophelia, she had to shake Elizabeth's shoulder for some time, after discovering her under a bench, curled up in the fetal position. Puffy eyelids half-opened onto a chink of bloodshot eye.

"Oh, my head . . . The Brats forced me to drink. I'd never before . . . Hmm. I've got a feeling I called Lady Septima many, many forbidden words. It'll make tons of sins to confess."

Ophelia helped her up.

"Later. We've got visitors."

The country folk were now flooding in from streets and vineyards, until they encircled the village square, making any escape impossible. It was a shock to wake up to, for the Babelians. There was a long showdown, as the two groups stared at each other, the one unsteady and hungover, the other standing firm and alert.

Bleary eyes against piercing eyes.

Were the inhabitants of this ark waiting for explanations? Apologies? Would they send the outlaws back to where they came from, but without an airship this time? Ophelia exchanged a tense look with Thorn. She got the feeling that it would take just one word to trigger hostilities.

"There really is no peace anywhere."

Professor Wolf's voice had cut though the silence like a cleaver. He was biting a cigarette while struggling to light it with an old lighter. It wasn't his usual sarcasm. He just seemed to be disappointed.

"Peace is everywhere, and here more than anywhere! Come now, *cher ami*, when will you be cured of your lamentable pessimism?"

Professor Wolf's cigarette fell to his feet.

Ophelia couldn't believe her glasses when she saw Lazarus barging through the country folk. His fine white frock coat was smeared in soil stains, and his silver hair sticky with sweat, but he was beaming with delight. The old man was certainly ever the magician, ready to pop up where least expected. His name circulated among the Babelians, across the village square: of all the powerless, he was the most famous, as an explorer and inventor. Indeed, Walter, his mechanical butler, was at his side, but moving so slowly that Lazarus got out a giant key to wind him up.

"Father!"

Ophelia turned to Ambrose, struck by the spontaneity of this exclamation. He might have a funerary urn that was forty years old, but he was sincere in his role of son. Lazarus was much less so in that of father. He dusted off his pink spectacles without a glance for Ambrose. On the contrary, he scanned all the faces around him, lingering, in a friendly way, at those of Blaise and Wolf, his former pupils, and then that of Thorn, whose ill-concealed mistrust seemed greatly to amuse him, before stopping, with a beaming smile, at Ophelia's face, as though it was hers he was hoping to find.

"*Tiens, tiens, tiens*, you, here? What a darling coincidence!"

"Coincidence?" she repeated.

She believed none of it. If Ambrose was an imposter, who, then, was he? He had spoken to her about the Deviations Observatory, but had omitted to specify that he had himself, long ago, been a boarder there.

As if the scene wasn't unreal enough, all the country folk approached Lazarus, irresistibly drawn to him, to touch his arms, his cheeks, his ears, his hair, without him seeming put out by it. Apparently, he was used to it.

That wasn't the case for the Babelians, who drew back at the approach of all those soil-blackened fingers.

"Don't let yourself be intimidated by my new friends," said Lazarus. "They don't have a sense of privacy, but they are *tout à fait* harmless. In fact, it's the most fascinating civilization I have ever had the chance to study. I've been sharing their everyday life for days . . . unless it's weeks?" he asked himself, rubbing his hairless chin. "I've lost count. They welcomed me into their midst with unparalleled hospitality. Their curiosity is as insatiable as my own! What serves as their camp is located beyond the fields. We were all gazing at the stars together when we spotted your firework. My friends immediately took to the road; I had to walk with them, or be left behind. I've parked the Lazaropter back at the camp. Walter!" he cried, as his voice became hoarse. "Some water!"

Of all his automatons, Walter was at once the most faithful and the least accomplished: he pushed Lazarus into the fountain. The country folk had observed the scene without even trying to hold him back, despite their outstretched hands, but their eyes had widened. Ophelia found them downright peculiar.

Blaise and Wolf combined forces to get Lazarus out of the fountain, and sit him on its edge.

"Father," said Ambrose, handing him his spectacles, which had fallen in the water with him, "you've been here all this time? I'm reassured to see you in good health. I was afraid a landslide might have swept you away."

"A landslide?" asked an astonished Lazarus, when he had finished spluttering and coughing. "There was a landslide in Babel?"

"Two," Professor Wolf corrected, bitterly. "It caused all of us, here present, to be expelled."

"That is *très* regrettable . . ."

Lazarus had said that while drying his long hair, but Ophelia saw the lines on his forehead twitch when he noticed the empty bottles lying on the cobbles.

The Babelians crowded around him.

"Professor, where are we?"

"Professor, who are these people?"

"Professor, what is this ark?"

"I haven't the foggiest idea!" he exclaimed, jauntily. "On the evening of my departure, I got caught out by Nina's Breath. It's not the first time that happened to me, but it's the first time I've been dragged to a new land, and one that's inhabited, what's more! At first I thought I had discovered, *miraculeusement*, the concealed location of LandmArk, the dream of every self-respecting explorer. I soon realized it was nothing of the sort. This, my children," he declared, stretching his arms out wide as if wanting to embrace the entire village, "is officially the twenty-second major ark of our planet! An ark without a family spirit, populated by folk who have evolved cut off from our civilization since the Rupture, can you imagine? So, naturally, I stayed on, to deepen my anthropological knowledge."

From an inside pocket of his frock coat, he pulled out a notebook, which dripped all over his shoes. While he was pontificating from the edge of the fountain, the locals had moved in among the Babelians, to feel their clothes or stroke their skin. They were particularly intrigued by Ambrose's inverted hands, Elizabeth's swollen lips, Blaise's pointed nose, and Professor Wolf's neck brace. Thorn, whose scars fascinated them the most, was going to great lengths to keep them at a respectful distance from his claws.

Ophelia was of most interest to the young girl she had seen at the bus stop. Her eyes were trained on her like the lenses of a telescope, and once Ophelia had got over the awkwardness of being stared at so blatantly, they made her feel, yes, important. It was the same wide-eyed look that Domitilla, Beatrice, Leonora, and Hector had all given her when she had leaned over the cradles of her sisters and brother when they were merely an observing presence, unable to translate the world into thoughts. Having said that, it was with that same look that they stared at the animated mobile endlessly turning above their heads.

"Professor," said Blaise, twisting his fingers guiltily, "we . . . we found this village deserted. Does it belong to these people?"

Lazarus shook his head, vigorously, as if his own ignorance delighted him.

"There again, I have no idea! There are other villages such as this one for kilometers around. I have visited several, and they had all been abandoned, but when I question my dear friends about them, they don't answer me. They never answer. Since I've been around them, I have never heard them speak, or seen them write once. They are disarmingly simple! There's no hierarchy among them, no one relies on the work of another. The servitude of man by man just simply doesn't exist here. They feed themselves on whatever they come across—fruit, roots, insects—and spend their days . . . feeling," decided Lazarus, seemingly searching for the appropriate term. "We have so much to learn from them."

Saying this last sentence, he had turned his spectacles toward Ophelia, in particular the letters "AP" on her arm. Right then, she glimpsed, behind the thick varnish of joviality coating everything he did, the real depth of his gravity. She then grasped the fact that had been under her nose all along: Lazarus wasn't a mere supplier of automatons for the Deviations Observatory. Neither was he merely one former boarder among so many others.

It was he who was the brains behind it.

Thorn, who had reached the same conclusion, and probably well before her, limped over to the old man to say something into his ear. Ophelia could guess the words without hearing them. *All three of us need to have a talk.*

To which Lazarus, smiling, agreed.

"Without the shadow of a doubt, dear partners."

THE COUNT

They left the square as discreetly as possible, no mean feat in such a crowd. Lazarus seemed to have unusual appeal. To Thorn's exasperation, he kept answering numerous questions, getting lost in endless digressions, and embracing many people, before he could leave the two civilizations to get acquainted without needing to be an intermediary.

He pointed out a building to Ophelia, all stone and tiles, different from the rest in only one respect: a flag, buffeted by an already torrid wind, flapped on its roof.

"If this village is like those I've visited, that's equivalent to a Familistery. We can chat comfortably there, without having to enter anyone's home. And also because, I don't know about you," he said, walking more briskly, "but I wouldn't mind finally using a bathroom worthy of the name."

"Father? May I come with you?"

Ambrose arrived in the narrow cobbled street they were just going down, clipping every doorstep with his wheelchair.

"No, dear boy," Lazarus replied to him. "Go back to our friends now, I won't be long!"

Ambrose opened and then closed his mouth. Lazarus's flamboyance cast a shadow over him far more stifling than that between the stone facades, this early morning. He looked dully at Walter, still walking, jerkily, along the street alone, unaware that his master was no longer following him.

"He goes everywhere with you. Why not me? Why never me?"

"Walter, that's different, come now! You are far more important. You always have been. I won't be long," repeated Lazarus, "wait for me."

Ophelia noticed how the scarf had tightened around Ambrose, as he laboriously reversed, head sunk between shoulders. She had seen this boy push away the limits of his own world and build real relationships with real people—people who weren't automatons—but there was nothing for it: as soon as Lazarus was there, he no longer knew where his place was.

Ophelia stopped herself from turning back to Ambrose, as she followed Lazarus and Thorn to the building with the flag. Given what was soon to be said between those walls, it was better that he not be with them.

The door wasn't locked. They entered a vast room that, if one ignored the dead plants, had a certain distinction, with its long meeting table, many chairs, and standard lamps. Time, in there, seemed to be suspended. Lazarus disappeared briefly behind a door, through which the sound of flushing could be heard. Ophelia paced up and down a little. Why did the inhabitants of this ark prefer to live in the fields rather than in the villages? There were no posters or notices here, either, but an impressive collection of pottery along the windowsills. She frowned on discovering, pressed to one of the windowpanes, the young girl from the bus stop. She had followed them, but her curiosity wasn't enough to make her go inside.

Thorn closed all the curtains, releasing a cloud of dust. He wedged a chair against the door to prevent any intrusion, and then turned to Lazarus with a grinding of his leg. His expression was fierce, but he didn't utter a word. Ophelia did so for both of them:

"Liar."

Lazarus put the cookie jar he had found down with annoyance, on noticing that its contents were moldy.

"By omission only. I have never distorted the truth, but neither have I revealed it entirely, either. That is a notable difference. I sense that you are displeased," he said, with a half-smile. "Is that because you haven't yet found the Other? Don't be hard on yourself, *ma chère*, you have done something far better. Walter!" he shouted, clapping his hands, "Disc No. 118!"

The automaton, who was tilting an empty teapot over an equally empty cup, started to produce a mechanical rumbling noise, as if his innards were changing place. After a few seconds, two croaky voices burst out of his middle:

"WHAT ARE YOU . . . YOU GOING TO DO WITH . . . WITH THE HORN OF PLENTY?" asked the first.

"YOU HAVE ACHIEVED . . . ACHIEVED A MIRACLE, *MADE-MOISELLE*," replied the second. "NO CANDIDATE . . . CANDIDATE BEFORE YOU HAD ACHIEVED . . . ACHIEVED CRYSTALLIZATION. WE WILL MAKE SURE THAT . . . THAT YOUR MIRACLE GOES ON TO ACHIEVE . . . ACHIEVE NEW MIRACLES."

"Thank you, Walter, that will do."

Ophelia's glasses had turned yellow on her nose.

"That was my last conversation with the observer. How did you . . . Is it that beetle?"

Lazarus smiled, euphorically.

"My automatons are all linked, one to the other. Trade secret," he explained, with a wink. "I can thus keep an ear to the observatory, and beyond, while continuing with my exploring."

It seemed to Ophelia that she was encountering the real Lazarus for the first time. This old man, with his exaggerated gestures, sparkling, down to the enamel of his teeth, had ceased to be a pawn on the chessboard. He had become a major chess piece. From the start, he knew. He knew that this God he served was Eulalia, that the Other was her echo, and doubtless many other things about which neither Ophelia nor Thorn had the slightest idea. Things he had deliberately kept from them.

Walter pulled chairs out from the meeting table so everyone could make themselves comfortable—he pulled out far too many, in fact—but Lazarus was the only one to sit down.

"The last time we saw each other, I told you that the echoes were the key to it all. I'm flattered to see that you followed my lead to the very end. I was sincere when I told you that I wanted to offer my services to Lady Gonde—I presume that all of us here know the secret of her true identity, so let's call her by her proper name. I want to make her *parfait* world even more *parfait*! A world in which man won't ever again be forced into servitude by man, or be alienated by material needs. Where do wars come from? What is the origin of conflict? Dissatisfaction. Behind the ideologies, there's always a material motive."

Lazarus kept crossing and uncrossing his legs, and twiddling his thumbs, as his excitement grew. He was addressing only Ophelia, as if Thorn was to her what Walter was to him.

"So, the Horn of Plenty," she murmured, "has always been you."

"Not always, and not only me," Lazarus corrected her, sounding modest. "All the observers you encountered belong to the powerless. We unified. There was even a time, which, *malheureusement*, I didn't know, when Mademoiselle

Hildegarde worked in concert with the observatory, but she later dissociated herself from it over a difference of opinions."

Ophelia thought back to the beetle woman, the lizard man, and the young girl with the monkey. So, they were all power-less. That was why the Deviations Observatory had given itself non-existent directors. Babel was one of the most egalitarian arks—it had been before the landslides, at any rate—but rare were the powerless who reached responsible positions over there.

"The Knight, that was you, too," said Ophelia. "You were in the Pole at the time of his arrest. You got him out of Helheim in order to recruit him."

"A most interesting boy! His family power suffered from a highly unusual form of deviation before his Mutilation. I had visited him at Helheim out of curiosity. I am, as you have dis-covered, *extrêmement* curious about everything." Lazarus's eyes began to shine behind his pink lenses. "We talked for a long time, he and I. The formerly powerless once again powerless. Don't take offense, but I wanted to find out about you. We had just learnt that you were linked to the Other, and that young boy had himself found out a good deal about you. It struck me that he would fit in far better at our observatory."

That's one, thought Ophelia.

"And Blaise," she added, out loud. "He once told me that you had been his teacher and confidant. That you found him *interesting*, too. Was it you who arranged for him to be enrolled in the Alternative Program?"

Lazarus nodded, with barely less enthusiasm.

"I have always thought, and still do, that there's a connec-tion between his bad luck and the echoes, but his stay at the observatory wasn't enlightening. I'm not at all surprised that you became close to him! As I've told you before, and tell you again: we inverts, we're all woven into the same destiny."

That's two.

"And Elizabeth," she continued. "The offer of a post at the observatory that the Genealogists wanted her to accept for them, it came from you."

Once again, Lazarus nodded. His zeal almost made his chair tip backwards.

"I witnessed her receiving the prize for excellence, and I thought how precious her talents would be to us. I may serve Lady Gonde, but she didn't reveal the secret of her code to me. Had Mademoiselle Elizabeth not been so submissive to the Genealogists, she could have been rallied to our cause . . . as you yourself were."

He seemed happy, genuinely happy, finally to be able to speak to her frankly, and to answer her questions. Impatient, too, to broach the subject she was intentionally delaying broaching. As for Thorn, his eyes were glued to his watch, as if he were counting every move of its hands. Ophelia was surprised at his silence, since he had got her used to him doing any questioning, but, just like him, she was silently counting.

That's three.

"And Ambrose?"

"*Quoi*, Ambrose?" Lazarus asked, with surprise.

"We found his funerary urn."

Lazarus uncrossed his legs to place his two white shoes squarely on the floor. His face showed no disappointment, just intense melancholy.

"I see. In that case, it's no longer necessary to keep from you what he really is. First, I must ask you a favor: don't speak to him about what I'm going to tell you. He's so very sensitive!"

Neither Ophelia nor Thorn promised anything. They stood waiting, silent and tense.

Lazarus had a quick look at the door, blocked by the chair.

"Ambrose is an echo incarnate. More precisely, he is the echo of an old friend of mine. A friend with whom I co-founded the Alternative Program. A friend who was committed, body and soul, to Project Cornucopianism. It is his funerary urn that you found."

"An echo incarnate," Ophelia repeated, her voice thickening. "Like the faulty objects of your Horn of Plenty?"

Lazarus put a hand on his stomach as he laughed, as though stabbed in the back.

"Faulty, now hold on a minute! Perfectible, let's say. Ambrose opened the way to some dizzying possibilities, all the implications of which maybe you don't yet understand."

Ophelia bit her tongue until it hurt. This conversation was really churning her up inside.

"Does he have a code, too?"

"He does have one, yes. On his back, so that he can neither see it nor touch it. This code pales into insignificance compared with the one invented by Eulalia Gonde, but it allows him to settle into his material form. For pity's sake, never mention it in front of him!" stressed Lazarus. "This code also prevents him from being aware of his nature, or his life expectancy. I find it upsetting enough already when he asks me questions about the mother he never knew—and for good reason."

That's four.

"And the original Ambrose, your friend, what became of him? Is he dead?"

A smile shone out against Lazarus's skin, now brown from the sun and the mud.

"Oh, no, *ma chère*, I'm convinced that he's still very much alive."

It was a rather strange response, but Lazarus caught Ophelia unawares by indicating the right side of his own chest, where his inverted heart was beating. His expression was so passionate, she almost feared an amorous declaration.

"I have spoken to you of my *situs transversus*. My body's symmetry is reversed, which meant that I, too, a very long time ago, before being approached by Lady Gonde, even before joining the Good Family, was a subject of the observatory. I was but a child. At the time, that establishment's only aim was to correct deviations, and I thought that such a shame! I didn't want to be 'rectified,' quite the contrary. I told you how my inversion made me receptive to other inverts, such as you, that it gave me intuitions. It also makes me receptive to echoes, and the observatory is full of them! I'm *absolument* certain that you sensed them, too, those echoes from the past. You're not a reader of objects for nothing."

Ophelia had to admit, she had experienced her most immersive visions over there. Her hands may have been out of order at the time, but her entire body had become like a sounding board.

"It was the echoes at the observatory that told me its story," explained Lazarus, his voice increasingly resonant. "the story of Eulalia Gonde, of the birth of the Other, and of that project I decided to start from scratch with my old friend Ambrose, when we were heading the observatory. There was so much to do to rid our world of its final impurities . . . Ah, forty years ago, already!" sighed the seated Lazarus, as his spectacles misted up with emotion. "It makes me sound old."

Ophelia felt a loathing so strong, she bristled all over. Forty years. It was around that time that weapon collections and war archives had been purged from Babel, as from Anima. Lazarus may not have spoken to Eulalia Gonde of his intention to recreate a Horn of Plenty, but he had no less influenced her approach by toughening censorship across all the arks. He had used the past to stop humanity knowing its own past.

Oh, yes, this old man with the pink spectacles and ridiculous ways was deplorable. Ophelia's museum had been mutilated, just as she had been herself, losing part of her family power, due to him.

That's five.

"The echoes of yesterday are not the only ones to have something to teach," Lazarus continued, warmly, impervious to her dislike of him. "The advance echoes have just as much, if not more."

Ophelia was really annoyed to realize how skilled Lazarus was at heightening her own curiosity. The more he spoke, the more she wanted to make him shut up and listen to him at the same time. As for Thorn, he was completely engrossed in his watch; he said nothing, didn't move.

Lazarus wagged his finger in a professorial manner.

"If you have conducted your investigation correctly, as I believe you have, you already know something of what I am talking about. We are surrounded by a gas that I, personally, have named 'aerargyrum.' That air has nothing in common with the oxygen that keeps you alive. *En fait*, it resembles no known chemical element. It is extremely difficult to study, and rare are the scientists who are aware of its existence. So subtle is it, our finest observation instruments can only detect it in its condensed form, for example when we produce waves of it and they return to us as echoes. So subtle," Lazarus insisted, stressing each word, "that the very fabric of time is different around it. You sense the echoes of the past. Me, powerless as I am, I sense the echoes of the future. An advance echo whispered to me in a dream that we would meet again in an unknown land. In other words, I was expecting you."

Lazarus's crow's-feet deepened around his eyes. With delight, he accepted the cup served to him by Walter, without noticing that it had been filled with dead flies.

"If I stayed here all this time, it wasn't merely to study the locals. It was also, and specifically, because I knew that our paths were going to converge here. Because I knew that I was destined to accompany you back to Babel, and reveal to you, personally, the secret of the third protocol."

Ophelia wondered how Thorn managed to remain so calm. She bluntly refused the cup of flies that Walter held out to her.

"Your observatory delivered me to Lady Septima, who put me in an airship that came down beside this ark . . . so that you yourself can take me back to where I started? It makes no sense."

Lazarus nodded his chin in agreement with every word, but his eyes clouded over for a split second, before regaining their former brilliance, and that was enough for Ophelia to derive some satisfaction. Despite appearances, he had his doubts, too.

"The logic of the echoes is not our logic," he stated, with exaggerated conviction, "but be sure that there is a reason. A reason that we can't yet discern. *Zut!*"

Lazarus spat out the flies that he had inadvertently sipped. Walter's faceless figure stood back impassively, like an inscrutable butler. Ophelia found them as absurd as each other. In fact, everything seemed absurd to her, suddenly: what she and Thorn had faced at the observatory, the investigation that they had conducted at the risk of compromising themselves as the world collapsed all around them, the death they had come so close to in that long-distance airship . . .

That's six and seven.

"Why tell us this only here, and only now?"

Ophelia's voice had changed. Lazarus must have noticed because his own voice changed, too, when he replied to her:

"The entire process depended on the choices you would make. It was my duty, in the interest of all of us, yours included, to keep quiet about anything that could influence your crystallization."

He leant on his knees to get up from his chair, as if his bones were suddenly showing the weight of the years.

"And you succeeded. You have created a new Other. No one, not even my old friend Ambrose, managed to do that. All those echoes converted into matter, that poor boy I call 'son,' and the family spirits themselves, aren't half as perfect as what you have given birth to."

He moved toward her, leaving the imprint of his soles on the floorboards. His white frock coat, still damp from his fall into the fountain, was weighing him down. And yet, there was a fieriness about him that made it seem as if there was lava beneath his wrinkled skin.

"If you knew how much I'm burning to meet your echo! You may think that I'm in possession of all the truths, but I'm missing the most significant of them all: the one that holds the secret of the echoes and of our world, the one my old friend Ambrose took with him, the one that will allow me to give humanity what it's missing in order finally to feel complete. For me, finally, to feel complete myself. See what Lady Gonde became, alone, thanks to her echo! Imagine what you in turn could become, what we could all become, together this time, thanks to yours! That would certainly give some sense to what has been sacrificed, don't you think?"

Some sense to what has been sacrificed. Ophelia turned these words over and over, until she herself was turned over by them.

Eulalia Gonde had lost first her entire family, then half her life expectancy, and from those ashes the Other had been born. She had obtained from him, in return, a knowledge that had freed her from the limitations imposed by an aging body. If there was one thing Ophelia definitely didn't want, it was to turn into Milliface, or to allow others to do so. No, none of that would make any sense of the death of Octavio. What had plunged into the void was irreplaceable.

She found the way Lazarus eyed her hungrily as he advanced, step by step, hands outstretched, unpleasant. There was something possessive about his behavior, as if she and her echo belonged to him.

"No, really, *ma chère*, don't reproach yourself, above all, for not having found the Other yet," he whispered, wrapping his palms, as warm and soft as his voice, around her bare shoulders. "In truth, all that you have been through was destined to draw you nearer to him. He is there, really close to you, from now on! I can almost feel his presence," he concluded, with an excited pant. "And I'm convinced that you feel it, too."

What Ophelia felt was Lazarus's breath. He coudn't have used any toothpaste for weeks.

"Have you finished?"

A silence fell on the room, heavy as the air that had been stagnating there since the village had been abandoned. It was Thorn who had just asked this question, as the cover of his watch closed itself.

Lazarus, still clinging to Ophelia's shoulders, seemed only then to remember his existence.

"Oh, I've never really finished," he guffawed. "I'm an incorrigible chatterbox!"

A ray of sunlight turned a curtain crimson, cut through the floating dust, and shone a bloodred light on Thorn's face.

"You are exactly like her," he said, in a voice that came from deep inside him. "You are like Eulalia Gonde. You are toxic."

Ophelia was chilled by the look he was giving Lazarus. It was the look of his father's clan; of a hunter confronting a Beast. For months, years, Thorn had fought relentlessly against his own claws. For the first time, Ophelia could see that he felt like giving in to them, even though he despised them, and, whenever he had used them, despised himself that bit more.

She had promised herself to change that look.

Lazarus studied Thorn through the spectacles that made him see a rose-tinted world. Did they, too, allow him to detect the shadows?

"Come, come, dear boy, I know that, despite appearances, you loathe violence as much as I do. You've already got your hands dirty for your little wife. I'm sure she would hate for you to do so again."

Ophelia at least agreed with that. She connected her claws to Lazarus's nervous system, and he let go of her shoulders due to the electric shock. She didn't allow him time to recover from his surprise before giving him a second electric shock, which threw him backwards. Then a third that flung him against Walter. Then a fourth that made him roll on the floor. Then a fifth that stopped him from getting back up.

At each shock, Ophelia was counting inside.

The Knight.

Blaise.

Elizabeth.

Ambrose.

My museum.

She hurled Lazarus against the back wall, and all the shelves, thanks to the animism working in the room, tipped all the pottery they held down onto his head.

Thorn and me.

Ophelia was overcome by profound disgust as she contemplated this old man curled up on the floor. The silver of his hair had turned into rust. It was she who had done that to him. However much she repeated to herself that he deserved it, there was an acrid taste in her mouth. She swallowed it as soon as her eyes met Thorn's eyes, which had lost all murderous rage and were staring at her in astonishment.

No, it wasn't always him who had to dirty his hands. She accepted what she had done.

"You are going to take us back to Babel and lead us to the Horn of Plenty," she ordered Lazarus.

He looked up at her with a face contorted with pain, but in which fear was absent. Even in this state, groveling amid the broken pottery, he was consumed with curiosity, as if the experiment was taking an even more fascinating turn than expected.

"*Bien sûr!* That was my intention, Mademoiselle Oph—"

"Over there," she interrupted him, drily, "you will give me back my echo. It is not, and never will be, the property of the observatory. Game over."

At this precise moment, just as Walter was pathetically flicking a feather duster over his master's bloodied head, an unexpected voice burst out from his middle:

"WHO IS I?"

THE REUNION

The bench stood in the shade of a giant fig tree. Ophelia recognized the backs of Blaise and Wolf, although it took her a few seconds to be quite sure: the former was far less hunched than usual, the latter, on the contrary, far less rigid. They weren't talking. They just sat side by side, jackets over arms, gazing together at the vineyards that stretched out from the edge of the village. Wordlessly, they shifted a little to allow Ophelia to sit between them. It was so peaceful on this bench, she forgot, momentarily, what she had come to tell them. She watched, with them, the languorous procession of clouds; breathed in, with them, the sweet scent of grapes and figs; felt, with them, the flashes of sunlight filtering through the foliage; and welcomed, with them, the breeze, as it slipped through her hair, beneath her gown, and between her sandals.

"We will miss you, Mademoiselle Eulalia."

Blaise's watery eyes seemed about to spill over, but it was hard to tell whether from sadness or joy, or both at the same time. Ophelia didn't need to say a word.

"You shouldn't go back to Babel," grumbled Professor Wolf. "If the world is doomed to collapse under our feet, we might as well be on this bench, glass in hand."

He handed Ophelia what was probably stolen liqueur. Coming from him, it came close to a real declaration of friendship, so she accepted taking a swig. She found herself enjoying it.

"You know," Blaise murmured to her, "my bad luck hasn't struck once since we crash-landed near this ark. The tiles remain on the roofs, the benches don't break, and the weather's *fabuleux*! I'm starting to feel hopeful again, and to believe in a future without landslides or expulsions. A future, Mademoiselle Eulalia," he concluded, squeezing her little hand in his, "when we will meet again."

Ophelia would have liked to tell them, him and Wolf, that it was precisely to put an end to the landslides that she was returning to Babel, but to do so she would have had to admit the whole truth to them—a truth still incomplete, a truth that would dent their trust in Lazarus—and she no longer had the time. And yet they deserved it, that truth.

"My name is Ophelia. I will return," she promised, as their jaws dropped, "and I will tell you the rest of the story."

She left the bench, and the serenity she had felt on it. As she walked through the ghost village, she was struck by the new activity in its streets. Music was being played, fruit handed out, flirting going on, squabbling going on. The Babel exiles had launched into mimed dialogues with the locals, since they couldn't converse with them. They emptied their pockets to show them, proudly, some specialties from back home: a weightless fork, a phosphorescent razor, a chameleon-mouse . . . One man had even managed, when Pollux's guard came for him, to shrink his house to the size of a thimble and take it with him—but, he admitted, looking pained, he feared he had left his cat locked inside it.

Ophelia had to admit that the inhabitants of this twenty-second ark were very receptive. They showed the keenest interest in whatever was put before them, examining, prodding, sniffing each item, wide-eyed, as if nothing in the world was more extraordinary, and all without showing any covetousness.

She slowed down as she went past a pottery, abandoned, like all the buildings.

She didn't even look at the lovely plates gathering dust inside. She saw only her reflection on the window. She raised a hand; it raised a hand. She stepped back; it stepped back. She stuck out her tongue; it stuck out its tongue. It was behaving like a normal reflection And yet.

WHO IS I?

The echo hadn't remained at the Deviations Observatory, as Ophelia had thought. It had followed her, without her realizing it, like a second shadow, even into Walter's recording mechanism.

She now understood that she owed it her life.

In the airship, it was the echo that had drawn her attention to the belfry, just before a collision that would have been fatal, to her and all the other passengers. She found it frustrating not to manage to communicate with it; terrifying, too, to succeed in doing so; and particularly satisfying to imagine the observers hitting a little metal parrot that was now mute.

But what if Lazarus was right, she thought, as her face darkened on the pottery's window. If she was, indeed, following the same path as Eulalia Gonde? If, by imparting some of her humanity to her echo, it would pass a little of its nature on to her, in return? If she started to take on the appearance of every person she met?

Her eyes slid from her own reflection to that of Elizabeth, behind her. She hadn't noticed her, but the young woman was perched on the low stone wall around the garden of the house opposite. With one leg folded up against her and the other dangling, she looked like the grasshopper that had alighted on her knee, and at which she was staring, pensively.

"I come from a large family."

For a moment, Ophelia wondered whether it was her or the grasshopper that Elizabeth was addressing. Her eyelids hung heavy over her eyes; she seemed to be somewhere between asleep and awake.

"I was neither the youngest nor the oldest. I remember our house, always very noisy, the jostling on the stairs, the smells from the kitchen, the raised voices. An exhausting house," she sighed, "but it was my home. So I believed."

Elizabeth turned from the grasshopper to stare straight at Ophelia. Her long tawny locks, her finest feature, were in serious need of a wash.

"One night, I woke up in the home of complete strangers. My family had got rid of me. One mouth less to feed, you know? I ran away into the street. I'd still be there without Lady Helen."

She gave the wall a gentle kick with her boot, as if to make the Forerunner wings, which were no longer there, tinkle.

"I was so close to decoding her Book, so close to giving her back her memory . . . I couldn't care less who the family spirits really are. I just wanted her to remember my name."

Elizabeth bit her lip, revealing the gap left by the incisor Cosmos's elbow had knocked out. She had lost that tooth to come to Ophelia's rescue; Ophelia should be grateful to her for that, but all she felt was a desire to force her down from that wall.

"Is that really what you want?"

Elizabeth raised her eyebrows, taken aback by the harsh tone of the question.

"Hmm?"

"To stay here: is that what you want?"

"I don't know."

"Do you want to return to Babel with us?"

417

"I don't know. I don't know where I belong anymore."

Ophelia thought how they at least had that in common, but, unlike for Elizabeth, the person who was her anchor was still alive.

She softened.

"There are still twenty family spirits whose memories you could restore."

"I don't know," Elizabeth merely repeated, returning to the grasshopper with a perplexed look.

Ophelia left her to her dithering and made for the large fallow field full of flowers at the back of the village. Ambrose had parked his wheelchair there, in the middle of the dandelion clocks. He must have blown on quite a few to kill time while he waited: the scarf, around his neck, was covered in downy seeds. He had a start when he heard Ophelia's steps approaching. She scanned the sky as carefully as he did, which saved them both from looking at each other. It was still a little too soon to see the Lazaropter arriving. The camp where Lazarus had left his flying machine was beyond the fields, and Thorn, not trusting the professor, had insisted on accompanying him, despite his troublesome leg.

"It was a *grosse* bump my father had on his head."

Without averting her glasses from the sky, Ophelia rolled her eyes to their blind spot, toward that presence with its blurred contours. It was the first time Ambrose had spoken since their meeting with Lazarus. He had done so quietly, almost timidly, as if he sensed something had changed between them.

Should she tell him that he was the echo of a man who had been missing for forty years, and that his father had never been his father?

"I got a bit carried away."

"He didn't seem to be cross with you. Quite the opposite."

Lazarus had kissed Ophelia on both cheeks the moment her

echo had made its presence known, through Walter. He hadn't taken her at all seriously when she had told him not to count on her for his utopian dreams. But after all, as long as he led them, her and Thorn, to the Horn of Plenty . . .

Ambrose's eyes fell to his reversed babouches.

"Father confides little in me, but I know he expects a lot of you. Too much, no doubt. I don't dare to imagine how much pressure you must have felt, all alone, to find the Other, since the first landslide. When I think," he added, a little awkwardly, "that at one time I thought the Other was you."

Ophelia couldn't resist a glance at what showed of his nape, between the shiny black hair and the old three-colored scarf. Somewhere on that back, a code that Ambrose was unaware of kept him materially present. She should have felt uncomfortable about it. She felt only sadness, not because of what he was really, but because he was doubtless happier not knowing about it. Basically, Ambrose wasn't so different from Farouk, who, despite the political tensions he had caused to decipher his Book, was just a being in search of answers—answers that were bitterly regretted afterwards. They were two echoes who owed their arrival in the world to just a few written lines, on the back of the one, in the Book of the other.

Did Eulalia's echo also need a code to materialize? Or was that the fundamental difference between an echo born spontaneously from a crystallization, and all those that had come into being artificially?

"I have already found the Other," Ophelia declared, to Ambrose's amazement. "I found him and I didn't even realize it."

If she believed the Shadow, at least. Someone who resembled her.

What if the Other was actually me, she thought.

Ophelia's self-mocking smile at this hypothesis fell fast.

Pass through. On that night, when she had encountered Eulalia Gonde's echo for the very first time, in her bedroom mirror, she had entered into him, and he into her.

But had he actually ever exited?

Feet in the dandelions, Ophelia didn't move anymore. She was petrified. Her heart was in her mouth. Her hands froze under her gloves. First she felt very hot, then very cold, as if her organism had abruptly registered the invasion of a foreign body.

"Mademoiselle, are you alright?" Ambrose asked, anxiously.

Ophelia barely heard him over her chaotic breathing. No, she couldn't be the Other because she would inevitably have realized it, because the landslides had always occurred without her knowing about it, and because, quite simply, she didn't want to be. She rolled that thought up into a ball, as she would a piece of paper, and threw it as far away as possible. She was already stuck with one echo too many, she didn't need a second.

"I'll be better when everything's over," she replied.

She was relieved to hear the approach of the Lazaropter. Like a giant dragonfly, it soon stood out against the intense blue sky of the afternoon. The draft from its propellers blew the dandelion seeds in all directions as it landed in the field. Walter activated the mechanical gangway.

"*Bienvenue* onboard!" Lazarus shouted from the cockpit.

Inside, the Lazaropter was as dark, creaky, and cramped as the hull of a submarine must be. Blinded by the change of light, Ophelia found Thorn by bumping into the arm he was holding out to guide her to her safety harness. He was sitting on a sprung seat, with one hand gripping the security handle on the ceiling, and legs folded right in to avoid his feet being run over by Ambrose's wheelchair. The journey promised to be a long one.

"Wait!"

It was Elizabeth, hoisting herself up onto the gangway that Walter was bringing back up, and then taking up what little space remained to them. A new pride shone from under her heavy eyelids.

"I am a citizen of Babel. I belong over there."

They took off. Ophelia had already travelled by mirror, airship, train, sandglass, lift, birdtrain, and wheelchair; the Lazaropter was the most uncomfortable mode of transport of them all. The vibrating of the propellers spread to the security harnesses, shaking the bones, deterring any conversation.

But the Lazaropter was fast and, after a few hours, Babel could be seen.

"*Sacrebleu!*" Lazarus exclaimed.

Ophelia, Thorn, Ambrose, and Elizabeth undid their harnesses and twisted round to look at the windshield, on which the wipers were battling with the elements. The sea of clouds had gone crazy, here raising great walls of vapor, there hollowing out troughs of nothingness. In the space of two nights and two days, Babel had become barely recognizable. Gaping holes had appeared right in the middle of the major ark, one of them taking half a pyramid with it.

"The landslides are accelerating," said Thorn.

Elizabeth's pursed lips whitened.

"Lady Septima promised the citizens that they would be safe in the center of town. She . . . she was wrong."

Through the swamp of clouds, the Babelians, their cries drowned out by the propellers, could be seen jostling each other in the streets, and desperately gesticulating up at them, in the Lazeropter. The ground beneath their feet had become their worst enemy.

Not the ground, thought Ophelia. The Other.

She refused to ask herself why she hadn't yet been able to identify him. Mustn't think about that rolled up piece of paper at the back of her mind.

In the meantime, she couldn't see anywhere they could land in town, to drop off Ambrose and Elizabeth, as had been planned. Neither of them knew that they had both, in a different way, been Lazarus's playthings. Ophelia didn't want to drag them deeper into the machinations of the observatory.

"Look!"

Ambrose twisted in his chair to indicate some shapes through the windshield, blurred by the mist. They were all hovering around the huge, still intact, tower of Babel's Memorial.

Lazarus, who was tirelessly pulling levers and cranks, pressed his face to a periscope.

"Airships," he said, "and not any old ones. They all bear the arms of the family spirits of Corpolis, Totem, Al-Andaloose, Flora, Sidh, Pharos, Zephyr, Tartar, Anima, Vesperal, the Serenissima, Heliopolis, Leadgold, Titan, Selene, the Desert, and even of the Pole. An interfamilial meeting on this scale in Babel, it's never been seen before!"

Ophelia's pulse had quickened at the words "Anima" and "Pole."

"Our family spirits are here?"

Since the foundation of the new world, none of the spirits had ever left the ark for which he or she was responsible. Lazarus was right: it had never been seen before.

"They are probably there for Lady Helen," Elizabeth managed to get out, wedged as she was against Walter's unwieldy frame. "They must have felt her loss deeply. The family spirits are linked together by their Books, that's one of the few things I grasped from studying that code."

Ophelia felt hypnotized by the damp blobs through the windshield. One of them was Artemis's airship, another Farouk's. They must have mustered all possible resources, both technological and supernatural, to cover such a distance in such a short time. It was torture not to be able to join them and ask them if her family were all well.

Thorn leaned over her, as far as the cramped Lazaropter allowed. Despite the bristles invading his jaw and the shadows drowning his eyes, he was bursting with energy.

"Let's stick to the plan," he said into her ear. "If all the family spirits are at the Memorial, Eulalia Gonde will soon emerge from the wings—and maybe her echo will, at the same time. It's now, more than ever, that we need the Horn of Plenty. Take us straight to the observatory," he ordered Lazarus, raising his voice.

"The observatory?" queried Elizabeth, astonished. "They got rid of us, they certainly didn't want to see us return."

Lazarus winked at her from the cockpit.

"*Ne t'inquiète pas*, I have my contacts over there. We'll be safe there. After all, I'm their favorite automaton-supplier."

Ophelia couldn't help but admire the old man's nerve in relying on the true to disguise the false. The bump kept growing on his forehead; he owed it to Ophelia, and yet continued to behave like the victor. Much as she repeated to herself that they must combine forces to save what could still be saved, she didn't trust him one bit. Over there, at the observatory, they would be on his territory.

That, at any rate, was what Ophelia was thinking as she spotted the colossus, in the midst of swirling clouds. She was still thinking it as the Lazaropter landed on the crown of his head, on a landing platform she hadn't known existed until then. She was still thinking it when Lazarus made them take a secret lift, descending directly into the skull of the statue.

She intended to reassess her situation only once inside the directors' apartments.

Entwined on a boardroom chair, a couple was gorging on saffron cakes.

"Now, finally, we are reunited!" the Genealogists gleefully declared, as one.

PLENTY

Rain, mingled with sunlight, was tapping on the rose windows that served as the colossus's eyes. The drops' shadows played across the smiles of the Genealogists. They were embracing so passionately, they became one and the same body. Their golden glow eclipsed the world around them, so much so that it took Ophelia a moment to realize that they weren't alone in the directors' apartments.

Pollux's guards were emptying the bookcases of their contents. Inmates' files, medical imaging, it was all coming out. They had stopped everything, ready to seize the bayonet rifles slung across their shoulders, as soon as the secret door to the lift had opened on to Lazarus, Ophelia, Thorn, Ambrose, Elizabeth, and Walter. They were just waiting for the Genealogists' order.

With a casual shake of his slice of cake, the man indicated to them to continue clearing, while the woman licked her fingers.

"What a lovely surprise to be visited by you!"

"We were starting to feel a little lonely here."

"There's not a living soul left in this establishment."

"Not an observer."

"Not a collaborator."

"Not a subject."

"No one."

Ophelia glanced through the nearest rose window. Down below, the cloisters and gardens were, indeed, deserted. Where had the man with the dimple gone? And beetle woman? And the other inverts? And Second? And the Knight?

Beside her, Thorn betrayed no emotion, but it seemed to Ophelia that his watch had stopped ticking in his pocket. He had wanted to beat these Genealogists to it, having made, and then broken, a deal with them, and he had failed. The electrical tingling from his claws that Ophelia had finally got used to had suddenly stopped. Just the thought that he, after so many brushes with death, might be afraid made her feel panic-stricken.

Ambrose himself seemed scared, as he stroked the scarf to calm his increasing anxiety.

There was something threatening in the air, like a smell of gas. Something terrible was going to happen here, but what?

As for Lazarus, he looked neither surprised nor concerned by the Genealogists' intrusion into his observatory. As usual, with thumbs tucked under frock-coat lapels, he was excessively confident.

Simultaneously, the Genealogists turned their eyes on Elizabeth, who instantly drew back a step.

"It's a relief to see you safe and sound, virtuoso."

"Making you board that long-distance airship was an insult to your talent."

"Lady Septima showed herself to be *vraiment* unworthy of her position."

"Because of her, the uprisings became widespread in Babel."

"Indeed, she's paying the price as we speak."

"Our fine fellow citizens threw her into the void."

"The harder they fall!" they crowed, in unison.

Ophelia found them inhuman. Even when they smiled,

no wrinkle disturbed the smooth gold of their skin, thanks, probably, to their family power. She thought of Lady Septima, plunging relentlessly toward the abyss that had swallowed up her son.

Ophelia realized, from the way Elizabeth's dirty finger-nails were digging into the edge of her uniform sleeves, that she shared her terror. Her eyelids had lifted like blinds as she followed the comings and goings of the guards, carrying off boxes full of the private lives of hundreds of patients. The Genealogists had taken advantage of the chaos to take over this place, always out of bounds to them, by force. Babel was on its knees, and yet its highest dignitaries remained there, ensconced in a chair that didn't belong to them.

"The family spirits," Elizabeth said, with difficulty. "They are all at the Memorial to deal with the crisis. Why are you not with them?"

Of everyone in this room, Ophelia would never have thought that she would be the one to stand up to the Genealogists.

They rose up, as one.

"Because, henceforth, that task is incumbent upon you."

"Babel needs an exemplary and dedicated citizen."

"Just as Sir Pollux needs us, today more than ever."

"Someone must serve as his living memory, and ensure that he knows, along with all the other family spirits, his true status."

"So here you are, elevated to the ranks of the Lords of LUX!"

Incredulous, Elizabeth gazed at the sun the Genealogists had just pinned to her chest. Ophelia could have sworn that it was the very badge that Thorn had returned to Lady Septima. This wasn't promotion; it was alienation.

"An airship is moored in the enclosure," said the man.

"Take it, and see you at the Memorial," said the woman.

"*Maintenant*," they said, together.

Pollux's guards, who had just emptied out the last bookcase, formed a guard of honor up to the door, while still clutching boxes. A mapped-out path. Elizabeth had never liked either the pressure of responsibility or the limelight. This new title seemed like a bad joke.

With a final glance back at Ophelia, she left the apartments, followed by her armed escort.

After her departure, only five guards remained: two posted at the entrance to the apartments; two in front of the secret lift; and a final one watching over the still absurdly cheerful Lazarus, as if he posed the greatest threat among them. It was still five rifles too many to contemplate escape. Ophelia could tell, from the way Thorn's long fingers were quivering, that he was assessing all the options for turning the situation around. Since they had exited the lift, he had stopped either looking at her or coming near her, just like when he had wanted everyone to think that his fiancée meant nothing to him. She was, herself, avoiding raising her glasses in his direction, for fear of triggering an explosion of the noxious gas building up around them.

The Genealogists suddenly focused all their attention on Ambrose. Even their eyes were venomous. He winced when the woman, with a swish of silk, leant over his wheelchair. A tiger confronting an antelope.

"What a fascinating deformity . . . You're not ordinary, my boy, and I don't just mean your limbs."

"Father?" he called out, softly.

Lazarus, with a rifle still trained on him, smiled at Ambrose from a distance.

"Don't worry about a thing. It will all work out for the best."

"It will all work out for the best," repeated the woman.

She stroked Ambrose's palms, tracing every line on them, and soon both of their arms were covered in goose bumps. As she used her Tactile power to explore this unknown skin, the woman's eyebrows suddenly relaxed, as if she had found what she was looking for. Slowly, sensually, she slid her golden fingers under Ambrose's hair, under the scarf, which bristled at her touch, and under the collar of the white tunic.

Ophelia understood too late what was about to happen. Ambrose hiccupped with surprise; a simple hiccup. The next moment, nothing was left of him in the wheelchair, apart from the scarf, blindly thrashing about, and a ray of sunlight dotted with rain.

Gone, like a puff of smoke.

The woman now held, between thumb and index finger, an old silver plate on which there was a microscopic inscription: the code that, for decades, had kept an echo anchored in matter, and that she had removed like a simple label.

Everything had happened so fast, Ophelia hadn't had time to breathe, and still couldn't catch her breath now. Her lungs, heart, blood were frozen.

"Dear, oh dear," sighed Lazarus. "You have damaged the code. Was that *vraiment* necessary?"

The guards remaining in the room stared at an imaginary spot in front of them, without blinking, as though to convince themselves that they hadn't seen a thing.

The Genealogists, with the same gesture, indicated Walter to them.

"Leave us, and take that automaton with you."

The guards obeyed. As they left the apartments with Walter, who allowed them to move him but sprayed them with toilet water, their faces betrayed their relief.

As soon as the great ebony door was closed again, Ophelia felt something hard against both of her cheeks. Two golden pistols. With simultaneous pressure, they forced her to look up at Thorn.

"Pollux's guards are not the only ones authorized to bear preventive arms for peace," the Genealogists informed him.

"You made a very disappointing chief family inspector."

"We closed our eyes to all your little secrets."

"As long as you were on our side, in this observatory."

"But you abandoned your post for this little Animist."

Ophelia wasn't really conscious of the two guns pointed at her, or the proximity of the Genealogists, whose golden hair was mingling with her own, or even of Thorn's predatory stillness. All she could see was the absence beyond the scarf. Ambrose was there and, the next moment, not there anymore. He had welcomed her, guided her, fed her, sheltered her, advised her . . . and he was not there anymore.

Without relaxing the pressure of her pistol, the woman threw the coded plate she had pulled off to Lazarus.

"We are honored to meet the true creator of Project Cornucopianism."

"To be honest, professor, until recently, we didn't deem you worthy of interest."

"*Bien sûr*, we knew that Eulalia Gonde had made you another of her servants."

"But at no time did we think you capable of being in competition with her."

"Recently, it became clear to us how much we had underestimated you."

Lazarus averted his eyes from the plate in his hands. The shadow of a smile was still there, lurking around his lips. Ambrose's sudden disappearance hadn't shaken him.

"What made you change your mind?"

Ophelia couldn't see the Genealogists' expressions because they were right beside her. She did, however, see Thorn tensing up, even in his eyes, when they pressed their two guns harder into her cheeks.

"This little Animist, whom we came across by chance."

"During the census, at a counter in the Memorial."

"We had a quick look at her papers."

"'Eulalia' is *vraiment* not a common name in Babel."

"And it's a name particularly loaded with significance."

"So we conducted a little inquiry into her."

"And learned that, in your absence, she lived in your home."

"And in that way discovered the existence of your supposed son."

"A son who featured nowhere on your genealogical branch."

"Whom you were very careful to conceal in your shadow."

"Of whom we finally found, thanks to perseverance, a trace in our archives."

"A mere powerless individual, born in your childhood neighborhood."

"A boarder, along with you, right here, in this observatory."

"And who hasn't aged by even a single hair in forty years."

"Lady Septima, decidedly very misguided, expelled him without allowing us to meet him."

"Most fortunately," they concluded together, "it's you who returned to us!"

Lazarus had placidly agreed with each of the Genealogists' statements.

"And how about you telling me what you expect of me, and my modest observatory?"

The pistols shuddered with excitement against Ophelia's jaws. She could no longer move a muscle.

"Plenty!" replied the Genealogists.

"The only type that really counts."

"Plenty of time."

"Immortality."

The scarf wouldn't stop searching, deep in the wheelchair, for a body that was no longer there. Ophelia couldn't take her eyes off it. These Genealogists hadn't grasped at all what this Horn of Plenty was all about. They had obliterated Ambrose without knowing what he really was. They didn't deserve immortality.

They didn't deserve life.

Stuck in the vise of the pistols, Ophelia closed her eyes to connect with the Genealogists' spinal cords. She didn't want to push them back. She wanted to hurt them, to dig her claws into their flesh as deeply as her power allowed.

She couldn't.

By gritting her teeth to extend her range, she could detect the nervous systems of Thorn and Lazarus, but not those of the Genealogists. Their skin was an impenetrable fortress.

She opened her eyes wide, and they met those of Thorn, up above, telling her not to do anything. She understood now why he feared them. Killing and being killed wasn't a problem for them.

Their breath burnt her ears.

"We don't age visibly, but that's merely a façade."

"Under our skin, our bodies die every second."

"We're tired of wasting time."

"And we're tired of searching this place."

Ophelia felt a glimmer of hope when, through the rose windows, she saw the LUX airship appear, but the craft continued its ascent and disappeared into the distance, in the direction of Babel's Memorial. She couldn't see how Elizabeth could have avoided obeying the Genealogists, but she felt abandoned, all the same.

"I consent," Lazarus declared, humbly bowing his head. "I will lead you to the Horn of Plenty. On one condition: we all go there together. Don't give my partners any grief, alright?"

The Genealogists indicated to Lazarus to lead them on, and to Thorn to follow them, and pushed Ophelia forward with their guns. She had to force the scarf to let go of the wheelchair, so as not to leave it behind. Clutching this writhing mass of wool to her chest made her feel as if it was her own heart that had burst out of it.

She was under no illusion. As soon as the Genealogists were masters of the Horn of Plenty, they would get rid of all of them.

Lazarus didn't call the large lift in the antechamber. He made them go down the hidden stairway that Ophelia and Thorn had already used for their clandestine meeting. They all plunged deep into the statue, far from the sun and the rain. The flickering bulbs added their shadows to the spiderwebs.

Lazarus sometimes took a turning to the right, sometimes a corridor to the left, whistling all the while. Wasn't he getting them lost within the labyrinths of the observatory? Ophelia couldn't have said whom, between him and the Genealogists, she trusted less. He claimed that Ambrose was important, but his sudden, grotesque disappearance made no difference to him. He would sacrifice his own partners without regret if need be.

Even more insistently than the pistols, Ophelia could feel Thorn's silent attention on her, as he continuously analyzed, quantified, evaluated, and recalculated.

After endless meanderings, they reached an underground platform, where a train seemed always to have been waiting for them. When Ophelia climbed aboard, flanked by the pistols, she noticed that it had the same velvet-covered seats and lamps with shades as on her first journey. Would the destination be different this time?

"I recommend that you sit down," said Lazarus, doing so himself. "The gradient is steep."

No sooner had he uttered these words than the compartment door closed and they began their descent into the tunnel. Ophelia came from an ark where the carriages and trams occasionally just did as they pleased, but this train truly had a will of its own. Was it, too, an echo incarnate? With no choice but to sit between the Genealogists, she concentrated, in vain, on the guns hurting her ribs. Gold was a metal with a strong personality, even when faced with an Animist. It was easier to maneuver an airship than make these two weapons see reason.

As she risked a quick glance through the train's windows, she caught a smile on her own reflection. At first she thought it was a nervous rictus, before understanding that it wasn't she who was smiling, but her echo. It was there. It was still following her. This vision lasted but a moment, and, very soon, the smile vanished from the window, but Ophelia felt surprisingly comforted by it.

She hugged the scarf tight, and met Thorn's intense gaze, from the seat opposite. He was as fiercely determined as she was to come through this. One way or another, they would find a solution. Together.

A sudden jolt indicated that the train had stopped.

At first, once she had alighted from the train, Ophelia couldn't see a great deal, but she was hit by a very musty smell. It was like inhaling rock. It wasn't dark here—quite the opposite. The more she blinked, the less Ophelia could take in the contours of this place. It was a cavern with a dizzyingly high roof. Its walls were riddled with galleries in which convoys of small trucks were forever coming and going. The size of the stalactites and stalagmites gave the feeling of having landed in the jaws of a Beast.

Ophelia could almost have forgotten about the pistols.

She squinted at the two parabolic mirrors on either side of the cavern, facing each other, huge as Cyclops, turning like windmills. They were even crazier kaleidoscopes than all of those she had faced at the observatory, and judging by their vein-like cables, they were the ones devouring almost all of the electricity.

"The Horn of Plenty!" murmured the Genealogists, each turning to a parabola.

Lazarus, his eyes eclipsed by the glare from his spectacles, managed an indulgent smile.

"*En fait*, no. These machines are there just to optimize it. The only true Horn of Plenty is right here!"

With the flourish of an old conjuror, he indicated a cage in the center of the cavern, at the intersection of the two parabolas. The cage resembled an aviary. Apart from its generous size, it wasn't that impressive in itself, but what it contained was even less so.

There was nothing inside it.

THE FALL

It was only once Ophelia was close to the cage, hustled there by the Genealogists, that she realized that it wasn't as empty as it seemed. Something tiny and shiny, barely more than the point of a needle, was floating in the middle of it. She thought of those flecks of dust that catch the sunlight along the slats of shutters, except that this one wasn't frolicking around. It was still and steady. And a prisoner: the cage was padlocked.

The Genealogists tensed up beside Ophelia; she could sense their muscles, their breaths, their powder, almost their thoughts.

"Open it."

Their voices had lost all lasciviousness. They expressed raw desire.

"Patience, patience!"

Lazarus searched the pockets of his frock coat, one by one, before slapping his forehead with a chuckle, and extracting a key from his left sock. Ophelia couldn't believe that, all this time, he had had something so precious concealed on his person, and there of all places. Someone else must have a copy. She peered up at the crisscrossing tracks carrying trucks around the cavern's mining galleries. Although anything not lit up by the moving rainbows of the two giant kaleidoscopes wasn't that clear, she could make out objects overflowing everywhere, and, even more so, hear the creaking of furniture, clinking of crockery, all the telltale cracked sounds of faulty goods. It was a tiny spark that had created all that?

The click of the padlock drew her attention back to Lazarus, who opened wide the cage door, which was as high as him.

"Before proceeding any further," he said, puffing himself up, "I would like to make a statement."

Moving in perfect symmetry, the Genealogists pulled their pistols from Ophelia's side to point them at him. Two shots. Two golden bullets, right in the chest. The impact threw Lazarus far from the cage, as the two shots resonated, endlessly. Ophelia felt as if this sound was echoing inside her. Thorn suddenly pulled her backwards, while the Genealogists, in a reverse impulse, moved toward the open cage, hand in hand, their smoking pistols still in their other hands. They didn't so much as glance at Lazarus's body, lying amid the parabolas' fluctuating colors, his smile frozen. From now on, no one stood between them and the Horn of Plenty.

"He had a plan," Thorn whispered into Ophelia's ear. "He must have had one."

The Genealogists entered the cage, like two phoenixes ready to be reborn, their faces turned up at that tiny spark full of infinity. They had but to reach out.

"Give us eternity."

It wasn't a prayer. It was a command.

The Genealogists no longer moved. Thorn had stopped breathing, and the scarf wriggling. Lazarus was a corpse on the ground. The Horn of Plenty had expanded the very web of time by adding surplus seconds, minutes, hours, years to it. Or so Ophelia would have thought had she not heard her own heart pounding away, before something, at last, seemed about to happen.

That something was the appearance of an aureole around

the Genealogists, whose eyes, wide open in ecstasy, watched their own glorious metamorphosis. The aureole darkened into a golden cloud that filled the whole cage. Their eyes widened even more, the cloud turned crimson, and Ophelia suddenly understood that it was their bodies—makeup, skin, organs— that were scattering in thousands of tiny pieces. No cry came from their gaping mouths, and soon there were no more lips at all. The Genealogists had become a haze that the spark was sucking up, little by little, molecule after molecule, like a ventilation filter, until the cage was completely cleared.

The Horn of Plenty had devoured them.

The spark then began to shine even more brightly. It filled the cage with a new mist, silvery this time. With morbid fascination, Ophelia wondered if it might be aerargyrum. For it to be visible to the naked eye, it must be in highly concentrated form. Gradually, the mist changed appearance, took on colors, solidified, until men and women were materializing from it. The echoes incarnate of the Genealogists. The cage was full of them. Their bodies were misshapen, their faces hardly recognizable. Faulty copies.

Ophelia and the scarf shuddered. Was that, then, the true power of the Horn of Plenty?

"We've got company," Thorn said to her.

Footsteps could be heard from the depths of the cavern, where all the shadows overlapped. People were approaching. When they stepped into the electrical light of the kaleidoscopes, Ophelia's shock was even greater than all the shocks she had experienced up to now. Ambrose was heading toward them. He was contorting, more than walking, but he was there, upright, very much alive, in flesh and beaming smile. He wasn't alone. A second Ambrose followed him into the light, then a third, then a fourth, and soon a throng of lookalikes was emerging from the darkness. They all looked similar, and yet each was dissymmetrical in their own way. They were all the echoes incarnate of an original Ambrose, who had disappeared forty years ago.

They didn't say a word to Ophelia and Thorn, but greeted them with a friendly nod of the head as they passed. Many automatons escorted them, all carrying coded plates and toolboxes. They regrouped around the cage and, with gestures that had been repeated a thousand times, they cleared all the echoes out, without rushing them, but taking care, above all, not to linger inside, and then reclosed the padlock. As soon as an Ambrose placed a plate on the back of an echo, its appearance changed. The Genealogists' features faded away—nose, eyes, ears, hair, flesh, muscles—until they had lost their last remnants of humanity.

"Automatons."

Ophelia's voice was flat. She thought back to the implosion of Hugo in the amphitheater, and to the factory in which they had sought refuge, to escape the patrols. None of all that was authentic. It was all just artifice, to prevent the citizens from knowing the true nature of the automatons. Lazarus had probably never created a single one in his life. He had used a simple code to turn real echoes into fake machines.

Now that she was looking at them differently, Ophelia realized that the form of several of the automatons here was familiar to her. Some reminded her of Mediana, others the Knight. Some were hitting their left ear, mimicking a habit that had lost all meaning. And others carried on their shoulders a replica of the mechanical creature of their former proprietor: a beetle, a monkey, a lizard . . . Among them there was even the mechanical parrot, now mute, that had enabled Ophelia's crystallization in the chapel.

If there was no one left at the Deviations Observatory, it was because all of its occupants had passed through the door of the cage. Was that the last stage of the Alternative Program, or a desperate act to escape the final collapse of the world?

Ophelia had exhausted her capacity for surprise. She didn't even bat an eyelid when Lazarus's corpse sat up, coughing and chuckling, and then versions of Ambrose helped him to his feet.

"'Everything that enters into the cage transmutes.' That's what I was about to say when those two impolite creatures cut me short."

Lazarus straightened up his pink spectacles on his nose, and then pulled out a metal plate, concealed under his frock coat. The pistols' two bullets had lodged in it, but not managed to pierce it.

"You knew," said Thorn, his voice heavy. "You knew exactly what was going to happen."

It was hearing him say these words that made Ophelia aware of the abrupt reversal of the situation, and it wasn't in their favor. They were underground, far from everything, facing an unpredictable spark, surrounded by an army of echoes incarnate in the service of a single man—the most fearsome of them all. The danger was no longer the Genealogists; it had never really ever been. The danger was Lazarus.

"Only the broad outlines!" he responded, with a mischievous expression. "I mainly trusted my pinky."

He waggled the little finger in question, indicating to someone behind them to come hither. Second moved forward through the morass of rainbows. Was she the only person from the observatory not to have been turned into an automaton in their absence? Left to her own devices, she had lost her bandage, revealing a scabby gash cutting across her nose, like a gory smile. Thorn became even more tense, and Ophelia knew that he was forcing himself, above all, not to look away.

And yet there was a sudden harmony about Second, as if, despite their contradictions, all her features had finally agreed to express the same excitement.

For the first time, she wasn't carrying any drawing materials, no paper, no pencil.

She walked resolutely between Ophelia and Thorn, obliging him to limp to one side to avoid another claws accident, and made straight for Lazarus. She stared at him with her white eye wide open.

"The extreme horizontality escapes through all the veins of the side aisle . . ."

Paying no attention at all to Second's burbling, Lazarus proudly placed his palm on her head.

"If I can glimpse certain echoes in advance when dreaming, it's nothing compared with that eye. Second has never managed to establish a dialogue with the echoes and induce a crystallization, but she deciphers them better than anyone. At first, Lady Septima saw the deviation of her power as shameful, and then as a pretext to infiltrate my observatory. She thought that by doing so she was serving the Genealogists, but it was to me that she was giving a present that was *absolument fabuleux*!"

"And they kiss the cherries while striking insomnia . . ." Second continued, unperturbed.

From an inside pocket, Lazarus pulled out his wallet, its leather giving off a ghastly smell, and took out a photograph, faded by time, warmth and damp. He handed it to Ophelia. It was the snap of a drawing pinned to a wall. Its realism was disturbing. It depicted very clearly the Horn of Plenty's cage, and its spark glinting inside it, along with three people beside its wide-open door: Lazarus, Second, and a woman. A small woman in a gown, wearing glasses and a scarf.

Ophelia would have liked to do to this photograph what

441

she had done to the drawings that came before it—throw it into the toilet, tear it to pieces—but Lazarus took it back from her to return it to his wallet.

"It's thanks to my little Second that I've never lost faith in the future. I knew that what we are living through today was going to happen sooner or la—"

"You're a hypocrite," Thorn interrupted him. "'Putting an end to the servitude of man by man'? How many of them have you sacrificed on the way?"

Lazarus managed an indulgent smile, but it was to Ophelia that he directed it. He couldn't get to grips with Thorn.

"I have never sacrificed anyone. None of those who had the privilege of entering this cage died from it. They still exist, but in a way that your mind and your senses can't conceive."

"And it directs the spaces until the bottle contracts—"

"They have been turned into aerargyrum," Lazarus added, in an excited voice that drowned out Second's. "And the echoes produced by this transmutation have themselves been turned into solid matter. It always works like that, I presume it's a question of balance."

Ophelia's eyes were aching from popping out of her head. She was imagining molecules of the Genealogists floating all around her as gas. Maybe she was even breathing in some of it. What Lazarus described was, to her, worse than death.

The tone of the professor's voice suddenly became that of a storyteller.

"Thousands of years ago, in the Babel of old, an imperial city was built, above our heads. During the work, the builders discovered a cavern, and inside that cavern, a minuscule particle of light. For how long had it been there? No one knew, but whoever approached it was swallowed up by it, and then regurgitated in the form of two monstrous echoes. A cage was constructed."

Just two, Ophelia thought, surprised. The Genealogists had generated many more echoes than that.

"We don't know how our distant ancestors used this discovery, but they finally blocked up the cavern. The Horn of Plenty became legendary. And one day, much later on, in a Babel ravaged by war, the army accidentally found it when searching for deposits in the basements of the ancient imperial city."

Lazarus was telling his story as though reciting it to himself, and was so carried away he even forgot about the Index.

"It was the start of some *extrêmement* extensive experiments. The army observed that, in proximity to reflective materials, the particle expanded." Lazarus indicated, in turn, the gigantic parabolas that made the kaleidoscopes spin. "The more the particle expanded, the more numerous the echoes. Eulalia Gonde herself has stood right here!" he exclaimed, resisting the urge to kiss the ground at his feet. "The bombardments put an end to the experiments, the Rupture shattered the old world, and the Horn of Plenty sank, once again, into oblivion. Until I pulled it out! The concept of transmutation is hard to accept," he admitted. "That's why I planted a fake factory in the town center, and a self-destruction code in my automatons, in order to protect the secret of how they were made. The day when I will finally be able to make public my research, without shocking public opinion, is close. Ambrose!"

The adolescents fussing around the new automatons immediately turned to Lazarus.

"Let's give a little demonstration for our guest."

"Yes, professor."

Their gentle voices resonated like those of a choir, under the cavern's lofty vault. Ophelia felt the scarf tensing up at the same time as she did. None of them would ever be the Ambrose that they had both got to know. These Ambroses were content to imitate a defunct model: their eyes were empty, vacant even to themselves.

"And the wall is a white perfume that derails . . ." spouted Second.

One of the Ambroses took out a key, which was then passed from one deformed hand to another until it reached an Ambrose standing near the cage. The padlock was reopened. In a chain of repetitive movements, objects were brought over from a convoy of trucks.

It was the same ritual every time. They placed a perfectly sound object into the cage: a chair, a sack of rice, a pair of shoes. They waited for the object to be decomposed, and then recomposed by the spark. Next, they collected barely recognizable versions, which only took definitive form once a seal was applied: wobbly chairs, weevily rice, unwearable shoes.

Thorn studied the process with intense concentration. Even now, trapped in the bowels of the observatory, he was only thinking about how to use this spark for his own ends.

Lazarus delicately flicked his handkerchief over one of the cage's bars, as if dusting the frame of an old master.

"The code only serves to stabilize the echo in its matter, and correct its imperfections, as far as possible. Without it, the echo wouldn't last long. From just one offering, the Horn of Plenty produces a multitude of duplications. It's very economical. *En fait*, it can even reproduce new echoes from an already materialized echo, but, alas, the further one goes from the original model, the more the duplicates feature design flaws."

To illustrate what he was saying, he tapped the turban of an Ambrose with eyes where his ears should have been, and an upside-down nose.

"The Ambrose who lived with me for all those years belonged to the first generation of echoes. You see, my old friend had volunteered to enter into the cage. He wanted to be transmuted into aeragyrum, live the experience from within. His scientific curiosity was second to none! In truth, *ma chère*," he said, winking at Ophelia, "that echo of him that you got to know was but a pale imitation. Similar, certainly, touching, too, but an imitation all the same. In some ways, he was my very first automaton, long before Walter. For that alone, I will miss him greatly."

"And there are curtains that rain behind every comet . . ."

Ophelia felt totally disgusted, a revulsion caused by Lazarus alone. He was so absorbed in his own story that he paid no attention to Second's nonsensical one.

"But that's all in the past!" he exclaimed, rubbing his hands. "You are one of us, now, *ma chère*, you and your echo. You're going to reproduce the miracle that Eulalia and the Other performed right here, centuries ago: create echoes incarnate that won't be lackluster versions of their originals, but, on the contrary, will surpass them in every respect. If our family spirits were originally ordinary humans, just think what marvels we could achieve. Unlimited delicious food! Paradise-like lands as far as the eye can see! A society of men and women who can just dedicate themselves to the arts, philosophy, and personal fulfillment! Our names will go down in History forever, the History that matters, the one with a capital H."

All of Ophelia's weight had sunk into her sandals. This old, powerless man had counted entirely on her to set himself up as a heroic figure, but she hadn't the remotest idea what she was supposed to do. Communicate with an echo whose existence she had only glimpsed four times? Expect instruction from it that would initiate her into the universe's greatest truths, known and unknown? She wondered how she could have only envisaged using this Horn of Plenty to restore Eulalia Gonde's humanity to her, and send the Other back into the mirror.

She looked at Thorn, drawn up to his full height between her and the cage. His endless shadow was like ink spilling from his heels. He was silently staring at the tiny spark before him, so close and out of reach. He couldn't grab hold of it, or even approach it, and yet his body was taut as a bow that can't give up on its target. He was searching, at all costs, for a solution.

As for Second, she had gone quiet.

It was then that Ophelia was struck by something that was suddenly obvious. Thorn didn't feature in the drawing that Lazarus had shown her.

"Watch out!"

It was as if Second had been waiting for that signal. She rushed at Thorn, who swiveled round to her with a grinding of metal, eyebrows arched in surprise. He was twice her size, and not a man easy to destabilize. Had his assailant been someone else, he would have used his claws without any qualms, but Ophelia saw something flash across his wide-open eyes—an immediate choice to be made. He allowed himself to be pushed backwards. His leg brace exploded in a clatter of steel, screws, and bolts.

Thorn had fallen inside the cage.

Ophelia shot up like a spring. She had stopped thinking, she was now but a primal reflex. Get him out of there. Now. *Now.* Arms stopped her in full flight. It was the Ambroses, who, at the click of Lazarus's fingers, had grabbed hold of her. She beat them away with her fists, her teeth, her claws, but as soon as she got rid of one arm, two others took over.

Now.

"Get up!"

Ophelia could see very well that Thorn was trying to. She saw him struggling with his overly stiff body, snarled in a chaos of metal, hindered by an intractable leg. She saw him, yes, but she screamed at him, all the same.

"Get up! Get up!"

Now.

"Help him!"

Lazarus shrugged his shoulders, helplessly. At the threshold of the cage, Second stared with her blank eye at this man writhing at her feet.

"But this well was no more real than a rabbit of Odin," she said to him.

Thorn froze. An aureole appeared all around him; his own flesh was disintegrating. He turned his long, bony face toward Ophelia, who was fighting off the Ambroses with her elbows, desperate to reach out to him. He looked deep into her eyes, nailing them with his most resolute look, in ultimate defiance, and then he disintegrated into thousands of particles.

Ophelia stopped fighting, screaming, existing. She watched, without flinching, as the haze—composed entirely of Thorn—was sucked up by the tiny spark, and, seconds later, the materializing of several echoes, standing in the cage, watch in hand. Distorted and inexpressive caricatures who weren't Thorn. Who would never be him.

Just as the Ambroses were about to follow the usual procedure, Lazarus stopped them.

"No," he said, gently. "Not these ones."

The echoes, without a code to keep them materialized, gradually faded away. There was nothing left of Thorn; not even a bit of fingernail, or a single hair.

Ophelia was suffocating. Her veins were burning. She was on fire. Her survival instinct told her to control her breathing, fill her lungs with air, but she couldn't anymore. Her body's vital mechanism had broken down. Her vision became blurred, and she felt herself tipping inside herself, far, very far back, well before her birth, to where all is cool, and calm, and forgotten.

Standing in the middle of the cavern, Eulalia wipes her glasses for the sixth time.

As each new bomb smashes into the observatory, right up there, at ground level, the stalactites shower her with rock dust. There is no one around her, but the ground is strewn with rifles, submachine guns, grenades, flamethrowers, and antipersonnel mines. With the toe of her military boot, Eulalia pushes them away. All of these weapons are unusable replicas, failed echoes. Happily, they will never kill.

Those who wanted to use them are dead, somewhere up there.

She should have understood sooner the true finality of the Project, and its absurdity. She should have known that her superiors had never had any intention other than to produce ever more weapons. Their experiments were, in any case, destined to fail. The echoes aren't intended to make up for the shortcomings of human beings.

Eulalia shakes off the rock dust that settles on her lenses. She survived the deportation of her family, exile from her country of origin, famine, illnesses, and bombardments. Every night, before falling asleep, she repeated to herself that all this had a meaning, that she was destined to slip through the net of all catastrophes in order to save the world from itself.

Today, she understands that, above all, she had been very lucky. The luckiest thing of all was encountering her Other through a telephone receiver.

"You changed my point of view on things."

"*Changed things,*" crackles the echo from the walkie-talkie she wears on her belt.

Eulalia smiles.

"Conceited."

She slips off the straps of her satchel, and from it carefully takes out a thick exercise book. Her most personal manuscript:

a play. She has put all of herself into it. The ink contains her blood and sweat, and she used her hair to sew the binding. She wrote this play over recent weeks, without a typewriter, without her superiors knowing. Had they found it, what would they have understood? She encrypted the text using an old alphabet she had invented, her favorite one, the one with the lovely arabesques.

Hugging the exercise book to her chest, she advances slowly between the two giant kaleidoscopes, their perpetual motion splashing her skin with colors. At the point where their radiance intersects, within the makeshift barbed-wire fence, and barely visible to the naked eye, she finally glimpses it: the Horn of Plenty.

"A particle whose gravitational field takes apart any matter that comes near it, before turning it into a substance that can be modeled at will." That's the definition of it her superiors had given her. Thanks to the Other, Eulalia knows how mistaken they were, she knows why they only produced faulty copies of weapons and soldiers, and why she won't make the same mistakes.

She places the manuscript within the barbed-wire fence and moves back until she's out of the spark's reach. Already, the binding is disintegrating into a cloud of paper. These pages written by her own hand, with her own blood and her own sweat, contain the beginning of a story, that of her future children. That's what Eulalia gives to the spark: words. In return, she expects an intelligent life from it. Twenty-one lives, to be precise.

Because her superiors were wrong; the Horn of Plenty has never been a particle.

It's a hole.

Ophelia took in a big gulp of air; she had remembered how

to breathe. A variety of misshapen Ambrose faces peered down at her. In among them was Lazarus, smiling at her.

"I must admit, *ma chère*, you almost had me worried. I thought you'd had a heart attack. I may have a Horn of Plenty at my disposal, but you're the only person in the world I can't replace."

Ophelia became aware again of the ground beneath her knees, the scarf twitching around her neck, the commotion of the trucks in the galleries, the mineral smell of the cavern, and the light effects of the kaleidoscopes. She was there, once again, and yet she was missing what was most important.

Lazarus offered her his elbow, attentively.

"I rather envy your husband, you know? He is experiencing what every explorer hopes to experience one day. Contemplating our reality from a perspective that no human will ever be able to access! If we didn't have so many wonders to achieve, you, your echo, and I, I'd happily invite you both to join me there with him."

Ophelia stared intently at him, through the double glazing of their glasses.

"Bring him back."

Her voice, strained from screaming, didn't seem to be her own. Nothing belonged to her anymore, and she no longer belonged to anything.

Lazarus sighed, with understanding.

"The process is irreversible. *Honnêtement*, I don't know why Mr. Thorn wasn't part of our plan, but what could we do? The advance echoes are never wrong."

Ophelia wasn't listening to him anymore. She ignored the elbow he was so keen to offer her, made her way through all the Ambroses, and went up to Second, still standing on the threshold of the cage, backlit by the spark.

"Why?"

The young girl held her gaze without flinching, with her normal eye and her blank one.

"But this well was no more real than a rabbit of Odin," she repeated.

Then, after what seemed like a supreme effort, she managed to say:

"You . . . must . . . turn back."

The Horn of Plenty floated, indifferently, in the midst of the rainbows. Helen's words, in the stand of the amphitheater, came back to Ophelia: "You should go beyond the cage. Turn back. Really turn back. There, and only there, you will understand."

"We mustn't waste any more time," Lazarus said to her, his spine protesting as he straightened up. "We must establish communication with your echo as soon as possible, so it can reveal to us the real operating method of the Horn of Plenty. Telephone, *s'il vous plaît*!"

An automaton immediately brought a telephone, sitting on a cushion, its cable endlessly unwinding from the depths of the cavern. Lazarus unhooked the receiver to hand it to Ophelia. There was infinite tenderness in his every gesture, his every look.

"I'm sure your echo is just waiting for a word from you, *ma chère*. It will reveal to you not only how to create plenty, but also how to overcome your own limitations, so that you can, in turn, pass it on to what remains of humanity. Eulalia lacked ambition, content merely to give us family spirits. She should have guided every woman and man onto the path of crystallization, taught them how to awaken their echo's consciousness, and elevate themselves to a state of omnipotence! That may even be why she lost control of her Other. If there's one person in the world capable of stopping it, it's you."

Ophelia seized the receiver. She put it back on the hook, pushed Lazarus into the cage, and went in with him.

"No!"

Lazarus hurled himself at the door that Ophelia was just closing. Too late: she had already fastened the padlock. It was ironic to think that, if the observatory hadn't healed her of her clumsiness, she would probably never have managed to do so in time.

Lazarus rummaged in his frock coat, searching for the key. His pink spectacles fell off his nose, shattering as they hit the ground.

"You can't! The plan! You mustn't!"

It was the first time Ophelia was seeing him in the grip of rage, but that was as nothing compared with how she felt toward him.

So it was to Second that she addressed her last sentence, through the bars:

"I'm turning back."

A radiant smile emerged under that of the gash. For the first time, Second felt understood.

Ophelia hugged the scarf to her chest, ashamed and relieved that she had dragged it into this cage with her. She wondered if it was going to suffer, as she looked up at the spark, looming down on her.

Not a spark, no. A hole.

Ophelia held her breath. A mist was rising from her gown and her gloves. She readied herself for getting her body through the eye of a needle. Thorn had boarded that long-distance airship for her; now it was her turn.

Lazarus, still searching in all his pockets for the key to the padlock, froze when he noticed the drawing that Second was holding up, right under his nose. It was the one from his wallet. She tore it.

That was the last thing Ophelia saw before being blown to smithereens.

THE WRONG SIDE

A searing pain. The sensation of being turned inside out, like a garment. And then tumbling.

Ophelia falls upwards. Gripping onto her scarf, she passes through what seem like strata of atmosphere, and the higher she goes, the more the falling accelerates. And yet she lands on her feet without a bump or a sound. She is surrounded by fog. She's not hurting anymore, but she's not sure if she's still breathing.

Where is Lazarus? There's no more cage, or cavern, or Second: nothing anymore, apart from the scarf and her. Ophelia looks at her arms and legs to make sure they are still there. Her skin has turned a shade of verdigris, as if she has become an old brass statue. She tugs at some of her curls. Blond. She tugs at her gown. Black. Even the colors of her scarf have been reversed. A beauty spot that, until now, had sat in the hollow of her left elbow, now nestles in the hollow of her right one. What is most disturbing is to see, without needing special lenses, the shadow of her family power enveloping all of her like foam. Ophelia unbuttons a now pale-blue glove, and sees the shadow intensifying around her reader's fingers. At least she has been reassembled in the right order and all in one piece, already a miracle in itself. So the Horn of Plenty was, well and truly, a passage.

But a passage to what?

Ophelia swivels round a few times. There's fog everywhere. Where is Thorn? She wants to call out to him, but something inside her refuses to do so. She moves forward through this intangible, limitless whiteness. She thinks she can see a rectangle in the distance, dim as a star behind clouds. No sooner has Ophelia's attention been focused on it than it starts to get bigger, and bigger, as if it were rushing toward her, whereas it should really have been for her to approach it. The rectangle is, in fact, a half-opened door. Ophelia slips through it.

She enters into a room so foggy, she can only just make out the outlines of the furniture and the glimmer of the lamps. Fog aside, the colors of the place are natural, unlike those of Ophelia. The door she came through belongs to a wardrobe. With its chaos of disorganized files and its overloaded décor, she really struggles to recognize the treasury of the Pole. She has been transported to the other side of the world from Babel. Even the interfamilial Compass Roses can't enable such leaps across space.

In the midst of the layers of fog stands the large desk that had so impressed Ophelia the first time she sat on the other side of it. It still bears the stain from when she spilt ink on it.

There's a man sitting at it. A man who isn't Thorn. The new treasurer? His coloring, too, is normal. Ophelia wants to announce herself, but, once again, the words stick in her throat. The man, in an over-powdered wig, is slumped in his chair. There is such an accumulation of newspapers, blotters, and files waiting on the desk, it's like a fortress of paper before him. He doesn't look at it, any more than he notices Ophelia, rudely peering over his shoulder. He's doing crosswords; it's all gibberish to her.

Not only has she lost her ability to speak, but also to read.

She has, on the other hand, developed a new sense that

allows her to perceive the generally imperceptible. Something that's at once infinitely subtle and strong is making the surrounding fog undulate. At every instant, the new treasurer projects his image, his chemistry, his density around the space. These waves go through Ophelia, which is neither pleasant nor unpleasant. She senses the form of this man, along with his powdery smell and the scratching of his pencil against his chin. He shows more interest in his crossword puzzle than in the telephone, which he leaves to ring on his desk. It makes a dampened, distant sound, but Ophelia feels every vibration as if she was made of the same substance. With a flick, she manages to make one of the waves move in the opposite direction. The ringing of the telephone then releases an echo, causing the new treasurer to frown.

Ophelia shakes her fog-covered hand under his nose, but he is unaware of her presence. Her existence is too different from his.

In any case, it's not this treasurer she's looking for—wrong person, wrong place.

Space immediately stretches out under Ophelia's sandals. The new treasurer, the telephone, the crossword puzzle, the desk, the wardrobe move away from her until they are lost in the fog. This pervasive whiteness is aerargyrum. Ophelia herself is made up of it, from head to toe. She can no longer express herself, and yet her mind has never been clearer. She instinctively grasps concepts that were hitherto unknown to her. What Lazarus calls aerargyrum is in fact inverted matter. The Horn of Plenty doesn't transform those who pass through it; it turns them in on themselves. And the echoes produced by this inversion in turn invert themselves; a code only serves artificially to preserve the structure of their atoms, but, with or without one, balance is maintained.

New forms emerge around Ophelia. Motionless carousels.

She is back at the Deviations Observatory, in the old amusement park of the Alternative Program. Aerargyrum shrouds both the sky and the ground.

Ophelia goes past the Fakir's Game stand, in which she had sheltered with Thorn. If she knew how to, she would shout out his name.

She moves toward the tiger carousel. She can make out a figure, curled up between the wooden creatures. Mediana! The precious stones inlaid in her verdigris skin have taken on an unusual hue. She, too, was sucked up by the Horn of Plenty, and, just like Ophelia, has become a negative of herself. The mist of her family power floats around her body like her baggy pajamas. Unlike the Pole's new treasurer, Mediana becomes aware of Ophelia's presence and looks up at her. White irises stand out against the black corneas of her wide-open eyes. How long has she been hiding on this carousel? Her mouth can't emit a sound. She holds her hand out to a shaken Ophelia. Mediana had been a torturer and a victim, but never had she asked for her help.

The aerargyrum creates a milky curtain between them. Ophelia can no longer see either Mediana or the carousel. She wanders around alone once more. Here and there, between two blank spaces, she catches a brief glimpse of other figures in the negative. Lazarus. The Knight. The young girl with the monkey. The beetle woman. The lizard man. Each time, Ophelia loses sight of them within seconds. She even has a fleeting vision of the Genealogists, first the man, then the woman, both searching for each other in the fog, unable to call out to each other. They seem totally disoriented by this limbo that leads nowhere. They wanted Plenty, they sought the ultimate truth, and here they are, left to their own absurd meanderings.

Much as Ophelia perseveres, she doesn't see Thorn among them. She, herself, begins to be overcome by a fear that's as disembodied as she is. The scarf tenses all its loops around her, and, similarly, the aerargyrum clings ever more tightly to her, swallowing up what remains of the surroundings, even blotting out her sandals.

What if she were doomed never to find Thorn again? If she were doomed never to find anything at all again?

Suddenly, a figure appears through the fog and makes straight for Ophelia, without the slightest hesitation. The more the gap narrows, the clearer the figure becomes. A back? The individual approaching her is moving backwards. It staggers, wiggles its knees, folds and unfolds its arms. Even its overall appearance keeps fluctuating and blurring. When, finally, it swivels round, it turns out to be a little young lady with messy curls, rectangular glasses, and a three-colored scarf.

Ophelia's echo.

It's standing so close, it's almost touching her. Its colors, at first just like Ophelia's before the Horn of Plenty sucked her up, gradually mirror those she has now. From pink, its skin turns to verdigris; from brown, its hair veers toward blond. Her echo looks so much like her! Apart from the fact that its scarf doesn't seem to be animated. And that it is chewing something.

"Who is I."

It uttered these words between two chews, in a barely human voice, but Ophelia's voice, all the same. How does it manage to speak? It waits, impassively. What does it want of Ophelia? How does it feel toward her? And her, how does she feel about it? More than anything, she wishes she could ask it where Thorn is.

Ophelia moves forward. The echo sneaks away. The more she tries to approach it, the more it backs off, into the aerargyrum. Is it running away from her? In this realm of echoes, she is probably the only person to have a guide, and she has no intention of letting it slip through her fingers. She walks faster and faster so as not to lose sight of the absurd image of her own body contorting itself to run backwards.

After an endless, almost blind race, Ophelia bursts out of the aerargyrum. She has left a washed-out world for an explosion of colors. A red ocean stretches as far as the eye can see, beneath an orange-colored sky. Ophelia gazes at the beach of blue sand, into which her feet are sinking. It's no longer just her that's in the negative, it's now the entire seascape. Why? There's no ocean in Babel, and yet this one seems more real than the Deviations Observatory, which has remained shrouded in fog behind her.

"Who is I."

The echo is balancing on the moving surface of the water. It's still chewing, as if it had a sweet in its mouth that won't dissolve. With its finger, it points to an island in the distance, with purple vegetation. The distance separating Ophelia from this other shore instantly shrinks, until there's no distance at all. And now, here she is on the island, walking up an avenue, deep in the luminous shade of the trees. Her echo is still walking backwards in front of her, as though to it, all this was merely a game of tag. Nothing here is normal, neither the improbable colors nor the abstract aromas nor the liquid sounds, but Ophelia feels sure she has been here before. She becomes even more sure when she reaches some majestic buildings of glass and steel in the midst of the jungle. She had lived within those walls. If her heart had retained an organic logic, it would have started to beat faster and faster. She's afraid—afraid to hope. It's her echo's turn to follow her at a distance, as she takes the initiative of going inside, and starts climbing some stairs. She had fallen at this very spot, she remembers, striding up a step. It was on her first day.

She goes through the door of a university amphitheater.

Around a hundred apprentices in yellow frock coats are seated along its tiers, hunched over their notebooks, frantically scratching away on the paper with their fountain pens. They are all in the negative, like Ophelia, but not one of them cares about her. The shadows of their family powers quiver with hyperactivity. They all seem in the grip of some indescribable torment, tearing out the pages of their notebooks, and then starting their work all over again, from scratch. Judging by all the balls of paper littering the entire floor, this performance has been going on for a very long while.

Ophelia smoothes out a random piece of paper. The white ink on the black surface is just meaningless scribbles; even she, who has become a perfect illiterate, can see perfectly well that these are not words. For these young people, who all aspire to joining the elite, no longer being able either to speak or read or write must be a veritable nightmare.

Ophelia bursts out laughing. Her distorted voice bounces chaotically around the amphitheater, attracting furious looks from the apprentices she is distracting from their work. She has never laughed like this in her whole life. It's an explosion of joy in its purest form. She would so like to tell them all how alive they are!

The Good Family didn't plunge into the void.

Ophelia leaves the amphitheater, runs along the corridors, and leaps over the benches. Her echo tries to follow her in its dislocated way, but she can't slow down, propelled by the strength of her sudden understanding, freed from a weight that's been crushing her for a long time.

There never was a landslide.

She comes across students and professors, wandering around the establishment. They all look drained, pacing back and forth past doors, coming and going along walls and ceilings, avoiding meeting anyone's eye.

Ophelia feels like dancing with every one of them. She dives into a walkway, and between its columns she can gaze at the red ocean, the neighboring islands, and, in the distance, shrouded in fog, a mainland bristling with construction sites. Wherever she looks, land and water form a continuous horizon.

The Rupture never happened; not, in any case, in the way it has been recounted. The old world wasn't smashed to pieces. It has remained intact all this time, just like the Good Family, hiding behind the void, behind Ophelia's dreams. Behind behind.

It turned in on itself. It inverted itself.

The sea of clouds? Entire continents of aerargyrum! A formidable concentration of aerargyrum.

Ophelia suddenly stops running. In the middle of the walkway, in front of a newspaper distributor, behind a long white fringe, she almost didn't recognize Octavio.

Octavio . . . She would like to be able to say his voice out loud to convince herself that he is really there, that he has never ceased to be there. He is so focused on the newspaper distributor that he pays no attention to her. He lowers the lever, picks up a copy, tears it up, throws it into a garbage chute, lowers the lever again, picks up another copy, tears it, throws it into the garbage chute, and continues without the distributor ever emptying.

Ophelia grips Octavio's shoulder to stop him. She can barely feel him through her glove, as if he were very far away, despite being so close. He turns his eyes toward her, which are no longer red, but turquoise, projecting the shadow of their power like two beams of smoke. She expects him to be as happy as she was at seeing him, but his face expresses only pain. He hands her a newspaper, silently entreating her to help him destroy them all, and then returns to his task, so absorbed that he instantly forgets Ophelia. There is nothing printed on these newspapers. It's not their contents that matter, but what they represent: the lies of Babel.

All of Ophelia's euphoria falls flat.

Octavio and the others are alive, yes, but at what price? They have been trapped in their obsessions, condemned continually to repeat the same rituals, and remain ignorant of what had really happened to them. Will she suffer the same fate if she lingers too long among them? She remembers the unbearable guilt she had felt when the airship plunged into the void between the arks. She now knows why: because the land of the old world is still there, on the reverse side of the spatial web. And even now that Ophelia has been inverted herself, she realizes that her presence here remains an aberration.

Second knew it. Second saw it.

That was why she had shown her all those pathetic portraits of Octavio. She doesn't only detect the advance echoes; she wants to stop them. And she had always expected Ophelia to save her brother from this place—from this Wrong Side.

But how? Ophelia hasn't managed to find Thorn, and she has no idea how to save herself. She scans the walkway in both directions, looking for her echo, which had been her guide until then. Had she ended up losing it, too?

An echo. Ophelia realizes that she knows one personally, right here, at the Good Family.

She takes a final look at Octavio, relentlessly throwing one newspaper after another into the garbage chute. She is sorry to leave him. She cuts across the jungle of a garden, in which she glimpses mute birds and dozy marsupials. She dives into an administrative building and scales its marble stories. She no longer really knows whether it's she who is running, or the building that's carrying her to her destination.

She steps into the director's office.

Helen is an echo incarnate, like all the family spirits, but she is also the most intelligent of the siblings. If anyone can help Ophelia to penetrate the mysteries of the Wrong Side, it's her. The black bulbs barely diminish the dazzling darkness of the office. It's deserted. Ophelia had been summoned several times, as an apprentice virtuoso, to see the lady director; the giantess almost never left her post, she should have been here.

Ophelia knocks into a trolley and hears a damp sound under her sandals. She's trodden on some glass. Looking closely at it, she recognizes the lenses of an optical appliance. As for the trolley she had banged into, it is actually a crinoline on castors, onto which an enormous dress has been stitched. The bodice hangs limply on the support structure. Ophelia is alarmed. She opens the glass door to the bookcase in which Helen's Book is displayed. On its skin pages, Eulalia Gonde's beautiful handwriting has turned into scribbles. There is no coherent language on the Wrong Side. By losing her code, Helen has returned to her original state. Formless. All that remains of her now is an empty dress.

"Who is I."

The echo is sitting in Helen's chair, which is far too big for it. It has a strange effect on Ophelia, seeing a provocative expression on her own face. It's still chomping, insolently, on its sweet. No sooner has she ventured towards it, than it springs up and away. Ophelia has the curious impression that this echo wants both to help her and to test her.

The space surrounding them changes shape, like modeling clay. They are now between two skies, one that opens out above their heads, and the other that is reflected beneath their feet. It takes Ophelia a few moments to realize that they are standing on the gigantic glass dome of Babel's Memorial, at its highest point. The view is breathtaking. The Good Family is now a mere outcrop of land in the distance; the building containing Helen's office not even visible on it. Ophelia has a panoramic view of the ocean and the harbor, of the old and new Babel, of arks the wrong way round, and districts back to front. She feels as if she's looking at a badly developed photograph. Here, the landscape is foggy and incomplete; there, multicolored and confused; nowhere is it harmonious.

But what shocks her the most are the sailing ships, which she couldn't see from the Good Family. There are too many of them to count, all stationary in the water, frozen in time and space. An armada several centuries old, thrown over to the Wrong Side before managing to reach the shores of Babel.

Ophelia looks up at the sun, as it darkens the sky. Its black light floods her glasses, giving a paradoxical clarity to all her thoughts, and so what if she can't express them out loud. She is replete with an understanding that requires no words.

The Right Side and the Wrong Side are the two pans of a pair of scales.

Every time matter inverts on one side, a counterpart inverts on the other side. For all matter that is turned into aerargyrum, so aerargyrum becomes embodied in matter, and for every echo embodied in the world on the right side, the Wrong Side needs a counterpart. A symbolically equivalent counterpart. Eulalia Gonde created a generation of demigods just from a simple manuscript, but in reality, it was but the first act of her play. On that day, she made a deal with the world on the wrong side. And years later, once the family spirits had grown up, Eulalia Gonde had stood almost exactly where Ophelia now finds herself. She saw war returning to Babel. It was the final straw; she decided to honor her deal. Over to the Wrong Side she hurled all the armed forces, all the conflict zones, all those nations incapable of keeping the peace. She sacrificed half of the world in order to save the other half. How many innocents, soldiers enlisted against their will, civilians caught up in battles were thus inverted without there being anyone to explain to them how and why? And how did Eulalia succeed in causing an inversion on this scale, without even having recourse to the Horn of Plenty? To send such a quantity of matter over to the Wrong Side, a new counterpart then had to be extracted from it, a symbolically equivalent one, sufficiently strong to maintain the scales' balance. No?

Ophelia senses the scarf bristling. She turns from the ocean, and its armada of ghost ships, to see her echo brandishing a block of marble at arm's length.

Ready to bring it down on her.

(Sisehtnerap)

Thorn walks through the fog. It's aerargyrum, quite obviously. Everything is white, and this whiteness disturbs him (white, winter, snow, Pole). There's nothing to quantify here, no distances between objects; no time, either. His watch has stopped (white, paper, treasury, Pole). He doesn't like this nothingness that seeps into the pores of his skin, now an absurd verdigris color, and permeates his brain as an involuntary association of ideas (white, Book, Farouk, Pole). He's no keener on the inverted symmetry of his body that has changed the position of his fifty-six scars. And he likes even less this shadow bristling with claws that clings to him like a mass of brambles, reminding him, with his every move, of the hideousness of his family power.

Thorn quickens his pace through the aerargyrum, without trying to understand how he is still managing to walk. Here he has neither his leg brace nor a stick, and his leg is assuming totally illogical angles at every stride. He feels no pain, which doesn't gladden him at all (white, amnesia, mother, Pole). Grinding bones, inflamed joints, mnemonic migraines, all this organic information constituted contours that had now disappeared, along with the decor. Without these contours, his memory is overflowing like liquid (white, enamel, smile).

No.

Thorn refuses, categorically, to let that particular memory, even more than all the others, impose itself on him. He refuses that door that he waited outside for three hours, twenty-seven minutes, and nineteen seconds, and that was never opened to him. He refuses that keyhole, just at the level of his eye, before his bones had begun their excessive growth. He refuses the laughter of his mother, who is showering Farouk's new ambassador, barely more than a child, with compliments, and already inviting him to dine at her table. He refuses that boy who's not him, and who has all that he will never have: a respectable birth, a future that's all mapped out, beauty in every millimeter of him, and his mother's smile. Above all, with his eye pressed to that shameful keyhole, he refuses the loneliness he detects in Archibald's eyes in the light of the chandeliers, much like the loneliness he's feeling in the gloom of that antechamber.

White. Thorn quickens his pace, plunging deeper and deeper into the aerargyrum, and its absence of contours. He knows neither where he is nor where he's going, but he will keep walking until he finds the only door that hasn't remained closed to him, and behind which he really is expected.

Ophelia's door.

Overflowing yet again (door, room, Eulalia Gonde, Rupture), Thorn's memory drags his mind backwards, in inverse proportion to the forward movement of his strides. The more he advances into the whiteness, the more he goes back in time, to Farouk's past, which his mother had imposed on him.

In the beginning, we were as one.

But God felt unsatisfied with us like that, so God set about dividing us. God had great fun with us, then God tired of us and forgot us. God could be so cruel in his indifference, he horrified me. God knew how to show a gentle side, too, and I loved him as I've loved no one else.

I think we could have all lived happily, in a way, God, me, and the others, if it weren't for that accursed book. It disgusted me. I knew what bound me to it in the most sickening of ways, but the horror of that particular knowledge came later, much later. I didn't understand straightaway, I was too ignorant.

I loved God, yes, but I despised that book, which he'd open at the drop of a hat. As for God, he relished it. When God was happy, he wrote. When God was furious, he wrote. And one day, when God was in a really bad mood, he did something enormously stupid.

God smashed the world to pieces.

Thorn sees again, in a scene his mind has replayed a thousand times, that door that Eulalia Gonde slammed behind her on the day of the Rupture. She locked herself up in her room. She forbade anyone from following her. Farouk, whose trembling hand on the door handle Thorn can see as if it were his own, finally disobeyed her. He opened it; he went in; he looked. Half of the room disappeared.

Thorn walks ever faster in the whiteness, twisting and untwisting his leg, stuck in this incomplete memory's furrow. It's no longer just his claws sprouting from his shadow, but a tangle of roots and branches representing the internal ramifications of his memory.

Eulalia was there, facing a mirror hanging in the air, standing on what remained of the floor. (*Try your dears.*) So why had Farouk felt this abandoned? (*Dry your tears.*) Why had he felt the same as Thorn, peering through his keyhole? (*God was punished.*) Why had Eulalia Gonde decided to rip that page out of her Book, to amputate it from her memory, to condemn the family spirits to amnesia, as well as, effectively, all their descendants? (*On that day, I understood that God wasn't all powerful.*) And what's this mirror all about, hanging in the middle of the room, between floorboards and sky? (*Since then, I've never seen him again.*)

Thorn stops suddenly, in the middle of the whiteness, and in the middle of the memory—a sudden freeze-frame. From the doorway, Farouk, petrified, stares at Eulalia Gonde's back; she is on the very edge of the void, facing the hanging mirror, her long dress and thick hair billowing in the draft. She shows less interest in the apocalypse that has torn the world apart than in this mirror. Incredulous, Thorn observes the mental slideshow his memory projects inside his skull, through Farouk's eyeballs, over Eulalia Gonde's shoulder. A reflection briefly overlaid hers, as fleeting as lightning: Ophelia (Ophelia with shattered glasses (Ophelia in a blood-spattered gown (Ophelia fatally injured))).

An advance echo. Thorn has just seen the future inside a memory that is several centuries old. And what he has seen is unacceptable.

Swiveling round a full 360 degrees, he scans the aerargyrum that surrounds him, searching for a way out. Wherever he might be, if he's managed to get in, logically, he can get out. And even if he can't, he must. If need be, he will force open every door on every ark, and a little more than that, even.

He looks more closely at what, at last, seems to be the contour of something, behind some pretty thick fog. Fancy that. Thorn was looking for a door; he's just found a well. It's a very old structure, going by the crumbling state of its mortar, and the spread of moss between each stone. There's neither bucket nor chain nor pulley, but Thorn would never have considered drinking water that had touched everything unhygienic that nature can throw up. The smell coming from this well is indescribable. Had it not been the only feature of the decor, Thorn would have gladly avoided getting any closer to it.

He leans over the edge of it, making sure not to touch it. What should be murky inside is, paradoxically, light, almost dazzling, and that spares him no detail: fungi, miasma, worms.

And, right at the bottom, a kid.

She is up to her waist in water (is it just water?), and her skin, hair, eyes are so dark that Thorn can't see the features on the face she's turning up at him. She says nothing. Against all this darkness, only her eyelashes stand out, abnormally white, framing two wide-open eyes. Thorn has never met this child, and yet he recognizes her without hesitation. It's Berenilde's daughter.

At the sight of her, before even wondering, reasonably, how she could have ended up in such an unlikely place, nearly nine meters underground, in this supposedly nonexistent part of the universe, Thorn is gripped by a feeling of pure hatred that he is the first to be surprised at. He hadn't realized, until now, how much he had tried to deny the existence of this cousin, who, just by being born, had stopped him being indispensable to his aunt; how much he had begrudged that aunt for not being satisfied with just him; how much he reproached himself for not being able to fill the heart of any mother with joy; how much, finally, he had, in consequence, been tough on Ophelia, at the risk of dragging her down to the bottom of his personal well. And now that he's looking into his cousin's big eyes, him above and her down below, he realizes the true extent of his stupidity.

He must get a move on, before the future revealed by the advance echo, in the Memorial mirror, becomes the past.

Thorn clambers over the edge with big, awkward movements. Ever though he no longer feels pain that doesn't mean that his bones won't break if he falls. He supports himself using the sides of the well (one meter twenty-four in diameter), wedging his boots and fingernails into the gaps in the mortar, and slipping on the slime. Every contact he makes seems abstract, as if he were in an invisible diving suit, but the deeper he goes, the stronger his revulsion. Several times, his bad leg lets him down, almost making him lose his balance. He won't allow himself to think about what the journey coming back up will be like.

Having reached the bottom, he is up to his knees in a mire that is definitely not water. His thorn-laden shadow, betraying the shameful power of his claws, certainly isn't enhancing his appearance: his cousin has flattened herself against the side of the well. So here she is, this great rival (eighty-nine centimeters tall). Thorn can see her face better now, even if he has to bend over to do so. Despite the darkness of her skin, she looks undeniably like Berenilde; he hopes she doesn't share Farouk's IQ. Her eyes, looking up at him, are wide open.

How does one address a kid of that age so as to be understood? Thorn suddenly realizes that he's unable to do so, and it's nothing to do with how uneasy she make him feel. He who never forgets a thing can't even put together a coherent sentence, either semantically, or syntactically. What would he have said to her anyway? That even if she makes him late, on top of making him feel pathetic, he can't bring himself to abandon her in this well?

He thinks again of Ophelia, of her blood. Must be quick.

Thorn, who had always sworn never to adapt his height to that of others, crouches down in the mire. He holds out his arms. The blinding brightness of the well makes the darkness of his scars stand out; he should have buttoned up his sleeves, children get upset over nothing. He grabs hold of his cousin, who comes without a struggle, which is surprising, but preferable. The claws bristle all around him at just this contact, and pulling her out of the mire is no picnic. Thorn is taken aback by the weight of this kid—her lack of weight, in fact. But what amazes him even more, beyond all that he had prepared himself for, is how impulsively she clings onto him with her whole body, as if, despite the nasty claws and rough gestures, his presence here in this well, with her, were the most comforting thing in the world.

Thorn has the irrational feeling that this weightlessness against him is seeping between his ribs, spreading through all that he is, and freeing him of a heaviness he hadn't been aware of feeling.

He wants to find Ophelia, but first he must return Berenilde's daughter to her.

No sooner has this priority become clear to Thorn than the space around them starts to change shape. The well has suddenly widened, reaching the size of a room, and the mire has evaporated into a thick layer of aerargyrum. Figures move around nervously, without noticing Thorn and the child he's awkwardly clasping. Their voices and colors are muted. They would remind him of ghosts were he not convinced of having become one himself. Whatever this room might be, he understands that, as far as time goes, they are all on the same page—these people recto, Thorn verso, and his cousin between the two, like a little ink blot that has marked the paper without soaking right through it.

The aerargyrum engulfs the entire décor, apart from a large baby carriage, with another kid lying in it. She's white from head to toe.

Thorn was sure of it. What he has fished out of that well is a mental projection. His real cousin, physically speaking, has remained on the world's recto. She's contemplating, with glazed eyes, the hood of her carriage, pulled out above her, and, judging by how skinny she is, she can't weigh much more than the

471

little shadow clinging ever more tightly to Thorn. Doesn't she recognize herself, then? It would be easy, not to say expeditious, to place her in this carriage so she has to return to her body.

Thorn reviews the hazy figures coming and going around them, until he locates the only one standing still, very upright in her dress, and near enough to the carriage to keep an eye on it. The fog doesn't allow him to see her face, but Thorn doesn't need to. He points the figure out to his cousin, whose white eyelashes instantly open wider. If she doesn't recognize her own body, at least she will recognize her own mother. Thorn can feel her trembling, about to rush forward, but against all expectations, and instincts, she looks at him one last time. At him. Thorn is hardly sensitive to the human eye (that external organ that produces crusts, tears, eyelashes), but those eyes, dark and deep as the night, seem to see in him something that he has always been incapable of seeing.

The next moment, his cousin vanished from his arms, like a soap bubble. There's no more carriage, or aunt, or room, or anything. Nothing except for a mirror that returns an image of Thorn that he manages, for the first time in his life, to find acceptable. The shadow of his family power has drawn in all its claws. There is the immediate, staggering certainty that he will no longer have to suffer their tyranny, because a kid gave him, yes, him, the most absolute feeling a being can feel. And because another kid pushed him into a cage.

Second hadn't taken revenge on him. She had made sure that he would be in the right place, at the right time. She had repaired the man who had damaged her.

Thorn contemplates his arms, now empty, and yet full of a new strength. Arms capable of the impossible. A little more than that, even.

He now has an advance echo to catch up with.

THE COUNTERPART

In the Wrong Side, all perceptions are warped. Colors, sounds, smells, space, and time follow a different logic. As her echo is about to fling a flagstone at her face, Ophelia wonders whether it will be as unpleasant as it seems. At the same time, she also wonders where on earth it managed to find a block of marble in the middle of a dome made exclusively of panes of glass. Finally, she wonders why it wants to kill her, after having saved her life.

"Who is I."

The echo's face, a perfect reflection of her own, has a questioning expression, behind its glasses, as if waiting for a sign to decide whether or not it should split her skull open. It hasn't stopped its strange chewing for a second.

There is no sign. However, appearing from nowhere, a frail adolescent delicately removes the flagstone from the echo's hands. When he drops it beside his babouches, it goes right through the dome without breaking any glass. With that sorted, the adolescent bows in greeting to Ophelia and her echo, who are both flabbergasted. There is nothing natural about the discoloration of his skin, his eyes, and his hair; just as there isn't about his presence at the top of the Memorial, indeed.

It's Ambrose. An Ambrose with his colors inverted, without

a wheelchair, or any deformity. The Ambrose of the funerary urn at the columbarium.

The very first Ambrose.

His long, pale eyelashes protect lucid eyes; he doesn't have the lost expression of others encountered in the Wrong Side. He gives a nod of the turban to the echo, as though in thanks for having brought him Ophelia, and then turns his smile on her. There's the same gentleness in his manner, the same curiosity in his eyes. She's relieved that she's unable to speak to him; like that, he will be unaware of the suffering he causes her by this resemblance, and won't know, either, that for her, there will only ever be one true Ambrose. This adolescent in front of her is a stranger, and, moreover, forty years older than he looks.

He was Lazarus's friend. So he can only be Ophelia's enemy. She becomes as tense as her scarf when he raises his fists, but, mischievously, he just sticks his thumbs up. Only then does she recognize him. He is the Shadow. It's him she saw at the edge of Babel, him who guided her to the automaton factory, him she chased in the columbarium, him who visited her in the chapel.

Ambrose 1 indicates Ophelia to her echo, and her echo to Ophelia, mimes a reconciliatory handshake with his hands, and then cheerily invites them to follow him, as if the matter were closed. The glass structure instantly takes on the consistency of water under Ophelia's sandals. She feels herself sliding through it, just like the marble flagstone did, but never really feels like she's falling. Now, all three of them are descending a stairway that goes deep into the Memorial; a stairway presumed no longer to exist for centuries.

Ambrose 1 leads the way with jaunty little steps. For an individual who has been stuck in an inside-out world for forty years, he is strangely lacking in restraint. Ophelia doesn't know whether she can trust him, but she knows that he is the Shadow, and that will do her for now. He managed to communicate with her from the Wrong Side, and several times, at that; by doing so, he proved that the frontier between the two worlds is permeable. Maybe he will be able to get Thorn and her back over to the right side?

Ophelia can't stop nervously turning her glasses over her shoulder to check that her echo, walking backwards and silently chewing behind her, isn't still planning to smash her head in. She can't understand what got into it, back on the dome, but she also can't fathom her sense of déjà vu.

All around them, the Memorial is even crazier than everywhere else in the Wrong Side. Half of the building is shrouded in an aerargyrum haze, through which Ophelia recognizes the thousands of bookcases, the transcendiums, and the topsy-turviums winding, story by story, around the vast atrium. But the other half of the Memorial, in the negative, is unknown to her. It is all old parquet floors, rooms invaded by vegetation, and deserted classrooms. It is where the family spirits grew up.

Ophelia lingers at a paneless window. Of course. After the Rupture, part of the tower was rebuilt above the void, because the architects at the time thought it had gone down with the rest of the island and ocean. They didn't know that it was still there, but inverted. Ophelia remembers never feeling at ease when she browsed the bookcases in this section, a malaise that she put down to the precipice beneath that part of the foundations. She now understands that it actually came from the coexistence of the two spaces.

And Ambrose 1 is leading her to where the two spaces are most entwined: the heart of the building. On one side there is the weightless globe of the Secretarium, in which a second globe hovers, where Eulalia Gonde's secret room was immured.

On the other, there's a tangle of old spiral staircases. The two dimensions overlap so smoothly that the walls of the globes and steps of the staircases are as translucent as tracing paper.

In places, Ophelia can see, under her feet, a floor that is located two hundred meters further down. She even spots people in the atrium, tiny as nail heads in the midst of the fog. Could it be the great interfamilial meeting now taking place in the world's right side, on another plane of existence?

Ambrose 1 stops with a bow. With no architecturally logical transition, Ophelia realizes that they have arrived at Eulalia Gonde's room. She is disappointed. She was hoping to find Thorn there, by some extraordinary ricochet of fate, but no one's there. Half of the room is immersed in an almost aquatic blend of mist and cobwebs. The other half offers a spectacular contrast, with its highly polished furniture, floral wallpaper, and all of Eulalia Gonde's personal effects, including her typewriter, which had remained intact in the Wrong Side.

And, between these two halves of the room, straddling both worlds, the hanging mirror. When she had been in the Right Side, Ophelia had passed through it twice by accident. She finally sees the wall, inverted at the same time as the old world, to which the mirror has never ceased to be attached. Rather than a wall, it's more of a partition between Eulalia Gonde's bedroom and her writing study. How many hours had she spent sitting there, conversing with the Other, literally solving the world's problems together? Ophelia almost feels as though she's reliving them herself, those hours, as if two memories were superimposed inside her, like the two halves of the Memorial.

In the meantime, she hasn't got very far. She turns to her echo, which is having fun randomly tapping away on the typewriter, its letters having disappeared from its keys; and then to Ambrose 1, who is passively waiting in a corner of the room. Is this what he wanted to show her? An empty room?

He indicates the mirror to her, with an insistent smile.

Ophelia goes up to it. Looks at herself in it. Is transfixed.

She accepted the idea that the Wrong Side was governed by singular laws, more symbolic than scientific, but to see her reflection—her *authentic* reflection—gives her a terrible shock. This person, in the mirror, has nothing in common with her. She has neither her features nor her measurements nor her eyes nor her hair. And yet, she is the final piece missing from the jigsaw puzzle.

It explains everything. It explains absolutely everything. Ophelia now knows who the Other is, she knows what the counterpart was to the inversion of the old world, she knows the role this mirror played in history, and that it will still play. She also knows why it was imperative that she be aboard that long-distance airship, with those expelled from Babel, because otherwise the entire course of history would have been changed forever.

She rushes over to Ambrose 1, shows him the mirror, the door, the ground, the ceiling, trying to make him understand, with exaggerated gestures, that now he must help her to find Thorn, because they have something very important to accomplish out there, behind behind, together!

The old adolescent folds her hands in his, to contain their flapping. Black teeth glint through the gap in his smile, but something deep in his eyes, with far more experience than Ophelia, makes her calm down. She realizes that he, too, has something very important to convey to her, and has done for a long time, even before their first encounter on the edge of the ark. Ophelia may have been unaware of his existence then, but he was already aware of hers, even if he had to wait for the two worlds to be sufficiently merged in order to appear to her. He explains all that to her without uttering a word, with his eyes.

He gently swivels Ophelia's hands, right palm facing up, left palm facing down. Then, contrariwise, he swivels them again, right palm facing down, left palm facing up. And then again, facing up, facing down, facing down, facing up, faster and faster. The echo copies their movements, dislocating its elbows, as if it were a game with rules it would never understand.

As for Ophelia, she fears understanding them.

The scarf jumps on her shoulders. A flash has just sliced through the air, as if lightning had silently struck at the very heart of the Memorial. In a blink, half of the room disappeared and reappeared, as if trying to rejoin its other half in the world on the right side. Ophelia silently questions Ambrose 1, who concurs, confirming her fears.

She suddenly thinks of that unknown land where the airship came down, of that village with no writing, of those mute country folk, cut off from all civilization for centuries, until they had forgotten the very concept of language. They come from the old world. They are the old world. And if some arks are inverting today, it's because that old world is now reinverting itself.

Ophelia contemplates her hands, still hanging there, shrouded in the shadow of her animism. Palm facing up, palm facing down.

The equilibrium between the Right Side and the Wrong Side was undermined by Eulalia Gonde when she inverted half of the old world, but it's Ophelia who gave it the coup de grace, on the night of her very first mirror passage, by helping a creature to escape from the Wrong Side without giving it a symbolically equivalent counterpart. At first, this imbalance went unnoticed. It was probably just a pebble inverting here, a blade of grass reinverting there. Today—and Ophelia changes the orientation of her hands to illustrate—it's entire countries that are changing. More and more lands and populations will be precipitated into the Wrong Side, while others will be repatriated to the Right Side, all at the whim of a dysfunctional pair of scales, their weighing mechanism getting increasingly fast, and increasingly random. A chain reaction that will end up breaking the scales themselves, and with them, all that exists.

Ophelia no longer has either the time or the choice. She must get back to the other side, and get back there right now, alone, even if it means coming back later to look for Thorn. If she doesn't do so, he will be lost in any case, wherever he might be. They will all be lost.

But how? What use is her finally knowing everything if she can't change anything?

She looks up from her hands, silently to question Ambrose 1, who replies by indicating no. He has never had any intention for her to leave the Wrong Side, because he can't himself. Instead, he points to her echo, which has picked up an old comb from a shelf.

Ophelia doesn't understand.

Ambrose 1 mimes, once again, a reconciliatory handshake. The next moment, with a parting smile, he has disappeared. He left as he had arrived. Perhaps he has rejoined Lazarus in aerargyrum limbo.

Ophelia turns to her echo, which is attempting, without much success, to drag the comb through its tangled curls. Would it, then, be her key to getting out? Ambrose 1 is right. There's a dispute between them that hasn't been resolved, and she now remembers what it's about. That marble flagstone with which the echo had threatened her is the one Ophelia had almost used against it, when it was still but a voice inside a mechanical parrot.

No doubt the echo senses her focusing on it, as it puts the comb down and, with chin raised, defies her to come closer. It's chewing faster.

If Ophelia were to make a step toward it, it would just move back a step. So she doesn't move. She looks squarely at it, straight in the glasses, across the length of parquet flooring between them. Their standoff lasts an eternity but, as much as she's in a hurry, Ophelia won't break it. The more she sees of this double of herself, so familiar and so unknown, the more she fears what they really are to each other. Two separate entities that originally formed just one.

Her echo is the mirror visitor that she has ceased to be.

"Who is I."

Ophelia has no idea how it manages to speak, when all she can produce is inarticulate sounds. Maybe it's because it was born of a question to which it awaits the answer. Fine. With slow gestures, Ophelia indicates them both, first it, then herself.

You is I.

The echo considers her as it chews.

Ophelia does the same gesture in reverse. First herself, then it.

I is you.

Barely has she given her response than the echo finally starts moving toward her, with a contorted gait that is less noticeable when it is going backwards. For the first time, it stops its chewing and sticks out its tongue, to show her, finally, what it has in its mouth: a minuscule spark of darkness.

The Horn of Plenty.

The echo has taken advantage of Ophelia's entering the Wrong Side to bring the front door with it! It has stolen the Deviations Observatory's cornerstone, the energy source that allowed Eulalia Gonde to create the family spirits, and Lazarus to create several generations of automatons. That indomitable force that had inverted so many of the sacrificed, starting with Thorn, is right there, on the tip of a tongue.

The echo swallows the Horn of Plenty like a pill, and, without allowing Ophelia time to react, it grabs her by the scarf and plunges with her into the room's mirror.

The feeling is horrendous.

It is as if Ophelia has been forced into a different skin. Her echo's individual consciousness dissolves into her own. They form, once again, but one. She has the contradictory feeling of doubling in volume, and then of flattening, from the tip of her toes to the fringe of the scarf. Space no longer has either an in front or a behind, obliging Ophelia to just hover there. She is stuck halfway between the Wrong Side and the Right Side. The in-between. A mesh preventing each world from mixing with the other, and which Ophelia, despite her countless mirror passages, has never broken through; not on her own, at any rate. It is not within her power to create a new Horn of Plenty. How, then, is she supposed to reinvert herself? She would like to scream for help, but her throat is now thick as blotting paper. She sees nothing, hears nothing. The only thing she is conscious of is her left foot, which is hurting her terribly, as if an invisible force were trying to wrench it off her. The pain rises up her calf, and, suddenly, she understands that someone, out there, is trying to pull her out of the in-between. From a distance, hazy cries reach her. The voices of her family. She wants to be back with them, she wishes it with all her might, but something resistant stops her.

The counterpart.

To return to the right side of the world, Ophelia has to accept giving up a symbolically equivalent counterpart to the wrong side of the world. If she doesn't respect this rule, all she will do is worsen the cycle of inversions and reinversions.

It's a deal.

*

Ophelia felt ripped apart when, after a final yank, she was expelled from the in-between. She collapsed, with all her weight, into the midst of a flurry of Anima swearwords. With her glasses skew-whiff and the scarf in a panic, she opened wide her dazed eyes. She considered the face, sprinkled with freckles, of her big sister Agatha, collapsed on the floor beside her, clinging to her leg; then her mother, red-faced and wild-haired, clinging to Agatha's waist; and then her father, clinging to her mother's fulsome dress; and then Aunt Rosaline clinging to her father; and finally, clinging to Aunt Rosaline like the links of a lengthy chain, her brother-in-law Charles, her little sisters, Domitilla, Beatrice, and Leonora, her little brother Hector, and even, each clinging to one of Hector's legs, her young nephews! It was the combining of all these hands that had enabled Ophelia to return to the right side of the world. There was one more hand when her great-uncle presented his to her, his moustache hoisted by a smile such as she had never seen before on his old face.

"Old habits die hard, eh? Your specialty is still getting stuck in mirrors?"

Ophelia blinked. She was all mixed up, dazed, shattered, and, on top of it all, completely disorientated. Her natural coloring had returned. All around her, she recognized the public restroom at the Memorial. She had left the in-between through the mirror fixed above the sink, against which she had almost knocked herself out. What she couldn't explain to herself was what her entire family was doing in this precise place in the world. A naked baby was wailing on what seemed to be an improvised changing table.

It took all the presence of mind left to Ophelia to grasp the hand her great-uncle was still holding out to her. To try to, at least; her gloves, strangely limp, no longer grasped anything. A silvery vapor was leaking out of them. Great-uncle's smile collapsed under his moustache. The joyful exclamations turned into horrified screams in the Memorial restroom.

Ophelia no longer had any fingers.

"Ah, yes," she muttered, in a croaky voice. "The counterpart."

IN THE WINGS

And there we are. He has played his part in history. Sure, it definitely wasn't a leading role, but at least he had enabled Ophelia to understand what needed to be understood. She came out from the wings, and what awaits her onstage, even he doesn't know this time. The end of times—of time—is approaching. Only a single advance echo remains. Ophelia, the old woman, and the monster will finally meet again. The rest is but a blank page, recto and verso, that's about to tear. Everything and its opposite are simultaneously possible.

Yes, entering that cage really was a most interesting experience.

THE IMPOSTURE

"Quick, sit her here! No, not there, here, in the reading room, on the balcony, the seats are more comfy. My dear, you're pale as a lightbulb . . . Charles, go and get a glass of water, preferably drinking water! Right, my dear, let's get those gloves off, maybe it's not as ghastly as it seems . . . Trombones alive! Your hands, my dear, your poor hands! Agatha, stop whining, it won't make her fingers grow back. Maybe . . . maybe they . . . just fell off? Domitilla, Beatrice, and Leonora, go back to the restroom and look for your sister's fingers! Oh, my dear, do these things really only happen to you? And what have you done to your hair? I just wish I could have got there sooner, to protect you from every danger, starting with yourself. Why, oh why, did you run away from home, my dear? Not a telegram—I thought I'd die of worry!"

Ophelia was watching her mother's lips move. She had gone from a world without language to a torrent of words. Her mother was going from questioning her, to pitying her, to scolding her, to kissing her. Her father, more discreet but less scatterbrained, made her drink the glass of water Charles had brought, which she couldn't hold without help. Agatha was sobbing louder than the baby's wails—her youngest, whose nappy Charles had been busy changing when Ophelia's foot had burst through the mirror. As for Hector, now taller than her, he was considering her very seriously from under the sandy fringe of his bowl-cut hair.

"Why have you lost your fingers?"

"I had no choice."

"Why were you in that mirror?"

"It's complicated."

"Why did you leave home again?"

"I had to."

"Why did you never write?"

"I couldn't."

Each reply took Ophelia several swallows. She now remembered how to speak, but it didn't come naturally, for all that. Hector wrinkled his nose, and all his freckles raced up his face in pursuit. There was resentment behind each of his "whys," but he ended up bending his own rule by asking, in a gentler voice:

"Does it hurt?"

Impulsively, Ophelia squeezed her little brother's cheeks with the two halves of her hands. She gazed at the empty space instead of fingers. The skin was all smooth, without a cut or a scar, as if she had been born like that. No, it didn't hurt, but was that preferable? If she had endured the breaking of her bones, and tearing of her flesh, maybe she would have realized what was happening to her. Those ten little digits, which had made her the best object reader of her generation, had returned to the Wrong Side as soon as they were reincarnated. She noticed that at least her beauty spot was back where it belonged, in the hollow of her left elbow. She had been perfectly reinverted during her transition through the in-between.

Domitilla, Leonora, and Beatrice, who had returned from the restroom empty-handed, threw themselves on her. They were too big for her shortened arms, but she hugged them tight all the same.

Aunt Rosaline had sat down facing her. With eyes as stern as her bun, and her long teeth visible between her lips, she was sizing her up with a combination of disapproval and compassion. Her complexion was as jaundiced as ever.

"I would even prefer the days when you used to spoil your gloves."

That was all, but those simple words were enough to bring Ophelia's emotions flooding back. She was suddenly overcome with both joy and sadness, and she no longer had the fingers to brush away the tears caught in her eyelashes. The scarf took care of it for her by nudging her glasses.

Ophelia had so many questions to ask, but she kept to the most important one for now:

"Where are the family spirits?"

"Here, at the Memorial, nearly all of them. Fox has gone to inform Berenilde of your arrival," Aunt Rosaline added, after clearing her throat. "Yes, they are here, but I should warn you that you will find them changed, too. Especially our little Victoria. She is not at all well."

Ophelia's great-uncle struggled to make his way through to Ophelia.

"Give her some air, goodness' sake! Can't you see she needs to fix her pipes?"

From the internal balcony she had been settled on, Ophelia could see the rings of stories winding around the atrium, and within them, a totally abnormal commotion. The Memorialists were running between the bookcases, emptying display cabinets, filling trolleys with rare books. Some were shouting that everyone must evacuate, others that they must stay. The silent sanctuary had turned into an almighty hubbub. And just to add to the confusion, the high tide had shrouded everything in a veil of clouds.

Ophelia looked up at the globe of the Secretarium, where

she had ended up shortly before, as it hovered, unperturbed, beneath the glass cupola. What she could remember of the Wrong Side was as confused as a dream, along with a feeling of not walking in her own sandals. The only thing she felt very clearly was guilt. She had returned without Thorn. She knew why she had done so, but that choice lay heavy on her stomach. No more than a few hours had passed since they had both entered that cage, but each second was widening the distance between them.

"Where are the family spirits?" she repeated.

As she was trying to stand up, gently moving her sisters aside and awkwardly leaning her stunted hands on the arm-rests, her great-uncle forced her to sit back down.

"I didn't want to betray you, m'dear, I swear to you. Your ma gave me the third degree, every day of every week of every month after your dramatic departure with Mr. Holey-Hat, and I never breathed a word."

"Well, that's really nothing to be proud of!" her mother butted in, her face pinched. "My sister moves to the Pole, my daughter runs away to Babel, everyone leaves me with no explanation."

"The arks don't revolve around you, Sophie!" Aunt Rosaline exclaimed, with exasperation.

"And then there were the holes," her great-uncle continued, more loudly, as if he hadn't been interrupted. "Anima became a veritable colander! Holes smaller than those here, granted, but bloody great holes, all the same, so deep you couldn't see the bottom, and what's more, the Rapporteur almost fell down one in her kitchen, which wouldn't have been such a bad thing."

"A hole in Uncle Hubert's field," said Hector.

"A hole in Granny Antoinette's cellar," said Domitilla.

"A hole in Goldsmiths' Street," said Leonora.

"Plop," Beatrice added.

"We had some at the lace factory," said Agatha, tapping her baby's back. "Didn't we, Charles? It was *ab-so-lute-ly* terrifying!"

"At the Pole, too, we had landslides," added Aunt Rosaline. "A forest of fir trees and a frozen lake disappeared, from one day to the next. I don't know if that's why, but Mr. Farouk suddenly decided to leave the Pole for Babel. He wanted no escort, no minister, no aide-memoire. Just Berenilde, and although he didn't mention it specifically, his daughter. They're all more unreasonable than barometers," she sighed, between her teeth. "A journey like that in times like these . . . But anyway, it's not as if there's just one place to shelter in."

"Are we going to die?" asked Agatha's eldest son.

The great-uncle swore into his moustache to shut them all up, and, looking serious, returned to Ophelia.

"Artemis also lost the plot. She summoned all the Doyennes here, in the middle of the night, to entrust Anima to them, and got a bee in her bonnet that she had to go to Babel's Memorial. Right where you were supposed to be doing your little inquiry. I realized this was tricky for you, or would be. I couldn't hold my tongue any longer. I told you mother where you were. Like a shot, we all packed our bags and invited ourselves onboard Artemis's airship. A tub she animated herself, m'dear, and so fast I almost swallowed my dentures! When we arrived at the Memorial, in Babel, we saw that you clearly weren't there, but we decided to stick around all the same. And lucky we did, hey?"

Breathless from having talked too much, her great-uncle looked deep into Ophelia's eyes, careful to avoid looking at her fingerless hands; hands that he had personally trained, and that would never read objects again.

She smiled, at him, and at all of her family. Her echo's final act, before dissolving inside her, had been to bring her back to her loved ones. Without them, she would have remained stuck inside the mirror, for good this time.

"Thank you. For being here. For being safe and sound."

They all exchanged glances, almost embarrassed by this declaration, as if they no longer really knew what to add, after that.

"Where are the family spirits?" Ophelia then asked again, resolutely getting to her feet. "I must see them."

It was right then that Berenilde made her appearance in the reading room. Ophelia had seen her drink, smoke, succumb to every excess, without ever losing her splendor. Now she was barely recognizable. Her hair, of which she had always taken the greatest care, whatever the circumstances, fell on her thinner shoulders like grey rain. She was pushing a baby carriage in which there lay a pale little body, still and silent. With her hands gripping the handle, she seemed unable to keep upright without it. As soon as she let go of it, Aunt Rosaline rushed over to offer her arm, but Berenilde refused it with a friendly gesture, and, despite the emaciation stretching her skin over her bones, stood rigidly upright. Her eyes widened, nearly drowning her face, as she surveyed all the Animists, adults and children, present in the room, before they stopped at Ophelia.

"How is he?"

Berenilde had been concerned neither about her nor her fingers, but Ophelia felt a wave of gratitude sweep over her. She was the only one to have spared a thought for Thorn, and didn't seem to doubt for a moment that Ophelia would have found him. And yet, what could she say in reply to her? That she had lost him once again? That he now only existed as aerargyrum, somewhere in the Wrong Side? That soon there would be neither Wrong Side nor Right Side, if the two worlds continued to collide? That the only person capable of preventing the catastrophe was right here, in this Memorial, and that Ophelia absolutely had to speak to him? That made for a lot of explaining, and time was short.

A tiny murmur spared her from trying:

"M-a."

All eyes turned to the carriage. Victoria, her cheeks hollow, shadowed, waxen, had sat up inside it. Her mouth twisted as she managed, in a broken voice, to get the same word out, the very first one Ophelia had ever heard her say:

"M-a!"

Berenilde considered the little girl in the carriage with bafflement, as if her own child had been exchanged for another, and then her chin quivered, and she let out a stifled cry from the very depths of her lungs. She lifted Victoria up in her arms, reeled under her weight, fell to her knees as her dress billowed around her, and hugging her tight with a love full of rage, she burst into both laughter and tears.

"It's incomprehensible," whispered Aunt Rosaline, her voice shaky, her hands on her stomach. "Only an hour ago, we could barely get her to swallow a spoonful of soup."

The whole family crowded around Berenilde and Victoria. Ophelia took advantage of this diversion to give them the slip. Later—if there was a later—she would celebrate their reunion properly.

She made her way between the patches of fog, bumping into terrified Memorialists dutifully filling trolleys with books. She recognized the patent section, where she had spent hours cataloguing, along with her division colleagues. She went past several people in the uniforms of the family guard and the security-service Necromancers, but this time no one asked her for her identity papers. It was panic all around.

Ophelia's gown was restricting her movements—a fastener

had come undone and she couldn't rectify it alone. She wasn't that keen to witness the end of the world in her underwear.

As she leaned on a guard rail overlooking the atrium, she saw the void down below. The real void. It had swept away the entrance to the Memorial, its high glass doors, an entire section of wall, the forecourt with the mimosas, the statue of the headless soldier, and right up to the birdtrain station. The interfamilial airships were drifting off, their moorings severed. Ophelia better understood the panic of the Memorialists. The inversions were assuming cataclysmic proportions, and her whole family was trapped on a piece of ark that was crumbling away like sugar. Soon there wouldn't be enough ground left to support the weight of the tower. Through this opening, and two waves of clouds, in the distance, the city of Babel appeared even more fragmented than ever, eaten away by an invisible evil that was destroying it, district by district.

Ophelia thought of Second, out there, in some basement, alone among a crowd of echo-automatons, waiting for her brother to be saved. She had undoubtedly pushed Thorn into that cage for a good reason. But what was it?

Ophelia leaned further over the guard rail. She spotted the family spirits right down below, in the middle of the atrium. Reunited where they had spent their childhood, for the first time in centuries, they formed an almost perfect circle.

If Ophelia hadn't miscalculated, the person she was looking for was right there, before her very glasses, among them.

From the level she was on, it was hard to see them clearly, but she recognized Artemis by her long red braid, Farouk by his immaculate whiteness, and Pollux by the sparks shooting out of his eyes, even from a distance. She may have never seen the other family spirits before, but she had studied their portraits, and so managed to identify them, one by one. Ra, Gaia,

Morpheus, Olympus, Lucifer, Venus, Midas, Belisama, Djinn, Fama, Zeus, Viracocha, Yin, Horus, Persephone, Ouranos . . .

Absent at roll call was just Helen, lost forever. And Janus.

Ophelia was overcome with anxiety. Had she got it wrong, in the end?

"They're waiting."

Fox had just leant his elbows on the guard rail, beside Ophelia, to join her in gazing down below. Aunt Rosaline hadn't exaggerated: he had really changed, too, but whereas Berenilde and Victoria had become more fragile, he had become excessively sturdy. It was as if his body had absorbed theirs, and then some, to become more muscular than ever, so that his buttons were ready to pop. He was carrying an enormous hunting rifle—a model intended for big game—that would have got him instantly arrested in Babel, had things not been so chaotic. It was the first time Ophelia was seeing him armed. Fox was more a man to use words, or, if pushed, fists. It was his eyes that struck her the most, buried deep under his knitted brows, burning with such intensity, it consumed their greenness like a forest fire.

"They've been like that since we arrived in Babel. An interminable meeting. One might think that they're grieving over the death of Mrs. Helen, but I know they're still waiting for someone, at their little reunion. The big boss."

Fox had said that last word as if it pained him, like a raging toothache.

"I'm waiting for him, too, that big boss," he added, scouring every corner of the Memorial from his observation post. "Oh, yes, you bet I'm waiting for him. He'll soon be among us, he might already be so."

"You've met him," stated Ophelia.

The fire in Fox's eyes intensified.

"In Citaceleste, on a pavement corner. I was on guard while

493

Mr. Archibald was visiting Lady Berenilde. We had just found LandmArk, and sir wanted to convince her to go there, too, to help us influence Don Janus. Gail . . . she'd stayed over there. She's still there. With *him*. He took *my* place, *my* face, *my* cat, and I can't even get back to them."

His Northern accent seethed with contained rage.

"And you?" asked Ophelia. "Were you—"

"Hurt? No, and that's the worst of it. He took on the appearance of a Narcotic. Sent me fast asleep. Should have seen the way he looked at me, just before. As if . . . as if I wasn't really a person, as if I was so insignificant in his eyes, he wouldn't have even considered getting rid of yours truly. I was nothing to him, you understand? Nowt. I've served minor nobility nearly all my life, but never have I felt nonexistent like that, and yet I've done my time in oubliettes. Soon as he comes out of his hole, that one, I'll show him who I really am."

Fox clasped his enormous hands to calm himself, and then suddenly noticed Ophelia's. The angry barrier of his eyebrows softened, and without comment, with a slightly gruff tenderness, he readjusted her gown, which was threatening to fall around her sandals.

"And you, kid, what are you going to do?"

"Reestablish a truth," Ophelia replied, without the slightest hesitation. "In the hope that that truth reestablishes all the rest."

From the atrium, Elizabeth's tiny but distinct voice reached Ophelia. In the middle of the circle of family spirits, she seemed punier than ever among their imposing figures. None of them paid any attention to her, not to her, not to her LUX insignia. She was showing them, insistently but with no authority, the gaping hole in the entrance wall. "My friend is still over there . . . She's in danger . . ." Ophelia bit her lip. *My friend.* Elizabeth thought she was still in the Deviations

Observatory, with Thorn and Lazarus, at the mercy of the Genealogists. She hadn't abandoned her. She was concerned for her. Sincerely.

As Ophelia turned her head, looking for the nearest transcendium to get down all those stories, she froze.

Thorn stood there, drawn up to his full height, between the patent shelves. He had knocked his forehead on one of the suspended lamps, and its copper shade was swinging like a pendulum, throwing a frenetic light across all the surrounding display cabinets.

He was there. He, too, had managed to get away from the Wrong Side.

Ophelia was incapable of speaking to him. She had a sponge instead of a throat, a nose, eyes; all of her was turning into water. She no longer had any but the fuzziest notion of anything that wasn't Thorn, here, now. She saw him again inside that cage, vanishing from her sight in an explosion of particles. She had felt as if she were disintegrating at the same time as him.

He brought her back to reality with just one question:

"Did you find him?"

He limped in her direction, leaning heavily on the bookcases, at the risk of toppling them. Without its brace, his leg seemed dislocated, as if all its fractures had returned under his trousers. He unfolded an arm, his thin wrist sticking out of a sleeve that was too small for him.

"The Other," he said, with difficulty. "Did you find him?"

He was about to keel over. Ophelia held her fingerless hands out to him, but Fox beat her to it. With a single swipe, he swung the butt of his rifle so hard that Thorn's head was flung backwards, with a cracking of vertebra.

"The bookcase glass, kid!"

Ophelia was horrified. By Thorn's broken neck, first. By his lack of reflection on the bookcase glass next. This man with the shattered leg and ill-fitting shirt was a version of Thorn that was three years old, from the time when he was still in prison. The day when "God" had paid them a visit.

Ophelia had seen what she had wanted to see.

With a twist of the arm and a few bone-cracking sounds, the fake Thorn put his head back in place. He lowered his pale eyes on Ophelia, conspicuously ignoring Fox, as if he rated his butt swipe on a par with a gnat bite.

"I wanted us to gain some time, but never mind. For sure, nothing and no one will have trade my mask . . . made my task of saving this world any easier."

His angular forms rounded until they had assumed the appearance of an unknown woman wearing a very colorful uniform, and with a dozen compasses dangling from her belt. It was now a fake Arkadian who was standing between the bookcases of patents.

"Janus gave me this useful, but tardy, little present," she said, indicating her own face. "May I present Carmen to you."

"She" vanished, only to reappear instantly on Ophelia's left side, mouth pressed to her ear.

"I have the final power . . ."

She disappeared and then reappeared, right beside her other ear.

". . . that was missing from my repertoire."

"Move away from her!" Fox growled, under his breath.

He now had his hunting rifle on his shoulder, and it was clear, from his whole posture, that he had been drilled in this maneuver a thousand times. He was suffocating with rage.

"If you've touched her. Even lightly. I swear to you."

Ophelia knew that it was no longer about her. Fox needed just one excuse to pull the trigger. The fake Carmen, little inclined to take him seriously, pointed out a fixed sign saying

"SILENCE, *S'IL VOUS PLAÎT*." Ophelia saw Fox's eyes bulge with fury, and then saw him no longer. There was no more Memorial. A dazzling sky was reflected in kilometers of terraced paddy fields. In the middle of them, puncturing the landscape like some ravenous maw, a chasm was spewing out reams of clouds.

The fake Carmen stood right beside Ophelia, calf-deep, like her, in the mud of a paddy field. It was her family power that had brought them here.

"The ark of Corpolis. A charming place, not so long ago. But we can timely fork . . . finally talk without interruption, at least."

"Until the next inversion," Ophelia countered.

The sponge in her throat had completely dried up. Without her fingers, she couldn't control the furious flapping of the scarf, contaminated by the turmoil of her emotions. The fake Carmen threw her a sidelong glance. Her eyes, as black as Mother Hildegarde's had been, reflected no light. Nothing about her was authentic, neither her grotesque way of jangling her compasses nor her voice devoid of expression.

"It's long gone, the time when, like you, I was just a limited little woman. From now on, I can do anything and go anywhere. There's just one dead angle to my new power, and it's right there, in that Wrong Side, where you had to go and stick yourself. I had to wait until you deigned to emerge from your hiding place. I sense that you're on edge. Would you prefer a more familiar setting?"

A light autumnal drizzle tapped Ophelia's cheeks. The change in temperature was stark. She was now sitting on a public bench. The street before her was deserted, but she recognized it immediately. She was now on Anima. A carriage without a horse, driver, or passenger was struggling to extract one of its wheels, wedged in a ditch. They were everywhere, across the street and the gardens: countless underground chimneys, with silvery vapors rising up from them. It could have been a bombsite. Opposite the bench Ophelia was sitting on, there was a row of houses, all made of bricks and tiles. The lit lamps behind the curtains indicated that they were occupied, but no one dared to come out anymore, even if there were holes everywhere, including in the roofs.

"It was more animated in the past," commented the fake Carmen, sitting on the bench beside her. "I remember enjoying my stay, when I came with the Caravan Carnival . . . the Carnival Caravan."

Ophelia was barely listening to her. In one house under the rain, all the lights were out. The home in which she had left her childhood. There was a crater, right in the middle of the path. Its diameter was such that it could have swallowed up her brother and sisters at the first stumble.

"You're lucky, my dear, it's still a charming neighborhood. I, personally, grew up in a military orphanage. I daresay I'm not telling you anything new, you did your little inquiry into the Eulalia Gonde that I was then. Is that your bedroom, up there? The little upstairs window, with the closed shutters? Was it there that you released my reflection from the mirror?"

Ophelia turned from the crater in front of her house to look straight at this Arkadian who wasn't one.

"You were unable to locate the Other, despite all your powers. Do you know why?"

The fake Carmen remained impassive on the bench, but Ophelia sensed she had riled her. She was preparing to do far worse; to risk more than her fingers.

"Me, I do know why," she continued. "It was pointless

taking on Thorn's appearance to get that information out of me. You only had to ask."

"Where is the Other?"

There was more than impatience behind this question. Ophelia took a deep breath, full of drizzle, and replied:

"Here. It's you."

IDENTITY

The Other looked blankly at Ophelia. The rotation of her head toward Ophelia bore no relation to the alignment of her shoulders and chest, and would have resulted in a neck injury for any normal person. Even her eyelashes, hung with beads of Anima drizzle, didn't move.

"Are you insinuating, my dear," she said, stressing each syllable, that it's *me* you released from the mirror?"

Ophelia was uncomfortably aware of the lack of space between them on the public bench. For a long time, she had thought that the Other had been trapped in the narrowest in-between. She hadn't known, then, of the existence of the Wrong Side, she hadn't known that the Other had been born there, and had never been its prisoner.

"No. The person I released from the mirror, and became mixed up with, is the real Eulalia Gonde. She was confined to the Wrong Side, by her own choice, since the Rupture. You had both changed places, for all that time. For Eulalia to be able to invert, along with herself, half of the world, there had to be a symbolically equivalent counterpart, something coming out of the Wrong Side to redress the balance. That was you. An echo endowed with speech, conscious of itself, that was outside the repetitive cycle, but an echo all the same."

"Where is my Book?"

The Other managed an impersonal smile. She stood up and, without the slightest modesty, and with a jangling of com-passes, got undressed in the rain, to display Carmen's naked body. No sooner removed, the uniform just disappeared, like smoke. Ophelia noticed the faces of several neighbors—all relations of hers, more or less distant—pressed to their win-dows along the street. Their fear of coming outside remained stronger, however, than their curiosity.

"If I'm really just an echo, as you suggest," said the Other, turning slowly on the cobbles so as not to conceal any part of her, "where is the code that keeps me incarnate in matter?"

"I wondered about that myself," Ophelia admitted. "I think that that's what differentiates you, fundamentally, from the family spirits and all the forms of materialized echoes. By sus-taining a dialogue with Eulalia Gonde, you ended up crystal-lizing yourself. You woke up to yourself, while you were still in the Wrong Side. You developed *your* thoughts, with *your* words, within a dimension devoid of its own language. You don't need a code. You do, on the other hand, need Eulal . . ."

Ophelia's breath was cut off. The Other's arm had suddenly stretched, in a supernatural elongation of muscle and bone, to grab her by the throat. She still had the Arkadian's naked body, but her flesh had taken on the rubbery consistency of a Metamorphoser. She wasn't gripping Ophelia to the point of strangling her, but how firm her grip was! The strength of a crowd concentrated in just one individual.

"I am peacefully deepening . . . deeply peace-loving. I have always stood up to all worms of defiance . . . forms of violence. So please, my dear, don't force me to yurt who . . . hurt you."

The bench had disappeared; Anima had, too. They were now both in the middle of what seemed to be a schoolyard, on the ark of Cyclope. The place had been hastily evacuated. Hoops, marbles, and satchels were floating here and there, in a state of weightlessness, abandoned on the spot. A chasm the size of a volcano had swallowed up all the surrounding buildings.

Ophelia was alone facing the Other, whose every fingernail she could feel digging into her throat. She had to shift her feet not to lose her balance. She didn't know how she had the guts to keep speaking to her, but the words poured out almost despite her:

"You sincerely think you're the real Eulalia, don't you? You've appropriated her ideas, her contradictions, her ambitions, you've adopted her scenario to perfection for centuries, but it's merely a part that you're playing. This mask that you wear, you know, deep down, that it only covers up a void. You're a reflection that's lost its own reflection. That's why Eulalia's face wasn't enough for you, why you started reproducing more faces, more masks, always more . . ."

The Other dug her nails deeper into Ophelia's throat. At the other end of her elastic Metamorphoser's arm, at the top of her immodestly arched Arkadian body, it was her face's turn to change appearance. Her skin grew pale down to the neck, her hair became thick and curly, and a pair of glasses sprouted on her nose.

This head of a woman, who looked like Ophelia without really being her, was that of Eulalia Gonde.

"Who are you to seaside . . . decide who I am and who I am not?"

Ophelia was starting to run out of breath, but she kept going:

"Ask yourself where she *herself* is."

The Other's eyes contracted at the same time as her muscles. The setting itself started to fluctuate again, sweeping them from a grand skating rink to a department store, then from zoological gardens to a beach made out of mandalas. They were being carried from ark to ark, but whatever the location, the ground was pockmarked with sinkholes. These pieces of world, now on the Wrong Side, had left behind nothing but aerargyrum vapors.

Hanging from the fist around her throat, and seeing stars, Ophelia couldn't breathe anymore. The scarf struggled, in vain, to free her. Did one turn into aerargyrum when one died? She doubted it. She would never see Thorn again.

The Other finally murmured, reluctantly, with head hanging, as though addressing Carmen's naked body:

"Lead us to Eulalia Gonde."

Ophelia collapsed in a heap of scarf. Air surged into her lungs; she coughed for ages to get her breath back. The stars scattered. Above her, a globe hovered under a sky of glass. She was back in the Memorial, in the atrium itself, in the middle of the family spirits.

At the Other's feet.

His polymorphism had got worse: as well as the naked body of an Arkadian, the oversized arm of a Metamorphoser, and Eulalia Gonde's head, he now sported the long nose of an Olfactory, and was sniffing the air for a particular smell. He stood in the center of the circle of family spirits, and was casting his eye around suspiciously, from one to the next, as if the culprit he was after was hiding inside their very skins. They must have recognized who he was themselves, behind his eclectic appearance, and despite their bad memories, because they all backed away on seeing the Other. All apart from Farouk, who, having become like a statue of ice, was staring at his face with fascination and revulsion.

As the patriarch of Babel, Pollux greeted the Other with a timid bow.

"Welcome. I believe we were expecting you. With regards to . . . well . . . this."

Hesitantly, he indicated the perilously close abyss that had devoured the entrance to the Memorial, and distress clouded his golden eyes.

"Our sister . . . My sister . . . I've already forgotten her name. She has left us, but I know, yes, I know that she would ask you for an explanation if she were still here."

"That's not him."

Farouk seemed the first to be disconcerted by his own words, as if he himself didn't know where they came from. And yet he repeated them, extremely slowly:

"That's not him. That's not God. Not ours."

He had pressed a large white hand to his Book, secreted somewhere in the thick layers of his Polar overcoat. A part of him, deeply buried, remembered having already been desecrated.

The Other paid no attention, either to Pollux or to Farouk. "Where is she?"

It was more an order than a question, addressed only to Ophelia. She tried, awkwardly, to get to her feet, leaning on the halves of her hands. Her neck was hurting her. She searched all around for the real Eulalia Gonde, but didn't find her. Looking up, her eyes crossed those of Artemis, with their vaguely questioning expression, as if the family spirit suspected some kinship between them, but couldn't remember exactly what. Looking up even higher, she saw all the people crowding around the railings of each story, and, among them, on the top story, her family, all calling to her and gesticulating, frantically.

Stay up there, she felt like shouting back at them.

"I don't see Eulalia Gonde here," murmured the Other. "Would you have panel mutated . . . manipulated me?"

Just as Ophelia was wondering whether she would survive another strangling, she jumped, as a large cat dived between her calves. Twit?

"Come, come now, anger does nothing for your complexion."

Archibald had, literally, appeared out of nowhere, twirling his hat on his forefinger. True to character in all circumstances, he was smiling. Gail, who had likewise not been there a second before, dragged Ophelia as far away as possible from the Other, and then, without asking, lifted her chin. She swore when she saw the bleeding fingernail marks on her neck.

"Should have kept that scum under triple lock and key, not been content to spy on it out of the corner of some opera glasses. You've messed up, Don Janus."

The air in the atrium crumpled like fabric, and a giant half-man half-woman burst through it, landing on his feet beside the family spirits, as if space, to him, was merely a theater curtain. Ophelia now understood where Archibald, Gail, and Twit had sprung from. She also now understood why the Other had kept moving from ark to ark, to elude the surveillance he was under.

With Janus, the siblings were finally all present. This family spirit, of indefinable gender, made his high heels ring out on the flagstones and then planted himself in front of the Other, looking down on him from on high.

"You did not respect our agreement. You were supposed to maintain total neutrality in exchange for the power of my *Aguja*. You claim to be the only person who can stop the landslides? Fine. But don't interfere in our business, and, above all," he stressed, with a theatrical flourish in Ophelia's direction, "never again raise your hand to one of our children."

With a grotesque contortion of his legs, the Other turned to Janus. The inhuman sound that came out of his mouth reverberated across all the marble and glass of the Memorial:

"Until today, I have watched over each young of new . . . one of you, from the wings. I believed you to be capable of preserving the perfect world that I had created for you. I was too permissive. The moment I delegate, you go astray. Chins are going to range. . . things are going to change."

Murmuring spread around each story of the Memorial, but no one spoke out loud. Ophelia did, however, notice a man, too far away to recognize, charging down a transcendium.

"I will save this world for the second time," declared the Other, "and then I will devise new rules. Many rules. I will earnestly pleasure . . . personally ensure that everyone abides by them. No more intermediaries. I will be everywhere, I will know everything."

The family spirits exchanged uneasy glances. Farouk was visibly struggling to stay focused on what was unfolding here. The most distressing thing, thought Ophelia, was that they would all soon have forgotten what they were seeing and hearing right now. All infinitely malleable, they hadn't been deprived of their memories for nothing. Indeed, that was doubtless the first thing the Other had done, after taking Eulalia Gonde's place.

Only Janus seemed to be in full possession of his faculties. His dark eyes shone, as he pulled, ironically, on the curly end of his moustache.

"And what if we refuse?" he sniggered.

With nostrils flaring, the Other sniffed him out, like an animal. A third arm sprang out from one of his ribs, like a jet of water, plunged into Janus's skull like a blade, and then steadily continued its downward trajectory, with some crunching of bones, until it had sliced him right down the middle. Janus's entire body then went up in smoke, leaving on the floor just a Book, cut in half.

Nothing remained of Janus. It had taken the Other no more than three seconds to bring to a close several centuries of immortality.

Ophelia's astonishment was shared by Archibald, Gail, the

entire Memorial. Twit flattened his ears back and growled very quietly. The family spirits were all bent double, hugging their stomachs, and looking deeply pained, as if the death of their brother had affected them physically.

"What have you done?"

Elizabeth stepped out from behind Pollux, who was gently sobbing. Long and white as a candle, and unnoticed until then, she stared unusually wide-eyed at the Book that was torn in two. She made straight for the Other, so fast that her frock-coat flaps lifted, clicked her boots together while raising her fist to her chest, on which the LUX insignia gleamed, and glared at this protean creature, which now bore no resemblance to a human.

"I . . . I don't know who you are, or what you are, but, in the name of the power conferred upon me, I am placing you under arrest."

Ophelia had to admit that she was impressed. As for herself, like all those present in the atrium, she no longer dared to blink for fear of being sliced in two. She finally saw Elizabeth as she was, or, more precisely, as she herself could have been. Her tawny hair, her freckles, her tallness, her good sight, even her age: none of all that really belonged to her. Elizabeth had taken from Ophelia, just as Ophelia had taken from Elizabeth.

With the only difference being that Ophelia was now aware of it. It was her she had seen, instead of her own reflection, in the mirror in the Wrong Side.

The Other, whose third arm was writhing with tentacular spasms on the floor, suddenly reached the same obvious conclusion. What remained of Eulalia Gonde's face, under that prominent Olfactory nose, cracked into a smile.

"So it's you."

Elizabeth jumped when the Other disappeared and then reappeared right in front of her, deformed body against formless body, a mere breath away. Avidly, he studied the shadows under her eyes, her wounds, her shapelessness, feeding off all the weaknesses he discerned in her.

"It's you."

"Sorry?"

Elizabeth seemed completely lost. She tightened her knees to lessen their shaking. The Other's smile just kept on growing, tearing his skin as if it were a fabric mask.

"You are Eulalia Gonde."

Elizabeth instantly stopped trembling. Those four words, which should have restored her identity to her, had the opposite effect. Her body withered even more, her face emptied of all substance. It was as if her spirit had withdrawn deep inside her.

"It really doesn't matter who, of the two of us, is first, does it?" continued the Other. "I am superbly infinite . . . infinitely superior to you. Just look at yourself, you pathetic little thing, you don't even know who you are anymore. So I am going to tell you: you are a traitor. You belong with all that was corrupt about the old world. By returning, you engendered . . . endangered those you claimed to want to save. It is my duty to send you back into the mirror that you should never have left."

A third leg sprang out of the Other to give an almighty stamp on the ground. The atrium's flagstones exploded due to a violent seismic surge. The earth shook. The cupola rained down a torrent of glass shards. The bookcases spewed out their collections of books. Ophelia had been flung to the floor by the quake; roaring and screaming rang in her ears. When it was all over, her scarf wiped the dust off her glasses.

She couldn't recognize the atrium. The ground was carpeted in glass and rubble. The colonnades had cracked, some had collapsed. Several of the family spirits held fatally injured men and women in their arms, who had been sent flying from the stories above by the impact. Ophelia couldn't see any member of her family among them, but screams were still reaching her from all four corners of the Memorial. She hoped they were safe and sound up there. She suddenly realized that she would, herself, have ended up crushed under a block of marble had Artemis not used her animism to hold it back.

"Thank you."

In the middle of all the debris, there was a couple in a passionate embrace. The man Ophelia had seen charging down the transcendium, it was Fox. With his hunting rifle slung over his shoulder, he was clinging to Gail as tightly as she was clinging to him. He was covering her in kisses, she was covering him in insults. A bubble of joy in an ocean of chaos.

Ophelia kept at bay the vision of Thorn, left on his own in the Wrong Side. She couldn't allow herself to weaken; not now.

As for Archibald, he was covered in scratches. He had mainly Twit to thank for them, having squeezed him tight to protect him from the splinters of glass. He let out a long, appreciative whistle.

Ophelia's eyes followed his. Exactly where the Other's third heel had struck the ground, a combination of rough rock and carved stone formed a stairway that had not been there before. It reached, steeply, all the way up to the floating globe of the Secretarium, under a cupola now bereft of glass.

The hanging mirror, Ophelia realized. The mirror in which Eulalia and the Other had changed places on the day of the Rupture. It was there that everything would be decided.

THE SPACE

The void was gaining ground. It had swallowed up the automaton-statue from reception, and was continuing to eat into the Memorial, mouthful after mouthful, as if the Other's excessive use of his family powers was also powering the inversion of the world. The ever-stronger pull of the wind made Ophelia feel as if she were fighting against the current of a river. At this rate, there would be nothing left to save.

"I hope you have a plan, Mrs. Thorn," Archibald whispered to her, as he contemplated the stairway climbing up to the sky.

"I do have one."

Except that it relied entirely on Elizabeth. Ophelia had been relieved to find her virtually unscathed. She had fallen to her knees before the Other, her hair streaming over her shocked face. Without her, it would have all been over. With her, it might well be, too. Everything now depended on whether she was willing, or not, to accept the truth. She played along when the Other took her by the hand, like a little girl, and forced her to climb the stairway with him, no longer concerned with anyone else. At every step, new limbs and organs—arms, feet, noses, eyes, mouths, ears—sprouted from his body, making him lose any semblance of a figure. He was becoming ever more massive, ever more unstable, as though every identity he had stolen over the past centuries sought preeminence.

As he gradually made his ascent, the men and women at each level drew back, but couldn't look away. The Other could have transported himself directly, and discreetly, to the inside of the Secretarium, to send Elizabeth back to other side of the mirror, but he had gone for the dramatic performance. The stairway, this step-by-step ascent, was a public condemnation.

God had come out from the wings, and wouldn't be returning to them.

A shiver coursed through Ophelia, even beneath her skin. She thought of Janus, the immense, the elusive Janus, killed in an instant; and then she made straight for the stairway.

A giant hand gently held her back, by the shoulder. To her surprise, it was Farouk. He shook his head at her. Did he, somewhere deep inside, vaguely remember her, or would he have stopped anyone from doing what she was about to do? Ophelia held his icy stare, despite the mental pain this visual contact triggered, until he consented to let her go.

Gail, who was biting Fox more than kissing him, suddenly let go of him.

"Don't go. I tried countless times to bump him off, and, no offense, I had all my fingers. That creature is indestructible. You're not."

Her eyes, one a blue sky, the other a night sky, shone with contradictory emotions. As for Ophelia, she felt but one emotion. She was scared. But she would climb that stairway all the same.

"Eulalia Gonde no longer knows who she is. I'm the only one who can help her to remember that."

Puzzled, Archibald scratched the beard that had taken over his entire jaw.

"That's your plan?"

"I'm not asking you to accompany me."

Ophelia clambered up the steps as quickly as her sandals

511

allowed. It was the steepest stairway she had ever climbed. She was skidding on bits of glass and stone, and there was no banister to hold onto. She stopped looking down once the ground became too distant, just fixing her eyes on Elizabeth, higher up, forever higher up, stumbling pitifully in the Other's wake.

"You were born in a distant land, a very long time ago," she told her, in a loud voice. "You were recruited into Babel's army. You worked on a military project. You crystallized your echo with the help of a telephone receiver."

Ophelia's words seemed to bounce off the surfaces of the Memorial without reaching the person they were addressed to. Dragged unwillingly from step to step, Elizabeth was more expressionless than ever. Seeing her like that, one really might have thought that she was the echo.

Ophelia persevered:

"You created the family spirits with your words, and with your blood. For them, you founded a school, right here."

The Other suddenly stopped, at the top of the stairs, which was a dizzying height. In front of him, as imposing as a moon, the Secretarium let out deafening creaks. Affected by his many family powers, its red-gold cladding crinkled like foil, and then the globe burst open in an explosion of metal. Ophelia protected herself as best she could. A blizzard of beams, bolts, cylinders, cogwheels, vases, silverware, and punched cards came hurtling down onto the Memorial. The howling of those collections of antiques. The agony of the biggest database in the world. Countless hours of cataloguing classifying, coding, hole-punching, all swept away in an instant.

The Secretarium was like a planet that had been gutted. All that survived, at its heart, was a second floating globe, its replica in miniature. With merely a gesture from the Other, it in turn opened, showering dust and cobwebs everywhere, and revealing the secret room enclosed within it, and in the middle of that room, the hanging mirror.

The stairway extended even higher, pushed up by some underground mechanism in the rocks, to the level of Eulalia Gonde's room.

Elizabeth gazed at the punched cards fluttering down all around her. Ophelia, battling the vertigo that was knotting her stomach, climbed, one by one, the remaining steps between them.

"You invented the code of the Books. You wrote storybooks under the initials 'E. G.' You made friends with an old caretaker. You suffered from chronic sinusitis."

"Stop."

This order came from the mouths of the Other. They had erupted all over him, on his face, neck, back, and belly. By stretching his flesh, he grabbed Elizabeth by the hair and Ophelia by the scarf, and hurled them, together, onto the floor of the room. Double blow, doubled pain. The hanging mirror's surface was already darkening; the Wrong Side was reacting to the proximity of the two Eulalias, real and fake, demanding the surplus one.

The floorboards creaked like a raft under the Other's weight, as he advanced with his glut of legs and arms. The eyes popping up all over him were all focused on Ophelia. What she saw of him through her cracked glasses was even more multifarious.

She leaned on her grazed elbows to crawl over to Elizabeth, who was curled up not far from her, and white as a sheet behind her freckles.

"This was your room. You spent hours on your typewriter. From here you heard the children you had created growing up. You told me that you came from a big family, do you remember? It's they who were your family. You weren't abandoned at the home of strangers. It's you who went over to the Wrong Side. You asked me to release you, I created a breach, and you returned through the mirror of your choice, in Babel, in a random house. It was your decision, so accept it. You alone can make your echo hear reason."

Elizabeth stared at her from under her purplish eyelids.

"I am sorry," she stammered. "It's a terrible misunderstanding."

"All this is futile," the Other interrupted them. "This traitor is going back through the mirror. And you, poor child, you will die here. I vole litheness . . . loathe violence, but twice you have foiled the Wrong Side, and I won't permit a third time."

As soon as one of the Other's mouths uttered something, all the others echoed it. Ophelia was no longer afraid. It was beyond that; she was fear itself, in its rawest state. The old woman, the monster, the red pencil . . . She tipped her broken glasses up at the dozens of arms raised above her. Which one would cut her to pieces?

"Just look at me. I represent hall of temerity . . . all of humanity."

An enormous bang punctured the air; the Other's skull was blown to pieces. Hunting rifle on shoulder, breathless from his ascent, Fox stood, defiantly, on the top step of the stairway.

"You represent no one."

With his second shot, he didn't allow the Other time to collect himself. Fox was smiling, savagely, between his red sideburns. Gail, who was gripping him by the waist to stop the gun's recoil knocking him off balance, gave him a look that overflowed with pride.

She repeated with him:

"You represent no one."

Fox fired a third shot. Archibald took advantage of the diversion to slip between the Other's many legs. He pirouetted over to Ophelia and Elizabeth.

"The reinforcements have arrived, ladies."

He gave a faint smile of derision, as if he deemed himself irredeemably crazy. Ophelia was extremely grateful to him for risking death for them, but how was he planning to get them out of this? The Other's flesh was forever re-forming, and Fox would soon run out of bullets.

Archibald leaned closer to be heard over the thundering shots.

"Listen carefully to me, you two. Especially you, Miss I-Don't-Know-Who-I-Am-Anymore. I'm going to try, and I mean *try*, to establish a link between you. I can't impose anything on you, but you yourselves can use me to make yourself transparent, one to the other. We have very little time."

A deafening silence followed. Fox had used his last bullet.

"Correction," said Archibald. "We have no more time."

Ophelia retched. With an organic spurt of tongues, teeth, and entrails, the Other lost any trace of homogeneity. Not just one, but whole clusters of heads started to appear on him. One of them shot out from an outsized neck, like a plant growing at lightning speed. It reached Fox straight on, head-butting him and breaking his nose, an appalling sound that Ophelia felt in her very bones. Fox lost his balance. Dragged by his weight, Gail couldn't bring herself to let go of him. They fell from the stairway together, without a sound.

Ophelia couldn't close her eyes. They weren't dead. Not them, not so fast, not like that.

Shriveled up beside her, Elizabeth just kept repeating that all this was but a misunderstanding. Archibald wasn't smiling anymore.

"You represent no one!"

It was Aunt Rosaline's voice. With her glasses broken, all Ophelia could see of her was a patch of color—her old bottle-green dress—gesticulating from the top-story railings.

There was an insuperable gulf between her and the small weightless floor on which the Other stood, but she was hurling any books she could lay her hands on straight at him—she who so valued anything made of paper. Ophelia's mother, father, great-uncle, brother, and sisters added their hands and voices to hers.

"You represent no one! You represent no one! You represent no one!"

The books took flight. Propelled by all these animist wills, they gathered into a swarm that swelled by the minute. *You represent no one!* Fox's and Gail's words spread from story to story, from mouth to mouth. *You represent no one!* The Memorialists trying to save the book collections started to tip their trolleys over the edge. *You represent no one!* The animism spread from book to book, the swarm turned into a tornado. *You represent no one!* Thousands of books came crashing down on the Other, covering his faces, eyes, mouths, ears, hands in paper. *You represent no one!*

Ophelia didn't know whether she felt proud, furious, or terrified.

"They're going to bring his wrath down on them."

Archibald laid one hand on her cheek, the other on Elizabeth's. "They're buying us time." This thought had imposed itself on all Ophelia's thoughts. She had already experienced the power of the Web several times, but nothing as disturbing as this silent, powerfully personal invitation she felt quivering inside her. She was losing all notion of otherness, all distinction between outside and inside. The Memorial crowd was reverberating inside her head; her heartbeats were filling up the world. The very fabric of her individuality was becoming increasingly porous. She was acutely conscious of Archibald's skin against hers, and of Elizabeth's skin against Archibald's, as if all three of them were enveloped in one and the same epidermis. Archibald was ill. Elizabeth was old. Ophelia was infertile. She knew that the moment she gave in to the lure of transparency, there would be nothing else she could conceal from them. Needs must. There was that memory inside her that other memory that she had to return a memory full of winding corridors and secret gardens the memory of Eulalia who wanted to save her world but who hadn't been able to save her family those souls united and then divided so that from this schism another otherness would be born that echo that took the place of her family but never was her family that was part of me that was me that I miss I miss her I miss Thorn I miss myself.

Release me.

Two words. Two words too many. In the Wrong Side, speaking is an unnatural act. It took Eulalia time—a great deal of time—and practice—a great deal of practice—to relearn the rudiments of language. She came up with a new alphabet at six years old, devised a programming code at eight, completed her very first storybook at eleven, and here she is, having to make a superhuman effort for three wretched syllables.

Release me.

At least she has finally attracted the attention of Ophelia, who dragged herself out of bed and is gazing, groggily, all around her. Her eyes slide through Eulalia, despite her standing there, in the middle of the room. They see neither her distress nor her hope. It's the first time for a long time—a very, very long time—that an inhabitant of the Right Side reacts to her call. Eulalia only has a few moments at her disposal. It's sleepiness that, for the moment, is making Ophelia receptive to the Wrong Side.

Sleepiness, and a mirror.

Release me.

The mirror in the bedroom quivers like a tuning fork as the words hit it, and inverts their vibrations until they are almost audible:

"Release me."

In the other bed, the young Agatha sleeps deeply, her red hair fanning out on her pillowcase. Eulalia suddenly notices that someone else has sat down on the mattress. A boy whose every color is inverted, like the negative of a photograph. Him again. That young Babelian has got into the habit of following Eulalia everywhere, like a shadow—which they both are, in fact. His eyes are full of both sweetness and curiosity. Eulalia knows that he doesn't belong to the old humanity she inverted along with herself. No, he was recently sent into the Wrong Side, from the Horn of Plenty, which she thought was buried forever, and it's partly because of him that she's here tonight.

Eulalia must stay focused on Ophelia, who is reeling with tiredness in front of the mirror. Mustn't lose the contact that's finally been made between them.

Release me.

"Release me," the mirror weakly repeats, in echo.

Ophelia looks into it, in search of Eulalia, who in reality is just behind her. Behind behind.

"Sorry?"

Every inverted ounce of Eulalia tightens. After an eternity of silence, finally some dialogue.

Release me.

Ophelia turns round, looks at Eulalia without seeing her. She's so young! One foot in childhood, the other in adolescence, and pretty hands wrapped in the shadow of her animism.

"Who are you?"

With every movement, every word, Ophelia sends out vibrations of herself that Eulalia feels deep within her own vibrations. She finds giving a reply demands considerable energy.

I am who I am.

Release me.

"How?"

On Ophelia's sleepy face, there is something of Artemis as a child. In her veins, the same blood runs; the same ink that Eulalia used to write the beginning of their story. Quivering with nostalgia, she recalls the day when Artemis passed through her very first mirror. That was in another life, in another town. At the time when her children were learning to use their powers, before turning away from them.

Before being turned away from them.

The Other had torn out their memories as soon as he had left the Wrong Side. Eulalia had watched the scene from the wings. She saw her own echo pretending to be her, speaking in her name, and mutilating the Book of each of her children—except for Janus, who had the good sense to be absent on that day. She had never felt so betrayed. This wasn't how things were supposed to happen.

Fake.

Deep down, Eulalia knew it. She had known it as soon as the Other had whispered in her ear to take all wars with her to the Wrong Side, while he would act as a counterbalance by tipping over into the Right Side. Eulalia wanted to save her world; the Other wanted to leave his. By giving her word to an echo, she had given him the power to leave the Wrong Side, and to take her place. The power to create a way through, a temporary Horn of Plenty, in short. All that was required was a simple mirror. Eulalia delayed honoring her promise because she knew, deep down, that she should never have made it. The call of the Other had become so strong, over there, on their island, that she couldn't go near a reflective surface anymore without feeling drawn toward it. She had thrown away all the spoons, removed all the windowpanes, even hidden her own glasses for fear of being swept away before she had finished bringing up the future family spirits. She had kept only the mirror in her room in one piece.

A mirror that she did end up passing through, on the day that war returned to threaten the life of her children.

A mirror similar to the one in which Ophelia's questioning expression is reflected right now. Her lips still form her question: "How?"

Pass through.

"Why?"

Because one half of humanity doesn't know that it has lived off the sacrifice of the other half. Because now, all the wars sent to the Wrong Side have ceased. Because millions of men and women have finally laid down their weapons and left behind their never-ending conflicts. Because Eulalia, alone, knows no peace. Because the Other remains deaf to her calls. Because he brought no reconciliation to any heart, any home in the Right Side. Because they made the mistake, both of them, of taking themselves for God. And because— at this thought, Eulalia stares at the young man sitting on Agatha's bed—others are making the same mistakes right now in Babel.

Because it must be done.

"But why me?" insists Ophelia.

Eulalia isn't a mirror visitor, she herself has never had the slightest power. She has visited the descendants of Artemis many times in the hope of finding, among them, the one who would be prepared to reopen the path for her. She doesn't really know whether Ophelia can do that, but the important thing is to persuade her that she can.

Because you are who you are.

Ophelia stifles a yawn. Soon she would be totally awake, and it would be too late.

"I can try."

Eulalia trembles. She exchanges a final glance with the young Babelian, who smiles at her, giving her a congratulatory thumbs-up. And yet, something suddenly holds her back. She has the duty, here, in front of this mirror more than anywhere else, finally to be honest. To Ophelia, and to herself.

If you release me, it will change us:
You, me, and the world.

Eulalia fears she has let her chance slip away, but Ophelia is just deciding.

"Okay."

They dive into the mirror together. Their molecules collide, intertwine, and intermingle. They merge into each other inside a seemingly interminable interstice. The pain is absolute. Eulalia senses that she is reinverting, atom by atom, but those atoms are already not entirely her own. Her ideas become confused, her identity is diluted. She will soon be out of the in-between. She must quickly choose her destination, any mirror belonging to any Babelian.

She must, above all, not forget.

Forget what?

She must correct their mistakes.

What mistakes?

She must go back home.

Go back where?

To Babel.

The link was broken. Ophelia, struggling to redefine herself as a separate entity, understood why when she saw Archibald stretched out on the floor, his top hat toppled over beside him. He had ended up losing consciousness. She herself had come close to fainting. As for Elizabeth, she was curled up and groaning.

In the middle of the room, the Other was nonchalantly tearing up, with his hundreds of fingers, the last pages from books still covering him.

All around them, there were no more railings, or bookcases, and there was no more cupola; nothing but clouds rumbling with thunder and a nauseatingly salty smell. The wind made the scarf and Ophelia's ripped gown flap as she advanced to the very edge of the floor, to the frontier between solid and void. Had the Memorial disappeared?

Incredulously, Ophelia slowly swiveled round. An ocean, as lowering and turbulent as the sky, stretched as far as the eye could see. An armada of warships, from several centuries ago, were aimlessly drifting around. She lowered her head and squinted, bothered by the cracks in her glasses. The ocean stopped exactly where the Memorial ark had been, turning into a howling vortex around this void but without spilling a single drop into it, contrary to all the laws of nature. The planetary memory.

The Wrong Side had regurgitated a piece of the old world, and swallowed, in its place, what little remained of Babel. It had taken the Memorial, Farouk, Artemis, her family. Her entire family.

"I can bring them back," murmured the mouths of the Other.

Ophelia turned toward all the faces springing up across his body. He no longer had any molecular coherence. His dislocated arms, like a myriapod's legs, indicated the hanging mirror, in the increasingly agitated surface of which he wasn't reflected.

"Everything is your fault, yours and Eulalia's. It's up to you to ticks fit . . . fix it. And the world belongs only to me."

"You represent no one."

Elizabeth's voice had combined with Ophelia's. She had got up. Her hair lengthened when she lifted her chin. Her shapeless body seemed, little by little, to thicken, and finally reassert her presence in reality.

"Not even me."

All of the Other's eyes—and there were many of them—opened wide, and then closed again almost as fast, reabsorbed, one after the other, into his skin. Then, in turn, the faces, legs, and arms all retracted, as if some irresistible force was sucking them in. His body gradually shrank, shedding its plurality, regaining a human appearance, until it became, despite itself, an exact copy of Elizabeth, even down to her Forerunner's frock coat.

He gazed at his hands, dotted with freckles. Hands deprived of family power.

"I remember now," Elizabeth said to him. "I remember why I broke our deal and left the Wrong Side."

She was speaking with a gentle lassitude, but the look she directed at this other her was unyielding.

"The old humanity that I inverted, along with myself, no longer bears any relation to the one we have known. It has calmed down. Far more than the one I left in your care. Sacrificing half of the world to save the other half no longer makes any sense. And anyhow," she sighed, almost smiling, "who are we to decide on their behalf?"

For the first time, Ophelia detected a slight uncertainty in the Other's stance. It wasn't an expression of doubt, more a feeling of inferiority, a sense of dissatisfaction that Elizabeth's words did nothing to help. He was already striving to reject this weak body that she had imposed on him.

No question of allowing him the time to do so. Ophelia threw herself, headfirst. With all the strength in her fingerless hands, she pushed the Other into the mirror behind him.

The wide-eyed stare her gave her, as he tipped backwards, was dreadful. As he made contact, the mirror's combination of glass, silvering, and lead turned into a vortex. The path to the Wrong Side had opened up to obtain, finally, the counterpart it lacked. Not prepared to let himself be sucked in, the Other gripped onto the edges of the mirror. He struggled fiercely, he resurfaced. Ignoring his blows, Ophelia and Elizabeth pushed him with all their might to force him through.

They couldn't do it. They were exhausted. Even diminished, the Other was defying them.

He was going to kill them, spill the blood, and fulfill the red pencil's prophesy.

Two arms surged out of the mirror. Ophelia thought it was some new metamorphosis of the Other, but the arms locked around him like jaws to drag him deep inside. They were hatched with scars.

They were Thorn's arms.

He had taken advantage of this temporary breach in the in-between. Sinking behind the surface of the mirror, the Other's face distended in surprise. He lost his freckles, his eyebrows, his nose, his eyes, his mouth, until there was no face left at all.

He let himself be swallowed up, like a faceless puppet. Along with Thorn.

"Not this time."

Ophelia plunged her hand into the mirror. She felt Thorn's hand grabbing hers, somewhere in the in-between, but she no longer had the fingers to grip onto him. The call of the Wrong Side was as irresistible as a tidal wave. Had Elizabeth not held onto her by her scarf, she would have been sucked in herself. Ophelia cried out when her shoulder dislocated, but still didn't let go. She would pull Thorn out of the Wrong Side, even if it meant giving up half of her body as the counterpart.

He mustn't let go of her.

He let go of her.

Reeling, Ophelia fell back onto Elizabeth, who herself fell back onto Archibald, who was just regaining consciousness. The wrinkled surface of the hanging mirror smoothed out until it was properly solid again. The path to the Wrong Side had closed up again.

Ophelia gazed at her hand. Worse than a hand without fingers, a hand without Thorn.

All around them, the structure of the Memorial was gradually reappearing. At first, it was but a filigree image against a backdrop of sky and sea, almost an optical illusion, and then the stone, steel, and glass solidified. The remains of the Secretarium, the great stone stairway, the main entrance, the garden with the mimosas, the transcendiums, and the circular stories were all reinverting themselves. Ophelia's family was there once more, every one of them, all exchanging wary glances with the Memorialists.

"Oh, no," exclaimed Archibald.

Ophelia saw it, too. Behind the hanging mirror, some old wallpaper was gradually losing its transparency. Sending the Other to the Wrong Side had broken the contract. The old world and the new were realigning on the same plane. The second half of the room, having remained in the Wrong Side until then, was gradually reemerging from invisibility, and with it, the second half of the Memorial; a half that Babel's builders had entirely rebuilt, since they believed it to have collapsed. The two structures were going to clash with each other.

Elizabeth cupped her hands around her mouth. With a new authority, she gave the order:

"Everyone evacuate! *Everyone!*"

Ophelia refused to do so. With her arm dangling from its dislocated shoulder, she watched as, all around her, the room re-created itself, one piece of furniture at a time. The wood was cracking, the stone exploding, the whole edifice roaring. What if Thorn was right there, nearby, about to reappear himself? She felt her shoulders being gripped. Archibald's eyes searched deep into her own, behind her broken glasses. He was telling her that they had to leave. Now.

There was a bang. The next moment, everything went dark.

THE MIRROR VISITORS

Pollux's botanical gardens were just as Ophelia remembered them. The air vibrated with heat, aromas, colors, birds, and insects, but there was also a new wind in the mix. That wind came from over the horizon, and smelt of salt. Where the void had once been, beyond the last palm trees of the arboretum, there now stretched an ocean.

There were no more arks; all was either land, or water.

"All this will mean considerable paperwork."

Octavio's eyes glowed red from the shadow of his fringe. It wasn't the gardens he was seeing, but Second. She was playing cards on the lawn with Helen and Pollux, along with a swelling crowd of strangers, all peering over their game. Men, women, and children from the old world viewed everything with curiosity. They were in perpetual movement, flowing in from across the continent, expressing the same silent amazement, unaware of how uneasy they made the current generations feel. The void might have disappeared, but a gulf remained.

"Two different humanities for a single land," commented Octavio, as if he had read Ophelia's thoughts. "I'll be amazed if this cohabitation proceeds without a hitch. Everything will depend on each person's choice, but I'd rather be here, choosing with them, than over there, going through hell myself.

Désolé," he muttered, almost immediately. "I shouldn't have said that to you."

Ophelia gave him a smile, which grew when she noticed the uniform he was wearing: without gold braiding, without an insignia, without prestige. Apart from the wings on his boots, it was the garb of a citizen like any other.

"You have the right to say what you think. We're in Babel-the-New, after all, and that's partly thanks to you. Lady Septima was hard to like," she added, after a pause, "but she loved you in her own way."

Octavio didn't take his eyes off Second's face, with that long scar running across it. She was laughing. No need to be a Visionary to see that she was winning easily against Helen and Pollux. She had put away her pencils for good, doubtless because there were no more advance echoes to draw. She had prevented one, the most important one, from happening. If she hadn't pushed Thorn into the cage, he wouldn't have been able to drag the Other into the wrong side of the world; indeed, he wouldn't have been able to do it, either, if he hadn't been a mirror visitor himself. Second and Thorn had saved Ophelia from the red pencil. Not only her, but also plenty of other lives.

"Will you go home to your parents?"

Octavio's question was detached, but Ophelia still sensed the word hiding behind it, and her heart sank. *Stay*. She watched, in the distance, every member of her family, busy drinking coffee under parasols that spun round due to all the animism. They had delayed their departure until she was out of the hospital. Now they were making the most of their last few hours in Babel-the-New, in no hurry to board the airship again and return to the rain. The world had changed, but the weather had remained true to itself.

"I'm not going home yet. I'm not staying, either."

Octavio frowned.

"Where are you going?"

Ophelia answered him with another smile, disconcerting him even more.

"And do they know?"

"I've already said goodbye to them."

"Oh. *Eh bien* . . . my break's over. Forgive me, but I've got enough work to last me a lifetime. If you return to Babel-the-New, you are duty-bound to knock on my door."

Octavio made his Forerunner wings jingle, and spared them both from any backward glance. Second stopped her game instantly to take the hand he held out to her. Helen and Pollux gazed at the playing cards abandoned on the grass, incapable of playing with them without someone there to explain the rules.

Ophelia remained alone under the trees. After her prolonged stay in the confines of the hospital, everything dazzled her. She could still feel a painful throbbing under her turban. Her hair had had to be shaved, but it was already growing back. To be killed by a beam after surviving the red pencil, and the apocalypse, would have been too ironic. She was doing well, according to the doctors. A nasty bump, a dislocated shoulder, ten fingers less, a still sterile belly. Ophelia wasn't sure whether it was down to her successive inversions, or the reabsorption of her echo, but she'd got her good old clumsiness back. Yes, she was doing really well.

Not everyone had been as lucky as her.

"You're abandoning me."

Ophelia looked down. Archibald was stretched out under the tall ferns, with his top hat propped on his nose, and Twit curled up against him. His remark was all the more strange since he hadn't visited her once in the hospital. Ophelia didn't hold that against him. She owed having got out of the

Memorial alive to him, and since they had been linked, she understood him better than she would have liked. They now knew their mutual secrets. She'd never be able to give life; he wouldn't be able to keep his own for long.

"I know it's not your philosophy," she sighed, "but take care of yourself all the same."

As on every day since she had woken up in that hospital bed, Ophelia couldn't help thinking about the living, the ghosts, and especially those who had disappeared. About Fox. Gail. Ambrose. Janus. Hildegarde.

About Thorn.

"Stop," Archibald told her.

"Doing what?"

"Thinking. Listen instead."

So Ophelia listened. Through the mingled sounds of parrots, cicadas, and conversations, she picked up the senseless prattling of Victoria. Close to the aviary, she was throwing a ball to Farouk, which would then bounce off his forehead. Every time, he lifted his arms too late. Victoria didn't give up, offered him some garbled advice, and then trotted along behind the ball. Every time she stumbled, Berenilde leapt up, impulsively, from the bench she had sat on to keep an eye on her, but Aunt Rosaline gently pressed her shoulder to urge her to sit back down.

Ophelia was missing them already. She would miss all of them. She might not be able to start a family, but the one she had created for herself, over time, made her feel as if she had several homes now. She gave a final wave to her parents, her brother, her sister, her great-uncle, to each one of them. If the gloves, which she had animated during her convalescence, gave the illusion of fingers, it was the scarf that had really replaced them. It helped Ophelia to get dressed, get washed, grip her cutlery, not because it was animated to do so, but because it had decided to, for itself. The time when they were as one was over. They were now two, separate from each other, freely together. And it was good that way.

"I already told you," Archibald warned her, from beneath the ferns. "If you don't return to the Pole, the Pole will come to you."

"We will return."

Archibald lifted the edge of his hat.

"We?"

She moved away without replying. There was one last person she had to see. She was waiting for her in front of the gate, clinging to its bars like an old lady, her eyelids heavier than ever. An invisible clock had starting working again, along with her memory.

"You're not looking too great," Ophelia said to her.

"You're not looking too presentable, either."

"What should I call you? Elizabeth, or Eulalia?"

"Elizabeth. I haven't been Eulalia for a very long time. In fact, my name isn't that important. They are."

Together, they turned toward the botanical gardens, where the family spirits were clumsily frolicking about. Helen and Pollux were trying to grab hold of the playing cards, scattered by the wind. Farouk didn't catch Victoria's ball once. Artemis, looking very pleased with herself, had broken the cup of coffee that Great-uncle had served her. Giants that had slipped back into childhood. No family spirit had returned unscathed from the Wrong Side. After the great reinversion, all that had remained of them were erased Books. Elizabeth had dedicated what energy she had left to give them a new code, a simplified code.

"The ink that I used this time for the Books won't last forever. No immortality, no powers, I want a new story to begin for my children. It's up to them to create what comes next without me. I would have liked to bring back Janus, but his Book was too damaged."

"And their own Books?" asked Ophelia. "Where are they now?"

Elizabeth's aged face turned enigmatic.

"Where no one will find them."

Where no one will tear out their pages, Ophelia understood.

Spontaneously, they both turned their eyes toward the distant tower of the Memorial, beyond the city's building sites. It stood partially demolished on its island. The bookcases hadn't returned unscathed, either, from their inversion. The pages of several hundreds of thousands of books had been erased, just as the letters "AP" had been from Ophelia's shoulder. The Wrong Side was a world in which writing had no place.

As for the hanging mirror, it had shattered into a thousand pieces.

"Nothing to report," replied Elizabeth, in anticipation of the question. "I spend half my days scrutinizing my reflection, but no sign of the Other anymore.

Ophelia nodded. The shadow of Ambrose 1 hadn't reappeared to her, either. He had only managed to show up thanks to the collision of Right Side with Wrong Side, where the veil between the two worlds was flimsiest, and probably by himself concentrating as much aerargyrum as was humanly possible. In one sense, no longer seeing him was proof that everything was back to order. Almost everything.

Ophelia noticed the white hairs now entwined in Elizabeth's long tawny braid. She and Elizabeth were linked to each other by a mirror passage. Their paths had continually crossed and re-crossed, like twin trajectories, but now they would each be going in a different direction.

Elizabeth forced a smile.

"You know, my return to the Right Side was horrendous. I

had lost half of my identity, and of my appearance. I terrified a couple of Babelians by turning up in their sitting room, but I was even more afraid of them. I ran off, I wandered the streets, unable to remember why I was there. Perhaps not wanting to remember, either. The weight of all Eulalia Gonde's responsibilities was too crushing, I suppose. And then your memories, Ophelia, were superimposed onto mine. An animated house, a large family. It wasn't just my past with the family spirits; there was also a bit of your childhood. I convinced myself that I had been abandoned. When the authorities asked me for my name, it was impossible to remember it, too. I mumbled something like 'Eula . . . Ela . . .'. They decided it would be 'Elizabeth.' I'm sorry I won't be able to see what comes next in your story," she added, suddenly changing the subject. "I won't be there when you return from your travels. In fact, I will be dead before this evening."

Ophelia looked at her, solemnly.

"I'm joking. I expect to last a few more weeks."

Pleased with the reaction she had got, Elizabeth went off, limping, to rejoin the family spirits, chuckling like an old woman.

Without Ophelia, she would already be dead. If the Deviations Observatory train had driven Ophelia directly to the third protocol, she wouldn't have been handed over to Lady Septima at the same time as Elizabeth. She wouldn't have boarded that long-distance airship with her. She wouldn't have been able to resort to her animism to save her from going down in it. They would never have discovered, together, the twenty-second ark. They wouldn't have both returned to Babel on the Lazaropter. Elizabeth would never have been in a position to regain the upper hand with the Other. The Wrong Side and the Right Side would have been off balance until that definitive collapse.

In short, the story would have had a somewhat less happy ending.

Ophelia crossed the bridge that now overlooked the ocean, and walked through the spice market. There were many more people here than in the gardens. The Babelians of today mingled with the Babelians of the past. They perused, sniffed, tasted everything that was within reach, much to the exasperation of the stallholders. There were many calls for the family guard. Octavio was right, cohabitation wouldn't be easy.

Not easy, no, but beneficial. Ophelia recalled the young girl she had encountered in that distant land, with its abandoned village. Those returning from the Wrong Side had the same look in their eyes. It was a look of total acceptance, without labeling anything, or comparing anything, affording each thing special value. A look that redefined otherness. Lazarus had spouted plenty of nonsense, but he had at least been right about one thing. *We have so much to learn from them.*

Ophelia herself looked as far away as the crowd and the city allowed, taking in the ocean on one side, and the continent on the other, the new world, and the old. Her heart was racing. There was so much to see, so much to discover!

She crossed over the streetcar rails, and kept going, before finally diving into the store bearing the sign:

GLAZING – MIRRORS

The scarf closed the door, discreetly, behind them. The store was pretty much deserted. The storekeeper was on the telephone with a client. On the counter, the radio was playing a well-known old song—Ophelia could never remember its name:

The bird you meant to surprise
Flapped its wings and flew away
Love's far away, you can wait for it
You stop waiting for it, and it's here

There were no more echoes to break up the melody; that was a rare occurrence now. As Ophelia walked along an aisle of mirrors, trying, above all, not to break anything, her image was endlessly duplicated. The Wrong Side was the reflection of the Right Side, but what if her own Right Side was someone else's Wrong Side?

Still on the phone, the storekeeper hadn't noticed her. That was preferable. Ophelia reached the back of the store, where he wouldn't be able to see her. She then moved toward the largest mirror, almost twice her height. She looked pretty strange, with that fat turban on her head, her twitchy scarf, her gown mended by her sister, and gloves impatiently wiggling at the end of her arms, animated by her feverishness. Hands that were incapable of grasping, incapable of reading objects. Incapable of holding on to Thorn.

Ophelia looked deep into her own eyes, but what she was looking for was far beyond them. Behind behind.

"You let go of my hand on purpose, didn't you?" she whispered. "You didn't want to drag me over to the other side with you."

Thorn, Lazarus, the Genealogists, Mediana, the Knight, Ambrose: they had all remained in the Wrong Side, because they had entered it through the Horn of Plenty. Such people weren't included in the counterpart; they had never been implicated in the deal between Eulalia and the Other. They were now out of reach, neither really dead nor totally alive.

As soon as Ophelia had been able to get out of her hospital bed, she had dived into the mirror in the bathroom. She had immediately returned through the one in the corridor. She had tried again, and again, wanting to slide into the in-between, but no longer managing to. It was as if the frontier between the two worlds was avoiding her. The nurses had finally attached her to the bed, to oblige her to rest. As soon as she had left the hospital, Ophelia had gone back to the basement at the Deviations Observatory, but, as she had expected, the Horn of Plenty had disappeared. Her echo had swallowed it to allow her, and her alone, to reinvert herself.

There was no longer a path to the Wrong Side, no more communication between the two worlds, for better, or for worse.

Thorn had given humanity its dice back, but who would give his own dice back to him?

"Us," said Ophelia. "You and me."

It wasn't a promise. It was a certainty. She would never give up. And if she had to pass through all the mirrors in the world, she would do so. There was no more past to understand, no more future to conquer. It was in the here and now that she would find Thorn again.

She closed her eyes. Breathed. Rid herself of all expectation, all desire, all fear. Forgot herself, as she did when reading an object. The final reading of them all.

"Because we are mirror visitors."

She plunged into her reflection.

A little more than that, even.

ACKNOWLEDGMENTS

My thanks to you, Thibaut, for having lived with me—sometimes with even more strength than I—the whole story surrounding this story, to the final period; and beyond. You are there behind each letter of each word of each sentence that I write.

To you, my precious and inspiring families, in France and Belgium, of flesh and quill, of silver and gold. You are a more intrinsic part of my books than their own pages.

To you, Alice Colin, Célia Rodmacq, Svetlana Kirilina, Stéphanie Barbaras, for all that you have taught me and brought me through your words.

To you, Camille Ruzé, who so delighted me with your drawings, and your humor, and without whom this final volume wouldn't be what it is. A little more than that, even.

To you, Evan and Livia, for being who you are. Emotion in its purest form.

To Gallimard Jeunesse, Gallimard, and all my interfamilial editors, for having carried the Mirror Visitor from ark to ark.

To you, Laurent Gapaillard, for having sublimated my settings.

To the whole *Clique de l'écharpe*, for the incredible creativity and inimitable good humor that you cultivated around the Mirror Visitor.

To you, Emilie Bulledop, Saefiel, Déborah Danblon, and to every bookseller, librarian, researcher, teacher, columnist who has passed on, and passed round, my mirror.

To you, Carole Trébor, for your friendship, and for your books.

To you, Honey, for having created *Plume d'Argent*, and for having believed in me.

To you, Laetitia, who was the first to encourage me to write.

To you, dear reader, for passing through my mirror, and sharing this adventure, page by page.

And finally to you, Ophelia, for having accompanied me so closely, from the first mirror visit to the last. I'm missing you already.